The Long Winter

Don Scribner

Copyright © 2025 by Don Scribner. All rights reserved.

For Samantha —

Your kindness, imagination, and strength inspire every page.

May you always find light in the longest winters.

Contents

The Long Winter 1
1 – Loss 6
2 – Crash 11
3 – Callahan 25
4 – Grubs 40
5 – Dangerous Encounters 50
6 – The Road to Rio Dell 68
7 – Miracle 83
8 – Live or Die Trying 100
9 – Captives 106
10 – Rescue 119
11 – Dogs 138
12 – The Face of Evil 150
13 – A Place in the Mountains 160
14 – Down the River 169
15 - Martin's Ferry 177
16 – Hope Rekindled 192
17 – Hunted 199
18 – Crescent City 218
19 – Patrol 242
20 – The Farm 263
21 – Enslaved 275
22 – The Man in the Poncho 303
23 – Changing Sides 316
24 – The Search 332
25 – Allies 340
26 – Warning 345
27 – Ultimatum 354

28 – The Battle of Martin's Ferry	359
29 – Evolution	368
30 – Moving Day	374
EPILOGUE	380

1 – Loss

Ian Hammond lost all hope the day he saw a woman toss her infant into the sea.

The movement was almost casual—like she was passing a basketball. No hesitation. No second thoughts.

He stopped dead in his tracks, crouching low behind a jagged outcrop of shale. His breath came shallow and ragged, misting the cold air. Did she know he was there? Did she even care?

The woman stood on the edge of a cliff, staring out at the gray horizon as if it might offer her an answer. The wind tugged at her tattered clothes, lifting the strands of dark, tangled hair that framed her hollow face. If she noticed him, she didn't show it. No flinch. No fear.

There should have been fear. To allow a stranger this close was to invite rape, death—or worse.

Ian rose slowly from his crouch, boots scraping against the frost-crusted earth. He kept his arms loose at his sides, projecting indifference, though every nerve in his body braced for violence.

The woman didn't move. She just kept staring, her gaze locked on the churning sea below.

Ian followed her line of sight, squinting against the biting wind. A hundred feet down, white-capped waves smashed against jagged rocks, sending up bursts of spray that hung in the air like ghostly mist. There was no sign of the infant.

"What did you do?" His voice was rough, hoarse from days of disuse.

The woman's eyes flicked shut, and a solitary tear carved a path through the dirt on her cheek. "I'm his mother. It's my job to protect him."

Ian stared at her, unblinking. "So, you threw him off a cliff?"

"It's quick," she whispered.

"It's final."

Her lip trembled. "I'm his mother," she repeated. "It's my job to protect him."

Ian's jaw tightened. He'd seen this kind of madness before—the hollow, haunted look of someone who'd lost everything. And then kept losing. She wasn't dangerous, not anymore. She was already gone.

"You killed him," he said, though there was no judgment in his tone. He just needed to understand.

"No!" Her voice cracked, and suddenly she was on him, pummeling his chest with weak, frantic fists. "How can you say that? I saved him!"

Ian didn't move. He let her hit him until her strength gave out and she crumpled to the ground, sobbing into her hands. His fingers brushed the hilt of the knife strapped to his thigh, but he didn't draw it. Nor did he reach for the rifle slung barrel-down and across his back. There was no point.

After a long moment, the woman looked up, her face streaked with tears. "Do you think God will judge me for this?"

"If there is a God," Ian said, "I don't think he cares much what you do. Or what any of us do."

The woman flinched, then rose slowly to her feet. She swayed for a moment, steadying herself with one hand on her knee. Ian offered his hand, but she slapped it away.

"Would you rather he starved?" she demanded. "Or was eaten by marauders? Should I have let the bloody flu rot him from the inside out?" She leaned in close, baring caramel teeth. "I saved him."

Ian held her gaze and saw it—the exhaustion, the surrender. The look of someone who had fought too long and just wanted it all to end.

Without another word, she turned and stepped off the edge of the cliff.

Ian didn't move. He just stood there, listening to the wind howl up from the sea like a mourning cry. After a long moment, he walked to the edge and looked down. There was nothing left of her but churned foam and shattered spray.

For a fleeting moment, he considered following her. The lure of misery's end was a song from Odysseus' sirens. But something stopped him.

He turned and headed back toward the woman's camp.

It wasn't much—just a threadbare bedroll and a battered backpack tucked among the tall, brittle grass. Smoke drifted lazily from a dying campfire, mixing with the salty tang of the sea air. Ian knelt and rummaged through the pack. There wasn't much left—a hand-operated can opener, some baby blankets, two empty water bottles.

No food. No weapons. No hope.

Ian shoved the can opener and a pair of nail clippers into his own pack, then rose and kicked the fire apart with the toe of his boot. The smoke had drawn him here. It would draw others, too. Better to let them waste their time searching the empty camp while he kept moving.

He adjusted the straps on his pack, buttoned the top of his olive-drab trench coat, and flipped the collar up to block the chill wind. It wouldn't be long before he'd have to undo the buttons again to let out the heat and sweat. Walking was his life now.

Everything was gray. The sky. The trees. The ground. It was the deathly pallor of a world choked off from its sun. Most of the fallout ash had blown away years ago, but the look of death lingered on the landscape.

Ian gave a wide berth to a long-dead pine surrounded by a bed of brown needles. He'd seen too many trees fall without warning in the last decade to risk getting too close.

It had been ten years since the bombs fell. Ten years since the Long Winter began. No one knew why, or even who. One day the world was standing, and the next it was ash. San Francisco had gone in a flash of light and fire. Ian hadn't bothered to check on what was left of the city. He didn't need to.

His wife, Shannon, and their son, Rusty, were dead.

The thought hit him with the same dull ache it always did, like pressing on an old bruise. There was no point in digging at it. He'd lost them, just like everyone else had lost someone. Just like the woman on the cliff had lost her son.

He kept walking.

The drizzle started around midday, soaking through his

ball cap and plastering his hair to his scalp. Once, he would have sought shelter from the rain. Now, it was just one more discomfort to endure.

It had been years since the last fallout rinsed from the sky. But the Long Winter raged on. Plants were dying from lack of sunlight. Animals were starving. The world was unraveling at the seams.

Ian adjusted the pack on his shoulders and kept moving. It was all he knew how to do.

2 – Crash

"They're hurting me."

Kylee's voice was small, but her eyes were wide and glistening, tears slipping down her cheeks. The words stopped Dee cold. She had been reorganizing the shelves in the children's dormitory, folding blankets, cleaning up discarded toys—just another mindless task in the underground compound. But at Kylee's words, her hands froze.

She turned sharply. "What do you mean, Kylee? Who's hurting you?"

"The doctors," Kylee whispered. "They test me. They hurt me and watch me fix it." The little girl wiped her eyes with her sleeve. "They poke me with things, cut me, burn me sometimes. But they say it's okay because I make it go away."

A sick, burning rage settled deep in Dee's gut. She had suspected the Petros' experiments weren't just about studying Kylee—they were about pushing her. Seeing how far she could go.

Her fingers curled into fists. She had to stay calm. "Did you tell anyone?"

Kylee gave a small, sad smile, as if Dee had asked a foolish question. "I told you."

That was it. The moment Dee knew—they had to leave. Tonight.

"I won't let them hurt you anymore," she said, grabbing Kylee's small hand in her own.

Kylee looked down, squeezing her fingers. "I know. But... there's nothing you can do."

Dee cupped Kylee's face, forcing the girl to look at her. "Watch me."

***

"Wake up, Kylee," Dee whispered, shaking the little girl's shoulder.

Kylee stirred, blinking sleepily. "What's happening?"

Dee glanced at the door. No alarms. No footsteps. Good. "We're getting out of here."

Kylee sat up instantly, her eyes bright despite the exhaustion. "We can leave?" Then doubt crept in. "But... it's poison outside."

"My family survived for months out there before I was taken. We can, too. We just need to stay away from the cities."

"What about the grubs?" Kylee's voice dropped to a whisper.

"We'll stay away from them, too."

Kylee hesitated. "How are we getting out?"

Dee took a breath. No more questions. No more delays. "Do you trust me?"

Kylee nodded.

Dee hugged her tight. "Then just come with me."

She grabbed the small backpack she had prepared earlier—warm clothes for Kylee, some food, a flashlight. Just enough to survive. Everything else was already at the airfield.

As they slipped through the dimly lit corridors, Dee's heart pounded so hard she was sure someone would hear it. But the compound wasn't built for security—it was built for science. The guards focused on keeping people out, not in. That was their mistake.

She and Kylee darted from shadow to shadow, finally reaching the outer doors.

Frankie was already there, pacing near a service exit. The scrawny pilot was jittery, wringing his hands. His dirty baseball cap was pulled low over his eyes.

"You're late," he hissed.

"We're here now," Dee snapped.

Frankie eyed Kylee. "This the kid?"

Dee's jaw clenched. "Yes."

"She doesn't look like much." He glanced over his shoulder toward the airfield. "Alright, let's move."

They sprinted across the open tarmac toward the small high-winged plane. A Cessna, Frankie had called it. Dee didn't care. It had wings. It would get them out of here.

Frankie did a quick walkaround, checking the engine. Dee scanned the darkness, heart hammering. Too much open space. Too many chances to be seen.

Once Frankie was out of earshot, Kylee whispered into Dee's ear. "He doesn't care about helping us, Dee. He just wants to kiss you. And other, even more gross stuff."

"I know," Dee said, suppressing a laugh. "Whatever his reason, as long as he helps us. Now stop doing that."

"Doing what?" Kylee asked with feigned ignorance.

"You know what I mean."

A voice behind them made her freeze. "What are you doing out here, Peters?"

A man in coveralls. A mechanic. He held a ratchet, frowning. "Why are you launching in the middle of the night?"

Frankie hesitated. "Petros' orders. Just moving some cargo."

The man narrowed his eyes. "Cargo?"

Frankie gave a stiff nod. "Yeah. Need to be quick."

"I need to check the manifest."

"No time—" Frankie moved to cut him off, but the man turned toward the maintenance shack.

Frankie panicked. He grabbed the mechanic and swung a wild punch, smashing his nose. Blood sprayed. The mechanic stumbled back, eyes wide.

The man lunged at Frankie, both of them crashing to the ground, wrestling.

Dee didn't think—she just acted. She grabbed a wrench from a nearby toolbox and swung it hard.

Crack.

The mechanic lay there, motionless.

"Shit," Frankie said as he squirmed out from under the big mechanic. "I think you killed him."

Dee dropped the wrench. "We ready to go?" There was no time for regrets.

The sound of sirens cut through the night.

They had been found.

***

Dee pushed Kylee into the back seat, then climbed into the co-pilot's seat. "Frankie, start the damn plane!"

The engine roared to life, the propeller spinning. The little Cessna lurched forward, picking up speed.

A Jeep appeared at the end of the runway. Flashes of gunfire. Bullets streaked past.

Frankie shoved the throttle forward. "Hold on!"

The Cessna shot down the runway. Dee braced. Kylee ducked low.

The plane rotated, and with a hop they left the ground. The runway ended at a cliff, and Frankie immediately angled the little plane downward to put the terrain between them and the assholes with the guns. He hugged the slope, gaining airspeed. Dee couldn't see anything outside the plane. Frankie pulled hard and she felt herself being pressed down as they transitioned from a descent to a climb.

"How can you see the ground?" she asked once they were safely in a climb out.

"I can't."

"Then how did you keep us from hitting the mountain?"

Frankie shrugged. "I've flown that departure a hundred times during the day. I know about how long I can stay in that dive before pulling up."

"What if you were off in your estimation?"

"We made it, didn't we?"

***

The clouds were like gray sheer curtains hanging over

the tall peaks to the east, filtering the predawn light. Dee could see the peaks on either side now, as the little plane hugged the eastern edge of the valley, keeping to the shadows created by the mountains.

"Why are you getting lower to the ground?"

"Actually, we've been climbing steadily. The ground gets higher on the northern end of the Owens valley." Frankie narrowed his eyes and scrunched his forehead as if lost in thought. "We don't have a lot of options up here. We've got to pick a valley and get through it before the weather closes in on us. I'm going to head to Tahoe, then pick my way up to eighty and follow it west through the mountains. If we get pushed down too low, I'm just going to land on the highway. If that happens, let's just hope there aren't any grubs hanging out in the mountains."

"Will they eat us?" It was the first thing Kylee had said since falling asleep shortly after takeoff from the compound.

"No, they won't," Dee said. "Most of them aren't going to be like that. Remember, I was out here for a while. You don't think I would eat you, do you?"

Kylee laughed at Dee's attempt to keep things light, although Dee was not sure herself. People who face death every day do desperate things.

Frankie cut straight north over Lake Tahoe. Dee thought she saw the house that her family rented one summer when she was a kid. The memory put a smile on her face. On the far side of the lake, the weather pushed them down into a valley. Frankie kept looking around nervously and at one point mumbled something about getting boxed in. But they found an Interstate just as the weather lifted and followed the highway west through the Sierra Nevada Mountains. They broke out of the mountains northeast of Sacramento and turned northwest to avoid the San Francisco hot zone.

Somewhere around Chico, Dee saw a long dust cloud forming below. At the head of it was a convoy of vehicles to include motorcycles, rusted out pickups, and an old box truck.

"Grubs," Frankie said. "You don't see too many with working vehicles anymore. These guys must be special." His thin lips curled into a grin.

Dee felt Kylee's scream as a sharp stab to the ears before she heard it. It was the type of scream that only comes from intense pain.

"What the fuck! You need to get a hold of her."

Dee ignored Frankie and turned around in her seat. Kylee was writhing, clutching her legs in pain, but there was nothing that Dee could see that was causing it. "Kylee, what is wrong?" She tried unsuccessfully to keep her voice calm.

Through tightly clenched teeth, Kylee breathed. "Their legs!"

"Who's legs?"

"The people in the truck, they're cutting off their legs."

"That little girl is looney. Why did we bring her, anyway?"

She is the whole reason we left, you moron!

"The truck down below us?"

Kylee nodded, still clutching her legs.

"You're imagining it, Kylee; just breathe."

"No, I'm not!" the girl yelled through clenched teeth. "It's happening right now!"

Dee wondered if Kylee was truly experiencing something that was happening down below. This was new.

Frankie reached his hand back and grabbed Kylee by the arm. "Knock that shit off! I can't fly with all that damn noise!"

Without even thinking, Dee punched Frankie in the mouth; he let go immediately. "Don't you ever touch her! You understand? You don't ever lay a hand on her!"

Frankie's hand was on his mouth, feeling for damage. He pulled it away to look at it, and a smear of blood oozed out of a puffed-up lip. She must have hit him harder than she thought.

"Dee," Kylee's head peeked up from the plane's backseat. "It's gone now."

Dee felt immediate relief that she was better. "What happened?"

"I think when he shook me, I was pulled back out."

"Back out of what?"

"Back out of whoever's head I was in."

Dee's face screwed up with confusion. "Has this ever happened to you before?"

Kylee looked down, searching her memory. Then, after a moment, she said, "I don't think so." This *was* something new.

A loud noise drew their attention back outside the aircraft. It sounded like a burp, but staccato, and much louder. The little Cessna banked hard to the left and dropped from the sky as Frankie pulled back the power and dove.

"What are you doing?" Dee asked.

"We're taking fire!" Frankie banked back to the right, still diving the little plane toward the ground.

"So why are you getting closer to the ground?"

"Because it's coming from *above* us! Above and behind."

It took a second for Dee to process what he was saying. There was *another* aircraft out there and it was shooting at them.

"If the two of you can shut up and let me fly this thing, we might survive." Then he muttered under his breath, "This piece of shit wasn't built for aerial combat."

Dee resisted the urge to ask more questions. She knew their best chance was to let Frankie do his thing. He eased the aircraft down in and among the trees. With the terrain rising rapidly in front of them, he slid the power lever forward and Dee could hear the engine spool up after a second's delay. The little engine gave it all it had, but it did not look like it was going to be enough to clear the ridge in front of them. Frankie pulled the nose back, and a horn sounded in the cockpit.

"What's that?" Dee asked reflexively.

"Stall warning." Frankie eased the nose back down just enough to quiet the horn. "I need to put her in best climb to clear this terrain."

Dee nodded. Frankie might be an asshole, but he knew what he was doing. Maybe she'd seduced the right guy after all.

They cleared the ridge safely, bunting over it and back

down into the next valley. It had been a few minutes since they had taken the initial burst of fire and Dee felt comfortable talking again. "What was shooting at us?"

"I didn't see it, but my guess is it was one of the drones from the compound," Frankie said, in a much calmer tone than he had used earlier.

"They have drones?"

"Yeah, it's the only thing they have that's armed."

Dee sat back and considered what had just happened. *That son of a bitch was trying to kill us!*

The radio crackled. "Cessna 538 Tango Bravo, this is George Petros on guard. Please acknowledge."

Dee's blood turned to ice.

His voice was calm. Too calm. "Listen, you have no idea what you've taken. That little girl is the key to everything. Return her, and no one gets hurt."

Frankie shot Dee a look. "What the hell is he talking about?"

Dee didn't answer.

Another voice cut in. Kylee's. "They won't stop."

"What?" Frankie snapped.

"They won't stop until they get me back."

The sound of gunfire. Loud. Close.

Impact. A burst of flame shot from the nose of the plane.

"The engine!" Frankie shouted.

They plunged.

Kylee screamed. Dee reached for her, but gravity yanked her back.

The trees rushed up to meet them.

The last thing Dee saw was a flash of green before

everything went black.

***

Patrick Riley shut his eyes and exhaled slowly, trying to steady the unease curling in his gut. This was his failure. The thought coiled around his mind, suffocating and absolute.

He should have seen it coming—a nanny going rogue, stealing the project's most valuable asset right from under his nose. Maybe he had let himself believe their security was airtight, that the compound was untouchable. Maybe he had gotten soft.

But none of that mattered now. He could sit in the failure, let the remorse burn through his gut, or he could move forward. Fix this.

Opening his eyes, he found George Petros watching the drone's sensor feed on the massive screen at the front of the compound's command center. Still composed. Still calculating.

"Any sign of life?" Petros asked, not looking away from the flickering infrared readout.

The technician seated one row below, her fingers poised over the console, hesitated before answering. "Nothing yet, sir."

Petros finally turned, his sharp eyes locking onto Patrick. "What now, Pat?"

Patrick straightened, pushing the doubt out of his mind. This wasn't the time for hesitation. "We launch a QRF," he said firmly. Petros knew the term—Quick

Reaction Force. They had discussed contingencies for a breach before, though neither had expected to need one. "I've already put the motor pool on standby. The trucks are being loaded with fuel barrels now. We'll have a team on the road in under thirty minutes."

He paused, doing the mental math. Two days up. Two days back. He didn't like it. It left too much time for something to go wrong.

Petros studied him, expression unreadable. "Why not take the hyperloop?"

Patrick shook his head. "The closest station is Sacramento. They'd have to go on foot from there through rough terrain. Hot zone. Radiation levels still spike near the valley, and we're running low on meds." His voice remained even, factual. "The trucks are the better option. Safer. Faster."

Petros nodded, not questioning the logic, but there was a flicker of something in his expression—dissatisfaction.

"Medical capabilities?" he asked.

"Each team has a medic. They train regularly."

"A doctor?"

Patrick hesitated. He knew where this was going. "No. But they're proficient in combat medicine."

"I want you to send a doctor with them."

It wasn't a suggestion.

Patrick kept his jaw locked, forcing himself to swallow the response that leapt to his lips. A doctor was a liability. A non-combatant. A risk. But there was no point in arguing. Petros was the kind of man who didn't make requests—he made decisions.

"Yes, sir."

Before Petros could respond, one of the drone techs stiffened at her console. "Sir, I have movement near the crash site."

Patrick turned sharply, scanning the screen.

The technician's voice carried an edge of disgust. "Grubs."

The word rolled off her tongue like an insult. The outsiders. The ones who refused to die.

Petros exhaled sharply, rubbing his jaw. "Looks like your QRF won't be quick enough, Pat." His voice was measured, but Patrick could hear the undercurrent of meaning. What now?

Patrick didn't hesitate. "We still send them." He turned to the drone operator. "How long can you keep eyes on the target?"

The man's fingers flew across the keyboard, pulling up fuel calculations. He frowned. "Thirty-six hours, maybe forty-eight if we stretch it. We don't have enough fuel for continuous ops, not on station."

"Make it forty-eight," Patrick ordered. He turned back to Petros. "We'll track them if they're taken. But in the meantime, we can use our outside contacts. Get people on the ground."

Petros didn't reply immediately. Instead, he leaned forward, resting his elbows on the metal railing that separated the upper command platform from the workstations below. He surveyed the room, eyes narrowing.

Then, he spoke. Not just to Patrick—to everyone.

"We all know then next phase," he said, his voice cutting

through the quiet hum of machinery. "That girl is humanity's best chance at surviving. Her recovery is priority one. Eliminate all obstacles to that objective."

The room was silent.

Then, he turned back to Patrick. And though his voice had been meant for the whole room, his eyes never left his former friend.

"Am I clear?"

Patrick felt the weight of those words settle onto his shoulders. He had been given his marching orders. Failure was no longer an option.

He nodded once.

"Yes, sir."

3 – Callahan

Ian smelled the camp long before he saw it.

The stench of wood smoke, unwashed bodies, and rotting refuse carried for miles on the cold wind, settling thick in the back of his throat. These places always reeked. Not just of human waste and sweat, but of desperation.

Most of these settlements had started as refugee camps in the chaotic days after the bombs. People had come looking for food, shelter—protection. Over time, those with guns and muscle had taken control, demanding labor, goods, or worse in exchange for their mercy. Some settlements tried to keep up appearances, electing councils or pretending at democracy. It never lasted.

Rule by intimidation always won out in the end.

This place didn't even bother with the illusion.

From the ridge, Ian could see the full sprawl of the camp. High ground, smart. It overlooked the wide, shallow basin of a river that cut west from the Cascades. The trees surrounding it had long since been cleared away, their remnants fueling countless fires, barricades, and pyres. What had taken their place was a patchwork of weather-beaten canvas tents, ramshackle wooden shacks, and even a handful of old trailers.

At the center of it all stood a single house, large and intact. A relic from before the war. The boss-man's house. The kind of place that people only lived in if they had the muscle to keep it.

The river was why this camp had survived. It had drawn people here, just as water always had since the first cities were built. Without it, Rio Dell would have collapsed long ago. Ian had heard rumors that a FEMA water purification system still functioned somewhere in camp, filtering out disease, radiation, and whatever filth the living and the dead left behind. If that was true, it was the camp's most valuable resource.

And if it was the most valuable, someone owned it.

Ian moved toward the entrance, passing through the gaping break in the rusted concertina wire that ringed the camp. Someone had spotted him long before he arrived—he was sure of it. Scouts would have seen the shape of him moving across the hills, assessed him for threats, and passed the word along.

The guards at the entrance—two men, both carrying battered rifles—watched him approach. A wooden signpost stood crooked in the dirt, scrawled with uneven black paint: "Rio Dell Trading Post."

One of the guards, a thick-bodied man with a scar carving down his jaw, held out a hand. "Weapons."

Ian spread his arms, palms up. "Don't have any."

The other man, leaner, younger, dead-eyed, stepped forward and patted him down. He found the knife strapped to Ian's ankle but didn't take it. A blade wasn't a problem. A gun was. The search was less about security and more about confiscation. If Ian had been carrying a firearm, he wouldn't have walked into Rio Dell with it anyway. His M-86 was buried under a fallen tree half a mile back.

The scarred guard jerked his head toward the open pathway. "Go on."

Ian stepped inside.

No one acknowledged him. That was how you survived places like this. You kept your eyes ahead, didn't stare, didn't hesitate. If you acted like you belonged, most people wouldn't question it.

The camp was teeming with activity. Figures shuffled between stalls, voices haggled over goods in hoarse, weary tones. Most people walked, but a few had bicycles, their chains clinking in uneven rhythm. He even spotted a rickshaw, one man pulling a cart piled high with sacks. A debt worker, probably. There was no official name for it anymore—before the bombs, people would have called it slavery. Now, it was just how things got done.

Ian's eyes flicked to the raised wooden platform at the center of the camp.

A man hung from a noose, his body swaying slightly in the cold wind. His eyes had bulged and clouded, his tongue dark and swollen, spilling halfway from his mouth. His skin had taken on the pale gray of death.

A cardboard sign was slung around his neck, dangling loosely from twine.

THIEF.

An example.

The people of Rio Dell didn't waste words.

A punishment like that wasn't just about justice—it was about reminding everyone who was in charge. A deterrent. A warning. If you stole from the wrong person here, the consequences were the same as if you pulled a gun on a guard.

One punishment.

Ian didn't look at the body for long. He already knew how it ended.

He moved through the crowd, scanning the buildings. He wasn't here to linger. He needed to trade for food, maybe whiskey, then get out.

You didn't ask for directions in a place like this. That was the same as announcing you didn't belong.

But he didn't have to search long.

A large canvas tent loomed near the center of the camp, just past the market stalls. A wooden pole held up the entrance flap, and nailed to it was a freshly painted sign:

"ILYA'S SHACK."

Beneath it, scrawled in blocky red letters:

"GOOD FOOD & GOOD WHISKEY FOR GOOD TRADE."

Ian adjusted the strap on his pack and stepped inside.

The plywood floor groaned under the weight of too many feet. Some sections were nailed down tight, others wobbled dangerously under shifting bodies. Tables were scattered across the tent in no particular order—old kitchen tables with missing chairs, flimsy card tables held together by rusted hinges, massive wooden spools turned on their sides. A crude attempt at order in a place where chaos ruled.

The air inside was thick, a suffocating mix of fried meat, tobacco, stale marijuana, and unwashed bodies. The smells clashed, one failing to mask the other. The farther in Ian walked, the more the stink settled into his clothes.

At the far side of the tent, a makeshift bar stood against a wall of scavenged plywood, its shelves lined with bottles of questionable liquor and cans with faded labels.

Ian felt the weight of stares on his back as he stepped inside. Sizing him up. Calculating. The kind of scrutiny that came from men looking for an easy mark and others measuring whether he was worth the trouble. He didn't stop walking, didn't make eye contact. If you didn't act like prey, most predators lost interest.

The low murmur of conversation resumed as he passed.

Except for one exchange at the bar.

An argument.

A man was selling something, voice eager, insistent. But the buyer wasn't interested.

"No." The word was flat, final.

The seller tried again, leaning in too close.

A hand shot out, grabbing him by the collar. The sound of fabric tightening filled the space, followed by a muttered threat. Then, with a casual shove, the seller was sent sprawling onto the floor.

The man who had thrown him down turned back to his drink, conversation over.

But the seller wasn't done.

Ian watched as the scrawny man clambered to his feet, face twisted with embarrassment. He dusted himself off, then turned sharply—not toward his aggressor, but to a girl standing behind him.

She couldn't have been older than twelve. Frizzy, dirty blonde hair. Blue-gray eyes wide with fear. Her face was painted with crude makeup, an attempt to make her look older, more desirable. She wore a yellow dress that was too clean, too neat—too out of place.

The seller grabbed her by the arm. Hard.

She gasped, her whole body going rigid.

Ian stilled.

The man yanked her close, leaned in, and whispered something in her ear.

She flinched.

Then he dragged her toward the exit.

Ian stepped in his way.

The scrawny pimp hesitated, then tried to shift around him. Ian moved too, blocking his path.

"Move," the man barked.

Ian didn't. Didn't blink. Didn't shift. Just let the silence stretch.

The pimp's fingers tightened around the girl's arm in a show of ownership. Defiance.

"Get out of my way, you moron," he spat.

Ian's voice was calm. Too calm. "Let her go."

The pimp snorted, eyes darting around the room, checking to see who was watching. "You don't have any idea who you're fucking with, do you?" Spittle flew from the corners of his mouth.

Ian let the words settle between them. Then, he exhaled.

"I have some idea."

The pimp's eyes flickered with uncertainty. His grip tightened, yanking the girl forward.

That was enough.

Ian moved fast—his hand latching onto the pimp's wrist, twisting. The man yelped, arm wrenching backward as Ian forced him into a lock. In seconds, he was being shoved toward the exit, his boots scraping uselessly against the plywood.

Ian threw him into the dirt outside, where he landed hard, spitting curses.

The pimp scrambled up, face red with humiliation. "This isn't over! You've fucked with the wrong crew!"

Ian didn't answer. Didn't even look at him.

When he turned back, the girl was gone.

A survivor, Ian thought. Smart. He only hoped she had somewhere safe to run to.

Inside the tent, the room had gone quiet. Conversations had stalled. People had paused, watching.

But only for a moment.

Then the raucous murmur returned, and Ian continued toward the bar like nothing had happened.

The bartender took his time walking over.

Thin. Like most were these days. His clothes were layered, probably to hide how little weight he carried. His breath stank of rotgut whiskey, and the way he moved told Ian he drank as much as he served.

He jerked his chin toward the door. "You must be some kind of stupid, bro."

Ian didn't answer.

The bartender wiped the counter with a rag that looked dirtier than the surface beneath it. "That pimp works for Callahan."

Ian shrugged.

The bartender let out a dry chuckle. "Your problem, I guess. What do you want?"

Ian eyed the menu tacked to the plywood wall behind him.

WHISKEY - BEER - MEAT ON A STICK.

He leaned forward slightly. "What kind of meat?"

The bartender didn't hesitate. "Dog."

Ian studied him. Watching his face.

The bartender didn't flinch, didn't shift. Used to this kind of scrutiny. "Look, we don't do that here. It's dog or squirrel. Take it or leave it."

Ian nodded. "I'll take one... and a beer."

The bartender held out a hand. "What ya got?"

Ian reached into his coat, pulled out the can opener he'd taken from the dead woman's pack.

The bartender turned it over in his fingers, then shook his head. "One or the other. Unless you got something else."

Ian considered. Then exhaled. "Just the beer."

The bartender poured a dark, bitter homebrew from a dented tap, setting the cup down with a thunk.

Ian took a long sip. It was rough, but not the worst he'd had.

Around him, voices rose and fell, conversation flowing without threat. The usual drivel—bets, rumors, half-baked conspiracy theories.

One man was louder than the rest.

"They're still out there," he was saying, voice filled with certainty. "Still running things."

A skeptic scoffed. "Who's still out there?"

"The government. Who do you think?"

A woman's voice cut in. Sharp, edged with frustration.

"Where the hell are they, then? What are they running? You got people dropping dead from the bloody flu, no radiation meds left anywhere, men out there eating each other—and those bastards in the big house"—she jabbed a thumb toward the camp's center—"think they own everything." She exhaled, shaking her head. "I don't see any damn government stopping any of it."

"They're not stopping it," the man countered. "They're keeping themselves alive. Their own clean zones. The rest of us? We're nothing to them. Just more bodies to keep out."

"Oh, here we go." The skeptic rolled his eyes. "Another clean zone nut."

The conversation continued, but Ian wasn't listening anymore.

Because he heard the shrill voice of the pimp from earlier.

"There's the asshole, right there!"

Ian didn't turn. Just stared into his beer.

A larger, heavier voice followed. "I've got it from here."

A barstool shifted beside him.

"Get him whatever he wants." The man's voice was calm, measured. "It's on me."

Ian sighed. Didn't even look up.

"Thanks," he muttered. "I'm not doing it."

Jenks chuckled. "Come on, Hammond. You could use the extra scratch."

Ian finally turned, locking eyes with Callahan's right-hand man.

"I told Callahan I was out."

They both knew that wasn't how it worked.

Jenks was a big man, well over six feet and north of 250 pounds, with dark hair and a thick dark beard that gave him a mountain man look. His size provided the intimidation that Callahan needed, but he was also smart. Unlike most guys that worked for Callahan, which was probably why Jenks was his right-hand man, his deputy and most trusted advisor. Not that Callahan really trusted anyone. "Look, order what you want," he said. "I can tell you're hungry."

"I'm good," Ian said. Then after a moment, "That piece of shit you walked in with working for Callahan now?"

Jenks kept quiet.

"He was pimping out a kid, Jenks."

"I don't do the hiring, Rog," Jenks said, wincing and cradling his left hand.

"Still bothering you?" Ian asked.

Jenks nodded and looked Ian in the eye. "It could have been a lot worse. I still owe you for that."

"You don't owe me shit, Jenks."

"Look, just meet with the man, Hammond, is that so hard?"

The bartender passed carrying two sticks of dog meat and two beers for a couple seated at the end of the bar. Ian got a good whiff of the meat as it passed. "That's all, I'm just meeting with him."

"That's it, no strings attached. If it doesn't work out with Callahan, consider the meal my thanks." Jenks held up his bad left hand.

Ian nodded. "I'll take some meat on a stick and another

beer."

"My man!" Jenks clapped Ian on the shoulder and nearly knocked him from his stool. They both knew how persuasive Callahan could be. Meeting with him meant you were working for him.

***

Callahan conducted business out of one of the few mobile homes in Rio Dell—a luxury only a handful could afford. He wasn't the boss-man here, not officially. But he knew how to stay in the good graces of the real power, offering kickbacks, brokering deals, never stepping on the wrong toes.

Ian followed Jenks inside.

Two men flanked the door. No weapons visible—but they were armed. Ian didn't need to see the guns to know they were there. The way the men stood—spines straight, hands relaxed but ready, eyes tracking every movement—meant they had their orders.

Ian ignored them. Sizing them up wasn't worth the trouble.

The interior was sparse but functional. A dented gray metal desk, rust creeping along the edges, dominated the space. Callahan sat behind it, all business. He looked like hell warmed over—dirty blond hair an unkempt mess, skin taut from long days and short nights. From behind, he might've seemed boyish—until you saw the narrowing of his eyes, the hooked predatory nose.

A young woman stood beside the desk, clutching a

stack of papers. Pretty. Not afraid. But not comfortable, either.

Jenks stepped aside, letting Ian take the center of the room.

Callahan's grin was immediate, broad, practiced. "Ian Hammond. Damn, it's good to see you, boy."

Ian hated when he called him that. Callahan was only a couple of years older, but he spoke like Ian had crawled out of the dirt looking for guidance.

Ian didn't take the bait. Didn't match the grin.

"How'd you know I was here?"

Callahan leaned back, lacing his fingers behind his head. "Not much goes on in my little outpost that I don't know about. You should remember that. Haven't I always said the key to survival is staying one step ahead? Eyes open. Ears open." His grin widened. "If you didn't want to be found, Hammond, you shouldn't have come here."

Ian considered arguing, but what was the point? He hadn't known Callahan was operating out of Rio Dell, or he would've kept moving. But nothing good ever came from arguing with Callahan in his own place.

"Fine," Ian said. "Why am I here?"

Callahan leaned forward, resting his elbows on the desk. "I need someone I trust to do a job for me."

Ian glanced at Jenks, then the two goons by the door. What, you don't trust these turds? He didn't say it.

Callahan picked up on his body language anyway. His voice tightened. "I need them here."

Then, his tone softened—calculating, conciliatory. "Look, I know things got... messy last time. Things happen.

We do what we have to. I figured you needed some time. Go off. Clear your head. That's fine."

Ian let out a slow breath. "What's the job?"

Callahan exchanged a glance with Jenks, the shadow of a smirk forming. "Good. I need something delivered."

Ian kept his face unreadable. "To who?"

"The usual. Associates of mine. Up north."

That meant Free Militia territory. And getting there meant crossing through bandit strongholds, marauder-infested wastelands, and cannibal country.

Ian nodded slowly. "What's the cargo?"

Callahan gestured to the woman beside him. She turned, opened a safe behind the desk, and pulled out four shoebox-sized packages, each sealed with duct tape.

Jenks took them and stacked them inside a nylon backpack.

Ian raised a brow. "You're sending me all that way to deliver shoes?"

Callahan's laugh was sharp, raucous. "Still funny, Hammond. No. Seeds."

Ian frowned. "Seeds?"

"Yup. Carrots and broccoli. Two boxes each. Our friends up north are setting up some indoor farms. They've got other crops but are lacking in these. Too many mouths to feed."

Ian exhaled through his nose. "An army travels on its stomach."

Callahan's smirk lingered. "Exactly."

Ian tilted his head. "You worried about where that army wants to travel next?"

Callahan grinned wider. "Every damn day. That's why I'm two steps ahead. Always." He tapped his temple. "Got fallback plans to my fallback plans. And besides—if I don't sell to them, someone else will."

Jenks chuckled. "Truer words, boss."

Ian leaned back slightly. "So you want me to drag these seeds through a hellscape filled with murderers and cannibals, just to hand them off to a prepper army—an army that's brought back drawing and quartering and thinks they're some holy crusade to save the country from itself. And you want me to do it—because you don't want to risk your regulars."

He motioned to the guards, then to Jenks.

Callahan's grin never faltered. "See, Jenks? I told you Hammond was the guy. He gets it."

Jenks rolled his eyes. "I was the one who said that boss."

Callahan waved him off. "Nah, pretty sure this was my idea."

Jenks sighed. "Yeah, boss. Whatever you say."

Ian ignored their back and forth. "Where's the drop?"

Callahan let the moment linger—that smug satisfaction of a man who just got exactly what he wanted.

He pulled out a map.

The spot was marked deep in the mountains, east of I-5. Just past the Oregon border.

Ian studied it. "I'm gonna need a map of my own. That's outside my usual range."

Callahan slid the paper toward him. "That one's yours."

Then, as Ian reached for it, Callahan added, "One more

thing."

Ian stilled. "What's that?"

Callahan's grin returned, but this time, it was sharper. Hungrier.

"It's not a what I want you looking for."

His eyes gleamed.

"It's a who."

4 – Grubs

Dee woke to the metallic tang of blood on her tongue and the relentless pounding in her skull. The world around her tilted, and she sucked in a sharp breath, tasting gasoline and burnt metal.

She reached up, fingers brushing over a wet gash on her forehead. The pain shot through her skull like a hammer strike. Blood trickled down her face, blurring her vision. She wiped at her eyes, blinking hard.

"Can you walk?"

The voice was urgent, unfamiliar. A man's voice, accented. Not Frankie.

She blinked through the haze. "Frankie?" Her own voice came out hoarse, weak.

"I don't know no Frankie, lady, but we gotta get out of here. Now."

Dee's mind was fighting through molasses, slow and heavy. Something wasn't right. Then, like a lightning strike—

Kylee.

Her chest tightened. "Where's Kylee?"

"She's clear," said another voice—a woman, steady and calm. "Now we need to get you."

Dee felt hands at her seatbelt, yanking. The tension released, and a strong arm hooked around her waist, pulling her free.

Pain exploded from her left forearm.

She barely had time to scream before the nausea hit, her vision tunneling.

"Omar, careful—her arm's broken," the woman warned.

"I see it," Omar snapped. Impatient. Focused. "She burns if we don't move. Now, lady, use your legs."

Dee barely processed the words, but some survival instinct kicked in. She braced herself against Omar's grip and stumbled out of the wreckage.

"Run!" Omar barked.

Her legs were wobbly, but they worked. She ran, cradling her arm against her chest, choking on the acrid air.

She felt the shockwave before she heard the explosion.

A wall of heat slammed into her back, knocking her forward. She hit the ground hard, rolling onto her good side, gasping for breath. The pain from her arm was white-hot, unbearable.

Kylee lay nearby, motionless.

Dee crawled toward her.

"Where's Frankie?" she rasped.

"Told you, lady—I don't know no Frankie," Omar said.

"She means the pilot, genius," the woman muttered.

Omar jerked a thumb toward the wreckage, now a roaring fireball. "He was in there. He's gone, bro."

"Sorry, honey," the woman said, quieter now. "He was dead before we got here. Was he your man?"

Dee shook her head. "No. He was just a guy."

She barely registered the words as she reached shaking fingers toward Kylee's throat, feeling for a pulse.

It was there. Faint, but there.

"She's alive," the woman said, kneeling beside her. "But I don't know for how long. She took a bad hit."

Dee felt her eyes burn, but she swallowed the emotion down. Crying wouldn't help.

A warm hand settled on her shoulder, squeezing gently. "My name's Jenna."

Dee turned slightly. The woman had sharp, sun-worn features, dark hair pulled back into a loose knot.

Jenna gestured to the man beside her. "This is my friend Omar."

"I'm Dee."

"And I take it the little one is Kylee?"

Dee nodded, still hovering over the girl.

Jenna's brow furrowed. "We haven't seen a plane flying in years, Dee. Where did you come from?"

Dee's mind whirled for a lie. "We stole the plane from an airstrip near Bishop."

Jenna and Omar exchanged a look.

They didn't believe her.

That was fine. As long as they didn't guess the truth.

Jenna didn't press. Instead, she turned to Omar. "Go find two straight sticks for a splint."

He nodded and jogged toward the tree line.

Jenna rolled up her sleeves, retrieving a coil of twine from a pushcart nearby. "The break in your arm is clean, at least," she muttered, cutting the twine with a pocketknife. "If we keep it immobile, it should heal."

Dee barely listened. Kylee still wasn't waking up.

Then—

"Dee?"

The voice was small. Weak.

Dee whipped her head around.

Kylee's eyes were open, glassy and unfocused.

"I'm thirsty," the girl whispered.

Relief crashed over Dee like a wave. "Kylee!" She smoothed the girl's hair back, trying to steady her shaking hands. "How do you feel? Are you hurt?"

Kylee blinked slowly. "I'm just tired... and thirsty."

Dee turned sharply to Jenna. "Do you have water?"

Jenna hesitated, eyes flicking to Kylee like she was seeing something impossible.

Then, she snapped back to reality, yanking a plastic water bottle from the pushcart and handing it over.

Dee examined the clear plastic.

"It's clean," Jenna assured her. "The place we filled it tests safe."

Dee nodded. "Thank you." She unscrewed the cap and handed it to Kylee, who gulped it down greedily.

Jenna still looked troubled. "She looked worse off than she was."

Dee forced a smile. "Adrenaline, probably."

Jenna didn't look convinced.

Omar returned, two straight sticks in hand. Dee got a **proper look at him now—**a wiry frame, deep tan, and a small black tattoo of two teardrops under his left eye.

Kylee noticed it too.

"What's that for?" she asked, pointing at the splints.

"For your sister, honey," Jenna said. "She broke her arm."

Dee didn't correct her.

Kylee's brows furrowed. "What?"

Before Dee could react, Kylee lunged forward, grabbing Dee's injured arm.

Pain shot through Dee's body. She gritted her teeth, barely holding back a cry.

Kylee's small fingers traced the break. "Sorry," she murmured.

Then, she closed her eyes.

A wave of warmth pulsed from Kylee's hands, spreading down to Dee's bones. The pain dulled.

Kylee moved her hands lower, feeling the break, then adjusted it slightly.

Dee's breath hitched. "Kylee, don't—"

Kylee ignored her.

Jenna's eyes widened in alarm. "You can't do that! She'll pass out from the pain!"

Kylee trembled. A soft moan escaped her lips, and she slumped backward.

Dee caught her. "Kylee? What's wrong?"

Kylee's eyes fluttered open. She was tired—but fine.

Jenna wasn't buying it. She crouched beside Dee, inspecting her arm.

Then, her brows pulled together.

"...It's healed."

Omar, still oblivious, held up the sticks. "You ready for the splint?"

Dee pulled her arm back, too slow.

Jenna's voice was a whisper. "It's completely healed."

"No," Dee said quickly. "She just set it for the splint. I

have a high pain tolerance."

"I know what a healed bone feels like. What did she do?"

Dee kept her voice even. "She didn't do anything. What do you think she could do?"

Jenna's lips curled into a slow smile.

Her eyes weren't smiling.

"Keep your secrets, Dee."

Then she stood. "We need to move. The explosion's gonna attract attention."

"Attention from who?" Kylee asked.

Jenna slung the pushcart's straps over her shoulders.

"Bandits," she said.

Then, with a knowing smirk—

"Or worse."

"We're trying to get to Crescent City," Kylee said, before Dee could shush her.

"What's there?" asked Omar.

"Just some friends," Dee said before Kylee could reveal anything else. "People we can stay with."

"We can help you get there safely," Jenna said.

"We can't ask you to do that," said Dee. She knew these grubs were not about to help them out of the kindness of their heart.

"It's not like we've got anything better to do. Plus, I'm guessing there will be some kind of reward for us when we get there," Jenna said.

"I don't know about that," Dee said. "We'll be fine on our own, really."

"Nonsense, we insist," Jenna said with a smile.

Omar lifted his shirt, revealing the pistol tucked into his

waistband.

***

They walked most of the afternoon.

The terrain sloped downhill, which told Dee they were heading west. If the sky had been clear, she would have been sure, but no one had seen the sun since before the bombs.

A thought struck her—Kylee had never seen the sun.

Not once in her life.

She had only seen videos—flickering images in the sterile compound, used as educational tools for the experimental children.

She doesn't even know what warmth from the sun feels like.

The thought sat heavy in Dee's chest as they trudged forward.

Omar led the way, deliberately avoiding roads. He kept them low, following ravines and canyons, staying out of sight. He moved like a man who knew exactly what he was doing.

As dusk settled, they stopped in a clearing shielded by fallen pines. The air was getting colder.

Jenna handed Dee a coarse wool blanket. "You two should share," she said. "Body heat's your best friend out here. Keep your clothes on—especially your socks. If you think it's cold now, just wait till three a.m."

Dee took the blanket, nodding but saying nothing.

It smelled like old sweat and dirt, but it was wide

enough to fold underneath them, offering some thin protection from the rocky ground. Small roots and stones pressed through the fabric, but it was better than freezing on the bare earth.

Kylee fell asleep quickly.

Dee didn't.

She lay still, staring at the black sky, empty of stars.

Jenna and Omar lay across from them, bundled under a blanket of their own. Dee could feel Jenna's occasional glances, checking to see if they were asleep.

Dee closed her eyes, breathing evenly, pretending.

A while later, Jenna's low whisper broke the quiet.

"Tomorrow, start leading us to Rio Dell."

Dee froze.

Omar shifted. "I thought we were taking them to that city place."

Even without seeing her face, Dee knew Jenna was rolling her eyes.

"That's what we tell them, genius. But tomorrow, you lead us to Rio Dell. They won't know the difference."

A beat of silence.

"You wanna sell them to Callahan?" Omar asked.

Jenna's voice was thoughtful, calculating. "Maybe. If he pays top dollar. If not, we go to another buyer."

Dee felt her stomach twist.

Jenna exhaled. "There's something about that girl... This might be my break."

Omar's voice turned greedy. "You mean our break, right, baby?"

A pause.

Then Jenna's voice, silky smooth. "Of course. It's you and me."

A rustle. Omar moving closer. "It's been a while, baby, I just thought—"

"Not tonight. Get some sleep."

Dee stayed still as stone.

Her mind raced. They had to get away. But how?

***

They walked in silence for an hour.

Then Kylee said, flatly, "You're not taking us to Crescent City."

Dee's breath caught.

Jenna's head turned slightly. "What makes you say that?"

Kylee's eyes were sharp. Too sharp. "Because you know people who would pay a reward for us. People who aren't kind."

Jenna's smile was slow. Amused.

"She overheard us last night," Omar muttered.

Kylee shook her head. "No. I went inside—"

Dee cut her off. "We both overheard you."

Jenna's amusement faded. "Good." Her tone turned cold. "I was getting tired of playing make-believe."

Omar grabbed an old bungee cord from the pushcart and yanked Dee's wrists forward, binding them tight.

"No need to tie the girl," Jenna said. "What can she do?"

Dee bit her tongue.

You'd be surprised.

Kylee's voice trembled with rage. "How can you do this?"

Omar snorted. "Keep it down, kid. There's worse people

out here than us."

Kylee's jaw clenched. "That's hard to believe."

A new voice cut in.

"You should listen to the man."

The world tilted.

Omar barely had time to reach for the pistol in his waistband before a baseball bat cracked against his skull.

The sound was wet.

Omar crumpled.

The man with the bat giggled.

Thin. Twitchy. His eyes wild with amusement.

But he hadn't been the one who spoke.

Dee's gaze snapped up—

A second man stepped out of the trees, an assault rifle resting easy in his hands.

A black ski hat atop his head sprouting strips of fabric twisted into long, dangling shapes—

Like tentacles.

The rifleman cocked his head, grinning beneath the mask.

"He was talking about me."

5 – Dangerous Encounters

The rain had been falling steady for hours, soaking through Ian's trench coat, masking his movement in the dense woods. It was a smart tactic, using the sound of rainfall to move unseen. Most marauders knew that trick. The ones who lasted this long weren't just thugs; they had street instincts, a predator's patience.

A twig snapped.

Ian flinched. Sloppy.

But the mistake didn't matter. It was already too late.

The click of a hammer cocking cut through the rain, freezing Ian mid-step. A man stood ten feet away, half-concealed behind a gnarled pine, a 9mm Browning leveled at Ian's head.

Ian's muscles tensed. His breathing quickened. A familiar, sickening clench formed in his gut—an animal instinct, old as time.

"Delightful morning for a walk, friend."

The voice came from the gunman. He stepped out of the shadows, revealing yellowed teeth and a patchy beard, unkempt and matted. His black knit cap dripped with rain, a few strands of greasy dark hair clinging to his forehead.

He smirked. "Just keep them hands where I can see 'em. Reach for that rifle, and I'll decorate that tree with your brains."

Ian didn't move.

To the left, a giggle.

The second bandit stepped forward, grinning. "Brains? Ain't much meat up there anyway."

The sick feeling in Ian's stomach turned to ice.

Cannibals.

The giggle stopped. A sharp smack followed as a third man emerged, cuffing the giggler on the back of the head.

"Shut the fuck up, Jerry. Watch where you're stepping, dumbass! You 'bout gave us away."

Ian's eyes flicked to this third man. He was different from the others—calmer, confident. His ski hat was ridiculous, a jester's nightmare, tentacle-like strips of felt sprouting from the top. But despite the absurdity, it broke up his silhouette, making him harder to spot in the woods.

A smart touch.

A leader's touch.

Ian met his gaze.

Tentacle Hat grinned. "Out for a stroll? Damn shame you don't got a lady with you. Ain't had nowhere decent to stick my dick in months."

Jerry giggled again.

Tentacle Hat snapped his fingers.

Jerry moved in, ripping Ian's rifle from his back.

Tentacle Hat chuckled. "You're a cool one, bro. Here we got you dead to rights, and you ain't said a word. No begging, no crying." He tilted his head. "That's rare."

"Makes it kinda boring," Jerry muttered.

Tentacle Hat ignored him. "What d'you think, Stiles?"

The gunman, Stiles, gave a small nod. "Yeah. Looks like he can handle himself." His voice was smoother, more educated than the others. "And no signs of the flu."

Jerry's grin vanished.

Tentacle Hat smirked. "Exactly what I was thinking. We could use someone like that. Good replacement for Jerry, even."

Jerry stiffened. "Come on now, Sanchez! I done everything you wanted!" His voice cracked. "You can't do me like this!"

Tentacle Hat—Sanchez—burst out laughing. "Relax, Jerry. Just funnin'." He clapped Jerry on the shoulder. "For now."

Jerry looked relieved—but not entirely.

Sanchez turned back to Ian. "What you say, bro? Come back to camp. Prove yourself on a few grabs, and you might even get that rifle back."

Ian looked over his shoulder at Stiles, the Browning still aimed at his head.

He forced a smirk. "You guys look like you eat well—except for this guy." He jerked a thumb at Jerry.

Sanchez roared with laughter.

Stiles stayed silent.

Sanchez motioned with his hand. "We'll talk through the deal on the way back."

Ian knew what that meant.

They didn't even check his pack. They weren't after supplies.

Why waste time robbing a man in the woods when you could get him to walk himself into camp?

Jerry tied Ian's hands with frayed rope. Sanchez explained it was just until they could trust him.

Obvious lie.

Jerry's pat-down was half-assed. He missed the knife strapped inside Ian's right leg.

Ian kept his face blank.

That was his one advantage.

***

They moved through the drenched woods, the rain slowing to a cold drizzle. Jerry led the way, with Ian behind him. Taking up the rear were Stiles, still carrying his Browning and Sanchez, who now had Ian's rifle in his hands.

Ian delivered the seeds to the Free Militia patrol two days ago. They had met him in Oregon, right at the location marked on Callahan's map. The Militia Lieutenant in charge of the patrol was a clueless prick. But they took the seeds without as much as a thank you and moved on. The entire trip had been uneventful . . . until now.

Ian kept pace. Watched. Waited.

The forest was too quiet.

No wind.

No birds.

A dead place.

They weren't the only hunters out here.

Jerry led them down into a narrow ravine, following the remains of an ancient, dried-out riverbed.

Ian's gut twisted.

A choke point. A kill zone.

They've done this before.

They climbed a small ridgeline when Jerry stopped suddenly, dropping into a crouch.

A sound carried over the hill. Voices.

Sanchez slid past Ian, crouching next to Jerry. "What we got?"

Jerry peered over the ridge. His giggling was gone. "Four of 'em. A guy, two women, and a kid." He licked his lips. "Walking meat sacks."

Sanchez grinned. "Day just keeps getting better."

Jerry chuckled. "Dumbasses are just sitting there, arguing."

Sanchez motioned for Jerry to follow him. "We'll cross over and get behind 'em." He turned back to Stiles. "Keep our new bro company."

Stiles nodded.

Ian saw his chance.

He flexed his fingers. "Cut me loose, and I'll give you a hand. Four's better than two."

Sanchez paused. Looked intrigued.

Then, a smirk. "Nah. Stay here."

He and Jerry disappeared into the trees.

Ian turned to Stiles. "What'd you do before all this?"

Stiles didn't even glance at him.

"Shut the fuck up."

So much for that angle.

Ian shifted slightly, scanning the ground. He spotted a small, round rock a few feet away.

Might not cut the rope... but it'd crush a skull.

He rolled onto his side, stretching casually.

His fingers closed around the stone.

Stiles didn't notice. He was too busy staring up the ridge, picking at his nose.

Then—

A woman's scream.

Stiles' head snapped toward the ridge.

Ian moved.

In one fluid motion, he rolled, swung, and brought the rock down with full force.

Crunch.

The blow hit Stiles' eye socket, not his temple. Not a kill shot.

But it was enough.

Stiles yelped, clutching his face.

Ian didn't stop.

He swung again. And again.

Stiles slumped.

Ian kept going. Until his skull caved in.

Panting, Ian knelt over the body.

He grabbed the Browning, flicked the safety on, and tucked it into his belt.

Then, he pulled the knife from his boot and sliced through his bindings.

Another scream.

A woman's voice. Pleading.

Ian froze. Then swallowed hard.

He could run. Get away.

No. That wouldn't work. These men knew how to track. If he ran, they'd come for him. Hunt him.

The only way to be safe…

Was to finish them first.

***

Ian slid onto his stomach, dragging himself forward over the damp, root-laden forest floor. The scent of rotting leaves and damp earth filled his nose as he inched toward the clearing.

Through the underbrush, he spotted Jerry, standing beside a small two-wheeled cart, bolt cutters in one hand, Ian's rifle slung over his back. The cart was packed with someone's gear. But Ian's focus wasn't on the supplies.

It was on the two figures tied to it. A woman and a girl. Both sobbing.

A useless gesture. Men like these thrived on fear, fed on suffering.

Near them, a man's body lay sprawled in the dirt. Knives jutted from his arm and chest, his corpse a human pincushion. The way they were placed—casual, careless—it wasn't a fight. It was practice.

A rustle on the far side of the cart.

Then, laughter.

Ian's gaze snapped toward the sound.

Sanchez. The tentacle hat bobbing with rhythmic motion.

Screams filled the air. A woman's voice. Raw. Agonized.

Ian's stomach twisted. He knew that sound. Helplessness.

Then, a sudden stop.

Silence.

Sanchez let out a satisfied groan, stretching like a man finishing a meal. He gripped the wooden cart, using it for balance as he lifted one leg, bent his knee toward his chest—

And stomped down.

A sickening crack.

The woman's body went still.

"Whoa!" Sanchez barked a laugh. "Jerry, bro, you gotta check this out."

Jerry turned, frowning. "What'd you do?"

"I must've pushed her nose into her brain or some shit," Sanchez mused, eyes flicking over the lifeless body. "Blood's coming out of her ears."

Jerry whined. "Come on, man! You said I could go next!"

Sanchez snorted. "Quit whining, dumbass. There's another one."

Jerry's excitement returned as his gaze locked onto the woman tied to the cart. Blonde. Healthy.

"I go first this time," Jerry declared.

"No way," Sanchez shot back. "Cut her loose. Bring her over here."

Jerry hesitated. "Be careful this time."

Sanchez turned, face twisting. "You telling me what to do, Jerry?"

Jerry backed off immediately. "No, man, I just—"

"Relax. I won't stomp this one till you're done." Sanchez grinned. "Besides, if I mess up, you get first go at the short one."

A sharp, terrified cry tore from the young girl.

Jerry and Sanchez laughed like children.

That sound—Rusty's face flashed in Ian's mind.

His son. Fear-stricken. Helpless.

Just like them.

Caution turned to rage.

Jerry slung Ian's rifle over the cart so he could cut the blonde woman loose.

Sanchez, still facing the other way, wiped himself off.

Ian had to move. Now.

He pulled the pistol up, braced his arm against the log, sighting Sanchez.

Deep breath. Steady.

Click.

No shot. Ian froze. No round in the chamber.

His heartbeat thundered in his ears.

He dropped back behind the log, forcing his breathing steady. He froze until he was sure neither Sanchez nor Jerry heard the click, then pushed a button on the side of the pistol grip to drop the magazine.

Empty.

These guys captured him and took his M-86 with an unloaded weapon. He would kick himself in the ass later for being stupid.

But not now. No time for frustration. No time for mistakes.

He drew his knife from the sheath at his ankle.

Took one deep breath.

And ran.

Jerry was talking, distracted, his head down as he worked the ropes.

He didn't see Ian until it was too late.

Ian caught the rising bolt cutters in one hand, using his momentum to slam Jerry's skull into the cart. The impact stunned him.

Time to finish it.

Ian ripped the bolt cutters away, gripping them like a hammer.

One swing.

The metal cracked against Jerry's temple. His head snapped sideways into the wheel of the cart. Limp.

Before Ian could react, a shadow lunged from the side.

Sanchez.

A human wrecking ball.

Ian barely had time to brace before beefy arms wrapped around his waist, tackling him to the ground.

His knife flew from his grip.

The impact knocked the wind from his lungs.

Then—pain.

The heel of Sanchez's palm smashed into Ian's face, slamming his head into the dirt.

Then another blow. A fist. Then another.

A crack. The taste of blood flooded Ian's mouth. His skull rang with each punch.

Sanchez was too strong. Too fast. Ian could barely think through the blows rattling his brain.

This was a mistake. Sanchez raised his fist for another—

CRACK.

The unmistakable snap of an M-86 firing.

Sanchez's body lurched.

For a moment, his face froze in confusion. Then he

slumped.

Sanchez's dead weight pinned Ian.

Ian gasped for breath, savoring the relief.

With an exhausted shove, he rolled Sanchez's lifeless body off.

The world tilted, his vision still blurry from the beating. He wiped blood from his face—then froze.

Because the barrel of his own rifle was now pointed directly at him.

The blonde woman. Fierce blue eyes locked onto his. Her grip on the M-86 was steady.

"Where's the rest of your crew?" she demanded. No hesitation. No mercy.

Ian swallowed. Didn't move.

"No crew." His voice was rough, his mouth full of blood. "I travel alone."

She studied him for a long moment.

"Anyone comes this way," she said, leveling the barrel, "and the first round goes through your head. Got it?"

Ian exhaled. "You're welcome."

She scoffed. "Don't think for a second—"

A small voice interrupted.

"Dee, untie me."

Ian turned his head. The girl. Her eyes wide, curious.

The blonde woman—Dee—glanced at her. The ice in her expression thawed slightly. "Just a minute, Kylee."

Dee pulled a pair of old scissors from the cart, cutting the rope one-handed—keeping the rifle aimed at Ian.

Kylee turned to the man tied to the tree. "He's dead." No sadness. Just a statement of fact.

She surveyed the clearing, scanning Jerry, Sanchez... then Ian. And frowned.

"Where are they all coming from?" Kylee asked, her voice thoughtful. "The Director said the outsiders were dying off. But we keep running into them."

Ian's pulse quickened. The Director?

Dee's grip on the rifle tightened. "We need to keep moving."

Kylee didn't look convinced. "Do you think this one can help us?"

Ian blinked. They were talking about him like he wasn't even there.

Dee scoffed. "Not a chance. We need to find our own say to Crescent City."

"Dee, he's hurt," Kylee said, moving toward Ian.

"Kylee, don't!" Dee's command was almost a squeal. "You don't know what he might do to you!"

It was almost like Dee had read Ian's mind. Although it didn't take a crystal ball to know he planned to grab the girl, use her as a shield and to barter for his own freedom. But as Kylee drew close, he relaxed almost involuntarily.

Kylee's expression didn't change. She stepped forward, placing a small hand on Ian's bloody lip. The cloud-filtered light gave her a cherubic glow.

He flinched.

A tingle ran through him—like static electricity after walking on carpet.

Kylee's fingers lingered, gentle. She smiled as if they had just shared an inside joke and stepped back.

Dee grabbed Kylee's arm, yanking her away. Still

pointing the rifle.

Ian barely noticed.

Because the pain in his head was fading.

He touched his lip. No fresh blood. No more throbbing ache. Just a faint, tingling pressure.

His stomach tightened. What just happened?

Dee glared at him. "Your boo-boo's better. Now get moving."

Kylee's gaze didn't waver. "He can help us."

Dee exhaled, exhausted. Ian saw the conflict in her striking blue eyes and the crinkle in her blemish-free forehead. "Fine." She jerked the rifle toward the cart. "You heard her, grub. Grab the cart and start pushing."

Ian rose slowly, using one hand to steady himself against the damp earth, the other clutching the tentacle hat to his lip, wiping away the last traces of blood. His head was clearer now, the fog from the beating lifting.

He spat a glob of dried blood onto Sanchez's lifeless body.

Dee kept the rifle raised, the barrel pointing toward the cart's push handles. "Get moving," she ordered.

Ian rolled his jaw, flexing his sore hands, and then shuffled forward. His limbs felt like lead, his ribs throbbing from the fight.

"Here's how this works," Dee continued. "You push the cart. We follow behind. Do what we say, and you might live through the next few days." Her voice hardened. "Once we get where we're going, you can get back to your business of preying on people."

Ian let out a breath, tired, annoyed. "Didn't I just save

your life?"

Dee let out a mocking laugh. "Oh sure, you were just being a hero, right?" Her words dripped sarcasm. Then her voice turned cold. "Don't bother, I know how it works out here. Tell me, what would've happened if I hadn't gotten free? Would you have stepped in? Or would you have just picked up where they left off?"

Ian's fingers tightened around the cart's handle.
Out here.

The way she said it. *Out here.* As opposed to where? Ian knew there was no point arguing.

He pushed the cart forward. It jerked, rocked, and refused to budge. He tried again—same result.

"It's stuck on something," he said, his tone flat.

"What?" Dee moved closer, her blue eyes flicking toward the wheel. "Must be caught on a root."

"Yeah," Ian nodded. "Just ahead of the left wheel." He pointed.

Dee stepped forward, crouching to check.

That was all he needed.

Ian snapped forward, grabbing the barrel of the rifle with one hand, the stock with the other. He twisted, using his body weight to swing Dee around, slamming her against the cart. The impact knocked the gun loose.

He grabbed it. Stepped back.

Dee froze.

Kylee let out a sharp screech, but didn't move.

Ian leveled the rifle, peering over the sights.
"Back up."

Kylee's gaze darted between them. "What's he going

to do?"

Dee didn't take her eyes off Ian. "He's going to take our supplies, then kill us." Her voice was steady, deadly calm. "If we're lucky, he'll make it quick. Isn't that right, grub?"

Ian exhaled. "I told you—I have a name."

Dee's expression didn't change. "Then let's hear it. Always wanted to know the name of the man who was going to kill me."

Ian hesitated.

A dozen times in the last ten years, he had done things he wasn't proud of. But killing a woman and a child—even ones pointing a gun at him moments ago—was a step he had never taken.

Finally, he said, "Ian."

Dee tilted her head slightly.

"Ian," he repeated, his voice calmer. "And no, I'm not going to kill you."

"But you'll take our food," Dee said flatly.

Ian hesitated, then nodded. He hadn't eaten in two days.

"Then you might as well kill us now," Dee said. Cold. Matter-of-fact.

Ian frowned. "What?"

"If you take our food," Dee continued, "we'll be dead in a week. Might as well save us the suffering."

Kylee watched the exchange with wide, unblinking eyes.

Ian let out a slow breath. He glanced at the cart, at the cans of food, the packs of supplies.

"Back up."

Dee stared him down. After a tense moment, she stepped away from the cart.

Kylee followed.

Ian motioned for them to sit, then knelt beside the cart. He rummaged through the supplies—cans of vegetables, ravioli, chicken soup. Tarps. Tools. A few scattered odds and ends.

And then he saw them.

Eleven packets of military-issue MREs.

His stomach tightened.

These weren't scavenged. These weren't years-old leftovers from bombed-out settlements.

These were pristine. Unopened. Fresh.

Ian's fingers brushed the packs. "Where did you get these?"

Kylee opened her mouth immediately. "They were part of our survival kit—"

"Kylee," Dee cut in sharply.

But it was too late.

Ian narrowed his eyes. "Survival kit?"

That didn't add up. Nobody had stockpiles like this anymore.

"From our plane," Dee added, her voice carefully neutral.

Ian's head snapped up. "Your plane?"

He stared at her, searching for any sign of deception. Nothing flew anymore. Not in years.

Dee held his gaze. "Listen, Ian. If you help us, we can get you more."

Ian scoffed. "How?"

"We have a destination," Dee said. "And resources waiting there."

Kylee perked up. "We're going to the Crescent City clean zone."

Ian barked a short, sharp laugh. "Right. A clean zone."

He shook his head. "I've heard that bullshit before. No one's had clean food, clean water—clean air—for years."

Dee's face remained neutral. "Then explain this."

She tilted her head slightly.

"Look at us," she said. "Look at our skin. Our hair. Our teeth."

She bared her teeth.

White. Straight. Clean.

"No one out here looks like this," Dee continued. "You know that."

Ian's mind reeled. He thought back to what Callahan had told him before he left Rio Dell:

I'm telling everyone this, Hammond. Be on the lookout for a woman and a young girl, nine or ten. The woman's blond, the girl has black hair. They'll look like people used to look—healthy and clean. Someone wants them real bad... bad enough to pay.

Ian's grip tightened on the rifle.

Could these be the two? Even if they weren't—they had to be worth something.

He let out a breath. "I don't buy the 'clean zone' shit."

Dee just watched him. Silent. Calculating.

He scratched his jaw, thinking. If he tied them up at

night, they wouldn't be a problem. He could make it back to Rio Dell in two days.

"I know someone who would love to discuss it with you, though."

Dee's face darkened.

Kylee shifted uncomfortably.

Ian lowered the rifle slightly. "Start walking."

6 – The Road to Rio Dell

"We need a fire," Dee said.

Kylee shivered beside her. The girl had handled the cold fine while they were walking, but now that they'd stopped, the sweat from the day's endless trek had turned to ice against her skin. Each frigid gust of wind cut through their damp clothes like needles.

"No fire," Ian said. Final. Absolute.

Dee already knew he'd refuse. The bodies of Omar and Jenna were proof enough that fires attracted the wrong kind of attention. But the request had just been an opener—a setup for what she really wanted.

"Then at least cut these ropes," she said, keeping her voice measured. "She needs to wrap her arms around herself. It'll help keep her warm."

Ian's eyes narrowed, assessing her.

"No."

Dee clenched her jaw. "She's a child."

"She's survived this long, hasn't she?" Ian said.

Dee's frustration flared. "She's never been outside before."

That got his attention.

"She's never had to endure a night like this," she pressed. "And if you're taking us somewhere, don't you think whoever you're selling us to will want us both alive?"

Ian's expression flickered. Just for a second. Then he

exhaled through his nose, reached into his nylon pack, and tossed a blanket at her.

"Make do," he said.

It wasn't much, but Dee would take what she could get.

Then Ian came over, pulled a length of twine from the same pack, and fastened their ankles to the tree before slicing through the ropes binding their wrists.

The moment Dee felt the strain on her arms release, she inhaled deeply, rubbing at the raw skin. She stretched her fingers, shaking out the numbness, and then pulled the blanket over herself and Kylee.

Ian smirked. "Anything else you need, princess?"

Dee considered. "A six o'clock wake-up call would be nice."

Ian's nostrils flared. For a moment, she thought he'd snap at her—but then, the corners of his lips curled, just slightly.

A stifled laugh. His shoulders relaxed.

"Alright," he muttered, shaking his head. "That was kind of funny."

He settled down against a fallen log, shifting to find a comfortable spot.

Kylee tilted her head, confused. Dee realized why—the girl had never stayed in a hotel. She'd never heard of wake-up calls, never experienced that part of the old world.

To her credit, Kylee didn't ask questions. She was probably used to accepting things she didn't understand. Unless, of course, she went inside their heads.

Dee had asked her not to.

The night settled into a quiet stillness, the wind hissing

through the bare trees.

Then Kylee spoke. "Ian?"

Ian let out a low sigh, as if already regretting responding. "What?"

"Why do you live out here?"

Ian's voice was flat. "Not all of us had the luxury of hiding in bunkers. The rest of us had to survive."

Dee's spine stiffened.

"Luxury?" she repeated. "You know nothing about what she's been through." Her voice came out sharper than she intended.

She expected an angry retort, a snap, a fight.

Instead, Ian frowned, brows knitting together in thought. A beat of silence. Then, he exhaled. "I guess you have a point."

His calm, introspective tone surprised her. For a moment, she didn't know what to say.

Kylee, of course, had no such hesitation.

"What else have you done to survive?" she asked.

Ian stared into the darkness. Stayed silent.

Kylee's voice softened. "I think it's okay to hurt people who are trying to hurt you first."

Ian's gaze snapped to her.

"But," Kylee continued, "if you hurt people for no reason, or just to get something, that makes you bad."

Dee tensed.

Kylee wasn't done. "If you're with bad people and you don't stop them, that makes you just as bad as they are."

Ian's jaw clenched.

Kylee kept going. "You have to make up for it. Even if it

doesn't help you."

Ian's hands curled into fists. His expression hardened. "Do you ever shut up?" he snapped. "Go to sleep, girl!"

Kylee blinked. Then, just like that, she closed her eyes. Within seconds, her breathing slowed.

Dee watched, knowing Kylee hadn't obeyed him out of fear. She'd said what she needed to say.

And now, she was done talking.

***

Ian took longer to fall asleep. Dee watched him, eyes barely open, waiting.

He lay stiffly at first, staring at the sky, shifting as though he couldn't find a position that didn't hurt. Then, finally, his breathing slowed. Soon after, he began snoring.

Dee listened to the rhythm of his breath. Watched his body language. Then, when she was sure, she moved.

Slowly. Carefully.

She reached down, feeling for the twine around her ankles. Her fingers searched for the knot, working at it with her nails.

It was tight. But not tight enough. After a few tense minutes, she felt the first loop loosen.

She pulled. Felt it slip.

Her heart pounded.

A snort from Ian.

Dee froze.

Ian mumbled something unintelligible, then shifted.

Dee held her breath.

Waited. Counted her heartbeats. One. Two. Three.

Nothing. He was still asleep.

She turned to Kylee, tugged at the twine around her ankle. Kylee's was tied tighter. It took longer.

She worked quickly, barely breathing. Finally, it came loose.

She glanced at Ian. Still asleep.

Good.

She reached over, touching Kylee's shoulder, ready to wake her—

And her own exhaustion hit her like a weight.

Just a couple more minutes, she thought. Just to let him drift deeper into sleep. Her head leaned back against the tree.

Just a few minutes.

Her eyelids drooped. The darkness pulled at her. And before she knew it—

She was gone.

***

"Dee. Dee, wake up."

A small hand shook her shoulder. The voice was Kylee's.

Dee's eyes fluttered open, her body still heavy with sleep. The world around her was gray and muted, the sky stretching pale over the jagged peaks to the east.

Across the clearing, Ian was rolling up his bedroll, moving efficiently, like a man used to breaking camp before dawn.

"It's morning," Dee murmured.

"Yep," Kylee said, grinning. "And you didn't want to wake up, did you?"

Dee rubbed her eyes, groggy. "I don't even remember falling asleep."

Kylee gave a small shrug. "Do you ever remember falling asleep? I don't."

Dee sat up, her mind slowly catching up. "No, I mean—I was supposed to stay awake."

Kylee watched her carefully. "You must have needed sleep, Dee. Yesterday was a long day."

But Dee wasn't listening anymore.

She grabbed Kylee's arm, pulling her close. "You don't understand. He was asleep. We could have escaped. I screwed up."

Kylee didn't react like a child who'd just heard they missed a chance for freedom. She wasn't upset. Wasn't even disappointed. Instead, she held Dee's gaze, her expression calm, steady—too steady for a nine-year-old.

"You didn't screw up, Dee," she said softly. "This is right. Our path lies with Ian."

Dee's stomach tightened.

"What path?"

Before Kylee could answer, Ian's voice cut through the clearing.

"If you two are done gossiping, I'd appreciate it if you gathered your stuff."

Dee's heart lurched.

The ropes.

In her panic, she had forgotten. The blanket still covered them, but she could feel the loose twine around their ankles. They had untied themselves before falling asleep. And now, Ian was watching.

Dee fumbled under the blanket, desperately trying to re-tie the bindings before Ian could—

"Don't bother."

Her hands froze.

Ian exhaled, shaking his head. "I already know you untied yourselves." He slung his pack over his shoulder. "Not sure why, though—if you were just gonna sit there all night."

Dee hesitated.

Before she could come up with an answer, Kylee jumped in smoothly.

"My leg went numb," she said. Completely casual. "I couldn't move it right. Dee untied mine, and then it just made sense to untie hers too."

Ian narrowed his eyes. "And then you just sat there. All night."

Kylee nodded. "We decided our best chance was to stick with you."

Ian held Dee's gaze for a moment longer, then exhaled sharply. "Whatever. Can we get moving now?"

He turned away, but something caught his attention. He tilted his head, squinting at something above them.

Dee followed his gaze.

High up, near the top of the tree they had slept against, was a cluster of leaves.

Not dead, brittle ones. Not gray, shriveled remnants like every other tree in the Long Winter.

Green leaves. Healthy. Alive.

Ian's expression hardened. His voice was almost disbelieving. "I'll be damned," he muttered.

Kylee tilted her head. "What?"

Ian didn't look away. "This tree is still alive."

Kylee's face lit up. "I think it was just sick from not getting enough food from the sun. Don't you like it better this way?"

Ian's jaw tightened. "Of course," he said. "But it's just... unusual."

Kylee smiled. "Well, I hope they all get better."

Dee barely breathed.

Ian's brows furrowed slightly.

Something wasn't right. Whether Kylee had anything to do with the tree or not, Dee wasn't about to let Ian think about it too much.

"We ready to go yet?" she asked, forcing nonchalance into her voice.

Ian glanced at her, then back at the leaves.

After a moment, he tore his gaze away. "Yeah. Let's move."

As they set out, Dee risked one last glance at the tree. A single thought nagged at her.

What else is Kylee not telling me?

***

Dee's feet ached. The tennis shoes she had thought were comfortable offered little protection from the cold, no support on the uneven ground. Every step felt like walking on bruises.

She wasn't sure how much longer she could keep up with Ian's relentless pace.

Kylee, on the other hand, showed no signs of slowing. The girl moved like she could go forever. If a nine-year-old could keep pushing forward, then Dee would too.

They came upon a river, cutting directly across their path.

Ian stopped, scanning the water, his gaze sharp and calculating.

The current was swift. Cold. The water looked shallow, but Ian hesitated, which meant it wasn't as easy a crossing as it appeared.

Dee sighed with relief. At least it gave her an excuse to sit down. She dropped onto the damp ground, peeling off her shoes to rub her sore feet.

Ian hadn't tied their hands this time. Travel was easier that way. If he thought that meant she wouldn't try to run, he was wrong.

She had no idea who he was taking them to, but she knew she didn't want to meet them. The first opportunity that came up, she and Kylee were gone.

Dee wanted to discuss it with Kylee, come up with a plan. But the girl just kept following Ian like a puppy as he searched for a place to cross.

A splash.

Then a gasp.

"Ian!"

Dee's head snapped up. Kylee stood at the riverbank, eyes wide with panic. Then—

"Dee, he needs help!"

Dee hesitated. Her muscles tensed. Then she saw him.

Ian was in the water. His head barely above the surface, his arms flailing against the current.

The river was deeper than it looked. He couldn't get traction.

Dee's breath came sharp and fast.

Downstream fallen tree jutted from the riverbank, its half-submerged trunk reaching toward the center of the current.

"Grab that log!" Kylee shouted.

Ian didn't react. Or maybe he didn't hear. The river dragged him closer.

Then—a desperate lunge. His arm hooked around a branch. The current yanked at his legs, pulling hard, trying to rip him free.

He held on. But his grip was failing. His hands clumsy, useless from the cold. He wouldn't last long.

Dee stood motionless. She felt Kylee watching her.

"We have to go," Dee said.

Kylee didn't move. "No, Dee. We have to help him."

"No, we don't," Dee snapped, grabbing Kylee's arm. "This is our chance. We run now."

Kylee's face was defiant. "He'll die."

Dee's pulse pounded in her ears. "So what? He's dangerous. He's going to sell us to worse men. He got himself into this. We don't owe him a damn thing."

Kylee yanked her arm free with surprising strength. And then—she ran. Straight toward the fallen tree.

"Dammit." Dee bolted after her.

Kylee was already climbing out over the water.

"Kylee, get back here!"

"I can reach him!"

Dee cursed under her breath. If Kylee fell in, she'd be swept away in seconds. "Come back," Dee ordered. "I'll get him."

For once, Kylee listened. She climbed back to shore.

Dee took a deep breath. Then she climbed onto the log. One step at a time. The bark was wet, slick with moss.

Ian's grip slipped. His body lurched, his hold on the log nearly lost.

"Hold on!" Dee called. She kept moving. Carefully. Steadily. The farther out she went, the thinner the log became. Her balance wavered.

Then—the log buckled. Her foot slipped. A broken branch stub jammed into her ribs, stopping her fall. Dee clung to it, breathing hard.

Carefully, she pulled herself back up onto the log. No time to rest. No room for mistakes.

"Ian," she called.

No answer.

Then, his eyes lifted. He saw her.

Dee extended her hand. "Grab on."

He moved sluggishly, his body unresponsive from the cold. But when he saw her hand, he reached for it.

His touch was like ice. His grip was weak.

"I can't pull you up," Dee said. "But I can pull you along. Hold onto the log. I'll move you back to shore."

Ian gave a barely noticeable nod.

That was enough. Dee pulled. They slid inch by inch, moving against the force of the current.

Ian kept his arm hooked, shifting his grip with every pull.

The hardest part came when they reached the broken branch.

"Go under it," Dee instructed.

Ian shifted. His body half-submerged for a moment before he pulled himself past the obstacle.

Dee's arm burned from the strain. Her grip was giving out.

But then—

She felt him get lighter. His feet touched the riverbed. From there, he stumbled the rest of the way.

Dee held on until he collapsed onto the bank.

Kylee ran to his side. "Ian?"

Nothing.

Dee crouched beside him. "Ian."

No response.

"Ian!"

Kylee's hands hovered over him. "I think I can help."

Dee grabbed her wrist. "No. Not yet."

Kylee looked at her. "Then what do we do?"

Dee's first instinct? Leave him. But they were past that now. She had learned about hypothermia back when she was a scout. Back when the world still made sense. "We need to warm his core," she said.

Kylee hesitated. "Do we build a fire?"

"No. Too risky. Even in daylight."

Dee thought for a second. Then—"Run back to his pack. Get the blankets."

Kylee nodded and sprinted off.

Dee turned back to Ian. His skin was pale, almost gray. The first thing she had to do—get rid of the wet clothes.

Kylee returned, arms full of blankets.

Dee didn't hesitate. She stripped Ian's jacket, shirt, pants.

"Turn around," she told Kylee.

Kylee obeyed.

Dee yanked off his soaking boxers and rolled him onto the dry blanket. She wrapped it around him tightly, tucking it close to his body.

His face was still pale. His breathing too shallow.

Kylee turned back around, watching. "What now?"

"Now," Dee said, "we let his body heat do the rest."

Kylee bit her lip. "Should one of us—"

"No." Dee cut her off. "That's where I draw the line."

Kylee looked like she wanted to argue. But she didn't. Instead, she knelt beside Ian. "Can we at least pray?"

Dee hesitated. Then, for the first time in a long time— She nodded.

She reached out, took Kylee's hand, and they both knelt.

***

Kylee sat cross-legged beside Ian, watching over him as he drifted in and out of consciousness.

Dee stood a few feet away, wringing the water from his clothes, laying them across a flat rock to dry. She wished the sun was out. At this rate, it would take forever.

Kylee murmured softly as Ian's eyes fluttered open.

Dee glanced over.

Kylee smiled. "You're awake."

Ian blinked groggily, shifting under the blanket. His body was still shaking from the cold, but his breathing had steadied.

Kylee explained what happened—how they pulled him from the river, how Dee wrapped him in blankets to keep him warm.

Dee listened without comment, keeping her eyes on the tree line. She was still wary. Just because Ian had nearly died didn't mean he wasn't still a threat.

Ian, for his part, watched Kylee as she talked. She spoke as if she'd always been by his side, as if they were old friends and not captor and captives.

Finally, after a long silence, Ian turned to Dee.

"I don't get you," he said. His voice was hoarse, his throat raw.

Dee stiffened. "What's there to get?"

"Twice now, you could have gotten away." Ian's gaze was sharp despite his exhaustion. "Twice. And instead, you—" he exhaled sharply, shaking his head. "Why did you help me?"

Kylee answered before Dee could.

"We couldn't just let you die."

Dee shot her a look. Kylee made it sound so simple.

Ian's tired eyes shifted to Dee.

She sighed, motioning toward Kylee. "She can be very persuasive."

Ian studied her, his expression unreadable.

Then he grunted. "Good thing I left your hands untied."

He exhaled, shifting slightly under the blankets. "Thanks."

Dee hesitated, then nodded. "You should thank Kylee."

Ian looked at Kylee.

Kylee beamed.

Ian grumbled something under his breath and looked away.

Kylee just kept smiling.

7 – Miracle

The afternoon light was fading fast. Somewhere beyond the thick, permanent cloud cover, the sun sank toward the Pacific. It would be dark soon.

They had made a few more hours of progress toward Rio Dell after Ian had recovered from his near-drowning. But now, it was time to find a place to bed down for the night.

Ian's mind still churned over what had happened at the river.

He could understand why Kylee had insisted on saving him. She was a child—too innocent to know better. But Dee? She knew.

She might not have known Callahan specifically, but she could guess his type. A flesh peddler. A trafficker. A man who traded in people.

She knew what was waiting at the end of this road. So why had she stayed to pull him out?

Ian shook the thought away. Didn't matter. It wouldn't change where this road led.

Something flickered through the trees. Ian stopped. Eyes scanning.

Through the branches, he could see them—houses. A whole development.

His gut tightened.

He tapped Dee on the shoulder, then put a finger to his lips.

Her eyes widened.

She bent down, whispering in Kylee's ear. The little girl nodded, looking toward the houses but staying silent.

This could be perfect. A house meant shelter, maybe even supplies.

Or it could mean something worse. Cannibal clans liked places like this. They used the lure of a warm bed to trap the desperate.

Ian shrugged off his small pack.

"You two stay here." He pointed toward a low rise in the earth. "If I'm not back in ten minutes, keep moving. Follow the frozen streambed—get as far from here as possible."

Dee nodded, but there was something in her eyes. Concern? For him?

Ian hesitated.

If something happened to him, they wouldn't last long out here.

He walked back, wordless, and handed Dee the rifle.

She blinked, stunned.

Then he turned and headed toward the houses.

***

Ian moved low and quiet, slipping between fences long rotted by time.

Movement caught his eye.

A house—yellow siding, peeling paint. Two figures crossed the dead grass of the front yard.

Ian dropped to a crouch, watching.

Something hung from a second-story window. A

tattered red sheet, flapping in the wind.

His blood ran cold.

The symbol was unmistakable. The Bloody Flu.

His mind flashed through the memories—the coughing fits, the blackened fingertips, the blood seeping from mouths, noses, eyes.

Even the most ruthless brigands wouldn't go near it.

Ian didn't waste another second. He turned and made his way back to Dee and Kylee.

The moment he emerged from the trees, Dee handed the rifle back without question.

"Let's go," Ian muttered, slinging his pack over his shoulder.

"Is it occupied?" Dee asked.

"Yes."

"And?"

Ian looked at her. "They've got the flu."

Dee's eyes tightened. She grabbed her pack. Got ready to follow.

But Kylee smiled and started walking toward the houses.

Ian's heart lurched. He reached out, grabbing her shoulder. "Didn't you hear me, girl? I said they're sick!"

Kylee didn't stop.

Dee let out a slow breath. "She knows."

Ian's chest tightened. "Have either of you seen what that flu does?"

"Yes," Dee said, without hesitation. "We've both seen it."

"Then you're both insane."

Ian turned, ready to put as much distance between

himself and that red banner of death as possible.

Then Kylee spoke. "Don't be afraid, Ian." Her voice was calm. Sure. "It will be okay."

Ian stopped mid-stride. His jaw clenched. Then he whipped around, marching straight up to her.

"NO. It will NOT be okay." His voice was low, sharp as a blade. "You walk in there, and within days, your joints will ache. Then sores in your mouth. Then—" He stepped closer, towering over her.

"By day five, blood will be leaking from your eyes, your ears, your skin. The virus will break down your body from the inside out."

Kylee just stood there, smiling.

Ian's breath came fast and uneven. "That's what will happen," he said, voice shaking with anger. "It will not be okay."

Kylee's smile didn't falter. "That's not what I meant," she said softly.

Ian's pulse pounded. "Then what the hell did you mean?"

Kylee reached out—gently. Her small fingers wrapped around his hand. And suddenly—

It wasn't Kylee holding his hand. It was Rusty.

A parking lot. A grocery store. A little hand in his. A memory. A lifetime ago.

Kylee's voice was barely a whisper. "He went quickly," she said. "He's in a better place now."

Ian's body locked up. His throat clenched. His vision blurred. "Who?"

Kylee's dark eyes met his. "Your boy. Rusty."

Ian staggered back. His knees almost buckled.

Kylee kept walking.

"Ian?" Dee's voice cut through the haze.

Ian couldn't breathe. How could she know? He had never told anyone.

A tear slipped down his cheek. His first in years. He wiped it away before Dee could see.

But she had. And she was smirking.

"She knows things," Dee said simply.

Ian's mouth was dry. He swallowed. Found his voice. "That's..." He stumbled over the words. "That's... impossible."

Dee just nodded. "Yeah. It was."

Then she glanced toward Kylee, who was already approaching the house.

"But that's nothing compared to what she's about to do."

***

They were spotted two rows from the house with the red banner.

Shouts rang out. Scrambling. Movement. A man limped out of the dilapidated front door, a shotgun in hand. His head was wrapped in filthy bandages, blood seeping from his nose. He was sick—but not weak. If he had the strength to walk, he had the strength to pull the trigger.

"Stay back!" His voice was hoarse but firm. "We've got the flu here!"

Ian and Dee froze.

Kylee didn't.

"Shoot her, Dad!" a voice—young, panicked—came from somewhere behind him.

The man hesitated. "She's just a little girl. The others haven't moved."

"It's a trick! Shoot her!"

"Shut up, Conner."

The man shifted his attention back to Ian and Dee. "We've got nothing you want," he warned. "And we're all sick." He pointed to the blood dripping from his nose. "So I doubt our flesh will do you any good either."

Kylee kept walking.

The man tensed. "Don't come any closer." His grip on the shotgun tightened—but he didn't raise it.

Kylee's voice was soft, certain.

"It will be okay."

His brow furrowed. "What are you—"

Kylee reached him before he could finish. She placed both hands on his chest.

The man stiffened. Then—they convulsed. Both of them.

Kylee and the man shook violently, bodies locked in some unseen force. Then, as suddenly as it began, they collapsed.

"Dad!" Conner ran toward his father, panic in his voice. Another boy—**younger, wide-eyed—**followed. Conner grabbed the shotgun, leveling it at Kylee.
Ian reacted instinctively.

"Don't shoot her!"

The man on the ground coughed, struggled to push

himself up. "Wait!" he gasped. "Don't hurt her."

Conner's hands trembled on the shotgun. "What?!" He turned on his father, voice tight with disbelief. "After what she just did to you?"

The man was already sitting up, wiping his nose. No more blood. He touched his face, his breathing steadier.

"Son." His voice shook, but not from pain. He grabbed Conner's arm, gently pushing the shotgun down. "Don't."

His eyes found Kylee, who still lay weak on the ground. "Did you do this?"

Kylee was too exhausted to speak. But she nodded.

The man's eyes welled with tears. Without hesitation, he pulled Kylee into a hug.

Ian had seen enough.

He stepped forward, ready to pull her away, but Dee grabbed his elbow.

Her eyes pleaded. Wait.

"Dad, what's going on?" Conner's voice wavered.

"She's the only hope your sister has," his father whispered. "The only hope any of us have."

Conner's hands shook. His father pried the shotgun from his grip. "Help me get her inside."

At Kylee's insistence, they allowed Dee and Ian to enter as well. But Ian had to surrender his weapons.

Inside, the air reeked of sickness. Four sick people. The father, the two boys, and a teenage girl lying on the couch. She was barely conscious, her body fevered, blood crusting at her nose, her ears, the edges of her closed eyes. Ian thought she was already dead.

Then she moaned. Shifted slightly. Not yet.

The boys carried both Kylee and their father inside.

"Toad, get me a towel," the man said.

The younger boy—**Toad, apparently—**scrambled away, returning with a small, damp washcloth.

His father wiped his now-clear nose, staring at the red stain on the towel. Then he turned back to Kylee.

"Can you do it again?" His voice was careful. Guarded. Hopeful.

He motioned toward the girl on the couch.

Kylee nodded. Rose slowly to her feet. Dee moved to steady her, but Kylee shook her off. She crossed the room. Laid her hands on the girl.

Ian tensed. He knew what was coming now.

The girl's body convulsed. So did Kylee. She trembled violently, then collapsed.

Dee rushed forward, catching her.

Kylee's chest rose and fell quickly. She looked drained.

Ian exhaled. He understood now. She had done this before. To him.

Back when they first met, when she had placed her hand on his bloody lip—when his concussion and wounds had disappeared. She had healed him. Just like she was healing them.

A cough. A rustle.

The girl on the couch shifted, her breathing easier. Her father's jaw tightened, his eyes burning with relief. Kylee took a deep breath, then turned to him.

"She was bad," Kylee murmured, her voice tired.

"Give her eight hours. Then make her drink as much water as she can. In two days, she'll be strong enough to travel."

A stunned silence fell over the room.

Conner took a step forward, eyes wide with disbelief.

"What... are you?"

Kylee smiled, small and sheepish. "I'm Kylee."

***

It was a family, of sorts.

Jack, the father, was still recovering from the bloody flu—weak, but on the mend. His daughter, Elizabeth, slept on the couch of the abandoned house, her body slowly healing. They already knew the son, Connor, and the younger boy, Toad, who was no relation. Jack and his wife—before she passed—had taken in the feral child who called himself Toad. That had been about six months ago, according to Jack.

Despite Connor's protests, Jack had agreed to let them stay. There was plenty of room, and Jack saw no threat in them. Ian didn't take Jack for a fool, but there was something in the way Jack looked at him, something left behind from Kylee when she had healed him—like a sixth sense about people.

Connor, however, refused to trust so easily. He kept Ian's rifle, and Jack, for all his fatherly authority, had relented to his son's skepticism.

As night fell, Ian and Dee helped Kylee into the bedroom. Jack handed Ian a candle to light the way. The house, though blanketed in dust, was intact. Kylee sat on the bed and tested the mattress with a small bounce. "It's comfortable," she murmured.

Dee kissed Kylee's cheek before stepping outside, needing fresh air. Ian lingered. Rusty had always been afraid of the dark, terrified of being left alone in a room without light. He wasn't sure if Kylee felt the same, but he couldn't bring himself to leave her—not while she was still awake.

"Ian," Kylee said softly. "Give me your hand."

He hesitated but then offered it without question.

Kylee held it for a moment, closed her eyes, and then let go.

"You'd like it in Crescent City," she murmured.

Ian blinked. "What?"

"The clean zone," she said, a faint, knowing smile touching her lips.

"You don't believe us," she continued, her voice teasing yet certain. "But we all have our part to play. It might take you some time, but I know you'll figure it out."

"Figure what out?"

"That despite everything, you're still a good man."

Ian stood there, mouth slightly open, words failing him.

Kylee rolled away, drawing the blanket over her shoulders. "Blow out the candle or take it with you," she said, her voice drowsy now. "I'm tired. I just want to sleep."

Ian lingered another second before blowing out the flame. Then, without another word, he stepped out of the room and closed the door behind him.

***

Feeling unsettled, Ian wandered outside. The ground seemed to glow with a pale light, and for a moment, he thought someone had turned on a battery-powered lamp. Since the bombs fell, the electrical grid had been nothing but a memory. But this was too much light for a candle or even a lantern. His stomach clenched with unease—light meant attention, and attention meant danger.

He looked up, searching for the source.

Through a ragged hole in the roiling clouds, something he hadn't seen in years poured down its silvery light.

The moon.

Almost full, it bathed the world in cold, white brilliance. Ian blinked, half-expecting it to vanish, swallowed by the clouds, returning the world to its usual oppressive darkness. But it didn't. The moon hung steady in the sky, silent and unwavering.

He inhaled deeply, savoring the crisp night air. At some point, he realized his mouth was open, a goofy grin stretching across his face. *Does anyone else see this?*

In the moonlight, Connor stood watch, staring up at the sky. Farther off, Dee stood on the stone patio, her back to the house. The light played against her hair, turning it into strands of molten silver.

Hearing footsteps, she turned. When she saw Ian, she relaxed.

"Can you believe it?" she asked, her voice edged with something close to wonder.

"It's been at least ten years," Ian murmured.

"She fall asleep already?" Dee asked, tilting her head

toward the house.

"She did."

"She's a weird little girl."

Ian chuckled. "She is. But she's more than that, isn't she?"

Dee hesitated, kicking loose a small rock with the toe of her boot. "Much more." A beat passed before she added, "I'm not one of them, you know."

Ian frowned. "One of who?"

"The people who run the compound where we lived. I'm not with them."

"Okay. I'm not even sure who *they* are."

"They took me about nine years ago, shortly after the bombs." She didn't try to make her timeline exact—no one kept perfect track anymore, not without clocks, phones, or calendars.

Ian folded his arms. "What do you mean *took* you?"

"I was with my family, on a ski trip in Mammoth when the bombs hit."

Ian's chest tightened. He'd been to Mammoth as a kid. He'd always planned to take Rusty someday—teach him how to ski. But there had never been time.

"We made our way down the Owens Valley, trying to survive," Dee continued. "We knew going back home to Irvine wasn't an option. The radiation would have been too high. Somehow, the valley was shielded from the worst of it, so we stayed there for months. I was scavenging through an old Vons grocery store when they grabbed me."

Ian's jaw clenched. "What did they take you for? What did they make you do?"

He wouldn't have been surprised if the answer was something horrific. He'd seen enough men like Callahan, who took what they wanted, especially from girls like Dee. But from what she and Kylee had said, this compound was different.

"We were nannies," Dee said simply. "We took care of kids like Kylee."

Ian stared. "That's it?"

"That was it. When we weren't working, we had access to the gym, the media center, the library, and the cafeteria."

"They had a *cafeteria*?" Ian shook his head. "Sounds nice. Is the rest of your family there?"

Dee's expression dimmed. "No. They just took me."

"What happened to them?"

She shook her head. "I don't know. They're probably dead."

Ian nodded. A decade ago, he would have tried to say something comforting. But now? Everyone had a story like that. No one wasted breath on sympathy anymore.

"So, are there people in Crescent City who can get you and Kylee back to this compound?"

"I don't even know if there's *anyone* there," Dee admitted. "But Kylee's convinced there are people who can help us. Not to go back. We barely escaped the first time."

Ian frowned. "Why? It sounds like they took care of you. Why risk leaving a place like that for... *this*?"

Dee met his gaze. "Because we weren't guests. We were *captives*." She let that sink in before continuing. "Comfort doesn't mean freedom. We weren't allowed to leave."

Ian exhaled. "Still sounds better than most places out

here."

"They're no better than the people scavenging and killing out here," Dee said. "They're just *better equipped*. They think they're superior because they live underground, protected from the flu, the radiation, the warlords. But they're not *good* people, Ian."

For the first time, he really saw her. Dee wasn't soft or privileged. She had been through hell, just like him. And she'd made it out.

"I guess I can dig that," Ian admitted. "But why did Kylee beg you to take her away? I assume that place was the only home she's ever known."

"If you can even call it a home. It was more like a prison. And recently, they were hurting her." Dee's voice hardened.

Ian bristled. "Why?" It wasn't a question—it was a demand.

"They call her an *experimental*." Dee made air quotes with her fingers.

Ian frowned. "What does that mean?"

"She's not the only one," Dee said. "She's part of a group—kids they experimented on."

"You mean the way she heals people?" Ian asked. "And how she seems to *know* things?"

Dee nodded. "She was born that way. Or so they claim."

Ian's stomach churned. "Radiation?"

Dee actually laughed. "Did you watch a lot of sci-fi as a kid?" She shook her head. "No. It's *nanobots*."

Ian blinked. "Like... little robots?"

"Microscopic," Dee clarified. "They live inside her. They were designed to help the body's immune system fight diseases."

"The bloody flu," Ian whispered.

Dee nodded. "Not just that—cancer, bacterial infections, even genetic defects. They repair injuries. They replicate themselves using food and waste."

Ian's mind reeled. "Someone with those inside them would *never* die. Not from natural causes."

"Maybe," Dee said. "They're still growing. Physically, they seem normal. But we don't know what adulthood will look like for them."

Ian exhaled sharply. "How many?"

"Twenty-five, maybe thirty."

Ian ran a hand through his hair. "That's... *insane*. But that still doesn't explain—"

"Kylee is different from the others," Dee cut in. "She can *control* the nanobots. She can *send* them into other people when she heals them."

Ian touched his lip absentmindedly.

"But they don't stay," Dee continued. "They deactivate once they've done their job. A failsafe, I guess."

Ian exhaled. "So she's the only one who can do that?"

"She's the only one *so far*." Dee's face darkened. "That's why the Director won't let her go. He wants to figure out how she does it—so he can replicate it."

Ian's stomach twisted. "Who *is* this Director?"

"The one who controls the compound," Dee said. "And maybe more."

Ian's mind spun. Kylee could heal anyone. But why had she healed *him*? She had seen into him, into his past. She *knew*.

Dee placed a hand in his. "You seem different."

Ian smirked. "You mean from the other grubs?"

"I'm a grub too," she said with a grin. "Just a domesticated one."

He laughed, but his thoughts remained heavy.

"I'm not as different as you think," Ian admitted. "I've done things…"

"So have we all," Dee said. "But the past is a trap. Where we're going matters more than where we've been."

She squeezed his hand and walked inside. Ian watched her go, her scent lingering in the cold night air.

Was he leading them?

Or were they leading him?

***

Ian found his way to the den, his limbs heavy with exhaustion. He couldn't remember the last time he had slept on something as comfortable as a futon. Five solid hours before dawn—if he was lucky—sounded like a gift.

Stripping down to his boxers and undershirt, he slipped beneath the thick down blanket Jack had left for him. The air was cold against his skin, and he shivered at first, but soon, his body heat filled the cocoon of fabric, warming the space around him.

He inhaled deeply, willing himself to let go, to sink into sleep. But no matter how drained his body was, his mind refused to shut down.

Kylee. The compound. The Director.

There was something new happening here—something

different, something *important*.

There had been a time when that would have mattered to him. When he would have cared enough to get involved, to do his part, to stand for something.

But that wasn't him anymore.

Or was it?

It was his choice, wasn't it?

Callahan would have his head if he ever found out Ian had located the two he was looking for and *didn't* bring them back. With Callahan, "hell to pay" wasn't just a phrase—it was a promise. And Callahan wasn't a sadist. Well, maybe he was, but his cruelty always came with a twisted sort of logic. A necessary evil. Examples had to be made. A man perceived as weak didn't last long—not unless he wanted to end up as livestock for some cannibal clan.

That was the world now. Short, brutal, and cruel.

But if that was a given—if his life was going to be short and painful no matter what—why *not* do something that mattered?

Why *couldn't* he be the good guy again?

It was his choice. Not Callahan's. Not Jenks'.

His.

As soon as they were rested, he would take them north instead of east.

He would take them to Crescent City.

8 – Live or Die Trying

They left Jack and his family the next morning.

Elizabeth had woken up, unable to stop thanking Kylee for curing her of the bloody flu. On their way out, Connor handed Ian his rifle back, his expression a silent warning: *Don't even try it.*

They walked for about half a mile before Kylee turned to Ian and said, "Thank you."

"For what?" Ian asked.

"For taking us to Crescent City."

Ian stopped in his tracks and stared at her, half-expecting to see something—some tell, some flicker of awareness—that explained how she *knew*. Kylee just kept walking, oblivious to the weight of what she had just said.

He had only decided last night. Lying awake, staring at the ceiling, his mind turning over the last few days. He *couldn't* bring himself to play the traitor, to hand them over like some biblical Judas. He was taking them north, to safety—or at least, what Kylee *believed* was safety.

But he hadn't told anyone yet.

And Kylee already knew.

"What?" Dee asked, picking up on the shift in the air.

"She's right," Ian admitted. "I don't know how, but she's right. We're not going to Rio Dell."

Dee's face flickered between confusion and relief. "What brought this on?"

Ian shrugged. "I don't know."

"Won't the people you're supposed to take us to be angry? Are you setting yourself up for problems?"

"They have to find me first," Ian said. "And let's be honest, you've got a much better shot at making it with me around."

Dee exhaled sharply, crossing her arms. "Why would you risk your life for people you don't even know? Doesn't that kind of thinking get you killed out here?"

"It does." Ian hesitated. "But I wasn't always like this. I don't fully understand what's happening here, but I know one thing—this little girl," he gestured toward Kylee, "changes things. Maybe everything. If I can play a small part in that, well... that's worth a few years of wandering through this dead world."

Dee studied him for a long moment, then nodded. "Okay. Let's go to Crescent City."

The sky remained clear throughout the morning, sunlight warming their path for the first time in weeks. Ian tilted his head back, soaking in the feeling—*a forgotten thing.*

Kylee walked alongside him, peppering him with questions. Everything from how he survived to what he did before the bombs to whether he'd ever tasted ice cream. As miraculous as her gift was, in a lot of ways, she was just a regular nine-year-old.

"What was Rusty like?" she asked, her voice bright with curiosity.

Ian smiled. "I wish you could have met him. He would've liked you."

And just like that, the day passed with more laughter and warmth than Ian had felt in ten years.

Dee took notice. When Kylee was out of earshot, she murmured, "She's really thriving out here. And she's taken to you. I've never seen her like this around a man before."

"I guess character judgment isn't one of her abilities," Ian joked.

Dee smirked before her expression turned serious. "I need you to understand something before we go any further. The Director—the man who ran the facility we escaped from—will want her back. He'll send people after us."

Ian nodded. "Then we stay ahead of him."

Dee hesitated. "He has drones."

"We can hide from those. Thick forest canopy will mess with their sensors. And there's plenty of forest around here."

She exhaled. "You might be right. But he's not stupid. I wouldn't be surprised if he's already contacted the local warlords, put a bounty on us. People *will* be looking."

Ian stiffened. *Of course.*

That explained Callahan.

That's why he wanted them. That's why he was willing to pay.

"Then we stay away from people," Ian said. "We've got enough supplies to get to Crescent City without stopping at camps or trading posts. But once we're there, what's to stop him from waiting for us?"

Dee hesitated before saying, "No. I think we'll be safe there. The people who run the safe zone... well, let's just say they *don't* see eye to eye with the Director."

That confirmed Ian's suspicion. Crescent City had *some* connection to the compound—but not a friendly one.

The morning passed quickly. When it was time to eat, they broke out the venison jerky Jack had sent with them, washing it down with fresh mountain water.

Then, as they were gathering themselves to move on, Ian froze.

Something was moving through the forest.

He crouched low behind a tree, motioning for Dee and Kylee to do the same.

Two men walked along a streambed—one holding a machete, the other a rifle.

Ian's grip tightened around his own weapon. They hadn't been spotted *yet*, and they wouldn't stick around to be found. He motioned for Dee and Kylee to back away slowly. If they could get up and over the ridge behind them, they'd be out of sight.

Then—

A muffled squeal.

Ian's head jerked around.

Two more men had come up behind them.

Kylee and Dee struggled in their grip.

And Ian *knew* the man holding Dee. Jenks. Callahan's enforcer.

Jenks' gaze met Ian's, unreadable. "You're going the wrong way, Hammond." His voice was all business. "I was hoping you could introduce me to your friends."

Ian said nothing, his mind racing for a plan.

Jenks cupped his hands around his mouth and called

out, "Pritchard, Solo! Over here! We found 'em."

The two men near the streambed acknowledged him with a wave and started heading their way.

Jenks shook his head at Ian. "How the *fuck* stupid are you, Hammond?"

Pritchard stepped up, yanking Ian's rifle from him.

For a moment, Ian thought he saw regret in Jenks' eyes.

Dee wasn't looking at Jenks, though. She was glaring at *him*. "You *know* these grubs?"

Ian wanted to explain. But now wasn't the time.

Jenks exhaled, rubbing the bridge of his nose. "You know what I gotta do now, right?"

He turned to Pritchard. "You're in charge. I've got business to handle."

Pritchard smirked. "You got it, boss."

Jenks grabbed Ian's arm and dragged him into the dead forest.

"Why not just do him here?" Solo grumbled.

Jenks ignored him.

They walked deeper into the woods until the others were out of earshot.

Ian swallowed hard. "You trust those perverts?"

"Pritchard's solid. Like *you* used to be."

Ian didn't flinch. "You know what you've got back there?"

Jenks shrugged. "Some guy's paying Callahan top dollar for the kid."

"And the woman?"

"She'll end up in Callahan's stable," Jenks said flatly. "She'll earn her keep."

Ian closed his eyes. He knew what that meant.

He thought of Rusty.

He thought of Kylee.

He thought of Dee, fighting like hell against a future she *knew* was waiting for her.

"All right," Jenks muttered.

Ian didn't move. He knew what was coming. He wouldn't fight it.

"Jenks," he murmured. "Look after them."

Jenks sighed. "You know I can't."

"Just do what you can. You owe me that much."

Jenks hesitated. Then—

The Beretta fired.

Three shots.

Ian flinched. But he was still breathing. Then he felt his wrists loosen. Jenks had cut the zip-ties.

"We're square now," Jenks said. "Stay the fuck away from Rio Dell."

Ian let out a breath.

Jenks gave him a look. "And don't *make* me regret this."

Ian turned away, bolting into the trees.

By the time he stopped running, his body was shaking. Not from exhaustion. From something deeper.

He stared back toward the direction of Rio Dell.

He made his choice.

9 – Captives

At first, there was shock. Then fear. Then despair.

But what finally settled in the pit of Dee's stomach was something worse—*failure*. It took root like a sickness, making her nauseous. She had failed. Failed herself. But worst of all, she had failed *Kylee*.

And now, there was the awful anticipation of what came next.

She didn't recognize the name *Callahan*, but the fear and hatred in Ian's eyes at its mere mention had told her everything she needed to know. She had heard stories—whispers passed between survivors, half-truths shared over rationed meals in the cafeteria. Cannibal gangs, warlords, criminals—men who had seized what was left of the world and ruled by sheer brutality. Out here, *success* was often measured by how cruel and savage a person was willing to be.

By that measure, Callahan was thriving.

The large bald man leading their captors went by *Jenks*. He had *killed* Ian. Just like that. And from what Dee could tell, he barely lost a wink of sleep over it. If there was any remorse behind that stone-cold expression, he hid it well.

Jenks was a killer. But he was a *controlled* one.

That control was the only thing keeping her and Kylee safe from the two younger men—Solo and Josey—who made no effort to hide their depraved thoughts. They joked openly about what they would do to Dee *if* Jenks wasn't around, their voices dripping with cruelty, unchecked by conscience or decency. They had the impulses of most men their age—only sharpened by sadism and stripped of restraint.

The fourth man, *Pritchard*, checked them from time to time, throwing out the occasional warning. But the real reason they held back was *fear*—fear of Jenks and, through him, Callahan.

Dee had no illusions. These men *knew* about Kylee.

That was why they had been hunted.

But how? Had Ian said something before he decided to take them to Crescent City? That seemed impossible—he had been with them almost the entire time. Unless he had a radio. *Or maybe Omar and Jenna?*

Jenna had seen her broken arm heal. But had she truly *understood* what she had seen? Or had she just assumed the injury wasn't as bad as it looked?

Too many unknowns.

Kylee's voice pulled her back to the present.

"Dee," she whispered, seizing the first chance to speak during their long march. "Are you okay?"

"Don't worry about me," Dee murmured. "How are you holding up?"

"I'm fine," Kylee said, though her small voice betrayed a hint of uncertainty. "A little scared, maybe. What do these men want?"

Dee hesitated. "Can't you *read* them?"

"I can," Kylee admitted, "but they only know what they were told."

"And what *were* they told?"

"To bring a girl and a woman matching our descriptions back to their boss." Kylee's expression darkened. "But they don't know why. Jenks knows *something* about me and my... quirks, but all he understands is that someone is paying Callahan *a lot* of money for us."

Dee's stomach twisted. "Whatever their plans, they're willing to kill for it."

Kylee nodded. "You're probably right."

Dee frowned. "There's no *probably* about it. They *murdered* Ian."

Kylee shook her head. "Nobody murdered Ian."

Dee's breath caught. "What?" Her voice rose before she remembered to keep it low. "Didn't you hear the gunshots?"

Pritchard snapped his head toward them. "No talking."

"Hey, *Prick*," Solo sneered. "I got something we can shove in her mouth if you want."

The words had barely left his lips before *Pritchard slammed the heel of his palm into Solo's face.*

Solo staggered back, clutching his nose as blood streamed through his fingers.

"You *motherfucker*," he snarled, his voice now thick and nasal.

Up ahead, Jenks didn't even turn around. "Shut the fuck up."

Solo wiped at his nose. "This asshole *broke* my—"

"You're lucky *he* got to you first," Jenks cut in, his tone unreadable. "Now shut your suck before *I* shut it."

The forest fell into uneasy silence.

Dee risked a glance at Kylee, but the girl didn't seem fazed. She met Dee's gaze and, ever so slightly, *smiled.*

Nobody murdered Ian.

The words echoed in Dee's head.

What did Kylee know?

***

The settlement they entered was little more than a sprawl of tents, trailers, and makeshift lean-tos clustered near a sluggish river. A single house stood at its center like a crumbling relic of the past, the only real structure left. Barbed wire surrounded the camp—a tangled, rusting slinky of twisted metal meant to keep the desperate *out* and the unfortunate *in*.

The people here were filthy, their faces gaunt, their eyes hollow. Some coughed into their hands, their bodies hunched with sickness. *Why the hell would anyone stay here?* Dee thought. The bloody flu alone should have been reason enough to keep moving. Then she understood—security. However crude, however brutal, it was *something*. Food, shelter, protection. For those who had something to trade, it was better than nothing.

At the entrance—a simple break in the barbed wire—Jenks handed a guard a small, lumpy sack. Payment. Bribery. Tribute. Whatever it was, it was enough. The grub barely glanced at Dee and Kylee before stepping aside, no questions asked.

Jenks led them through the camp quickly, keeping them out of sight as much as possible. It wasn't until they neared a larger trailer that Pritchard, Solo, and Josey peeled off, disappearing into the maze of shelters. Jenks alone knocked at the trailer's door—a precise rhythm, one rap, three quick raps, then repeat. A signal.

The door creaked open. A toothless man peered out, gave Jenks a nod, then stepped aside.

The moment they entered, the stench hit Dee—stale sweat, old tobacco, weed, piss. The air inside was thick, oppressive. Blackout shades smothered the light from the six small windows, leaving only thin slashes of sunlight cutting through the darkness. A large, filthy rug covered most of the floor, doing little to muffle the creaks beneath their feet.

Jenks guided them through the gloom, past a heavy blanket strung across the space, dividing the trailer into separate rooms. Beyond it, an old metal desk sat at the far end, flanked by two grizzled men and a woman holding a stack of papers.

But it was the man *behind* the desk that Dee focused on.

His face was sharp, angular—almost wolfish. Dirty blond hair, thinning at the top, stuck out in unkempt clumps. His cold eyes flicked over Kylee, studying her like she was an item off a manifest, something to be assessed, not a child to be regarded.

"Well," the man drawled, finally leaning back in his chair. "So this is what all the fuss is about. Somebody wants you *bad*, little girl."

Kylee met his stare, her face unreadable, offering nothing.

Callahan. It had to be.

Callahan's gaze shifted to Jenks. "Where's Hammond?"

Jenks exhaled slowly. "He's dead."

A silence stretched in the dim room. Callahan's expression didn't shift, but something in the air tightened. He flicked his fingers, a simple gesture. The two men and the woman took the hint and stepped out, disappearing beyond the dividing blanket.

Once they were gone, Callahan locked eyes with Jenks. "How?"

Jenks barely hesitated. "I shot him. Double tap. Back of the head."

Callahan's jaw worked, teeth grinding against each other. He swallowed hard, then reached into a desk drawer and pulled out a small flask. Tilting it back, he took a long, deliberate sip before offering it to Jenks.

Jenks took it without question, taking a shallow pull before handing it back.

After a long pause, Callahan spoke. "You're a good number two, Jenks. So I'm gonna let this slide."

Jenks didn't move, didn't breathe.

"I don't wanna see Hammond suffer any more than you did," Callahan continued. "But examples have to be made. *Targeted application of extreme violence*, right? We've talked about this before. People test you, *that's* when things start falling apart. What we would've done to Hammond—ugly as it would've been—would've *saved* lives."

"I know, boss," Jenks said, his voice measured. "Won't happen again."

Callahan studied him for another moment, then nodded. "I know it won't." He leaned forward, tapping a finger against the desk. "This is salvageable. People liked

Hammond. He was cool, but a hothead over the weirdest things." His eyes flicked toward Dee and Kylee. "We'll say he didn't come in quietly. That you had to put him down. That's the story, yeah?"

Jenks nodded. "Absolutely, boss."

Callahan's lips twitched into something that wasn't quite a smile.

Dee watched the exchange, noting the subtle shift. Jenks wasn't the groveling type. But something about Callahan—the way he controlled a room, the way his words slithered into the mind and *coiled*—made men like Jenks bend.

Callahan tilted his head. "Those idiots you had with you—gonna be a problem?"

"Pritchard won't," Jenks said. "The other two might go off-message when they get high."

Callahan sighed, rolling his eyes. "Well, there's a cannibal clan up north offering five gallons of refined gasoline for every head of two-legged cattle."

Jenks didn't react.

Dee's stomach twisted.

Solo and Josey were *already dead.* They just didn't know it yet.

Jenks exhaled. "What's to stop them from running their mouths *before* we hand them over?"

Callahan smiled. "You ever read *Message to Garcia,* Jenks?"

Jenks frowned. "No... never heard of it."

Callahan shook his head, amused. "Bet your boy Hammond knew it. It's all about doing *whatever* it takes to accomplish the mission." He leaned back in his chair. "But I'll help you out on this one. They can't spread rumors if they don't have tongues."

Jenks gave a slow nod. No shock. No hesitation.

Dee felt ice in her veins. *These men were monsters.*

Jenks glanced toward her. "Where do you want them?"

Callahan barely spared them another glance. "Put them in storage for now." Then, as if dismissing them entirely, he turned his attention to the papers on his desk.

It was over. They had just been *filed away.*

Jenks nodded and grabbed Dee's arm, steering her toward the door.

Kylee followed without a word.

As they stepped back into the light, Dee fought the rising panic in her chest.

They were running out of time.

***

Jenks led them back through the hanging blanket, motioning for the two men at the door to reenter Callahan's makeshift office. With a grunt, the toothless man helped Jenks roll up the worn rug in the center of the trailer's floor.

Beneath it was a crudely assembled trapdoor—rough wood slapped together with two-by-fours and scavenged hardware. It was clearly not part of the trailer's original design. Jenks unlocked a combination padlock and hauled the hatch open, revealing a ladder that descended into blackness.

He gestured. "Down."

Dee went first. The air grew colder with every rung. As her eyes adjusted, she saw the walls of a tight concrete room—no more than twelve feet square. Four cots were spaced evenly around the perimeter.

Two of them were occupied.

Two young women, maybe in their late teens, lay shackled to the wall by thick iron cuffs. Neither moved. One had her eyes open, staring blankly at the ceiling, unblinking.

Dee's skin crawled.

Jenks guided Kylee down behind her, then led them to the two empty cots. He shackled Dee first, then Kylee—each cuffed by one ankle, just like the others. The metal was cold against her skin.

As Jenks stood, Kylee pointed to his left hand. "What's that?"

Even in the dim light, Dee could make out the mangled skin—scarred and twisted, like melted wax.

Jenks looked down at it. "Old burn."

"Does it still hurt?" Kylee asked softly.

"Sometimes."

There was a pause.

"I fell into a fire a while back," he added.

Kylee tilted her head. "Why are you lying, Carl?"

Jenks stiffened.

"I'm not," he said quickly. Then his brow furrowed. "Wait... I never told you my first name."

Kylee didn't blink. "Someone held your hand in the fire. Over and over. Until Ian stopped them."

Silence.

Jenks stared at her, his face a storm of confusion and memory. He pulled his hand away like it had been burned all over again.

He turned to Dee. "Hammond tell you about that?"

Dee shook her head. "No. First I've heard of it."

"I guess... I guess he told her when you weren't around."

Dee shrugged. "Maybe."

Jenks didn't answer. He turned and climbed the ladder in a hurry, like the room had suddenly gotten too small.

Then the trapdoor slammed shut.

And darkness swallowed everything.

***

In the trailer above, all was quiet.

Below, in the cellar, there was no light.

No shadows.

Only the dense, suffocating dark—the kind that swallowed sound and breath and hope.

Then came the creak of the trapdoor.

A slice of pale light spilled in, followed by the glare of a flashlight.

Three faces peered down.

Dee recognized the first two instantly—Callahan and Jenks.

The third took longer to place, but the memory came—Patrick Riley, the chief of security from the Owens Valley compound. She'd seen him around before, always in the background, always watching.

He didn't say a word. Just stared.

Then he nodded, once.

Kylee was the one.

The trapdoor closed again.

Darkness returned.

"He's here for me," Kylee said. Her voice was level. No fear. No sadness. Just fact.

"I'm afraid so," Dee murmured. "I'm sorry, Kylee. I failed you." She exhaled slowly, her voice cracking. "Looks like you're going back."

It was too dark to see Kylee's face, but her voice carried a smile.

"You don't know that yet, Dee."

Dee's throat tightened. "I don't see another way out of this that isn't worse."

Kylee's answer was calm. Certain. "Ian will come for us."

Dee paused.

She wanted to believe it—but she couldn't. Not after the gunfire. Not after the river.

"Ian's dead, Kylee."

There was a long silence.

Then, softly:

"He will come for us."

***

The wind howled through the skeletal remains of what had once been a parking lot, carrying with it the dry dust of a dying world. Patrick Riley stepped away from the dilapidated trailer, his boots crunching over gravel and broken glass. The late afternoon sky was the color of rusted steel.

He kept walking until he was out of earshot. Then he pulled the handheld transceiver from his coat pocket. The casing was scratched, the antenna wrapped in electrical tape. Still, it worked.

He keyed the mic.

"Control, this is Handler-One. Over."

A moment of static. Then:

"Go ahead, Handler-One. This is Control." George Petros's voice was calm, smooth as ever.

Patrick exhaled slowly.

"I just got out of Callahan's compound. We made contact. Visual confirmed—the anomaly is here."

A pause. Then, "Intact?"

"She's fine," Patrick replied. "But there's a problem."

Another pause. Sharper this time. "What kind of problem?"

Patrick glanced over his shoulder toward the trailer. He lowered his voice.

"Callahan's changing the deal."

Silence crackled back at him.

Patrick continued. "He says the girl's value has increased since our last arrangement. Claims he's got offers coming in from other buyers—real ones. Clean zone names."

"And you believe him?"

Patrick hesitated. "Callahan doesn't bluff. Not when it comes to product."

Static buzzed, followed by George's voice—lower now, like a storm building in the distance.

"What's he asking for?"

"Double. Plus transport security."

"Transport to where?"

"He didn't say. But I think he's trying to force a hand. He wants leverage."

George was quiet. Too quiet.

Then: "Let me make something very clear, Patrick. Callahan doesn't dictate terms. He delivers. We control the corridor. We control the logistics. If he thinks he can walk this back, he's forgetting who put him in that trailer."

"I understand, sir. But the situation's delicate. We push too hard, he might burn it all—walk away, or worse, sell her out from under us."

George's voice hardened. "Then remind him why we're still interested in doing business. And remind him what happens when someone makes us regret that."

"Yes, sir."

"Stay close. Don't lose sight of the girl. I want eyes on her at all times."

"Understood."

Patrick released the mic and let the radio drop against his chest. He stood there for a moment, staring out at the empty horizon.

Callahan had just moved the pieces.

Now it was Patrick's job to stop the board from flipping over.

10 – Rescue

Ian ducked behind a tent as he watched a pimp drag a young girl into Callahan's old trailer-office. It was the same guy he had a run in with during his last visit to Rio Dell. From what little Ian knew, the guy was a coward who enjoyed holding power over pretty girls and hurting them. But he was also terrified of Callahan. Terrified enough to report back immediately with any earnings. Which meant Callahan was in the trailer now. And if so, Dee and Kylee would be with him.

There were no guards outside the trailer, but the lights were on. The windows, the ones that were not held together with duct tape, were covered with a thin layer of mud and had window coverings on the inside. Ian sat in the shadows, debating what to do next.

He felt a tingle in his hand. It felt as if Kylee had slipped her hand in his, just the same way Rusty used to. He had watched Callahan and his crew do horrible things to people for all kinds of reasons and done nothing to stop it. But he could stop this.

He knew how it worked; people were sold for many reasons. It could be anything from slavery to food. But Kylee was special. She could do things, help people. She would go to the highest bidder. Callahan would probably keep a woman like Dee in his stables and pimp her out for top trade value. Ian felt a chill as he considered Kylee's and

Dee's likely fates. He could not let any of that happen. He would not.

Ducking back into the shadows, Ian found a suitable spot to surveil the trailer where they were being held. He needed to get an idea of how many people were in there and how they were armed before he just kicked in the door with nothing but a knife in hand. Ian toyed with the idea of getting right up to the trailer window and looking in, but there was too much chance he'd be seen.

He needed to be patient. After all, everyone had to take a leak sometime. And sure enough, after about forty-five minutes, the door opened. It was harder to see now that the moon was setting, and the night was growing darker. But he could tell by the size that it wasn't Jenks. Ian thought he had a good chance at taking anyone else in a straight-up fight.

The figure made his way to the nearest wooden outhouse and walked in. Never even looking behind himself. *This guy must feel safe.* Ian slinked through the rows of tents and positioned himself on one side of the outhouse. He gripped the knife in his right hand and crouched down, staying on the balls of his feet.

The outhouse door swung open. There was Ian's prey, starting back to the trailer. Before he got more than a couple of steps, Ian pounced. Flexing his legs, he took two strides, wrapping his left hand around the man's mouth and pulling him to his chest. With his right hand, he slipped the knife up to the man's side and pressed the point home, just enough to let him know it was there but not enough to break skin.

Now that he was close, he could see that he had hit the jackpot; it was Callahan. Keeping a tight grip, he pulled Callahan back to the far side of the outhouse to get out of sight of the trailer just thirty yards away.

"Okay," Ian said. "I'm going to ask you a question, and then I'm going to take my hand off your mouth. The only noise you're going to make will be to whisper the answer ." He pressed the knife point a little harder. "Got it?"

Callahan nodded.

"Good," Ian whispered, and loosened his hand slightly.

"I thought you were dead, Hammond."

Ian had known he'd likely screwed Jenks by showing back up here. But he didn't care. Jenks had taken them; he was just as guilty as Callahan. "Are they in the trailer?"

Callahan let out a laugh. "You got a hard-on for that blonde, don't you?"

Ian pressed the point of his dagger into the man's ribs, not sure if he was drawing blood yet.

"Yeah, they're in there, Hammond. But look. You know you don't want to get on my bad side, right?"

Ian interrupted, "I'm already on your bad side."

Callahan ignored the comment and continued, "You've been a good earner so far. I can overlook this; I know how horny a man gets running outside the wire. Let me go now, and we'll forget the whole thing. Hell, I'm in such a good mood today, I may even let you take her for free to get your rocks off. It'll get your mind straight."

Callahan was lying.

Ian pulled him to his feet, keeping the knife steady at the jugular. "All right, you already told me what I need to know. Let's go."

Ian's plan was to take Callahan inside and barter with Callahan for the girls. They would have to hold on to Callahan for a while to make sure they wouldn't be followed. After that, he would kill Callahan.

Ian felt the elbow before he saw it. His muscles clenched in his knife hand, but he didn't know if there was any damage before his nose exploded in a gush of blood. In what was almost an instant reversal, he was lying on the ground outside of the outhouse with Callahan on top of him. He made a stabbing motion with his knife hand before he realized the knife wasn't there anymore.

Callahan's fist came down on Ian's face, crunching his already once broken nose and knocking his head into the hard, foot-worn ground. Through blurring vision, Ian saw the tip of his knife just a centimeter from his eye.

"Chill out, Hammond, or you lose it." Callahan's voice was both calm and threatening.

Ian let his arms go limp in surrender. The throbbing in his nose and the river of warm blood streaming down his cheek were all he felt. "Jenks," shouted Callahan. "Come out and help me with this prick." A large figure appeared from the trailer.

Jenks snapped his head in surprise, and Ian heard him mumble, "Shit."

"You told me this asshole was dead." Callahan stood up. "Then he tries to jump me. How the fuck is he here if he's dead?"

Jenks kept quiet. What could he say? Ian thought he saw fear in the big man's eye.

Callahan turned back to Ian. "Jumping a man on the shitter Hammond? What the fuck, you think I'm cute? Didn't even offer a reach around." Ian felt a sharp pain in his ribs as Callahan landed a kick. "Get up."

Ian stood slowly and then felt himself being yanked up roughly by Jenks. "I told you to stay away," he whispered into Ian's ear. "What happens next is on you now." Then louder, "What we gonna do with him?"

"Bring him in and tie him down. There's a market for good meat. We'll cut nice steaks out of his legs and keep him breathing so the rest of the meat don't spoil. Then you and I need to have a chat."

Callahan and Jenks brought Ian into the dimly lit trailer. Ian tried to staunch the flow of blood from his nose with his hand, but Jenks yanked it back down. The river of blood continued to flow freely.

A third man with a gun sat just inside the door. On the far side of the trailer sat a group of captives on the floor with their hands and feet tied with old wires. They were mostly girls, but there were a couple of boys as well, probably a dozen in all. They ranged in age, but none of them looked older than twenty. Sitting among them with their backs against the wall were Kylee and Dee. Ian knew enough about Callahan's operation to know that if they were out of the cellar, they were being prepped for delivery.

Ian shrugged, almost embarrassed.

Jenks grabbed Ian by the arm and spun him around to zip-tie his wrists. Once he was done, he shoved him back to the ground, grabbed his ankles, and zip-tied them, too.

Kylee tried to whisper something to Ian but was cut

short by Callahan. "Shut up! Next tongue I see wagging I cut out." He looked around, making eye contact with the captives to make sure they knew he was serious. Ian knew these guys wouldn't hesitate to cut out a tongue, but he doubted they would in this case. That might damage the merchandise. But there were ways to inflict pain without permanent or visible damage.

The slavers spoke quietly, and Ian strained to hear what they said. Callahan's voice rose in anger. "That Poindexter thinks he can get over on me? Fuck that prick. We got other buyers!"

Jenks spoke. "He knows we have them now. His man Riley said to hand them over or face dire consequences."

"What's he going to do? Throw his pocket protector at us?"

Ian shot a look at Dee. He could see that she was listening too and nodded to confirm his unasked question. They were talking about the Director—the man she and Kylee had run away from. So, Callahan did have a deal, and it looked like it had gone south.

What little Ian could hear of the rest of the conversations gave him the impression that they would be selling them to some kind of enclave instead. It was somewhere in the mountains to the east and supposedly paid top dollar for kids, teenage and younger. For what purpose they didn't know and didn't care.

"I thought you were dead." It was Dee's voice. "Kylee kept telling me you were alive and coming for us. She must have sensed it was your plan all along."

"I was coming this way anyway." A smile broke through

the blood still seeping from his nose.

She smiled in return.

Exhaustion got the best of Ian, and he fell asleep where he sat.

He was only out for a minute when he was awoken rudely with a kick from one of Callahan's men. They were getting the prisoners up and preparing to move. The slavers probably wanted to get out of camp before first light to avoid drawing too much attention. The thugs that ran this place probably knew exactly what was going on under their noses but allowed it to happen anyway. They probably got a kick back from Callahan to look the other way. The only reason they would hassle these guys was if they wanted to present some appearance of safety within the camp. Just so people would stop here.

Jenks squatted down next to Ian. He assumed Jenks was going to tell him again how badly Ian had screwed him by coming back. Jenks stared at him a moment, then said, "When you told me I didn't know what I had back there, what did you mean?"

Ian looked down. "Does it matter? Callahan's already got them sold off. Besides, you wouldn't believe me, anyway."

Jenks raised his left hand, the bad one, and showed it to Ian. At first Ian wondered why. He already knew what had happened to that hand; Ian was the one who put a stop to it. But the hand was fine, no burn scars and fully functioning. It was as if Jenks' hand had never been shoved in a fire. "Did she do this?" Jenks asked.

"Yup," Ian said with a smile. "Now you know what I

meant."

"Get them moving, Jenks!" Callahan said with his signature impatience.

Ian slowly got to his feet as Jenks rousted the rest of the prisoners. Callahan came over with a knife and cut the zip-ties around Ian's ankles. "You're not the score here, so fuck with me, and I'll end you right in front of them."

Ian nodded and wondered why this man was wasting his breath. They both knew he was dead either way and would take the first chance of escape he got. Maybe they just wanted to get out of camp before they killed him.

As the prisoners filed out the door, Kylee looked back at Ian. She even risked a smile. Stepping down out of the trailer, Ian could see a maroon glow over the mountains to the east. There was not much time before the dim morning light filtered through the clouds to light the camp. He knew his captors would want to move quickly.

Ian could make out the concertina and the guard platforms. It would have been a peaceful morning if it not for the zip-ties around his wrists and the armed men surrounding him.

Boom. The world exploded without warning.

A tremor knocked him to the floor. The northeast tower was gone.

Another blast—southeast tower obliterated.

Smoke. Screams. A white glint in the sky—a drone. Armed. Accurate.

"The Director's here," Kylee said in an even monotone.

Automatic weapons fire erupted on the east side of the camp. Most of the camp defenders ran west. They were not paid enough to stand up to this. The few who stayed continued to fire into the tree line east of the camp. Motor vehicles, the first Ian had seen operating in years, appeared through the smoke. The vehicles were small pickup trucks reinforced with crude armor and one or two military-style Ultra-Ts. Rounds from the camp defenders bounced off the armor, having no effects.

People poured out of tents and trailers to see what was happening. Some ran from the vehicles, others hesitated. They were in shock or still half asleep. The other prisoners and their captors looked on, stunned. Callahan was yelling, trying to get them to move west, still thinking he could get out of the camp and get his payday.

As the smoke cleared; Ian could see there were six vehicles. Each had a large plate, maybe two to three meters square. All six stopped with simultaneous precision in a rough line as the defenders continued to waste their ammunition. Within a few moments, the firing stopped. The remaining camp defenders, and nearby onlookers, rubbed their skin, confused and frightened. Moments later, they screamed and ran away from the vehicles with the large plates.

Ian recognized the reaction. The attackers were using an active-denial system, which puts out a high-frequency microwave burst that made the targets feel like they were on fire. They wanted to subdue people, not kill them.

At least not until they got their hands on Kylee.

Figures in reflective metallic silver suits appeared alongside the Ultra-Ts. These figures walked past the vehicles, unaffected, carrying a variety of automatic weapons. Their reflective suits apparently providing protection from the active-denial emitters. The vehicles moved forward at the same pace as the men in the silver suits, and people ran from them as the affected area crept closer.

Grasping the danger, most of the slaver guards ran west, as did the prisoners. Callahan implored his men to wait, but there was no stopping them.

Ian stared at the surreal scene until Dee stepped up and shook him by the shoulders. Not out of anger, but to jumpstart his survival instinct. "We can't stay here," she shouted at him. "Let's go!" Kylee said nothing but nodded. There was no fear in her face. Ian looked at Dee, who motioned for him to lead the way.

They only made it a few feet when Ian felt a hand on his shoulder spin him around roughly. It was Callahan, brandishing Ian's knife. "I told you not to f—"

That was all he got out before Ian's fist landed square on his mouth. Callahan stumbled back, stunned, a stream of blood flooding down a split lip. Ian punched him again, causing him to stumble back even faster, tripping on his own feet and landing on his rear.

"Get down!" Ian said, kicking him in the chest, pushing him all the way down and slamming his head into the ground. Callahan swung the knife up to stab Ian in the side. Before it could land, Ian grabbed the knife arm and twisted the knife free. "And give me my knife back," he said, giving the man one more kick to the head.

Ian turned to walk away when he heard, "Hammond, we're not done here!"

He spun around to see Callahan pointing a Glock at him. He jerked at the pop of a pistol firing and looked down to where he had been hit. There was no wound. Maybe Callahan had missed. Instead of firing again, the slaver boss slumped over and collapsed into a growing pool of his own blood.

Jenks came from inside the mobile home with his own small pistol in hand. Was he making a play for the head of Callahan's organization? Maybe Jenks would follow through on Callahan's deal with the Director. Instead, Jenks lowered his weapon and yelled, "Get her the fuck out of here Hammond!"

That was all Ian needed to hear. "Go," he said to Kylee and Dee, who both ran ahead of him and away from the silver men, along with the rest of the camp.

They moved through the chaos, checking behind periodically to see if the attackers were gaining ground. Visibility was cut by lingering smoke and the thick dust from the westward stampede of camp dwellers. The scene was full of panic as people ran from the attackers, driven by a collective fear.

The attackers fired occasionally to either side of the camp. They even gunned down a man who tried to break from the crowd and cross the river on the north side of camp. But the people who ran west could go. Their plan was to gather up all the people in the camp. That way they could sift through and find Kylee.

He stopped suddenly, yanking at Dee's arm. Kylee stopped with them and was nearly flattened by the crowd. One man shoved Ian, not maliciously, just because he was in the way. Ian stumbled but kept his feet. He pulled Dee through a nearby tent flap out of the way, motioning for Kylee to follow.

"What are you doing?" she asked. "We have to keep going!"

"Listen to me. We're being herded."

"What?"

"Following the herd will just get us caught. We need to make for the river."

"But that water is freezing. We wouldn't survive an hour out there after going through that."

"We'll have to figure that out when we're through. The other option is to get in line to pick our way through that concertina on the other side of the camp."

Dee stayed silent.

"Look, you can follow me or follow them." Ian pointed to the mass of humanity running by the tent flap, screaming and shoving. "Your call."

She nodded and, after looking at Kylee for agreement, motioned for Ian to lead the way out of the tent. The crowd thinned, as most had already passed by.

The silver invaders moved slowly, gathering prisoners, and binding their hands and feet. Ian started toward the river, followed by Kylee and Dee, using the tents to mask their movement.

Reaching the last tent before the river without incident, they avoided notice. Ian crouched behind the canvas and motioned for the girls to do the same. "Okay," he said, speaking just loud enough to be heard above the clamor. "When we go for the river, we need to run hard. There's no cover until we get to the other side, so the quicker the better."

Ian put up a hand to tell them to hold for just a second as he peeked around the corner of the tent.

One man in silver was less than fifteen feet away, inching his way toward the tent. Ian jerked his head back reflexively. He could see now that the silver clothing was like a fireman's suit, with big silver boots and a large metallic helmet. The helmet had a clear window in front for the wearer to see out of, but it restricted peripheral vision. Ian could use that to his advantage.

He pulled out the knife strapped to his right ankle. Slipping around the corner of the tent, he surprised the man in the silver suit, grabbing his weapon before he leveled it. With the other hand, he drove the knife just under the man's ribcage with a swift punch. The silver suit was reflective, but it was not armor.

Ian could see the man's eyes grow wide and felt his grip on the rifle loose just enough to pull it out of his hands. It was an M-86, like the one that Jenks and his men had taken from Ian. He pointed it at its owner, who lay on the ground with his helmet now off, clutching at his wound, and no longer a threat.

Ian felt a pang of guilt as he realized this guy was not much older than twenty, with greasy bangs flopping down over a pimply, scrawny face. But he had no choice; this boy would give them away the second they ran for the river. It was him or them.

Ian raised his rifle and aimed at the boy's head, trying for a clean, painless shot. The boy's eyes widened. Ian squeezed the trigger when Kylee walked between his sights and his target.

His jaw went slack as Kylee walked right up to the young silver fighter and placed a hand on his head. His eyes closed, and his face changed from mortal fear to the complete serenity of sleep. Kylee then moved her hands down to his knife wound. After a few seconds' convulsion, she stood. The boy's wound was no longer bleeding.

"We need to go now." Kylee's tone was calm.

"Right." Ian nodded, regaining his wits. "Give me a five-second head start. If there are any snipers watching, that will flush them out."

"No! We go together or not at all," Dee insisted.

Ian allowed himself a smirk. "They won't hit me on the first shot. I'll be fine."

"He knows what he's doing, Dee," Kylee said.

Reluctantly, Dee grabbed his hand and squeezed. Ian took off toward the river. Excitement grew in his belly—they would get away. He waved Kylee and Dee out from behind the tent, and they followed him toward the river.

Suddenly, Ian's skin itched, then burned. Before he realized what was happening, he was on the ground, writhing in pain. He imagined this was what it felt like to be on fire. He could barely see Kylee kneel next to him, asking what was wrong.

Then he heard a muffled voice say, "We've got her."

Three silver figures closed in. One grabbed Dee from behind, and another yanked Kylee away from Ian, pulling her to her feet.

The barrel of a Chinese-made QBZ-191 infantry rifle

pointed at Ian's face and the fiery pain stopped as if the active denial had been turned off or turned away. The man holding the rifle said to one of the other silver men, "What do we do with him?"

"There was no mention of a man," the muffled voice said in return. The silver man weighed his options. "He's surplus population."

"No!" Dee wrestled herself away from the man holding her and lunged at the man with the rifle. He raised the rifle and was about to bring the butt down on Dee.

"Stop it!" commanded Kylee, her voice loud and filled with authority well beyond her years.

The man with the rifle froze for a moment and then fell to the ground, limp. The other two men in silver also dropped to the ground.

"Let's go." Kylee took off into the river without waiting for a response. Ian looked at Dee. She looked as shocked as he was. Then she met his eyes, shrugged, and ran after Kylee.

Once through the shallow river, the three of them moved into the woods on the far side. They were cold, wet, and tired, but they ran. A drone appeared overhead, causing them to stop and crouch. But once it passed, they kept moving.

***

They traveled eight miles before finally risking a stop. Their clothes, soaked in the river crossing, were dry now except for the sweat they had built up. The sun had broken through the clouds that were the hallmark of the Long Winter and hastened the drying. Ian sat leaning against a redwood, catching his breath. He looked up, allowing himself to savor the sight of the sun for the first time that day. The sight of that beautiful yellow ball was a clear sign that yesterday's appearance was more than a fluke. Holding up a hand to shield his eyes, he noticed two green leaves peeking out from a branch toward the top of the redwood.

Dee and Kylee rested with both of their backs on a fallen tree. "What did you do back there?" Ian asked Kylee.

She looked up and closed her eyes, soaking in the sun. "I don't know. I just told them to stop, and they did."

"Have you ever done that before?"

"No . . . first time."

"You really didn't know that would happen?" Dee joined the conversation.

Kylee shrugged, still enjoying the warm sun.

"You know who those guys are back there, don't you?" Ian asked.

"The Director sent them," Kylee said nonchalantly. "He has plans for me and the others. But I have plans of my own." She looked around and took a deep breath.

"Find Crescent City," Ian said.

"That's just step one," Kylee said, "not the full plan."

Dee looked perplexed, like she was also hearing this for the first time. "So, what comes after Crescent City?" she asked.

"Then we help."

"Help who?" Ian asked.

"Anyone who needs it," replied Kylee with the tone of someone answering a silly question.

"What about the Director?" Dee asked.

But by the time Dee got her question out, Kylee was already up and chasing after a butterfly. Ian turned to Dee. "That guy won't stop, will he?"

Dee shook her head. "No. He's not one to give up easily."

Ian nodded and threw a rock on the ground and thought for a moment. "So, what now, boss?"

"We get back on track to Crescent City," Dee said without hesitating. "Kylee believes her place is out here, helping what's left of humanity survive and maybe even live quality lives. If there are people there, like she believes, maybe they can help. If not, we move on."

"Look! Birds!" Kylee's excitement drew their attention to two hawks flying overhead. They circled over a grassy field, taking turns diving.

Before they knew it, Ian and Dee were on their feet watching too. One hawk came up with a mole or a small mouse. It struggled for a moment. Then, just a few feet off the ground, the mole wrestled itself free, then dropped and ran.

"Little guy kept fighting, didn't he?" Dee asked.

Ian nodded.

He felt Dee's hand slip around his. It was surprising but not unwelcome. He squeezed her hand in response. Soon, they would be in Crescent City. There they would really see what Kylee could do. But for now, there was no place he would rather be.

***

Patrick approached the vehicle as it was shutting down and watched as the assault force commander stepped down from the passenger side of a mud caked Ultra-T. The motor pool bay was not a place Patrick normally found himself, but he needed to get a firsthand account of the raid on Rio Dell. George would want a full report soon.

"Captain," said Patrick, getting the man's attention. "The reports we received have been conflicting. What happened?"

The exhausted man exhaled loudly and said, "We can confirm she was still at Rio Dell, but she managed to get away."

"How?" said Patrick, with a bit more anger than intended.

"She and the nanny had help. A man, looked like a drifter."

"You saw him?"

The captain shook his head. "No, but some of my team had apprehended the anomaly along with this man and the nanny."

"Please tell me they didn't let them go," said Patrick.

"Look, sir, my team did everything right. They had the anomaly and the nanny ready to be bagged and tagged, and were about to dispose of the drifter, when something happened."

"What?" said Patrick.

"They lost control of their bodies and fell

unconscious. When they woke up again, the three of them were gone."

"Did they say how this happened?"

The assault commander hesitated. "They believe the girl did it."

Patrick stared back at the man for a moment, trying to process what he had just heard.

"Look," said the exhausted man, "I don't know if I believe it either… "

Patrick cut him off. "No, I think that's exactly what happened." Then speaking more to himself than the man in front of him, he said, "This changes the equation a bit."

He turned to the assault commander and said, "Talk to your men. Keep this information quiet for now. Got it?"

"Yes sir."

Patrick left the motor pool bay without another word. George would want to hear about this immediately.

11 – Dogs

Dee's eyes fluttered open, chilled by the damp morning mist. For a moment, she dreamed the warmth on her face was sunlight—but reality set in fast.

There was no sun today. There hadn't been for days.

Above, boiling clouds churned, sealing off the sky like they had since the bombs fell. The dense fog clung to the ground, promising drizzle... then rain. The same miserable pattern she'd come to expect since leaving the compound.

They called it the Long Winter—a world left to wither after humanity had poisoned its skies.

Hope had teased her just days ago when she'd glimpsed the moon for the first time in years. The next day, sunlight. She'd dared to believe things might change. But now, under this suffocating gray, Dee knew better.

The rustle of wind through dead trees and faint birdsong couldn't drown out Ian's snoring nearby.

She glanced over. Ian lay sprawled on the cold dirt, trench coat pulled tight, a faded Giants cap low over his face. His arms, crossed beneath his head, served as his only pillow.

Dee shifted on her thin foam mat—a luxury compared to Ian's bare patch of ground.

Her thoughts drifted, as they often did, to her family. Were Mom, Dad, and Carole still out there somewhere? It had been years, but hope was hard to kill.

Another snore rumbled from Ian.

Dee watched him breathe, chest rising and falling. Grubby. That's what they used to call people like him in the compound—grubs, the ones left outside to rot. But now, looking at him in sleep, there was something... peaceful. Almost humanizing.

He'd saved them from Callahan. Risked everything.

Maybe not all grubs were monsters.

Her musing shattered as she glanced at Kylee's mat—empty.

Her heart seized. "Kylee!"

She lunged for Ian, shaking him violently. "She's gone!"

Ian snapped awake, disoriented. His eyes locked onto the empty mat. He was on his feet in seconds.

"Was it my watch?" he asked, voice sharp.

Dee swallowed hard. "No. Mine."

Ian's jaw clenched. "Get your shoes."

They geared up fast. Ian shoved the rifle into Dee's hands.

"Head south to the ravine—follow it west. I'll go north. We meet at the bottom."

"I don't think we should split up—"

"We don't have time to argue." His glare said the rest: Because of you.

Dee nodded, guilt burning in her chest.

She pushed downhill, weaving through skeletal trees and patches of ash-laced snow.

"Kylee!" she shouted, risking the noise. If marauders were nearby, so be it. Finding Kylee mattered more.

The ravine offered no signs—no footprints, no broken

branches. Just silence and fog.

Her foot plunged through a patch of slush into icy mud. She yanked it free, feeling cold seep into her bones. But she pressed on.

Panic gnawed at her thoughts.

Where are you, Kylee? "KYLEE!"

From the distance—

"Dee, over here!" Ian's voice, urgent.

Relief flooded her as she sprinted toward him. When she reached the clearing, the relief vanished.

Ian stood, knife drawn, shielding Kylee—who looked completely unbothered. Surrounding them was a pack of half-starved dogs, growling and circling.

A husky lunged. Ian caught it mid-air, but its teeth sank deep into his arm. He fought to drive his blade into its throat.

Dee's breath caught. She fumbled the rifle from her shoulder, chambered a round, and raised it—but Ian and Kylee were too close. No clean shot.

The other dogs barked wildly—a twisted chorus of hunger.

Dee shifted her aim to a snarling Labradoodle.

"No!" Ian barked between gritted teeth, wrestling the husky. "Shoot the alpha!"

Dee spun—her stomach dropping.

Atop the ridge stood a massive Doberman, muscles rippling beneath its coat. Well-fed. In command.

It locked eyes with Dee and growled—a deep, resonant threat.

Then it charged.

Dee raised the rifle—clicked off the safety just in time.

Her first shot missed. The Doberman closed the distance in seconds.

Dee fired again—the crack of the rifle echoed through the trees.

The beast crashed into her, knocking her flat. She braced for teeth—but felt only dead weight.

It twitched once, then went still.

Gasping, Dee shoved the body off and scrambled to her feet.

The pack was fleeing, yelping as they scattered into the ravine.

Ian stood victorious over the husky, blood dripping from his arm. Kylee sat behind him, legs crossed, as if she'd been waiting for them to finish.

Dee's arms trembled from adrenaline. She lowered the rifle, heart racing.

Ian turned to Kylee, panting. "What were you doing out here?"

Kylee shrugged. "I wanted to talk to the doggies."

Dee stared at her, incredulous.

"They're not ready," Kylee added with a sigh. "They just wanted to be mean."

Ian exchanged a glance with Dee—equal parts exhaustion and disbelief.

"Next time," he muttered, clutching his bleeding arm, "wake us up first."

***

They packed up their mats in silence, rolling them tight and stuffing what little they had into Ian's backpack. As always, Ian insisted they erase every trace of their camp. No fire. No footprints if they could help it.

It had been a frigid night—again. But warmth was a luxury they couldn't afford. They were being hunted.

George Petros wouldn't stop. The Director's reach was long, and Kylee was too valuable to his twisted vision of the future. The attack on Rio Dell had proven that Petros would raze entire settlements just to reclaim her.

And if not Petros, there were always marauders—the desperate remnants of humanity, willing to trade anything—or anyone—for another day of survival in the Long Winter.

Despite it all, Kylee had handled the cold better than either of them. Dee barely slept through her shivering, but Kylee? She was unfazed. Nanotech had its perks.

Ian said little that morning. After Kylee healed the bite on his arm, he'd gone quiet. Dee wasn't sure if it was anger or thoughtfulness. Either way, she couldn't blame him. She'd fallen asleep on her watch. Kylee had wandered off. If anything had happened…

They moved down the western slope, the sky a blanket of dull gray. Dee had to admit—Ian knew how to pick a campsite. Hidden, elevated, with a clear view of anything approaching. His paranoia had kept them alive this long.

"Dee, Ian's not mad at you for falling asleep."

Kylee's voice snapped her from thought.

"What are you talking about?" Dee asked sharply—then

realized.

"Kylee! Get out of my head!"

"Mine too!" Ian grumbled, his first words of the day.

Kylee ignored them both. "You shouldn't feel guilty. You didn't fall asleep. I put you to sleep."

Dee blinked. "Wait... really?"

Kylee nodded, almost sheepish. "I just wanted to talk to the doggies."

Dee felt a strange mix of relief and frustration. "Kylee, you have to trust me. Those dogs weren't your friends—they could've killed you."

"I know," Kylee murmured, eyes downcast. "I'm sorry."

Ian cut in, rubbing his arm where the bite had been. "Can you... do that anytime? Put people to sleep?"

Kylee shrugged. "Sometimes. Not always."

Ian gave her a look—half impressed, half concerned. "If you figure out how to control that, it could come in handy."

Dee smirked, but then caught Ian drifting into thought again.

"What is it?" she asked.

"Nothing."

She raised a brow.

"Alright," he admitted, "was that really your first time firing a rifle?"

Dee rolled her eyes. "Yeah, why?"

"Because you're terrible at it."

"I killed the dog, didn't I?"

"After three shots."

Dee shrugged. "Guess I could use some practice."

Ian grinned. "We'll fix that—if we ever get enough ammo

to waste."

***

By midday, they reached flat ground, following a shallow stream westward. The trickle of water was a welcome sound—a lifeline in the dead world. They filled up their water bottles and followed the stream west.

"Dee, look!" Kylee pointed upward.

Dee followed her gaze to see a towering oak, its branches bursting with fresh green leaves. Not dead. Not dying. Alive. Most of the trees near this stream were greening up, as if spring were finally trying to push aside the ten-year winter.

Her breath caught. "Wow..."

Ian stared too. "I'll say wow."

"The farther north we go, the greener it gets," Dee whispered, hope stirring in her chest.

For once, Ian didn't correct her optimism.

She turned to him. "That's a good sign, isn't it?"

"It's a great sign," he said, not taking his eyes off the greening branches. "It seems the farther north we go, the healthier the trees get."

***

Hours later, the stream had become a river, wide and deep. The sun broke through, warming their backs as they shed layers of clothing. Dee could hardly believe it—real sunlight, real warmth, and ahead... a forest of green.

They reached a rocky embankment where the river cascaded into a clear pool below.

Ian glanced at her with a mischievous grin. "I could use a bath."

Before she could respond, he was stripping down to his boxers and diving in with a splash.

"How is it?" Dee called.

"Cold enough to shove my balls up into my throat!" he shouted.

Dee laughed—a genuine, full laugh. She hadn't heard herself do that in... she couldn't remember when.

"I don't see any balls," Kylee said as she looked around the pool with confusion. At that, Dee laughed even louder.

"But man, does it feel good," Ian said while treading water. "Why don't you try it?"

Dee looked at him skeptically.

"All right, I'll turn around until you get in." He turned to face away from her. "Good?"

Dee wanted to get in the water. It had been at least a month since she had anything resembling a shower. But she couldn't very well leave Kylee on the shore alone. After all, the girl was raised in captivity. She never learned to swim.

Splash. Before Dee could finish her thought, Kylee had jumped in and was swimming out to Ian. "Kylee!" Dee shouted in panic.

Kylee looked back at her. "What?"

"You can't swim."

"Looks to me like she's doing just fine," Ian said, who had turned at the sound of the splash.

"I saw how to do it," Kylee said.

"What do you mean? Saw how to swim?" Dee's panic became confusion.

"Yeah," Kylee ducked under water then popped back up. "I saw it in your mind. It's easy."

Dee wanted to scold her but instead found herself smiling. One less thing to worry about.

With a playful glare at Ian, she shouted, "Turn around, pervert!" and stripped down to her bra and panties before joining them.

The water was frigid at first when she entered. But she got used to it quickly. Ian would occasionally try to sneak up on her underwater and grab her foot. He had been doing the same thing to Kylee, who started doing it back to him. They raced from one side of the river to the other. Kylee won, but Dee could tell that Ian let her.

Dee got out after getting her fill, followed by Ian. Kylee stayed in the water. She would stay there all day if they let her.

Dee stayed in her bra and panties, keeping the rest of her clothes off until they were dry at least. She found a nice flat rock to lie out on and dry in the sun. Ian, still in his boxers, plopped down next to her.

"Look at her," Ian gestured toward Kylee who was practicing swimming under water.

"I've never seen her have so much fun." A warm feeling came over Dee as she watched Kylee swim back and forth. What a contrast to her miserable life at the compound.

Inside the compound she was subjected to test after test. Once they found out that Kylee had the unique ability to project the nanobots out to other people and heal them, the testing intensified.

Dee wished she could have gotten all the children out. But that would have been impossible. Besides, Kylee had it worse than any other experimental because of her ability to project. Maybe one day Dee would go back there and get the rest of them. But first, she had to keep Kylee safe and keep them both alive.

"She's been through so much."

"Yeah," Ian nodded, then looked away. She had confided in him what the Director and his people were doing to Kylee through their experimentation into her abilities. Ian's jaw clenched several times, and she could tell he was thinking about it. Although she felt safe around him, there was something in this man, just below the surface, that he kept barely contained. Dee was sure that if Ian ever met the Director, that thing would break loose.

"So, who are these people in Crescent City we're going to find? You still haven't filled me in completely. How does Kylee know about them?"

"She probably pulled it from the Director, the same way she read us."

Dee hadn't kept Ian in the dark intentionally about their destination. Things had happened so quickly since they met that she hadn't had time to explain. And to be fair, this was the first time Ian had really asked about it.

"I don't have all the details myself. Bits and pieces of things I've overheard, or things Kylee shared with me. They are a medical research team, once part of the Director's organization, in fact. They broke away from him about five years after the bombs fell. Some disagreement between him and their team lead, Dr. Schumacher, I believe her name is."

Ian's face screwed up in a look of skepticism. "If they used to work for this Director . . . does this guy even have a name? Calling him *The Director* all the time makes him sound like Darth Vader or something."

Dee nodded. "Yes, he has a name."

The look she got from Ian implored her to continue.

"George Petros," Dee said flatly.

Ian let out a sharp breath. "No shit."

"I take it you've heard of him."

"Who hasn't?" Ian asked. "Look, I know you were still a teenager before the bombs fell, but there were only so many billionaires out there. And this guy especially was all over the news. He was pretty . . . let's just say he was eccentric."

"He's brilliant," Dee said, "and extremely focused. That's what makes him such a danger to Kylee. He wants her back and he won't stop until he gets her. He couldn't care less about anyone who gets in his way."

"So, if this Schumacher woman and her team were working for him, what makes you think they can be trusted?"

Dee shrugged. "Kylee believes they broke away from Petros because they didn't agree with his methods. And that they feel their talents should be used to help the survivors out here, not shun them."

"It's an enormous risk to take based on the opinion of a nine-year-old girl," Ian said.

"You know as well as I do that Kylee is so much more

than your average nine-year-old."

Ian held his hands up in a gesture of surrender. "Fair enough. Crescent City it is then."

They sat quietly, soaking in rare sunlight—until Ian suddenly tensed, eyes scanning the sky.

"Kylee! Out of the water—now!"

Dee shot up. "What is it?"

Ian pointed upward, his voice low. "I thought I saw... yeah, there it is again."

"Saw what?"

"A wing flash. An aircraft."

12 – The Face of Evil

"Down!" Ian barked, pointing to a boulder large enough to shield all three of them.

Dee and Ian grabbed their clothes in a rush, meeting Kylee just as she swam to shore. There was no time to get dressed—survival came first.

Soaked and barefoot, Kylee didn't hesitate. The girl moved straight for cover, her resilience as uncanny as ever.

Ian cursed under his breath, sliding back down the rocks to snatch up his rifle. He waved them on—don't wait—before sprinting back up the incline toward the boulder.

They crouched low behind the jagged stone, chests heaving, skin slick with water and fear.

A faint, high-pitched buzz cut through the air.

Dee's pulse quickened. The sound was getting closer.

"It's going away," Kylee whispered, peering skyward with unsettling calm.

"Not yet," Ian muttered, eyes scanning the horizon. "Give it a minute."

Dee caught sight of it—the glint of metal slicing through the gray sky. The drone hovered overhead, then veered south, disappearing beyond the ridge.

Relief surged as she started to rise—

But Ian yanked her back down. "Wait."

The buzz returned, sharper now. The drone banked

hard, circling back.

"What's it doing?" Dee whispered, her throat tight.

"Search pattern," Ian said, voice flat with experience. "Sweeping the valley floor."

Kylee's voice was quiet but certain. "He's looking for us."

Dee didn't need to ask who he was.

The minutes stretched into an hour—the longest of Dee's life.

The drone crisscrossed the valley in methodical lines, each pass feeling closer than the last. Dee shifted, trying to stop the numbness creeping into her legs, but every movement felt like a risk.

Kylee didn't flinch. She sat still, patient—as if she'd done this a hundred times before.

Finally, the buzzing faded. The drone glided over the southern ridge and vanished.

Ian held them in place for another tense ten minutes before standing. He stretched, rolling his shoulders and shaking out stiff legs.

Dee tried to rise but stumbled, collapsing back onto the damp earth. She rubbed circulation back into her calves, wincing. Kylee, as always, moved like nothing had happened—untouched by fatigue or fear.

"Where do you think it's headed?" Dee asked, still catching her breath.

Ian scanned the ridge. "Probably sweeping the other side now. Those drones run for about twelve hours before they've got to head home. Depending on when it launched, it's still got fuel to burn."

Dee shivered, pulling her damp clothes around her

shoulders. "And when it's done?"

Kylee answered, her voice soft but resolute.

"There will be others. He won't stop until he gets us back."

Neither Ian nor Dee had a response to that. Because they knew she was right.

***

Once the drone was gone, they grabbed a quick bite—just enough jerky to keep moving—then followed the river west, sticking to the cover of trees. The weight of exhaustion pressed on all of them, but Ian kept his eyes scanning the ridgelines.

After hours of tense silence, Ian finally spoke. "We need to get back to high ground before nightfall."

Dee sighed, her voice edged with fatigue. "Why? So we can freeze again?"

Ian didn't bite. He just glanced up toward the southern ridge. "We need a vantage point. You never know who's out here."

Dee exhaled sharply, irritation bubbling over. "Fine. But maybe we rest before we start climbing your 'vantage point.' Kylee's only nine, remember?"

Ian smirked, unfazed. "You're cute when you're pissed."

Dee tried to hold onto her anger but felt a laugh slip out despite herself.

Ian's smile broadened, deepening the dimples in his cheeks. "All right Dee, point taken. We'll keep the pace reasonable."

"Dee?" They both turned to see Kylee pointing toward movement in the trees just ahead of them.

Ian reacted instantly, signaling them to get down behind a fallen redwood. He pulled binoculars from his pack, scanning the undergrowth.

"See anything?" Dee whispered.

A beat passed. Then Ian relaxed, lowering the binoculars with a smirk. "Family. Two adults, two kids. Let's stay low and let them pass."

Dee let out a shaky breath as fear drained from her body.

"Nothing yet . . . wait. Yeah, someone's out there all right." Dee felt an electric fear move up and down her spine. Ian put his rifle down quickly and smirked.

"What?" Dee asked, perplexed by his sudden relaxation.

"Looks like a family. Four of them, two adults and two kids. Let's just sit tight here and let them pass. My guess is they don't want to be bothered any more than we do."

Dee exhaled as fear drained from her body. She almost laughed but did not want to give them away.

She felt Kylee get up from behind the tree. "Did you say kids?" she asked—too loud. Dee turned to shush her, but before she knew it Kylee had left the safety of the fallen tree and walked straight toward the family.

"Kylee, no!" Dee hissed.

Ian cursed under his breath, but it was too late. Kylee stepped out into the open, waving like she was greeting old friends.

There were four of them, just like Ian had said, a man, a woman, a boy, and a girl. The boy looked to be about nine, same age as Kylee, and the girl looked a little younger. The two adults appeared to be unarmed. But she knew by now that just because you don't see a weapon doesn't mean it's not there.

"Hi," Kylee said, waving her arm as if trying to get the attention of a friend.

Her sudden appearance startled the adults. They looked around for the best direction to run. The children looked up, hopefully, and then looked back at their feet.

"Good morning," Dee said nervously, waving her hand in a friendly gesture. She wanted to diffuse whatever situation Kylee was creating. Even gentlest of people could be dangerous if they feel threatened, especially if they have kids with them. "We're not going to hurt you," she added. "We're just passing through."

The man pulled out a knife and said, "That's close enough." He was tall and scrawny, with a frizzy, unkempt beard. He looked to be in his late forties or early fifties, his face weather worn. Dee knew he was probably younger than he looked. The outside aged people.

"Hey!" Ian said. "Take it easy. Our little girl here just wants to say hi to your kids."

"We've got nothing you want," said the woman. "We barely have enough to feed ourselves." She appeared younger than the man, maybe in her thirties. Her hair was stringy, and her teeth were blackened.

"It's okay," Dee said. "We won't come any closer. We're heading northwest. Where are you coming from?"

"Up north, near the Oregon border," said the man, lowering his knife.

"Oh, well, that's close to where we're headed," Dee said. "Can you tell us what we can expect?"

The couple relaxed when they saw Dee and Ian keeping their distance. The children kept looking down, seemingly uninterested. Kylee walked right up to the two kids, but still got no reaction. She touched the boy on his shoulder, but still nothing.

"You don't want to go too far north," said the man, a little less shrill than he had sounded a moment ago. "Some assholes up there trying to control everything and everyone."

"Marauders?" Dee asked.

"No, more like an Army," the woman said. "They call themselves the Free Militia. Think they can make people do what they say." Ian shot Dee a look. It looked like he knew about this group.

"Just like the government back in the day," added the man.

"How far north?" Ian asked.

"Up in Oregon," the man replied. "Mainly west of Portland. But word is they're expanding south. So, watch your step. They like to roam around on horseback." A smirk appeared on the corner of the scrawny man's mouth. "I guess they think of themselves as cowboys or something."

"Appreciate the heads up, we'll steer clear." Dee said. Kylee appeared back at her side now. She was uncharacteristically quiet and stared at the other two children.

"Anything you can tell us about where we're headed?" the woman asked for a return on the favor.

"About thirty miles ahead southeast, there's an old FEMA camp near what used to be Rio Dell. It came under attack a few days ago, that's why we left. So, approach it carefully if you approach it at all. But it might be back up and running by now. Either way, though, I'd be careful going through this entire area. There are a lot of marauders and even cannibals between here and there.

Dee felt Kylee snuggle up to her arm and slip behind her, hiding. She looked down to see what was wrong as Ian bid goodbye to this small family. Kylee's face screwed up in anguish as her eyes watered.

"Kylee, what's wrong?" She had never seen Kylee this upset. Not even back at the compound.

Kylee squeezed her close and Dee could feel her little body shaking with fear. Through the sobs, she blurted out, "Dee, they're hurting them!"

"Who, Kylee, what are you talking about?" But Dee put it together before Kylee had to answer. The two children had been way too quiet. A quick glance at the four strangers confirmed it. While the two kids looked like brother and sister, there was no family resemblance to either adult.

Dee hugged Kylee close.

"What a weird little kid," the woman laughed nervously before shooting an angry look at the two kids beside her. The couple grabbed the two kids by the shoulders and backed away. Then they turned and started walking at a brisk pace.

Dee glanced at Ian, who stared back at Kylee, also becoming aware that something was wrong. At first, he looked confused. Then their eyes met. "Stop them," Dee whispered, her voice sharp with urgency.

Ian's eyes flicked from Kylee to the retreating strangers. Realization hit—and in one fluid motion, he unslung his rifle and moved. "Hold up!" Ian called, closing the distance with long strides.

The man turned his head and spoke over his shoulder, still moving away. "I told you, we got nothing you want–leave us be!" He had the boy by the scruff of his neck while the woman had the girl by the arm, twisting it.

Ian caught up to them easily. Dee admired his athleticism and physical courage. The scrawny man let go of the frightened boy to push Ian away with both hands.

The push didn't even budge Ian. But when he pushed back, the man stumbled and almost fell. Ian looked at the boy. "Hey little buddy, is this your dad?" As the boy looked at the unkempt man he shook, and a wet spot appeared on his pant leg.

The woman chimed in, "What do you care? They're ours–we paid for 'em." It was the wrong thing to say.

Ian snapped his head toward the woman, and Dee watched his face twist into a frightening regard. He turned back to the man, who had regained his footing, and smashed the butt end of his rifle into the man's face. Teeth flew as a painful cry bellowed from a ruined mouth. Ian reached out, gently pulling the little boy behind him. Then he raised his rifle toward the woman. "Let the girl go."

The woman glanced at her boyfriend, who was now writhing on the ground, holding his jaw. A flash of anger crossed her face.

"I said take your greasy fucking hands off her!" Ian raised the rear sights to his eye and steadied the rifle, now aimed directly at the woman's stringy head.

Not in front of the kids, Ian. Dee moved her hand to cover Kylee's eyes. The woman pursed her lips in frustration, tempered by fear and let go of the girl's arm. Without hesitating, the little girl ran to join her older brother.

The injured man reached his hand up to the woman for help, but she ignored him. Somehow, he made it to his feet, still holding his jaw and moaning in pain. He said nothing. Dee suspected his jaw was broken. The stringy-haired woman looked at her boyfriend in disgust.

Ian kept his rifle trained on the couple. "Leave your packs here." He referred to the day packs each of them had on their back, most likely filled with all this couple's possessions, along with some food. Dee was glad he was taking their food. It would make feeding two additional mouths easier, at least in the short term.

"Now get moving! If I find you trailing us, I'll kill you both. I'll make it slow if I find out you hurt these kids."

The woman spit on the ground in front of Ian but complied. Her injured boyfriend followed, moaning, and holding his jaw.

The siblings followed Ian as he grabbed the two packs and rejoined Kylee and Dee. Dee knelt to be eye level with the two children. "You're safe now."

The girl nodded and smiled. The boy, still shaking, turned back, and looked at the couple as they grew smaller with distance.

"What are your names?"

"I'm Anna," the little girl volunteered. Dee could tell she was relieved to be free of those two monsters. "My brother's name is Heath."

"Good to meet you Anna, Heath." Dee stopped short of asking about their parents. They needed time for their trauma to abate.

"Heath doesn't talk much anymore. Not since we were with Harriet and Zeke."

"Were those their names?" asked Dee, motioning toward the departing couple.

Anna shrugged, "I guess so, that's what they called each other."

Dee smiled and nodded. "Well, Heath, you don't have to say anything if you don't want to."

Heath looked at Dee blankly. No smile, no emotion.

"Do you want to come with us?"

"Yes!" said Anna. "Heath does too, he just can't say it– or show it."

After wiping away her remaining tears, Kylee walked up to Heath and Anna and gave each of them a tight hug. She looked Heath in the eye then touched him on the chest. Her eyes rolled back for a moment, and Heath looked confused. Heath felt his body with astonished eyes as she pulled away. Dee knew Kylee had sent her nanobots to heal Heath's wounds, the physical ones at least. The other wounds would be with him for the rest of his life. Heath looked Kylee in the eye, and Dee thought she saw the smallest hint of a smile on the boy's face.

13 – A Place in the Mountains

Ian wanted to go back and kill the two monsters who'd been with Heath and Anna. He would take his time doing it, minute by minute, piece by piece. He didn't know exactly what they'd done to the kids—he didn't want to know—but Kylee's reaction had told him enough. What held him back wasn't mercy. It was the fact that leaving Dee and the three children unguarded was an even worse risk.

At least Ian could take comfort in the fact that he broke that guy Zeke's jaw. They deserved to face justice for what they did. There were no more police to arrest them, no more courts to convict them. Vigilante justice was the only justice left.

Heath hadn't spoken since they found him. Anna insisted he could talk, just wouldn't. Ian had seen that kind of silence before—too many times. It wasn't something you could fix with food or kind words. It stayed with you. Like a scar on the inside.

They gave the kids a can of sirloin burger soup from Zeke and Harriet's stolen pack. Heath and Anna shared it quietly beside the riverbank while Kylee kept up a stream of light conversation, already bonding with Anna. Despite everything she'd seen, Kylee was still a child—and around Anna, she glowed. She even tried talking to Heath, but didn't push when he stayed quiet. Ian caught himself smiling. It was easy to forget that for all her abilities, Kylee was still nine.

Wisps of pure white clouds adorned the bright blue sky, making it stunning. A breeze carried the scent of pine and wet moss. Ian breathed deep, savoring the untainted air. Farther from the blast zones, nature was clawing back. Shrubs, birds, even squirrels—signs of life returning. He closed his eyes to it, let the tension ease from his chest—until Kylee's voice cut through.

"Ian," she whispered. "I see something. On the ridge."

Ian's eyes followed her pointing finger. Movement. Subtle, but there. He reacted instantly. "Down. Behind the trees—go."

They dropped behind a cluster of fir trunks, limbs low enough to break a silhouette. Ian unslung his rifle and crouched beside them, pulling binoculars from his pack.

"There's three," he whispered. "Two in camo. One in a dark poncho. All armed."

Dee crawled up beside him. "What are they doing?"

"The one in the poncho's got binoculars out. Scanning the valley." He lowered his voice further. "Stay low. Keep the kids flat."

Dee nodded and backed away, motioning to the children to hunker down. Ian gestured Kylee over. She crawled silently through the brush until she was close enough to hear a whisper.

"You can't put them to sleep?" he asked.

She shook her head. "I told you, it doesn't work like that."

"Well, then how does it work."

"That's the problem, I don't know myself how it works.

I just did it back in Rio Dell, but I don't know how or why."

He sighed. "All right. We wait."

Fifteen tense minutes passed. Ian never took his eyes off the ridgeline. To his surprise, all three children remained perfectly still. Even little Anna, who'd barely known them a day. Kids born into the Long Winter were different. Tougher. They had to be.

A small scraping noise snapped his attention back. He glanced over his shoulder—Anna had slipped, knocking a loose rock down the slope. It wasn't loud, but it was enough.

Ian whipped the binoculars back up. The man in the poncho had stopped scanning. He was looking directly at them.

"I think they heard that," Ian whispered. He slid the binoculars aside and lined up his rifle.

"If they start coming," he told Dee, "I'll draw them west. You grab the kids and run east. Head down the ravine. Don't stop."

She nodded, face pale but steady.

Ian pulled back the charging handle on his rifle just enough to verify a round was in the chamber, then let it slide back into place gently. He put his sights on the three men on the ridgeline.

Then—a low hum. Mechanical. Ian froze.

"Drone," he muttered. He glanced up. Sure enough, it flew above the valley, banking into a slow, deliberate arc. Whether it was a new one or the same drone from earlier, it didn't matter.

He pulled the binoculars up again. The three strangers

had vanished from view. He scanned the ridgeline until he spotted them—ducked behind a rock outcrop, motionless. Either they were hiding from the drone, or they'd decided to let it do the hunting.

"They're pulling back," Ian said. He crouched, then turned to Dee. "Stay here. I'm gonna check it out."

He climbed the slope like a ghost, rifle ready. From the top, he scanned the ridgeline thoroughly. No sign of the strangers. No sign of the drone. Just trees, rock, and the distant hush of wind.

Ian returned and gave a tight nod. "They're gone. Let's move."

They gathered their packs and slid into the trees, putting distance between themselves and the strangers on the ridge—whoever they were.

***

They pushed deeper into the mountains for the rest of the day. Ian wanted as much distance as possible between them and the three armed men they'd spotted on the ridgeline. The sun stayed out most of the afternoon as they followed a broad, winding river upstream. Ian guessed it was the Klamath.

Late in the day, they came upon a pair of weathered cabins perched above the riverbank, half-hidden among a grove of vibrant, healthy trees. Near the shore stood three canoes on a cracked wooden rack. A faded sign read: Six Rivers Canoe Rental. Nearby, a second rack held a few torn life vests bleached pale by sun and time. Two ancient fishing rods lay in the grass where someone had dropped them—maybe years ago. Ian figured this must've been a small recreation stop, long abandoned after the world fell apart.

They approached the cabins cautiously. Ian had Dee and the kids stay down by the river, out of sight, while he cleared both structures. When he was sure they were empty, he waved them up.

The first cabin had been a gift shop and snack bar. The shelves were bare, but on the counter sat a glass jar half-filled with dusty Fireballs, still sealed in their wrappers. Dee tested one, deemed it edible, and handed a few to each of the kids. What they didn't eat, they stashed in their pockets for the trail.

Sleeping rolls littered the wooden floor—signs someone had camped there after the collapse, but not recently. Ian couldn't understand why anyone had left. Far from the San Francisco blast zone, the land here was still fertile. The river teemed with fish, and he'd spotted deer tracks earlier. You could survive here. Most people back then didn't know how.

The second cabin looked like staff quarters—canoe guides, store clerks, maybe both. A small lounge greeted them inside: dusty couches, a cracked television, a mini-fridge, and a table cluttered with old board games. Dee opened the fridge and found lukewarm soda and bottled water. Still good enough to drink.

In the back, bunk beds sat in disarray beneath a film of dust. Dee searched the mattresses for pests. "Old bedbug casings, but they're long dead," she announced. "Killed a couple spiders too."

Kylee had found a battered copy of Chutes and Ladders and was teaching Anna and Heath how to play. Anna giggled as her cardboard figure zipped up ladders. Heath stayed quiet but followed along—his first real interaction since they'd rescued him.

"It's good to see him engaging," Dee said, sitting beside Ian on the couch.

He nodded. "Yeah."

"They taught us a little psych at the compound before letting us care for the kids. You know—signs of trauma, therapeutic play. What Heath's doing now? That's a healthy step."

Ian didn't need training to see the boy was broken. Some cracks didn't heal. Still, he let her have the optimism. "That so?"

Ian headed outside for a sweep of the area, scanning for fresh tracks, discarded trash, anything that suggested company. The woods were silent, the river steady. He returned with an armful of deadwood and laid it beside the fireplace. The temperature was dropping fast. Clouds had rolled in, dimming the sky.

"Think that's wise?" Dee asked, eyeing the pile of firewood.

He shrugged. "This place is remote. Those canoes wouldn't still be here if this was near a major route. But just to be safe, I'll wait until dark. No light until then. If anyone smells smoke, they'll already have to be close."

"What about drones?"

"They'd spot the heat signature," he admitted. "But

unless they've got tech that sees through walls, we're just a blip. And we'll be gone by morning."

"We won't get far on foot."

"Who said anything about walking?" Ian grinned. "You ever paddle a canoe?"

"Once or twice. When I was a girl."

"Think you can steer from the stern?"

"Sure. Like riding a bike." She smiled, but then asked, "Any decent life vests?"

"Found some in the gift shop. Even had kid sizes."

"This might actually be fun," Dee said. Then, hesitating, "But if it gets bad out there…"

"We pull off the river and hoof it again. Simple."

The kids kept playing as Ian lit the fire. Heath had apparently won the first game—no reaction, but Kylee celebrated for him and gave him a high five. He hesitated, then returned it. A small victory.

Dee leaned closer and dropped her voice. "Ian, should we try to find their parents?"

He sighed, watching the flames. "Even if they're alive, we won't find them. They'll be safer with us than bouncing around the wasteland looking for ghosts."

"We'll be dodging threats either way."

"Yeah, but at least we'd have a direction."

She didn't look convinced. "We haven't even asked them if their parents are alive."

"They won't know. They've probably been separated for weeks."

"I still think we owe it to them to try."

He rolled his eyes and muttered, "Guess you've already

made up your mind."

"I just want to ask," Dee said. She turned to Anna. "Sweetie, can you come here?"

Anna padded over, wide-eyed, Fireball bulge in her cheek.

"Where did Harriet and Zeke find you?" Dee asked gently.

Heath flinched at the names, but Anna answered. "They bought us from traders."

"Traders?" Dee echoed. "Who were they?"

"The ones the soldiers sold us to."

Ian straightened. "Soldiers?"

"The Freeliscious soldiers," Anna struggled.

"Free Militia?" Dee offered.

Anna nodded. "They took Mommy and Daddy too. Said they needed to make an example."

Dee's voice softened. "Do you know why?"

"Daddy had a gun. They said that was against the law."

"Do you know if your parents are still alive?"

Tears welled in Anna's eyes. "I don't know." Dee pulled her into a hug.

Ian retrieved a road map from the gift shop and spread it across the coffee table. "Anna," he said once she calmed, "can you show me where they took your parents?"

Anna hesitated, looking at the map with wide, uncertain eyes. "I can't," she whispered, eyes brimming again.

"That's okay," Ian said. He began to fold the map up—but a small hand stopped him.

It was Heath. He pressed a single finger to the paper,

firmly and without hesitation. Right over a name: Martin's Ferry.

14 – Down the River

Dee slipped off her sun hat to let the warm rays soak her face. It still felt like a miracle. Kylee, Anna, and she had all picked out hats from a display in the old gift shop—sun-bleached but intact. When she offered one to Heath, he made a face, so she found him a plain baseball cap instead. From the same shelf, she grabbed a half-used tube of SPF 50 sunscreen.

After some examination, she saw the expiration date was worn, but the seal was unbroken. "Surprised this stuff still works," she muttered.

Ian shrugged. "It might. No heat, no light—it's been in a cold, dark cabin for ten years. Like a walk-in freezer. Stuff keeps better that way."

Dee nodded. "Guess the Long Winter preserved more than just us."

She dabbed it on each of the kids' faces. They squirmed and wrinkled their noses at the greasy texture. None of them had ever used sunscreen before—until recently, none had ever seen the sun. The Long Winter had blanketed their entire lives in cold and shadow. They'd grown up thinking it would last forever.

Ian, of course, still wore his ratty San Francisco Giants cap, sweat-stained and salt-crusted from years of wear. When Dee urged him to trade it for a clean one, he scoffed.

"I'll rinse it in the river," he offered with a grin.

"Why not just take a clean one?"

"Loyalty."

"To a team that doesn't exist anymore?"

"I'm no fair-weather fan," he said, grinning wider. "I'm keeping the hat. End of discussion."

Dee laughed at the memory now as she paddled. Ian's canoe drifted just ahead of hers. He had stripped down to a blue North Face t-shirt, damp with sweat and river mist. When he looked back and smiled, Dee realized she'd been staring.

They traveled in two canoes: Ian and Heath in one, Dee with Kylee and Anna in the other. Anna sat in the middle, while Kylee perched on the bow with a paddle she barely needed. The river did most of the work. If Heath's map point had been accurate, they'd reach Martin's Ferry by late afternoon. Dee was skeptical—who knew if the boy could read a map—but it was the only lead they had, and it led them toward Crescent City anyway.

Up ahead, the water shifted and frothed.

"Rapids," Ian called over his shoulder.

"I see them," Dee replied, turning to the girls. "Okay, make sure those life vests are tight. Kylee, you remember what to do if I yell 'pull left' or 'pull right'?"

Kylee gave a quick nod.

Moments later, they hit the turbulence. The current surged around them, snapping tree branches and rocks just beneath the surface. Dee's heart raced. She'd been through whitewater before—but never like this. Not in a canoe, not with two kids, not with lives depending on her.

The bow veered right.

"Pull left!" she shouted.

Kylee dug her paddle in as Dee pulled opposite from the stern. They righted the canoe, barely dodging a sideways spin. The river roared louder as they slipped and jolted through the current. Dee was already exhausted.

She glanced over. Ian and Heath narrowly missed a boulder and vanished behind it. Her heart stopped.

"Ian!" she screamed.

Seconds later, they reappeared, upright but struggling. She didn't have time to feel relief—her own canoe rammed something underwater. The boat jerked sideways. She gritted her teeth and pulled hard.

Kylee must have sensed the danger too. She braced her paddle on a submerged branch and shoved. The effort nearly toppled her forward. Dee instinctively reached to grab Anna. The canoe teetered—then righted. They were moving forward again.

But the bow was empty.

"Kylee!" Dee's scream split the air.

"Where'd she go?" Ian shouted.

"She went in!"

Dee scanned the rapids, frantic. Anna cried out beside her. On the opposite bank, Ian's voice rose in panic. "No! Stop! Heath, sit down!"

Dee looked in time to see Heath strip off his life vest and leap from the canoe without hesitation. He vanished into the churning water.

"Shit," Ian muttered, helpless.

They had no choice but to ride out the rest of the rapids. Seconds later, they emerged into calmer water. Ian reached shore first, pulling his canoe up onto a sandy bank. Dee followed, trembling and soaked, her knuckles white from gripping the paddle.

Ian met her in the shallows, lifting Anna from the boat. The girl said nothing, eyes locked on the river. Dee stood frozen, scanning the water, hoping for a sign.

"I've never seen anything like it," Ian said, breathless. "He just jumped in. Like he was diving into a swimming pool. What the hell was he thinking?"

"He was thinking about friendship," Dee murmured. "Loyalty."

Ian looked away, rubbing a hand over his face. Dee wanted to cry but couldn't. Anna needed her steady. So did Ian.

Anna wept quietly at first. Her sobs grew louder. Dee wrapped an arm around her, unsure how to console someone so small, so broken.

Then came a voice, small but calm.

"Don't cry, Anna. Heath's okay."

Dee spun.

Kylee and Heath emerged from the trees, soaked to the bone but alive. She ran to them and pulled them into a hug, ignoring the cold, the wet, the shock. Anna followed, hugging her brother so tightly he nearly toppled over. Ian joined them, wrapping an arm around all three kids.

When he stepped back, he looked at Heath. "Don't you ever pull a stunt like that again. You hear me?"

Heath didn't respond, only looked from Ian to Anna, then out at the river.

"Ian," Kylee said softly, "he saved me."

And for the first time in weeks, Dee realized: someone had saved *her*.

***

They made camp a short walk from the river, at the edge of a dense grove where the trees offered shelter but still let in the golden afternoon light. None of them spoke much. After what happened on the water, everyone needed rest—physical and emotional. Dee built a small fire, low and smokeless. Anna clung to her brother like she was afraid he'd vanish again if she let go. Kylee sat close beside them, her hair still damp, her arms around both.

Ian stayed quiet as he peeled off his wet shirt and spread it on a low-hanging branch to dry. "I'm going to take a walk," he said at last, slinging his rifle over his shoulder. "I want to get a look at what's around us before it gets dark."

Dee nodded, understanding. "Be careful."

He moved quickly through the trees, climbing a slope that curved westward. The ground was soft with needles and leaf litter, quiet underfoot. From the top of the rise, he spotted something through the trees—a small cluster of rooftops in a clearing below. It wasn't on the map. Curious, he worked his way down toward it.

As he drew closer, the stillness grew heavier. The kind of silence that wasn't natural.

Ian stepped past a broken wooden fence into what had once been a village. Maybe two dozen buildings—cabins, sheds, a schoolhouse—now gutted and burned, blackened timber sticking up like broken teeth. The stench hit him then: old smoke, char, and something metallic and sour that turned his stomach. Blood.

Ash crunched underfoot as he stepped through the remains of a general store. Shelves had been stripped, walls riddled with bullet holes. He crouched and touched the ground—boot prints, deep and recent. A lot of them. Not scavengers. A unit. Disciplined. Purposeful.

He walked farther into the village square and found what he expected: spent shell casings, a broken rifle, and a painted mark on the charred remains of a water tower. A crude emblem—two crossed rifles beneath a star. The Free Militia.

Ian exhaled slowly, jaw clenched. Whoever lived here hadn't stood a chance. No bodies, but that almost made it worse. Either the attackers took them... or there was nothing left to bury.

He headed back toward camp as the sky began to bruise with twilight. When he emerged from the trees, Dee looked up from where she sat by the fire, concern already rising in her eyes.

"What did you find?" she asked.

Ian glanced at the kids, then met her gaze. "A village. Burned. Recent. Free Militia, no question."

Her expression darkened. "Anyone left?"

He shook his head. "Not a soul. Just smoke and ash."

Dee's eyes flicked to the children huddled together near the fire. "We camp here tonight," she said quietly. "But tomorrow... we move fast."

Ian nodded, his face hard. "Yeah. Before they come back

to finish the job."

***

The fire had burned down to a low, steady glow. The children were asleep, curled into each other under the threadbare blankets Ian had scavenged from the cabin the day before. Kylee's hand rested protectively on Anna's arm. Heath slept with his back to them all, but Dee noticed his breathing—slow, even. Peaceful. For now.

Dee sat on a flat stone near the fire, arms wrapped around her knees. Ian was beside her, staring into the embers, his jaw set tight. He hadn't said much since coming back.

"How bad was it?" she finally asked, her voice low enough not to disturb the sleeping children.

Ian's eyes stayed on the coals. "Worse than Rio Dell."

She swallowed. "Any sign of a fight?"

"No. No shell impacts, no barricades. They didn't defend themselves. Or didn't have time." He finally looked at her. "It wasn't a raid. It was an execution."

The silence stretched between them. Above, the moon filtered through the canopy, pale and distant.

Dee spoke softly. "You think that's what happened to Anna and Heath's parents?"

Ian gave a slow nod. "They took them to make an example. That's what she said. This was an example."

Dee exhaled shakily. "And the kids were spared."

"Sold off, probably. Just another resource to them."

He shook his head. "It's not just about survival anymore. These guys have doctrine. Orders. They're trying to build something. Their own twisted version of order."

She was quiet a moment. "You think Crescent City's still out there? Still safe?"

"I don't know," he admitted. "But if they're not... then we have to find somewhere that is. We can't keep running forever."

Dee looked over at the kids, then back at him. "We're not just running anymore. We're responsible now. Whether we asked for it or not."

Ian reached out, and she let him take her hand. He didn't squeeze. Just held it.

"I know," he said quietly. "I won't let anything happen to them."

"I know," she echoed.

The fire crackled between them. Outside the circle of light, the forest was silent and vast.

15 - Martin's Ferry

At dawn, they ate breakfast of venison jerky from they pack they took off of Zeke plus two fireballs each. Then they got back onto the river.

Ian and Dee agreed that this time they would stick to the plan and pull over at the first sign of whitewater. After consulting his map, he estimated another twenty miles to Martin's Ferry.

"How are we going to know when we're there?" Dee asked after about ten minutes back on the river.

"There's a bridge ahead, according to the map. This place should be just past it. Hopefully we'll see signs of people by then. If not, then we'll pull up and look around."

"What if we find nothing?"

"We keep going and take Anna and Heath with us to Crescent City. This river will take us within a day or two's walk south of it before dumping into the ocean."

***

The sun glinted off the surface of the water as their canoes cut steadily downstream. Birds chirped lazily in the trees lining the banks, and the current was gentle enough that Dee could rest her paddle in her lap. Kylee sat quietly at the bow, her eyes scanning the shoreline with an alertness Dee had come to trust.

Anna and Heath, in the canoe just behind them with Ian, were pointing at something in the trees—a large osprey circling high overhead. It might've been the first moment that felt remotely like peace since they left Rio Dell.

That was when Kylee's voice broke the stillness.

"Don't stop," she said sharply. "Don't talk to him."

Dee followed Kylee's gaze and saw a man standing on the eastern bank ahead, waving both arms over his head.

"Help!" he called out, staggering toward the edge. "Please—my boy's sick. He needs help!"

He was rail-thin, shirtless, with wild eyes and blood smeared across his chest. The sight might have been convincing if not for the unnaturally stiff way he moved, like an actor playing a part. Dee caught herself paddling slightly toward shore.

"Kylee?" she asked under her breath.

"It's a trap," Kylee said flatly. "I can feel it. There's more of them in the trees."

Dee's hands tightened on her paddle. "Ian—don't stop," she called back without looking.

"I see them," Ian replied. His rifle was already across his lap.

The man on the shore ran a few steps into the shallows. "Please! He's just a boy! You can't leave him!" His voice cracked into a sob—but it was too loud, too rehearsed.

Dee glanced at the trees just behind the man and caught the briefest glint of sunlight on metal. The tip of an arrowhead.

"Down!" Ian shouted.

Thwip. An arrow skimmed past Dee's shoulder, splashing into the river just inches from the canoe.

"Keep paddling!" Dee barked. "Hard!"

A second arrow arced out from the forest, striking the side of Ian's canoe and bouncing off. The bandits had poor aim, but they didn't need precision. One hit in the right place could tip a boat—or worse.

More arrows followed—some thunking into the water, others whizzing overhead. Dee bent low, digging her paddle in hard on the left. Kylee mirrored her stroke without being told, helping steer them in a wide curve away from the eastern bank.

Ian fired a warning shot toward the tree line. The report cracked like thunder across the water, scattering birds and silence alike. The arrows stopped.

"Did you hit anyone?" Dee shouted over the rush of the current.

"I wasn't aiming to," Ian said grimly. "Just wanted to let them know they picked the wrong river."

They paddled on for another mile before anyone dared to speak. When they finally pulled into a shaded cove to rest and catch their breath, Kylee turned to Dee and said quietly, "They've done that before. That man... he didn't mean a word he said."

Dee nodded. "I know, sweetheart. You were right."

Kylee didn't smile. She simply turned and looked back upriver. "They'll try again."

Dee glanced at Ian. He was scanning the tree line, rifle across his knees, jaw tight.

"They can try," he said. "We're not the ones drifting blind anymore."

***

Instead of the bridge marked on the map, they found a jagged ruin—twisted girders and splintered asphalt jutting out like broken ribs. Most of the span had collapsed into the river, swallowed by current and time. The roads on both sides now ended in empty ramps, leading to nowhere but open air.

Ian studied the wreckage. At first, he considered the shock wave from San Francisco's blast might've reached this far north—but that seemed unlikely. More probable, the bridge had either fallen to neglect or been destroyed deliberately.

Two men stood at the edge of the western ramp, watching. One held a baseball bat, the other cradled a hunting bow. Neither waved back when Ian lifted his hand in greeting. They stared in silence, eyes unreadable.

"Sentries," Ian muttered low enough for only Dee to hear. "We're getting close."

Dee followed his gaze. "Do you think it's safe?"
Ian gave a noncommittal shrug. "Well, they didn't shoot. That's something. If this is the place Anna remembers, it had a trading post. That means they're used to travelers, even if they don't like them."

"They don't *look* used to travelers," Dee said.

Ian didn't answer at first. Then, quietly, "Nobody looks friendly anymore. Not out here." He remembered again how new this world still was to Dee. For most people, the past ten years had been a long descent into brutality. For Dee, the fall had only just begun.

As they drifted farther downstream, more figures came into view along the bank—a man and woman hauling water in a rusted bucket, someone fishing off a log, others scattered in the shade of the trees.

Then they saw it. A makeshift wooden fence crowned the hill above the western bank, its logs sharpened into crude spikes. The wall stretched in both directions and enclosed what looked like a pre-bomb cabin surrounded by tents. From their vantage point on the river, Ian guessed the wall was about six feet high.

He slowed their pace and gestured toward a small cove tucked behind a bend. "There," he said. "Let's stash the boats, just in case."

They paddled into the inlet and slipped ashore. Working quickly and quietly, Ian and Dee, with the kids helping as best they could, dragged the canoes into the tree line and covered them with branches and leaves. It wouldn't fool anyone paying close attention, but it might buy them time.

"If they get stolen," Ian said, brushing bark off his hands, "they get stolen. Still put us days ahead of where we'd be on foot."

Dee nodded, eyes still fixed on the hilltop fence. "I just hope they trade food," she said. "Or answers."

"Let's find out," Ian said, slinging his rifle across his back. "But stay sharp. Places like this—sometimes it's not the outsiders you need to worry about."

***

It was about a twenty-minute walk to the small settlement. There was a gate in the fence-line that was manned by two sentries carrying crossbows. These guys differed from the mercenary thugs guarding Rio Dell. They were twitchy, nervous. They asked a few questions about their business here and Ian gave them a prepared story about being a family looking to resupply on their way to Free Militia territory in Oregon.

The sentries searched them for weapons. Ian had been to enough of these places to know he needed to hide any guns before showing up at the front gate. His M-86 was buried under a bush near where they had hidden the canoes. They found his knife but let him keep it.

Martin's Ferry was mostly tents and makeshift lean-tos. The cabin at the center served as a trading post and was probably an old ranger station. Ian guessed that in the early days after the bombs, it served as a beacon for people wandering the wilderness, trying to escape the radiation and the bloody flu. The rest was probably built up by those who stayed in what they perceived to be a relatively safe place. The settlement was small compared to Rio Dell, but there were enough people here that someone could recognize them and try to get word back to this Petros guy or one of his outside associates.

As they entered, a few people glanced their way. As Ian suspected, strangers were normal here. The tents were mostly populated by refugees. A few served as storage. Small fires inside old metal trash barrels were scattered throughout, surrounded by people rubbing their hands to keep warm. Clothes hung on makeshift clotheslines strung around the encampment. They stopped close to one of the burning barrels so that the kids could warm up.

Nearby, a cork board stood nailed into a wooden post with paper messages on it,

written in charcoal. There were offers of services for trade, two warnings about the end times, and even a notice of a community meeting at the trading post a few days hence. Among the messages, Ian noticed a poster tacked up in the top dead center. It was a wanted poster describing three fugitives, a man, a woman, and a nine-year-old girl. The physical descriptions matched him, Dee, and Kylee perfectly. The poster promised a reward of a week's worth of provisions and "Trade Credits" from the "Free Militia."

Ian cursed under his breath.

"I thought you said this Free Militia was up in Oregon."

"That guy Zeke did say they were looking to expand south." Ian wanted to rip the message down, but that would draw attention. "And it sounds like they know who we are."

"Petros," whispered Dee. "He must have struck a deal with this *Free Militia*. Should we leave?"

Ian nodded. "We need supplies first. You stay here while I check out that trading post." I want to get us enough to last out to a week, just in case . . ."

"In case what? In case there's nothing there? In case we made the whole thing up?"

"Just in case. You never know what can happen these days."

Dee frowned, but thankfully let it pass. Behind her, a

few tent rows down stood a man in a dark poncho warming his hands by one of the barrel fires. The poncho gave him a medieval look, like a sinister cloak. He looked in their direction and glanced away when Ian looked back. There was something familiar about him. Ian tried to get a look at the guy without making it obvious. Something protruded from his back, covered by the poncho. By the shape, it looked like a pack with a slung rifle, but it was hard to tell for sure.

Then Ian realized where he knew this guy from. This was one of the three men they had seen in the mountains a couple of days before. The group they hid from, the ones who were looking for something.

"We might need to get moving sooner rather than later."

Dee looked him, furrowing her brow with a question.

"Don't look," he continued, "but there's a guy in a black poncho scoping us out. He was one of those guys we almost ran into day before yesterday. My guess is he's looking to collect on that reward."

Dee nodded but kept her eyes straight ahead. "Well, get moving then. Get what you can and get back out here."

"I'll make it quick."

The heavy wooden door to the cabin creaked as Ian pulled it open. It was well lit inside from ambient daylight through several uncovered windows. Shelves and aisles were set up with miscellaneous trade goods arranged randomly. It reminded Ian of a convenience store from back in the day. But instead of taking cash, this place took its payment in trade goods, with nonperishable food being the most valuable of all currencies.

The shop keep was a middle-aged man, with a graying beard and wind-burned face. As he chatted with another customer from behind the counter, Ian scanned the displays for anything useful. He guessed the food and anything else with actual value would be in the back room behind the counter.

When the other customer departed with a bag of jerky and knit hat in hand, the shopkeeper turned his attention to Ian. "Can I help you, friend?" he asked with a smile.

"Yeah." Ian had become wary of people who smiled at strangers. "I'd like whatever I can get for these in trail food." He pulled a hand-cranked eggbeater, a pair of ski mittens, and a teakettle out of the bag he had taken from Zeke and Harriet. He knew he had a good hand to bargain with. The eggbeater worked fine, which he showed. The mittens were worn, but had no holes, and, other than some soot from sitting on a fire, the kettle was intact.

"Well," the shop keep said cautiously. "I'll give you half a pound of jerky and three cans of peaches for all of it."

Ian felt relieved. The guy was low balling him, which meant he was trying to take advantage of him the honest way. "I'll take the peaches, but I'll need a pound and a half of jerky." He pulled another item out of the bag, this one a flashlight. The batteries still had some juice in them, which Ian demonstrated for the shop keep by switching it on and off. "If you have a box of 5.56 ammo, I'll take that too."

Something, fear maybe, flashed in the shop keep's eyes. "You know we don't deal in firearms around here. They've all been scooped up by the Militia."

Ian suppressed a reaction. That confirmed it. That

poster was not just put up there by some random Free Militia patrol. They came around often enough to control things in the territory that included this little hamlet. "Good to know," Ian said, putting the flashlight back into the bag.

"Hold on," said the shop keep who probably owned the place. "I'll give you two pounds of jerky and the peaches for all of it, including the flashlight."

Ian looked the man in the eye for a moment. This was the best deal he would get. He pulled the flashlight back out, put it on the counter. "Deal," he said, concluding the transaction with a firm shake.

The shop owner went back to gather the food for Ian. Bells jingled on the cabin door. In walked the man in the black poncho from outside. After a quick glance at Ian, he turned his attention to the displays.

Ian turned back and leaned on the counter. Flat on the counter, held down with scotch tape, was another wanted poster describing Dee, Kylee, and himself. The description was vague, but not wrong. The sooner they got away from this place, the better.

"You looking to collect on that bounty?" said the shop owner, emerging from the back room with Ian's food.

"You bet," Ian said. "Anyone spot them yet?"

"No, not that I've heard," the owner said absently. "If they're up here from the south, they're probably headed for Crescent City."

"Sounds like an excellent place to start," Ian said. "Thanks for the tip. You think the Free Militia will make good on their offer."

"A week's worth of rations and trade credits? You bet . . . they can afford it. You know they've got indoor farming collectives set up all over Western Oregon, where they're growing all kinds of crops now with artificial light. Although if this keeps up," the shop keep motioned to the sun outside, "they might just be able to grow their crops outdoors. Run them with forced labor from what I hear."

Ian glanced at the man in the cloak who was watching him. Then he gathered up the food in his pack and said, "Thanks for the food."

"Yeah, safe travels to you, friend."

He left, avoiding eye contact with the man in the black poncho.

Dee and the kids were right where Ian had left them, huddled near the barrel fire for warmth.

"All right," he said in a low voice as he approached. "Let's ask around about Heath and Anna's parents—then we move. That guy in the black poncho followed me into the shop. We need to keep this quick."

Before Dee could respond, a voice rang out from a few tents down.

"Anna!"

A small boy sprinted toward them, about Anna's age, with another boy—slightly older—close behind. From the same family tent emerged a couple. The woman, healthy and middle-aged, beamed with recognition. Her husband, shorter than Ian and wearing black glasses, stared off into the distance.

"Charles," the woman gasped, "it's Anna... and Heath! Henry and Marion's kids."

The younger boy threw his arms around Anna, followed by his brother. Anna lit up with joy. Heath stood nearby, quiet and reserved.

"Where are they?" Charles asked, his voice eager but uncertain.

"Here," the woman said, guiding him forward carefully. Only then did it become clear—Charles was blind.

As Carole embraced the children, she glanced warily at Ian and Dee. "How did you get away from the Militia?"

The question was meant for Heath, but Anna answered. "Heath doesn't talk anymore. The Freeliscious men sold us to bad people. They hurt him. Then Ian and Dee helped us escape."

Carole's suspicion softened. She extended a hand. "I'm Carole. This is my husband Charles, and our boys, Ben and Jimmy."

Dee introduced herself and Ian. Charles offered his hand too, and they shook.

"So you knew their parents?" Dee asked.

Carole's expression dimmed. "Yes. They arrived a couple months ago."

Anna piped up. "Have you seen my mommy and daddy?"

Carole hesitated. "I'm afraid not..."

Charles cut in gently. "Let's talk somewhere more private. This might not be safe to discuss out here."

Carole nodded, but before she could lead them away, Kylee stepped up to Charles.

"Your eyes stopped working?"

Charles smiled. "They did. The light from the San

Francisco blast blinded me. I was too close."

"How did they stop working?" she asked, peering up at his glasses.

Charles chuckled. "The flash burned my retinas. Haven't worked since. And your name, young lady?"

"Kylee," she replied.

Charles reached out his hand. Kylee took it, then gently pulled him down to her level.

"What are you doing?" Carole asked sharply.

"Wait," Dee said. "She can help."

"Help? How?"

"Please," Dee urged.

A few onlookers gathered, including the man in the dark poncho. "Kylee, not here," Ian warned.

But Kylee didn't listen. She reached up, removed Charles' glasses, and stared at the lifeless cataracts behind them. Then, with both hands, she closed his eyelids and pressed her palms to them.

"Hey!" Carole lunged forward, trying to pull Kylee away.

"Daddy!" shouted Ben, rushing toward them.

Heath reached out and stopped the boy, silently urging him to wait.

Charles collapsed into a seated position, shaking violently. Kylee convulsed too, but Ian caught her and eased her to the ground.

Anna whispered, "It's okay, Miss Carole. Kylee's trying to help."

The crowd's murmuring grew louder.

"What's going on?"

"Is he okay?"

"What did she do?"

Two men seized Ian. He resisted only until Kylee's tremors subsided. A woman grabbed Dee.

The atmosphere thickened with panic and fear. Ian had seen this kind of mob before.

A man pushed through the crowd—a wool shirt, cargo pants, metal-rimmed glasses, and a pack. "What's happening here?"

"They did something to Charles, Doc!" someone shouted.

The doctor knelt next to Charles and Carole, grounding his backpack. He felt around Charles' face. Charles stopped shaking and slowly opened his eyes.

"Wait a minute . . ." said the doctor as he opened the top flap on his bag to pull out one of those angled flashlights that doctors used to look inside ears. To Ian's surprise, the thing worked, and the doctor flashed it into Charles' eyes. Charles blinked and looked at his wife.

Charles blinked. Then he looked directly at his wife.

Gasps erupted.

The doctor stood, shaking his head. He turned to his neighbors and said, "You can put away your pitch forks. I don't understand how, but he can see."

Carole clutched her husband in disbelief. Charles held her, tears running down his face.

The grip on Ian's arms loosened. Dee was released.

"Charles hasn't seen Carole or Jimmy in ten years," the doctor said. "He's never seen Ben at all."

He offered his hand. "Qassim Roy. Folks call me Case."

"Ian Hammond," Ian replied. "This is Dee, and this—"

he helped Kylee up "—is Kylee."

Case turned to Kylee. "How did you do it?"

Anna cut in. "They didn't do it. Kylee did. She's magic."

Case studied Kylee with growing wonder, then looked to Ian and Dee. They nodded.

He knelt before Kylee. "You've given him back more than sight, Kylee. Thank you."

Kylee beamed.

In the crowd, the man in the black poncho watched her, no longer hiding his interest. Then he turned and slipped through the tents, vanishing into the settlement.

16 – Hope Rekindled

"We haven't seen them since the day the Militia took you," Case said gently, trying to explain what little he knew about Heath and Anna's parents. "They took you one way and your parents the other."

Anna's voice cracked. "Did they kill them?"

Carole pulled her close into a maternal hug. "Honey, your mom and dad are smart and strong. If anyone can outwit the Free Militia, they can." Her reassurance quieted Anna's sobs, though tears still streaked the girl's cheeks. Dee glanced at Heath—he hadn't said a word, but his eyes were burning with barely restrained anger.

Dee looked around the old ranger station-turned-trading-post. The kids didn't need to hear the rest of this conversation, but she wasn't sure where to send them.

Clarence seemed to read her mind. He stepped forward and placed a hand on Anna's shoulder. "I've got some cake in the kitchen. Want a slice?"

Anna looked up, eyes still wet. "Is it chocolate?"

"Chocolate icing," he grinned.

She nodded and wiped her face. "Okay."

Clarence gestured to Heath. "There's some for you too, son."

Heath glanced at him, then shook his head.

"Heath, why don't you go with them?" Dee encouraged gently.

"He's fine," Ian said. "Let him stay."

Dee gave him a sharp look. "We need to talk freely."

Ian didn't budge. "Look at him. He wants to be here. And whatever we say won't be worse than what he's already been through. If he ever comes out of this—if he's going to protect Anna—he needs to know the truth."

"He won't be alone," Charles added firmly. "Not as long as we're around. Henry and Marion saved our lives more than once. We owe it to their kids."

Dee relented with a small nod.

Carole took a deep breath, her expression darkening. "They took them right in front of us. Hauled them off like animals, locked in a caged trailer. Henry tried to fight. They beat him down, nearly killed him. Would've, if one of the soldiers hadn't knocked him out first."

"Why?" Dee asked.

Charles answered, voice steady but low. "Henry had a rifle stashed in his tent. Most of us do, but they found his during a 'wellness inspection.' They said he was endangering the community. Truth is, they needed an example. Firearms threaten their control. Crossbows and blades? Fine. But guns? That's where they draw the line."

Carole shook her head, disgusted. "They took the kids too—sold them off like livestock to a couple of monsters. Like they're not even people."

"Anna mentioned something about blood draws," Case added, polishing his glasses absently. "Said the people who took the blood weren't Militia—they weren't in uniform."

"They'd never had blood taken before," Carole said. "It must've terrified them."

Case nodded, thinking aloud. "If those weren't soldiers, then who were they? What were they looking for in Anna and Heath? That might help us understand what comes next—if they come again."

"You think they'll come back?" Carole asked, alarmed.

"Maybe," Case said. "Unless they already found what they were looking for."

"But why the kids?" Carole pressed.

"We don't know," Case admitted. "It's just a theory, but there's a pattern forming."

He turned his gaze to Dee. "You never did explain how Kylee was able to do what she did for Charles."

Charles blinked slowly, still adjusting to his restored vision.

Dee exhaled. "I don't know how it works exactly. We were both at a facility—somewhere between Bishop and Mammoth. Underground. Built into the mountain. They called the children there *experimentals*."

"It was a research facility?" Case asked.

"Yes. The kids were born there, infused with nanotech while still in the womb."

"That's monstrous," Carole whispered. "Experimenting on babies."

"They were raised there. The nanobots stayed in their systems. The children can heal themselves."

"What was the purpose? Immunity to radiation? Disease?" Case asked.

"I don't know. I was brought there after the bombs. My family had gone to Mammoth on a ski trip. We were scavenging for supplies when guys in radiation suits picked me up. At first it seemed safe—food, shelter—but they never brought my family. They said they were looking, but I stopped believing that pretty quickly."

"And they kept you there?" Carole asked.

Dee nodded. "I cared for the kids. That's what we were made to do—caregivers for the next generation of whatever they were trying to build. Kylee was special. Not just in what she could do—but who she is."

"You said the children could heal themselves," Case prompted. "But Kylee healed someone else."

"She did. Somehow she developed the ability to project the nanobots. It's a conscious act—she has to touch the person she wants to heal."

"And this is something the researchers didn't anticipate?" Case asked.

"No. That's when the Director—Petros—took a personal interest."

"George Petros?" Charles interjected. "He was huge before the bombs. Entrepreneur, scientist, deep political ties. Pushed the boundaries of every field he touched."

"That tracks," Ian muttered.

Dee continued. "When Kylee's powers evolved, they ramped up the tests. It got worse. They hurt her. That's when I knew I had to get her out."

Ian finally spoke again. "You couldn't just watch it happen."

"No. I couldn't."

He looked at her with something new in his eyes—respect.

"That's an incredible story," Case said softly. "And I

believe you. There's no reason to make any of this up. I've seen people put research above ethics before—but this is something else."

"Which is why we need to leave," Dee added. "Petros will never stop. Staying here puts you all in danger."

Clarence returned from the kitchen with a tray of tea. "Well, hell. That's quite a thing to walk in on." He handed out mugs. "I've got harder stuff in the basement if anyone needs something stiffer."

"Thanks," Dee said with a weary smile.

"You're welcome to stay the night," Clarence added. "I've got cots in the back room."

"We're not married," Dee clarified, seeing the direction his offer was going.

"Doesn't matter," Clarence chuckled. "The cots are still warm."

"She's right, though," Ian added. "We've already drawn attention. Someone saw what Kylee did—and ran. We think he was part of a group we saw in the mountains. Probably scouts."

"That could mean Militia or Petros' men," Carole said. "But you don't know for sure."

"No," Ian admitted. "But it's too big a risk."

Case leaned forward. "Look—Martin's Ferry is remote. Nearest garrison's three days by foot. Even by horse, that's a four-day turnaround. And there's no GPS. No easy radios. I doubt anyone could call in reinforcements that fast."

"What if they already had a patrol nearby?" Carole asked.

"Possible," Case conceded. "But unlikely. I still think

you're safe for one night."

Ian rubbed his temples. "Maybe. But I'd rather move under darkness than wait for morning."

Before they could decide, a knock came at the cabin door. Clarence opened it a crack.

"Oh, hello, Tina."

"Is she here?" a woman's voice asked.

"She's resting—been through a lot today."

"We all saw what she did for Charles." The woman stepped into view, middle-aged, dark-skinned, wearing a gray sweatshirt and green jacket. Her eyes found Dee and Ian. "Are you her parents?"

"Not exactly," Dee said. "But we care for her."

"My son—Travis—he hasn't walked since one of those Militia thugs rode over him. Broke both his legs. His ribs. Crushed his knee."

Case added, "We can't help him. Not the way he needs. It's surgery or nothing."

Dee stood. "Tina, I'm so sorry. But I don't think Kylee can do something that extensive."

A quiet voice interrupted: "I can try."

Kylee stood in the hallway, eyes calm, determined.

"You're still exhausted—" Dee began.

"I've been resting. I'm ready."

Tina's face lit with hope. "He's outside. I'll bring him in."

She opened the door wide. Outside, a young boy no older than seven lay on a stretcher, his legs wrapped in splints. A teenage girl—his sister, perhaps—stood protectively nearby. Behind them, a growing line of villagers waited silently.

Kylee stepped forward, her small frame dwarfed by the moment.

Dee looked at Ian. He gave a resigned shrug. "Looks like we're staying a little longer."

Ian turned to Clarence. "How many cots did you say you had?

17 – Hunted

Through the window of the old ranger station, now converted into a trading post, Ian watched the field on the western edge of Martin's Ferry. A group of children played soccer beneath the jagged silhouette of the Cascades. Travis, whose legs had been shattered just days before, dribbled past Heath and passed to Ben—Charles and Carole's younger son—who booted the ball between two tree stumps for a goal. Anna was nearby too, more interested in picking dandelions than playing.

"Kylee would love this," Dee said softly as she stepped out of Clarence's bedroom. She had been checking on the girl, who had been unconscious for two days since pushing herself to heal nearly a dozen people. Dee slumped onto the cot near the door, her face worn, her voice tired. "She's never played soccer, but I know she'd be good at it."

Ian tried to lighten the mood. "As good as you are with an M86?"

Dee cracked a tired smile. Clarence had quietly handed over a box of 5.56 rounds from his private stash, and Ian used the opportunity to give Dee some weapons training. He'd expected her to struggle, but to his shock, she hit a man-sized log at 200 yards on her first shot—then again, and again. She was a natural.

"How is she?" he asked, nodding toward the back room.

Dee shook her head. "Still out. Charles practically

kicked me out. Told me to rest. I didn't argue."

Ian nodded. "He's a good man."

The last two days had been filled with both relief and dread. Kylee's gift had changed lives—some saved from infection, others from radiation poisoning or worse—but the strain was brutal. Each time she healed, the convulsions worsened. After curing a young man's cancerous growth, she collapsed and hadn't stirred since. Dr. Roy—Case—had called it a coma.

Charles and Carole had stayed close, checking in regularly. Ian and Dee had come to know them well. Charles, a former software engineer, and Carole, once a teacher, had survived the chaos by sheer instinct. They'd been camping with their three boys when the bombs fell. One of those boys, their eldest, hadn't survived the third winter.

The previous night, Ian had shared a bottle of Wild Turkey with Clarence, Charles, and Carole in quiet thanks. He hadn't had more than a sip—just enough to feel it in his chest and remember what it was like to be warm.

Dr. Roy came often, too. He had lost his own family—his wife on a rafting trip, his two sons vanished in the chaos. One had been a med student, the other a special operations pilot. He never found out what happened to them.

This place—Martin's Ferry—was more community than Ian had seen in years. The terrain offered protection, and so, apparently, did a cautious detente with the Free Militia. If circumstances were different, he might have wanted to stay.

Dee's voice pulled him out of his thoughts. "I've never seen this before," she whispered.

"What do you mean?"

"She's never been out this long."

Ian exhaled slowly. "She gave everything she had, Dee. We didn't know this was her limit. Neither did she."

"She shouldn't have pushed so far," Dee said, her voice breaking. "I should have stopped her."

Ian sat beside her and gently wrapped his arm around her shoulders. "Do you think she'd have listened? She's like you. Once her mind's set, that's it."

Dee buried her face in his chest, and the tears came quietly. He held her close, feeling her tremble, her breath catch, her grief spill out. Kylee was more than just a child in her care. She was family. Ian had always known Dee was strong, but this was the first time he saw how deeply she felt.

Eventually, her sobs gave way to a steady, rhythmic breathing. She had fallen asleep against him. Ian thought about slipping away, but he didn't want to wake her. So he stayed, letting himself drift off too.

When he woke, it was dark. Dee was quietly laying out extra blankets on the floor beside the cot.

"You could've taken the other bed," Ian murmured.

"This gives us more room," she said gently, lying down and patting the space beside her.

Ian hesitated, then joined her. Her hip brushed against his thigh as he settled in. He tried to ignore the warmth that stirred inside him. This wasn't the time.

"I checked on Kylee," Dee said. "She's still unconscious,

but Case says her vitals are stable. He's hopeful."

Ian nodded. "Good."

She rolled toward him. In the dim moonlight, her face was calm, peaceful. Then her lips were on his—soft, seeking. Ian froze for a beat, then drew back.

"I'm sorry," he said. "I don't know what I was thinking."

But Dee pulled him gently back. "I need this," she whispered.

Their kiss deepened. He felt her hand slide to the back of his neck, felt her body press against his. For the first time in what felt like a lifetime, there was no pain, no fear. Just warmth, breath, and presence.

The world outside was still broken, but in that moment, inside the quiet cabin, they found something whole.

***

"She's awake," Clarence said, poking his head into the room.

Those two simple words lifted Ian's chest like helium. Morning sunlight spilled across the foothills through the window's thin curtains, casting long amber streaks across the wooden floor.

"That's great news!" Dee said as she entered, carrying two steaming cups of coffee. The relief on her face was unmistakable, her smile radiant. She handed Ian a cup, then leaned down and kissed him gently.

"What time is it?" he asked, blinking the sleep from his eyes.

"Little after six," Dee replied. "Sun's just up."

Now that Kylee was awake, it was time to move. Ian had hoped they'd be gone before morning, but at least they weren't too late. "Let's get packed."

Within ten minutes, they were ready. Charles and Carole offered to take in Anna and Heath. It made sense—they knew the children better and had been friends with their parents. If there was any chance the kids' parents returned to Martin's Ferry, this was the place to be.

"Don't worry," Clarence said. "I've got space under the cabin. Old storage basement. I use it for supplies now, but I can hide three or four kids down there if the Freebies come sniffing around."

"Freebies?" Dee asked.

"Short for Free Militia. We try to make them sound friendlier than they are."

Case arrived just as Dee began asking questions. "Do you think she's well enough to travel?"

"I believe so," Case said. "She seems well rested."

"But what if it happens again?"

"I'd suggest limiting how much she uses her abilities for now," Case replied. "I've already talked to her about the risks. She understands—at least as much as any child her age can. But she's strong-willed, so it'll be important to keep a close eye on her."

Dee nodded, though it was clear she wasn't convinced she'd have much influence over Kylee's decisions.

"One thing I'll add," Case continued. "And this is just a theory, but I think the fatigue she experiences may lessen with time. Like building muscle, her system may adapt as she uses her abilities more. The key is to avoid overuse until she's strong enough to handle it."

That seemed to ease some of the tension in Dee's face, though she still said nothing.

"Makes sense, Doc," Ian said. "We'll keep a close watch."

The goodbyes stretched longer than Ian wanted. Clarence handed over cans of food and jerky from the trading post. Dee tried to refuse, but Clarence wouldn't hear it. Case told them to return if the heat ever cooled down.

Kylee received hugs, handclasps, even whispered prayers. People treated her with reverence, some wanting to touch her as though it might heal them too. The awe in their eyes made Ian uneasy. It was starting to feel less like gratitude and more like worship.

"This'll never end if I don't stop it," Ian muttered. "All right, folks," he said loud enough for the crowd to hear. "We've got a long road ahead."

He and Dee gently pulled Kylee away and started toward the trail back to the canoes.

Just then, a lookout ran up to Case, panting. "Militia spotted," the heavyset man wheezed. "Three miles out. Coming from the north."

"Signal came from the northern outpost," he added when Clarence asked for the direction.

"You need to go. Now," Case said to Ian and Dee.

Ian gave a sharp nod. "Understood."

Dee offered hurried thanks, giving Clarence and Case quick pecks on the cheek before grabbing Kylee's hand. Together, they ran for the river.

The sprint to the hidden canoes was frantic, but they

made it. Only needing one now, Ian left the second canoe for the villagers. With paddles biting into the current, they shot downstream, putting water between them and Martin's Ferry.

Kylee spotted them first—movement along the eastern bank. Ian followed her gaze and caught sight of four or five riders weaving through the trees on horseback, pacing them from an overgrown road.

"Do you think they've spotted us?" Dee asked, keeping her voice low.

"Not yet. Pull right."

They veered toward a low-hanging tree on the riverbank, its drooping branches cloaking them in shadow. Hidden under the leafy canopy, they watched the patrol pass.

For twenty tense minutes, the riders scoured the shoreline, then moved on.

Ian waited another half hour. "I think we're clear. But we should continue on foot. We're too exposed out here."

"That'll add days to the trip," Dee said, frowning.

"I know. But if they're combing the river, they'll spot us eventually."

"And you know this how?"

"Because that's what I'd do."

Barking erupted in the distance. Ian tensed. "Shit."

"They sound close," Dee said. "If they're wild dogs—"

"I don't think they are." Ian lifted a hand, signaling silence. Then he heard it—men shouting commands to the dogs.

Dee's expression darkened. "They've brought dogs."

"Exactly. We can't stay here. But if we push off now, we're spotted. If we run, they'll track us. Only one option left."

Ian gripped Dee's shoulders, steady and firm. "Take Kylee. Hide upstream in that thicket. I'll take the canoe out and draw them off."

"No, Ian—"

"They'll kill all of us if I don't. Let me pull them away."

Dee's eyes filled with dread. "There's got to be another way—"

"There isn't. Listen: wait until they come after me, then backtrack. Move through the riverbed to lose the dogs' scent. Hunker down for a day, then head west to Crescent City."

He handed her the M-86. Kylee, eyes glassy, looked up at him.

"Will we see you again?" she asked.

"Yes. I promise." He traced a line across his chest. "Cross my heart."

Dee's voice caught. "If you make it... how will we find you?"

"I'll find you," Ian said. Then he turned, slid the canoe into the current, and paddled into the open.

The last thing he saw before rounding the bend was Dee holding Kylee close, her eyes locked on him until the trees swallowed them whole.

***

Ian dug his paddle into the water and pulled hard. With

each stroke, the river's current did more of the work, sweeping him farther from Dee and Kylee. He made no effort to stay quiet—in fact, he banged the paddle against the canoe's edge, shouting and splashing, daring the patrols to notice him.

It worked.

A rifle crack split the air above his head.

"Shit," Ian muttered, ducking instinctively.

Around the next bend, three horsemen waited on the eastern bank. Two had bolt-action rifles trained on him. The third, seated in the middle with a gloved hand raised, wore a black field jacket with a red and gray armband cinched tight around his left bicep—gray background, red chevron, black star in the center. The mark of the Free Militia. Ian had seen them before. They were the new uniform, unofficial but unmistakable.

"Pull over!" the leader barked.

Ian glanced back upriver. He'd put decent distance between himself and the girls—he hoped it was enough. Flipping the canoe wouldn't stop a bullet, and trying to run would only get him shot. He angled toward shore, dragging the paddle lightly.

He grounded the canoe on the muddy bank just as more riders emerged from the trees, fanning out in a loose semicircle.

"Keep your hands up. On your head. Fingers laced," the leader ordered.

Ian obeyed slowly.

"Cox. Harris. Get our guest out of his boat," the leader said.

Two men sloshed forward and yanked Ian from the canoe. They frisked him roughly, finding the knife in his boot and tossing it to the leader, who examined it with a smirk. His jacket bore the same armband, though Ian noticed his was more worn—maybe a veteran among the scavengers.

"Nice blade," the man said. "Bet you've gotten real up close and personal with this."

Ian didn't flinch. "Why don't you climb down and find out?"

The answer came fast—a rifle butt to the gut. The breath left him in a painful grunt as he doubled over.

"There's something you need to understand, friend," the leader said from his saddle. "You're in Free Militia custody now. That means your mouth—and everything else—belongs to us."

Ian gritted his teeth and said nothing.

"Where are the others?" the leader asked. "The woman and the kid."

"I left them," Ian said. "They were slowing me down."

"Where?"

"Back near Martin's Ferry. Maybe they turned around. I didn't ask."

A younger rider piped up. "Want me to go check the village, Shube?"

Shube waved him off. "Nah. He's lying. I'll take a couple boys up the bank. He stashed them, then came paddling in loud to pull us off the scent."

He pointed down at Ian. "Get him back to the Farm. They always need more labor."

Then he spurred his horse into motion, two riders falling in behind him.

Corporal Taylor, left in charge, turned to a freckled soldier. "Harris, tie him to your saddle."

"Yes, Corporal."

Taylor glanced at Ian, grinning. His own armband was newer, the red chevron still bold against the gray fabric. "You know anything about farming?"

Ian shook his head.

"Good," Taylor said. "You're gonna learn."

The men laughed as Harris tied the rope around Ian's wrists, securing it to the saddle horn. Ian didn't resist. He just stared upriver and prayed Dee and Kylee had already disappeared into the trees.

***

The terrain forced the militia horses to slow to a walk, then surge to a trot, then slow again—an exhausting pattern for Ian, who was tethered like a reluctant pack animal behind Harris. The rope around his wrists bit deeper each time the line grew taut. His right leg throbbed where a rifle butt had caught him back at the river, and his knees ached with every uneven step. Only the pain kept him upright.

Harris glanced back occasionally to check on him. There were four riders in total: Harris, Corporal Taylor, Cox, and another named Jenkins. The men swapped lewd jokes and tales of violence—classic foot soldier bravado—but aside from Harris, none spared Ian a glance.

After a few grueling miles, Ian's boot snagged a root. He crashed to the dirt, hard. Harris stopped and yanked the rope. Ian rose with a grunt, testing his ankle. Pain shot through it—twisted, at least. He limped.

"Shit," Cox muttered. "He's lamed, Taylor."

Taylor turned in his saddle. "So?"

"He'll slow us down. Marauders work this stretch. Maybe even cannibals."

Taylor sighed. "You wanna give him a ride?"

"Hell no." Cox smirked. "Let's just kill him. The Farm's got plenty of grunts. One less won't matter."

Taylor pursed his lips, weighing the risk. "Schube'll throw a fit if he finds out."

"We'll say he fell. Cracked his head on a rock. Happens all the time."

Taylor didn't look convinced—but he didn't object either. "Fine. But no one breathes a word."

Cox was off his horse before the sentence finished, grinning. He approached Ian with the slow satisfaction of a man who enjoyed what came next. Ian stumbled back, but Harris yanked the rope, toppling him. Cox straddled Ian, pinning his bound hands with one leg, pushing his head into the dirt with the other.

The blade was cold against Ian's throat.

"Goodnight, pumpkin," Cox whispered.

A promise flashed in Ian's mind—his promise to Kylee. To see her again.

Then, a rifle cracked.

Cox lurched sideways, tumbling over Ian. Blood spilled from his shoulder.

"Get the bitch!" Taylor shouted.

Ian craned his neck toward the treeline. Dee stood at its edge, calm and focused, firing with precision. Her shots rang out steady, measured.

Jenkins spurred his horse toward her and was thrown from the saddle by a well-placed shot to the chest. Taylor dismounted behind a fallen tree and returned fire. Bullets punched into the dirt at Dee's feet, forcing her to dive for cover.

Harris, frozen, looked from Taylor to Ian—unsure.

Ian made the choice for him. With a vicious jerk, he yanked the rope. Harris stumbled forward, lost balance, and slammed face-first into a rock. Ian was on him in a blink, driving his head into the stone twice more until the boy slumped motionless.

He found a knife on Harris' belt and cut himself free.

Taylor's rifle barked again. Splinters burst from Dee's cover.

Ian tried to shoulder Harris' rifle, but Taylor was between him and Dee. No clean shot.

He turned to the horse, climbed onto the stirrup and, with a shaky breath, threw himself up. The horse reared, startled—but Ian gripped tight and urged it forward. He tore across the clearing.

Taylor adjusted his aim.

Dee was pinned.

Ian reached for the knife, flipped it into his hand, and hurled it.

The blade struck Taylor in the back.

He cried out, staggering, rifle swinging wildly.

Ian didn't hesitate. He galloped straight at him, then leapt from the saddle, tackling the corporal. Taylor's rifle discharged into the sky.

They rolled. Ian landed on top.

He drove his fist into Taylor's face—once, twice, a third time. The man's nose shattered. Blood sprayed. Ian rose, then stomped down hard on Taylor's head. Bone crunched. Blood pooled from his ears.

Dee peeked from behind the tree, eyes wide.

When she saw Ian, she ran toward him, smiling. He returned the grin, barely able to believe they were both still standing.

Then gunfire cracked again—more men bursting from the treeline.

Five riders.

Dee ducked. Ian sprang back onto the horse and raced toward her. She reached up—he grabbed her arm, hoisted her behind him, and they galloped across the clearing under a hail of gunfire.

Bullets bit into dirt. One struck a branch above them. It broke loose, bounced harmlessly off Ian's shoulder. They plunged into the trees, the horse weaving between trunks. Behind them, the militia pursued.

Up ahead, Ian spotted another clearing. If they could cross it before the militia reached the tree line, they might have a chance.

He kicked the horse into a full gallop.

They made it across just as the militia began to break through.

Ian pulled the reins, slowing near the next treeline.

"Let's get off here," Dee said. "I have an idea."

Ian dismounted, helped her down. Without hesitation, she slapped the horse's rump. It bolted into the woods.

"What was that for?" he asked, annoyed.

"Just follow me."

They dove into the woods in the opposite direction. Fifty yards in, Dee found a wall of brambles and slipped into them. Ian followed, just as the militia thundered into the clearing.

Hidden in the thick brush, they waited. Branches snapped. Horses whinnied. Then—silence.

"They followed the horse," Ian whispered. He looked at her, admiration plain. "That was smart. And that shooting—"

"I'm not useless out here," she said, voice soft but firm.

"Not even close," Ian said. "And I'd love to meet the fool who says otherwise."

She smiled, glancing back toward the clearing. "Think it's safe?"

"Maybe. Let's give it a few more."

Ian froze. "Wait—where's Kylee?"

"She's safe," Dee said. "We found a shack in the woods, covered in ivy. You'd have to trip over it to find it. She's probably in there making friends with the spiders."

Ian stifled a laugh. "That tracks."

After a few more minutes, they slipped from the brush. Dee led him to the shack.

"You know," Dee said as they walked, her tone coy, "that horseback grab was pretty impressive."

"Thanks," Ian said, still catching his breath. "I was

about to be dead. Appreciate the save."

"I meant the way you swooped in. Like a knight."

Ian smirked. "It was spectacular, wasn't it?"

She turned, stepped in close. "Like something out of a storybook." She kissed him, soft and lingering. Ian's heart pounded.

He started to pull back. "We should get to Kylee."

"She's fine."

Ian hesitated. "What if they find the shack?"

"They won't."

Then she smiled, full of fire, and drew him down to the forest floor.

For the first time in days, he didn't care what was coming next.

***

George Petros tapped the screen on his desk, and the armored shutters groaned open, revealing a view of the snow-dusted Owens Valley. Gloam filtered over the ridges—a dim, cold light that matched the long winter's pall. But even in this ashen age, the mountains retained a brutal sort of beauty. He took a deep breath and allowed himself a moment to admire it.

The data on the screen still flickered in the background: metrics, biomarkers, degradation curves. Most men in his position would delegate the analysis. Petros preferred not to. Finding patterns in raw numbers grounded him. It reminded him of who he had been before the world burned—an engineer, a builder. He still was. Only now, he was building something much bigger.

There were encouraging developments in experimental subject #5—Billy. But none of them came close to the potential of experimental #3. Kylee Daniels. The anomaly.

Her absence was a wound to the program. But he had faith. Recovery efforts were in motion. She would come home—soon.

The intercom chimed.

"Pardon the interruption, Director," came Vanessa's voice.

George arched a brow but kept his tone warm. "Vanessa, you are never an interruption."

He could picture her blushing at the compliment. Morale was manipulation—always be the sun they orbit.

"Mr. Riley is here, sir. Status update on the anomaly recovery."

George's smile returned. "Excellent. Send him in."

The door whispered open. Patrick Riley entered, leaner than he used to be but still carrying that weathered, disciplined air—an officer's bearing dulled only slightly by age and compromise.

"Pat," George rose, coming around the desk. He clasped both of Riley's hands, then gave him a quick shoulder-pat. "Good to see you."

"Likewise, sir."

"Oh come on. Not that 'sir' business when it's just us. You're my oldest friend."

"You keep saying that, George," Riley smirked. "But some of your oldest friends are buried under glass."

"Then you'd better stay useful."

They both chuckled. Riley pulled a dark bottle from his pack.

"Gift from our associates."

George raised a brow. "Tell me that's not—"

"California Cabernet. I know you preferred Malbec before the skies turned gray, but beggars, choosers, and so on."

George turned the bottle in his hands. "Hydroponic grapes. Miraculous what fascists can accomplish when they set their minds to it."

Riley's smile thinned. "They're efficient."

"Mm." He gestured to the chair across from him. "Let's talk about Kylee."

Riley's grin faded. "We almost had her."

George's eyes narrowed, but he kept his voice calm. "Let me guess. The vaunted militia fumbled it?"

"There was a breakdown in judgment," Riley said carefully. "We tracked her to a settlement on the Klamath. Martin's Ferry. The militia captured her associate—Ian Hammond."

"The drifter from Rio Dell."

"We believe so. But he escaped. With help from Delilah."

"The nanny." George's jaw clenched. "She's proving troublesome."

"She's also ex-staff, well-trained. And Kylee clearly trusts her."

"That's not a liability—it's an opportunity. Where are they now?"

Riley shrugged. "They're moving. Fast. But I still believe they're headed toward Dr. Schumacher."

"That's a dead end. We don't know where Jane went."

Riley's eyes flickered. George caught it. "Or do we?"

"We don't," Riley said. "But Kylee thinks she's still at the Crescent City site."

George leaned back, drumming his fingers. "Then we meet her there. Can the militia handle the pickup?"

"I already spoke to Silas Bray. He's mobilizing a detachment to the northern route."

"Good." George nodded. "The militia may be blunt instruments, but at least they're consistent. You've done well, Pat."

Riley said nothing, but his jaw tightened at the praise.

"I assume you made it clear to the General how vital this recovery is?"

"I did," Riley replied. "I reminded him that our alliance is conditional."

George's expression cooled. "Make sure he doesn't forget."

They sat in silence for a moment, two men bound by power, history, and shared ambition—though one carried it more easily than the other.

"She's special, Pat," George said at last, tapping the screen. The girl's biometric data hovered in digital silence. "She's the future. I won't lose her to sentiment."

"I know."

"Good. Because sentiment," he said, turning back to the window, "is a luxury the old world died clinging to."

18 – Crescent City

"This isn't right," Kylee said through an exhale as she stared down at the once idyllic Pacific coast town of Crescent City. Looking through Ian's binoculars, Dee had to agree. There was some movement in and around town, but nothing more than random scavengers dashing through vacant streets and empty buildings. Nothing to indicate the settlement they came here to find. This was supposed to be the place where things were coming back. The place where a local electrical grid was back up, vehicles were running again, and civilization was coming back from the brink. But from where Dee stood, it was just another dead town.

It was their third day out from Martin's Ferry when they finally arrived in the foothills overlooking Crescent City. The route took them through the giant redwoods, which were a big hit with Kylee. Some of the tall trees were still green. The farther north they went, the more resistant life was to the effects of the Long Winter. No wonder Dr. Schumacher and her people had come here to settle. Dee saw why this would be preferable to living underground and under the thumb of George Petros.

"Well, we might as well go down there and look," Ian suggested. "We came all this way."

Dee nodded absently. But it was Kylee who answered. "We might find something down there. Maybe a clue about what happened to Dr. Schumacher and her people."

"You sure they were ever here?" Ian asked.

"Of course," replied Kylee, as if it was a silly question. Dee was not so sure. She had based her knowledge of Crescent City on things she had overheard from the scientists and engineers at the compound, and, of course, on Kylee's unfailing certainty that the breakaway settlement was here. But what she was seeing now made her fear that the trip up here had been a waste of time.

It took them another two hours on foot to reach the first few buildings outside of town. They moved slowly and carefully at Ian's insistence. He said buildings were dangerous. Sure, you could hide in them. But so could other people. Someone could be watching you, and you would never know until it was too late.

"I don't see any sign of your Dr. Schumacher or anyone else," Ian said, breaking a long silence.

Dee nodded. "I thought I saw some movement from the ridge, but now I see nothing."

"Maybe it was animals, or an illusion, like a trick of the light," offered Kylee.

"Or maybe they saw us coming and are setting up an ambush," Ian said soberly.

The thought made Dee go cold with fear. "We should leave."

"That might be best. We're way too exposed here."

"We need to at least look around," Kylee protested.

Dee stepped in. "Kylee, it's too dangerous. We don't have any . . ."

She was cut short by a loud noise from a nearby

building. It sounded like something fell. Dee exchanged a look with Ian, who moved stealthily toward the source of the noise. He motioned for Dee and Kylee to take cover behind an overgrown hedgerow, which they did.

Ian closed half the distance to the building, an old school, when they heard footsteps running on the far side by the athletic fields. He ran back to join them and said, "Someone's got eyes on us. We've got to leave now!"

Without stopping to even acknowledge him, Kylee took off running toward the back of the school. Dee exchanged a look with Ian and reflexively ran after her. Ian followed, muttering a frustrated curse. Dee knew how he felt. She hated it when Kylee just acted without thinking. One of these days that impulsiveness would get her into trouble.

Kylee disappeared around the corner of the one-story building, and Dee raced to catch up. She and Ian turned a corner into a parking lot. On the far side, Kylee was already sprinting across an overgrown baseball diamond. In the outfield was a compact figure, small enough to be a child, a boy, climbing a mesh metal fence. It was only about four feet tall, and the boy negotiated it with ease.

Dee wanted to yell at Kylee to let him go but stayed quiet. The last thing she wanted to do was to alert anyone within earshot of their presence. If this boy was here, chances were there were adults nearby.

"I had no idea she was so fast?" gasped Ian. Dee didn't bother with a response. She was having a hard enough time keeping up with Kylee that she did not have the breath to waste on talking.

The boy disappeared into a line of trees twenty feet back

from the fence. Kylee hopped the fence and disappeared after him. When Ian and Dee reached the trees, they slowed. Dee feared they had lost Kylee's trail, but Ian tracked her easily through the woods.

Ian stopped short in front of her, squatting down and holding up a clenched fist to signal her to do the same and be quiet. They were just feet from breaking out of the trees, and about ten yards from a parking lot in front of what looked like an old city government building. There were signs that the area had been recently used. For one, it looked cleaner than most buildings in town; it did not show ten years of neglect. Also, the parking lot was intact. Most asphalt Dee had seen since she and Kylee escaped from the Director's facility was cracking and chunking up from ten years of freezing temperatures. There were signs of sealant and even repair work.

But that was not the reason Ian had stopped short. Out in the parking lot was a group of people, Dee estimated fifteen to twenty, who appeared to have set up camp in the building. They were all staring toward the tree line where Dee and Ian squatted.

They watched Kylee as she approached their makeshift camp. The boy ran up to a woman with the group and pointed back at Kylee. Kylee, who had slowed to a walk, was waving back at them with her typical oblivious friendliness. The adults eyed her with suspicion.

"You need to go out and get her," Ian suggested.

"Why me?" Dee protested. "If I go out there alone, they'll see me as an easy target."

"No, they're not marauders. They're scared of

something."

"How do you know that?"

Ian looked at her. "Look, there are two types of people out here: predators and prey. In ten years, I've learned to tell the difference. These people aren't predators, so they won't attack a lone woman looking for a little girl who ran away. But if they see a scruffy dude pop out of the woods, they're likely to go into full self-defense mode. And if they do that, then you and Kylee will really be in danger."

Dee sighed but reluctantly agreed. "Okay."

"But just in case I'm wrong, I'll be ready to pick off the first guy who gets frisky." He pulled back the handle on his rifle and checked inside to make sure a bullet was in there.

She gave him a look that said, *not helping,* and then stepped out of the tree line with her hands up in a gesture of surrender. "Hello," she said to announce herself. "I'm just here for my daughter."

All eyes went from Kylee to Dee. "I hope she didn't disturb you," Dee continued. "We're not looking for trouble."

"That's far enough," yelled the woman, who was now hugging the young boy. "We'll send her back to you and both of you can be on your way."

"That works for me." Dee was relieved. She did not want to get close to these people any more than they wanted her to.

A loud whistle pierced the calm from a few streets over. Frightened shouts erupted, and the group scattered as if on reflex. The whistle blew again, closer this time. Dee wasn't sure who was coming, but she could tell by the reaction of the scavengers that she didn't want to be caught out in the open.

She looked for Kylee in the maelstrom of panic but could not pick her out. Her heart jumped into her throat. *Where was she?*

Marauders, some riding bicycles, the rest simply running, appeared from around a nearby street corner. Dee dove behind an overfull dumpster, hoping no one spotted her. She held her breath before realizing how absurd it was to think that her breathing might give away her position with all the noise.

She got a better look at the intruders. Most were armed with small crossbows strapped to their arms. They had other weapons too, machetes, hammers, baseball bats, for close combat. But it was the crossbows that were the immediate danger as they began firing at anyone within range. Behind them came a large box truck, ambling through the street.

An older man, who was lagging, caught a crossbow bolt in his back. But it was smaller than a crossbow bolt, Dee realized. It was more like a dart. The old man stumbled forward a few feet, and then fell on his face, unconscious. The darts were tranquilizers. A few others had fallen to darts. Every time a scavenger fell unconscious, the box truck came by and loaded them up. *They want these people alive.* She recalled the box truck roaming the street below them the day they escaped from the compound, and the horror that Kylee sensed coming from within as they flew overhead.

There was still no sign of Kylee. Dee had to trust that

the girl had hidden herself. She knew that her best chance of protecting Kylee now was to not get herself captured. She glanced toward the tree line, looking for Ian, but he was also out of sight. Dee considered making a run for the trees, but the marauders were too close now. They would catch her before she reached cover. Her best bet was to stay hidden behind this awful smelling dumpster.

A young girl, no older than six, squealed in terror just yards from Dee. Her jet-black hair was in disarray and tears streamed down her face from large brown eyes, made larger from fear. She was alone.

The squeal drew the attention of one marauder, who ran in the girl's direction. He aimed his tranquilizer crossbow, steadying himself for accuracy. The little girl stood frozen and crying.

Before Dee realized what she was doing, she was out from behind the dumpster, exposed. She scooped the little girl up with both arms, without breaking her stride, before the marauder even noticed she was there. Moving on pure instinct, she looked around desperately for a way to escape. There was a narrow alleyway between the government building and an old convenience store next to it. She might disappear in the alley and give them the precious seconds they needed to escape. She just hoped there was an exit on the other side.

The marauders sprinted toward the alley entrance, trying to cut her off. Dee felt the added forty pounds of the girl she carried in her legs and in her lungs. Only the rush of adrenaline kept her moving. The sound of bicycle wheels squealing loomed closer, but Dee could not spare the time or energy to look behind her.

The alley entrance was just feet away now. Dee's body got bumped sideward by a kick from a cyclist as he passed, knocking both her and the dark-haired little girl to the ground. The marauder looked down, aiming his tranquilizer crossbow, his dirty face grinning in triumph.

Unsure what else she could do; Dee pulled the girl close and wrapped herself around the tiny frame to shield her from the inevitable sting of the dart. But it never came. Instead, she heard a meaty thud as the cyclist's body fell to the ground, lifeless. A red pool formed under the back of his head.

She glanced up to see the bicycle veering off and falling on the ground, now riderless. Sprinting toward her came Ian, pistol in hand. He reached down and yanked her to her feet, then pushed both her and the dark-haired girl into the alleyway. A dart skidded off the corner of the convenience store just as they ducked into safety.

"The door on the left," Ian barked, pointing to a small service entrance in the large government building. Dee twisted the knob. It was open. The three of them ducked through quickly.

"This way," said the little girl, speaking for the first time. She led them down a narrow hall to a stairway leading down into what appeared to be some kind of underground.

"What's down there?" Dee asked. The little girl didn't answer as she descended into the darkness.

Ian shrugged. "We know what's behind us. Guess we'll deal with anything that's down there when we find it."

They followed the dark-haired girl down three flights of

stairs to a large metal door. They took a moment to catch their breath, reasonably sure no marauders had seen them come down here.

The ambient light from above faded, and Dee's eyes were slow to adjust. The dark-haired girl banged on the door with her palm. At first it sounded like she was just knocking, but as Dee listened, she noticed that there was a distinct pattern to her knocking. It was a signal to whoever was inside.

The door flew open, and the little girl slipped inside. Ian and Dee followed close behind her before it could be closed. When the door closed behind them, they were in complete darkness. Then light panels illuminated as if triggered by the closing of the door.

Now Dee could see they were in a large room with bench seating. The walls were adorned with what looked like road maps, public service messages, and posters advertising movies and shows that had just started streaming the year the bombs hit.

On the far side of this vast room was a platform overlooking a tunnel that ended up in this room and disappeared into the dark in the other direction. They were in a hyper-loop rail tunnel. Dee rode one with her mother into LA when she was a kid. But she did not know that any had ever been built this far north.

They were not alone. In front of them were two men and a woman. The two men were armed with crossbows, which they kept trained on Ian. Dee backed toward the door and weighed their odds of evading the marauders above until two more people blocked the way behind them. A man and a woman, also wielding crossbows. Kylee sat just past the three people in front of them, next to the boy she had chased through the ball field and the woods. It looked like this group was a makeshift family.

The woman in front of them spoke first. "Take his rifle." Dee recognized her as the same woman who had spoken to her on the surface.

The man closest to Ian approached cautiously, keeping the crossbow trained. Ian raised his arms in a frustrated surrender and the man with the crossbow took the rifle from Ian's hand. Dee exhaled in relief that he did not try to fight his way out this time.

"Now," said the first woman. "Why were you chasing Manny out there?" She gestured toward the boy just in front of her. Dee saw now that the kid, Manny, had radiation burns emanating from his chest that scarred half of his face. She was shocked by the disfigurement at first, then immediately felt guilty for it. "Are you militia scouts?"

"What?" Dee was a little surprised by the accusation. "We weren't chasing him. We were chasing her." She pointed at Kylee.

"Bullshit!" said one man behind Manny. "If they're not with the militia, then they're perverts or flesh peddlers. Why else would they chase Manny, then grab Melissa?" He was referring to the dark-haired girl.

"Grab her?" Ian said indignantly. "Dee here saved her. She was almost taken by those cannibals."

"Yeah," Dee said. "After all of you abandoned her up there."

"Is this true?" the woman in front of them, who

appeared to be the leader of the group, asked Melissa.

The little girl nodded, then smiled at Dee.

"Look," Ian said. "All we want to do is get our girl back and leave here without running into those marauders again."

"*If* we let you leave, you're not taking this girl," said the leader. "She's under our protection now."

Ian stepped forward menacingly. But before he could do anything, Kylee spoke. "That will not happen," she said, looking up directly into the woman's eyes and smiling. "I'm going to leave with them, after I help Manny."

Confusion marked the faces of all the scavengers, including the woman Kylee was speaking to.

"Kylee, that's not a good idea right now," Ian said. "These folks don't look like they've got much patience."

As usual, Kylee ignored him and walked up to Manny. She reached a hand toward his face. None of the adults moved to stop her, apparently too confused by what she was doing to react.

It was only when Kylee touched Manny's face that the leader moved to stop her. "Don't touch him!" she yelled. But it was too late. The process had begun. Kylee was shaking when the woman pulled her hand away. Manny started shaking and fell to the floor in convulsions. The woman let go of Kylee and dropped to the ground next to Manny. "What did you do, you little monster?"

One man lowered his crossbow and reached forward to grab Kylee, who was still shaking, but stayed standing. Ian lunged at the man holding Kylee. "Get your hands off her!" he barked.

The other man with a crossbow aimed it at Ian's head, just inches away. Dee felt helpless. These people were armed and already agitated. Now, in their minds, they had justification for murder.

The woman holding Manny sobbed as she pulled his convulsion ridden body closer. "Kill them!" she said. "Kill them all!"

"No, Angie, don't." The voice was quivering and small. The woman, Angie, looked down at the boy in her arms. His shaking subsided, and he touched his hand to his face. "I feel weird, but . . . I think she was helping me."

Angie looked down at Manny, and her eyes grew wide. "Oh my God!"

"Angie, what is it?" asked the man holding Kylee.

"His face..." Angie's voice quivered.

"What about his face?" said the same man.

"His burns," Angie said, "they're gone."

"Gone? What do you mean, gone?" asked the other woman in the group, her crossbow still pointed at Ian.

The man holding Kylee released her and peeked around Angie's shoulder. "I don't know how, but he's completely healed."

Angie turned to Kylee. "Did you do this?"

Kylee nodded. "And I can heal you too, Angela. If that's what you want."

Angie touched both hands to her stomach. "You mean . . ."

"Yes, I can help you have children again."

***

Dee watched as Ian stuck two fingers into a can of corned beef hash, pulled some out, and crammed it into his mouth. There was only one spoon that the scavengers could spare, and Ian graciously allowed Dee to use it while he just used his fingers. She got the sense that he was used to eating canned goods this way.

There were fourteen of them down here, including Manny and Melissa. Two of their group had either been taken by marauders or found some place to hide above. At least that's what they hoped. Dee told them of the people she saw loaded into the box truck, but there were others on the surface that were not part of this clan.

Angie was their leader. She was a middle-aged woman with stringy blond hair and missing teeth. But she had strength and a good grasp on how to survive.

The group had moved about half a mile down the tunnel to what looked like an old maintenance room. Apparently, this was where the scavengers lived. There were a couple of rooms and an old restroom. They kept buckets of seawater by the toilets, which apparently still flushed if water was poured into them. It was a pretty cozy set up.

The canned goods had been left here by Dr. Schumacher's people. They gave one can each to Dee, Kylee and Ian after Kylee had healed whatever issue Angie had that made her sterile. Obviously, there was no visible evidence that Kylee had changed anything inside Angie's body. But they had all seen how she healed Manny's scars, and Angie claimed she felt different. Plus, there were a few others who had minor injuries that Kylee could heal. So, they believed it, and were more than willing to share what little food they had.

"They were good people," Angie said about Dr. Schumacher and her team. "The lights were back up in this part of town and everything while they were here. They were doing what they could to help the survivors in and around Crescent City with medicine, food, whatever they could spare. Of course, they couldn't pull off miracles, like our little messiah here."

Kylee paid no attention to the compliment. Instead, she was running around with Manny and Melissa playing *hide and seek,* now that she was fully recovered from the temporary exhaustion she always felt after using her healing powers.

"Ever since they left, the city above hasn't been safe," continued Angie. "You saw for yourself those marauders that now hunt wherever and whoever they like. Those animals raided shortly after Schumacher and her people bugged out."

"What made them leave?" Dee asked.

"They just up and left," said Joey. "One day they were here. When we came back through a few days later they were gone."

Angie nodded in agreement. "The rumors we heard from other folks in the area were that they were afraid of some cat they called *Petros.*"

Dee's face must have betrayed her because the other woman, Shanay asked, "Do you recognize that name?"

"Yes," Dee said. "Kylee, and I escaped from his people about a month ago. They've been after us ever since. They want Kylee back."

"Yeah," Angie said, "I'd probably want her back, too."

"He doesn't want her for her healing abilities," Dee said. "Well, actually he does, but he's running experiments on her and other children like her."

"There are others like her?" Shanay asked.

"Not exactly like her," Dee said. "Kylee's abilities far exceed anything the other children can do. That's why he wants her back, so that he can replicate her abilities in the others. I had to get her out of there. She couldn't take anymore."

Angie reached out and put her hand on Dee's arm. "You did the right thing. Not everyone knows what the right thing is. Even fewer people will do something about it when they do, especially when it puts them at risk. You are almost as rare a find as that little girl."

Dee smiled. She was at a loss for what to say. She had never thought about it in that way. In her mind, there was no option other than getting Kylee out of that situation.

Angie gestured toward Ian. "I just hope this knot head realizes that."

"Huh?" Ian said, looking up from his corned beef hash for the first time.

"I'll take that as a no," laughed Angie.

Ian shrugged and dug back into the near empty can to scrape the last of the hash from its sides. Dee laughed along with Angie. She didn't feel like explaining to them she and Ian weren't together, not really. She wasn't sure herself. But it felt good to laugh. It felt good to feel safe.

"Why don't you two get some sleep?" Angie suggested.

"We'll keep watch. You're perfectly safe down here, the marauders don't even know anything's down here. Even if they did, they would need dynamite to get through that outer metal door."

Dee looked at Ian, who shrugged and laid back. Within minutes, he was snoring.

***

Dee woke feeling rested—truly rested—for the first time since leaving the compound. The constant tension of life outside had kept her locked in a cycle of shallow, vigilant sleep. But here, in the dark safety of the tunnel station, her mind had finally allowed her body some peace.

Ian was still asleep beside her, his arm slung protectively near Kylee, who slept on the cot beside them. Others in the makeshift clan lay scattered around the darkened room, breathing quietly. Those on watch had already taken their posts.

Dee rose and stepped into the lighted antechamber. Angie and three others sat at a makeshift table playing cards. A single camp lantern cast long shadows on the wall.

"You want in on the next hand?" Angie asked.

Dee shook her head. "I don't know how."

"It's just poker, five-card draw," said a young man next to Angie. "You must have played."

"It's just five-card draw," said a young man seated to Angie's right. "You've seriously never played poker?"

Dee gave a sheepish shrug.

"Damn," Angie muttered. "That's a first. Well, pull up a

chair. We'll teach you."

"I'll just watch for now," Dee said with a smile. "Maybe I'll figure it out.

The table went back to their game, dealing, folding, bluffing with good-natured jabs. Dee found herself slipping into the rhythm of the group. For a moment, the world outside the tunnels seemed far away.

According to Angie, the tunnel went along the coast as far as San Francisco with stops in Klamath, Eureka, and other places in between. But the furthest they had ever explored in that direction was about ten miles, with no openings in the tunnel.

Ten minutes passed, and Dee had started to get the rhythm of the game. She was just about to ask for cards when Ian shuffled out of the sleeping room, yawning and stretching with an audible groan.

"You finally got some sleep?" she asked.

"I did," he said with a grin. "Felt like a decade's worth."

"Kylee's still out?"

Ian nodded. "She's hibernating. I was out cold too, but something woke me—a banging sound, like on a pipe. I came to see if anything was happening, but it stopped."

The poker table fell silent. Angie's eyes lifted sharply.

"What kind of banging?" she asked.

"Hard to say. Echoed, like someone hitting metal with a hammer. Figured someone was doing some plumbing."

Everyone at the table stood at once.

"Grab your gear," Angie said. Her voice was soft but urgent.

Without hesitation, the others reached for pipes, knives,

and makeshift clubs. Angie grabbed the group's only rifle.

"Sure," he said. "What's going on?"

"Hopefully nothing, but the signal we gave to our tunnel watch was to bang on one of the main valve pipes with a hammer. That pipe runs right into this station so we can hear it, even though the watch is a mile away. It's a signal that someone is encroaching on the tunnel."

"Ian, can you wake the others?" she asked.

"On it." He vanished into the back room, then emerged moments later, rifle in hand.

They all moved out on Angie's lead, weapons drawn and ready for those who had them. There were thirteen total, including eight scavenger adults, the two children, Manny and Melissa, then Ian, Kylee and Dee. Angie pulled out a flashlight and scanned in both directions up and down the tunnel. There was nothing out of the ordinary, at least nothing, that Dee noticed.

"All right," breathed Angie. "We need to split up here. Gwyneth, Pavel; take our guests and go up to the city hall entrance to warn Shanay. Take Manny and Melissa too. Wait until you get word from us it's safe. Give us an hour, if you don't hear anything, take everyone out of the escape ladder and get to the lighthouse. Hold up there if you can, but only a day. If we don't catch up with you by then, consider us dead and get the hell away from here. Got it?"

Ian chambered a round in his rifle and said, "I'm coming with you. If someone's coming down that tunnel with hostile intent, you'll need the extra shooter."

"No," Angie said with a tone of finality. "You're staying with them." She motioned toward Dee and Kylee.

"Wait," Dee said. "If there's anyone down the tunnel, you'll have a better chance of fighting them off with all of us. Don't you think?"

Angie looked at her and smiled. "I knew I'd like you." Then she stepped closer. "I don't know how it works, but Kylee is special. We will probably be fine, but none of our lives are worth losing her. She might be the most important person on the planet right now. Your job is to keep her alive. No matter what the cost, keep her safe, find Dr. Schumacher, and let her unleash that little girl's potential. It's only a feeling but I believe she might just pull us out of this mess that we've made of the world."

Dee swallowed hard and nodded. She didn't know what else to say. Angie kissed Manny and Melissa and then tussled Kylee's hair. Without another word, she moved out with five of her people in tow and made their way south in the hyper loop tunnel.

Ian put his hand on Dee's shoulder and gently nudged her in the opposite direction. "Come on," he said.

Pavel and Gwyneth led them north. Shanay met them halfway, sensing the urgency before they even spoke.

"What happened?"

"South tunnel signal," Pavel said.

"Might be nothing," Gwyneth added quickly.

"Or it might be someone who found the back door," Shanay said grimly, chambering a round.

Then came the knock.

Everyone froze.

"Anybody home?" a voice called out playfully from behind Shanay held up a hand for silence.

"Hey," said the voice again, "can Angie come out to play?"

Rough laughter followed.

"We've got a friend of hers out here. Says he lives here."

Another voice. Weaker. "It's me... it's James..."

There was a sickening thud.

"Speak up meat," said the disembodied voice. Someone outside grunted in pain and the voice spoke again, this time less playful, "I said speak up!"

Another muffled voice came from beyond the door. "It's me. It's James." Pavel and Gwyneth looked at Shanay whose face scrunched in anguish.

"And what is it you want to say, James?" asked the first voice.

"Check the south tunnel," said James. "They're sending . . ."

James wailed in pain after a thud and said no more.

"Listen up," said the voice from beyond the door. "Here's how this is going to go. You open this door, or we cut pieces off your pal Jimmy here. We'll make them nice little bite-sized pieces so that he'll last longer. You've got five minutes."

Shanay closed her eyes tight, as if trying to shut out the world. A tear streaked down her face. She opened her eyes and looked right at Kylee and then motioned for everyone to back away from the door quietly.

Once they had put enough space between them and the door, Shanay whispered. "Pavel, take them up the escape ladder. Get the kids out of here."

Pavel nodded and motioned for Dee, Ian, and the kids

to follow. Shanay and the rest of her team headed back to the entrance and looked for fighting positions.

Pavel led them back south into the tunnel. Ian took up the rear, making sure the kids could keep up. Pavel stopped at an access door and was about to open it when everything went dark.

"Shit," whispered Pavel. "Shit, shit, shit. They cut the lights."

"Come on man," Ian said. "Keep it together."

The door creaked open. Dee felt around for the door frame and went through. Once inside, ambient light from overhead provided some illumination. Between that and her eyes adjusting to the dark, she could see inside the room. It was small, little more than a closet, with mops, empty buckets, cleaning supplies, and trash strewn about. There was a thin layer of dust covering everything. In the center of the small room, a ladder shot straight up through a hole in the ceiling. That hole was the source of the light.

"Lucky this is here," Dee said.

"And lucky the eaters never found the exit up top," Ian said.

"It's well hidden, designed to blend into the surroundings. They built these emergency exits every few miles in case of flooding, earthquakes, or any other contingency that they just couldn't think of. From what I remember, the company that built the hyperloop claimed it was made to withstand any natural disaster, so they didn't want the public to know that their claim was false."

"I don't care why it's here, just that it is," Ian said. "Who goes first?"

Pavel ascended the ladder, followed by Melissa, Manny, Kylee, and then Dee. Ian took up the rear. It was about a four-story climb, but once the ladder entered the ceiling, there was just a shaft surrounding it, only wide enough for the ladder and a climber.

About halfway up, Melissa stopped and hugged tight to the ladder.

"What's wrong Mel?" asked Manny.

The little girl whimpered, "I want to go back down."

"You need to keep going," said Manny. "The more we wait the more tired my arms get."

"You can do it, honey, just one step at a time," Dee said.

Melissa didn't answer. She closed her eyes and tightened her grip on the ladder.

Ian stayed silent, but Dee knew what he was thinking. If the marauders broke in and found this room . . .

"You're not afraid of heights, Melissa," Kylee said, quiet as if she was announcing breakfast was ready. "You want to see the sun." Melissa opened her eyes and climbed the rest of the way to the top without stopping.

Once he reached it, Pavel manipulated a lever on a hatch at the top and pushed it open. A blinding flood of light from outside told them it was daytime, which would not help their chances of escaping undetected. After climbing out one at a time, they found themselves behind an old bus stop bench.

Pavel put his finger to his lips in a silent shush and signaled Dee to stay low with hand and arm gestures as she climbed out of the hatch. Dee was surprised to see that the children were all lying low and keeping quiet. They were experiencing just enough terror to keep them following directions.

Ian was the last to climb out. He scanned the area for threats, looking more like the hunter than prey. "Which way," he whispered to Pavel.

"Over here," said Pavel, pointing eastward down a wide street. He took two steps, then stopped. "Wait, no . . . this way." He turned south, stopped again, and then looked around.

"Jesus," Ian said. "Follow me." He moved toward a narrow alley when the piercing sound of a whistle shattered the midday quiet. A trio of bicycles sped toward them from the east. *Marauders!*

Ian ushered the kids into the alleyway with a renewed urgency. He stood at the head of the passage between the two buildings and fired two rounds from his rifle, one of which found a biker, knocking him off. The other two kept coming, barely noticing their fallen comrade.

A meaty thud from behind Dee prompted her to turn just in time to see Pavel fall from a machete that had been buried in his neck. Blood squirted from his carotid artery as he squirmed, then went limp.

The man holding the machete grabbed Melissa by the hair and held the bloody weapon to her throat. He wore dirty jeans and an overcoat and had a long beard that matched the color of his coat. Manny pounded the man's thigh with his fist, but the savage just chuckled.

"Ian," Dee said as she advanced on the lone machete wielder. Seeing what was going on, Ian pointed his weapon at him.

"Uh uh," said the marauder, tightening his grip on Melissa's hair and moving the blade of the machete closer to her throat.

Two other dismounted cyclists came up the far side of the alleyway with their wrist mounted dart crossbows trained on Ian and Dee. The remaining two bicycle riders were now at the alleyway entrance, blocking any possible escape. They dismounted their bikes, one holding a spiked baseball bat, and the other with a Winchester hunting rifle, pointed at Ian's head.

The man with the rifle spoke, "Drop your gun meat."

19 – Patrol

The lights were low, casting long shadows over reinforced steel walls and sleek glass displays. A giant, holographic map of the western seaboard glowed faintly in the background. At the center of the room stood George Petros, hands clasped behind his back, eyes fixed on a slow-rotating 3D schematic of Crescent City and its surrounding terrain.

Patrick Riley entered carrying a digital tablet under his arm.

Petros turned slightly but didn't look directly at him. "You're back sooner than expected."

"Riley handed over the tablet and said, "There's something you need to see."

Petros took it, his eyes scanning the screen. "Ian Hammond."

"Yes. The man who helped Dee and the girl escape from Rio Dell. I had our analysts pull everything we could from the pre-war DOD archives. He's not just another survivalist."

Petros' eyes sharpened.

"He served two deployments with the Marine Corps," Riley continued. "First Battalion, Fifth Marines—Pendleton. One combat deployment to the Philippines, joint operations with the Philippine Marines. That's where things get interesting."

Petros tilted the tablet slightly and scrolled.

"He was part of a team supporting anti-insurgency operations against Chinese-backed separatists in the region," Riley said. "Records indicate his unit was ambushed during a patrol outside Zamboanga. Five men dead. Hammond led the survivors through enemy territory for six days. No air support. No evac. They walked out alive."

Petros glanced up now, locking eyes with Riley. "He sounds... resourceful."

"More than that. A few months before the bombs, he was reportedly captured by Chinese forces during the Pacific collapse. Taken to a black site in the mountains—one of their gulags. He escaped. Alone."

Petros leaned against the edge of the command console, processing the information.

"This isn't some misguided refugee," Riley said. "He's trained, experienced, and clearly motivated. He knows how to survive in enemy territory, organize resistance, and inspire loyalty."

"Does he know what Kylee is?" Petros asked.

Riley hesitated. "I'm sure he suspects something about her. He's seen her abilities. He knows she's different. And he's not afraid of it. That might make him even more dangerous."

Petros placed the tablet down slowly. "A soldier with nothing left to lose. History is full of men like him."

"But none of them had access to Kylee Daniels."

Petros nodded. "We'll need to factor him into the containment strategy."

"I can have him taken out," Riley offered quietly.

"No," Petros said, voice even. "Not yet. Killing him would turn the girl against us permanently. She's still young. Impressionable. We need her trust—or at least her compliance. Hammond is leverage."

Riley nodded, though he didn't like it. "And if he comes after us again?"

Petros turned fully toward him now, eyes hard. "Then we teach her what grief feels like."

The room fell silent. Somewhere deeper in the compound, a generator clicked on.

Riley stepped back into the shadows. The war had already started. And Petros—calculating, relentless, visionary—wasn't just planning to win it. He was planning to *shape* what came after.

***

After taking Ian's rifle, the lead marauder casually swung the butt of his Winchester up and cracked it across Ian's face. The impact blurred Ian's vision and sent him stumbling, blood already flooding his mouth with a copper sting. He spat into the dirt, checking with his tongue to make sure his teeth were still intact.

The man holding Melissa barked an order to one of his companions. Dee's arms were yanked behind her, and her wrists were bound with twine. The children trembled but were, for the moment, unharmed.

"Cut that meat up and bag it," the leader grunted, jerking his rifle toward Pavel's body. "We'll cook it before it turns."

Then he turned back to Ian and leaned in close, the stench of his breath nearly as violent as the earlier blow. "Maybe we save one of the little ones for dessert, eh?" He flashed a grin full of blackened gaps where teeth should've been.

A sharp burst of gunfire echoed nearby—close enough to rattle nerves. The leader whipped his head toward the alley's western end, raising his rifle to look through the scope. He didn't get the chance.

His skull exploded in a mist of red as the shot hit, dropping him like a rag doll. His rifle clattered uselessly beside him.

The ground began to shake. Hoofbeats thundered in from the west.

"Militia!" someone shouted, panic crackling in his voice. The marauders bolted, scrambling over one another to escape. One tried to reclaim his bicycle but made it barely two steps into the open before a bullet punched through his chest. He crumpled beside the bike, blood soaking through his shirt in spreading arcs.

Ian turned to Dee. "Move!" he hissed, motioning for her and the kids to retreat down the alley. But they didn't get far.

Three horsemen thundered into the alley, rifles up and ready. Ian froze, one hand instinctively moving to protect Kylee, though he had no weapon left to wield.

The rider in front pulled his horse up sharply, the animal snorting and pawing at the ground. Beneath the wide-brimmed hat, Ian caught a familiar face—blond hair, steel-blue eyes. Schubert.

The Free Militia sergeant grinned down at Ian. "Well, I'll be damned," he said. "Good to see you again, friend. Didn't catch your name last time, but you left an impression."

Ian didn't answer. He held Schubert's gaze with quiet defiance.

"No matter," Schubert said, scanning past him to Dee and the kids. "Looks like you've been busy. Don't worry, the cannibals are gone. You're safe now."

He turned his eyes back to Ian. "You and your crew match the descriptions we were given. And the fact that you ran tells me our captain's going to want a word."

Ian stayed silent, jaw clenched.

Schubert's smile grew tighter. "You're all guests of the Free Militia now."

Dee's voice cut through. "And by guests, you mean prisoners?"

"Of course," Schubert said, like it was the most obvious thing in the world. "But you'll be treated well—so long as you behave.

***

They began walking at dawn, and except for the occasional water break for the horses, the Militia patrol didn't stop until sunset. They followed the crumbling spine of Highway 199 out of Crescent City, riding openly, without concern for exposure. These men were confident in their firepower—or arrogant enough to think nothing could touch them.

The children were seated in front of three militia riders, each perched on the forward half of a western saddle. Ian and Dee were roped together at the wrists, a short tether binding them side by side, connected by a longer lead tied to one of the soldier's saddles. The pace wasn't brutal, and when Dee stumbled once in the afternoon, Schubert called a ten-minute break. Humane, by comparison to the cannibals. Ian noted it.

But he also wondered—had they found the bodies of the militia men he and Dee killed near Martin's Ferry? Schubert hadn't brought it up yet, but vengeance often brewed quietly in men like him. Ian couldn't tell if Schubert was the pragmatic type who understood this was a war of attrition, or if he was just waiting for the right moment to settle a score.

There were ten riders in all—roughly squad size. Schubert seemed used to this role: a patrol leader operating independently, making life and death decisions for his men. Ian had expected a group like the Free Militia to be more centralized, run by amateur warlords trying to mimic power. Instead, they ran on something disturbingly close to doctrine.

By the time they stopped to make camp, the sun was hanging low in the sky, bleeding gold across the hills. The prisoners were gathered in a loose group under watch. Kylee was quiet—too quiet.

"This is fun," Melissa chirped.

Dee gave her a bewildered look. "What in the world is fun about this?"

"I've never ridden a horse before," the girl said brightly.

"Do you think they'll teach me to ride?"

"Of course we will," Schubert said, strolling by. "Once we get to Bray Ranch, you'll learn to ride, hunt, fish—all kinds of things."

"What's the Bray Ranch?" Manny asked, sitting on a flat rock and chewing venison jerky.

"It's our headquarters," Schubert said. "Used to be Silas Bray's personal estate. Now it's more like a small town."

"Is that where we're going?" Melissa's voice jumped with excitement.

"Eventually. We've got some stops first," Schubert answered with a smile.

Melissa squealed. Manny grinned.

Dee looked over at them, frowning. "Don't you miss your family back in Crescent City?"

Manny shrugged. "They weren't really our family. They just found us and took care of us. I was only with them a few months."

"They found me a couple weeks ago," added Melissa.

"Where's your family?" Dee asked gently.

"Dead," Manny replied simply.

"Mine too," Melissa echoed. Then she turned to Schubert. "How long 'til we get to the Gray Ranch?"

Schubert chuckled. "Bray Ranch, sweetheart. About a week." He gestured for two of his men to stay behind and watch Ian and Dee while he took the kids down to the river to wash up.

Dee watched them go, then turned to Ian. "I don't get it. Melissa and Manny seem thrilled to be here. And they don't seem to miss anyone."

Ian took a long breath before replying. "I think they do. But kids today—especially kids who've lost everything—they learn fast. They harden fast. The people in that tunnel meant well, but they weren't their family. These militia guys—awful as they are—offer safety and structure. That's a kind of comfort. The kids probably feel that."

Dee nodded, chewing her lip. "It still doesn't sit right."

"Me neither. And as for Kylee... I think they have different plans for her."

A militia man returned with the kids. Melissa and Manny were chattering. Kylee lagged behind, silent.

"Sergeant Schubert wants to talk to you," the soldier said.

He led Ian and Dee down to the other side of the camp. Two armed militia escorts stood back on the riverbank, scanning for threats. Schubert sat on a pop-up camp stool, shirtless and shaving. He had a mirror propped up on a nearby rock to help him guide the razor.

"You killed three of my men," Schubert said. The accusation took Ian by surprise, and he noticed Dee shift uncomfortably. Was this it? Did Schubert separate them from the kids so he could execute him and Dee?

Ian responded carefully, "They were about to slit my throat."

"That's not what my man Cox said when we found him."

"Not surprising," Ian said. "It was his idea."

Schubert eyed him for a second, then said, "That's kind of what I figured. Sounds like Cox. He's always on his own program, my problem child." Schubert dipped his razor in a metal cup of water on his lap to rinse it off. He raised his arm to shave, revealing an Eagle, Globe, and Anchor tattoo on his left shoulder.

"Where did you get that?" Ian asked, partly from curiosity and partly from indignation that one of these Free Militia turds might have served in the Corps.

Schubert winced. "What?"

"On your shoulder."

A hint of a smile crossed the militia sergeant's face, as if recalling a better time. "I was still on active duty when the bombs hit; home on leave."

"I'd been out for about a year when it happened," Ian said.

"No shit," Schubert said. "Semper Fi brother."

"Yeah, you too."

"You a grunt?"

"Yup, One-Five, Pendleton," Ian said, giving him the inside baseball title for First Battalion, Fifth Marine Regiment in Camp Pendleton, California.

Schubert fired back, "One-Seven, out in the Stumps." The "Stumps" was an endearing term for the Marine Corps base in Twentynine Palms, California; a remote spot in the desert, known to most people as a sign along Interstate 10.

"Oh man, I always felt bad for you guys."

"It wasn't so bad. Didn't see it much with all the deployments. In fact, we'd just gotten back from my third trip to the PI." Ian knew immediatly that Schubert meant the Philippine Islands when he said "PI".

"One of my deployments was to the PI." It was Ian's one real combat deployment, supporting Philippine Marines in operations against Chinese-backed insurgents. The conflict had only heated up after Ian left. Prior to that, he'd spent six months on a ship, mostly floating in circles in and around the Spratly Islands.

Ian caught a look from Dee that told him she was getting annoyed that he was reminiscing with the enemy. She wouldn't get it. Despite what this guy was now, they had a shared experience that few people could relate to. And when you ran across someone who had been where you had one of the toughest times of your life, you will want to talk about it. Besides, it might help to get on this guy's good side.

Ian got her point, though. "So, what's a real Marine doing playing toy soldier with these Free Militia nut balls?"

"Careful, friend," said Schubert, letting some of his jovial attitude fade. "These guys are my brothers now. Just like the Corps."

"The Corps never asked you to extort people for protection."

"We're restoring order. You know what it's like these days. Did you feel extorted when my guys gunned down those cannibals? Would you rather we have left you in their caring hands?"

Ian was happy that Schubert and his squad came along when they did. But he was not about to admit that now. "It's not like you did it out of the kindness of your heart."

Schubert ignored the jab. "We defend people from the savages. Pretty soon, we'll be feeding them too. We've got hydroponic farms set up all over southwestern Oregon, and into California. Within a year we'll be growing enough food not just to feed our own, but to distribute throughout the territory. Is it too much that we ask the people, whose lives we're saving, to help with supplies now and then? Maybe even lend a hand to rebuild order? At least until we get things up and running."

"Wow," Ian said. "You almost make it sound reasonable to subjugate a part of what used to be America. So, by 'lend a hand' you mean forced labor, right? From what I've heard these farms are nothing more than slave camps. And what happens if people can't afford to give up some of their supplies? Do you leave them alone, to defend themselves? Or do you come down on them like a mafia loan shark? Maybe make a few examples to keep the rest of the peasants in line?"

"Tough times need tough measures," said Schubert, a little quieter than he was a moment ago. "Whether they appreciate it or not, people are much better off with us than they are without us."

"Even the children you kidnap from their parents?" Dee asked, speaking up for the first time.

Schubert squinted a look of annoyance and confusion. "What the hell are you talking about?"

Ian took back over. "We came across two kids over a week ago who said they were taken from their parents by the Free Militia and sold to some perverts. Is that part of your protection plan?"

"That's bullshit," said Schubert. "Those kids were either lying or confused."

"We found them with those perverts," Ian said through clenched teeth. "For some damn reason we let the shit bags live but got the kids out safe."

"None of that matters," Schubert said, as he rinsed the shaving soap from his face. His tone turned dismissive. He appeared tired of the conversation and having his world view challenged. Or maybe he just had things to do. "Get yourselves cleaned up. We need to eat and bed down for the night. I want to be back on the road by sunup."

With that, Ian and Dee were escorted down to the nearby river for their own cleanup.

***

Dinner was venison jerky again—chewy, salty, and tough on the jaw. It was the staple for Free Militia patrols on extended runs. They kept a two-man watch through the night, switching out every two hours. The kids were left untied, but Ian and Dee weren't so lucky. Each wore ankle shackles just tight enough to hobble any serious escape attempt.

Ian slept well enough. Dirt and pine needles made a better mattress than the cold concrete he'd been used to during the worst of the Long Winter. True to his word, Schubert had his men up before dawn. Camp was struck efficiently and without conversation.

They rode half the morning before stopping in a broad grassy field where the militia handed out another round of jerky and shared a single canteen among the prisoners, rationed in brief sips. The stop stretched longer than usual, and Ian soon saw why.

Another mounted patrol approached across the field— eight more riders. A rendezvous. Probably pre-arranged by radio. One of Schubert's men carried an old PRC-117 military transceiver strapped to his saddle. Most electronics had been fried by the EMP that lit the skies before the bombs fell. The fact that this radio still worked meant it had either been shielded in a Faraday cage or carefully rebuilt. Either way, the Free Militia had more technical resources than Ian expected.

Two riderless horses followed the new patrol. After a brief exchange with Schubert, their leader turned his patrol southwest, leaving the horses behind.

Within minutes, Ian and Dee were hoisted onto the new mounts. Their hands were tied, and each of their horses was led by a militia rider via a trailing rope. Ian guessed Schubert was tired of the slow progress with them on foot.

They'd just started moving when one of the horses shrieked and reared up, spooked by a coiled snake slithering through the grass. The rider—young, red-haired, maybe twenty—lost his balance and crashed hard onto the ground.

"Wells!" Schubert barked, already dismounting.

A few men rushed to the fallen soldier. One knelt beside him. "He's not moving."

Schubert dropped to one knee. "Come on, kid. Wells—wake up."

Another soldier grimaced. "Schube... he's not gonna make it."

Schubert stood, jaw clenched. "Did someone at least kill that snake?"

"Sergeant Schubert," Kylee's voice came from behind. "Please untie my hands. I need to get down."

Schubert spun around. "Are you kidding me, little girl? One of my men's dying and you want to stretch your legs?"

"She can help," Ian said quickly. "Just let her try."

"A nine-year-old?" one soldier scoffed.

"You're all standing there like he's already dead," Dee added, voice sharp. "Maybe let someone try something."

Schubert stared hard at Dee, bristling. "Fuck you," he muttered, then nodded to one of his men. "Let her down."

Kylee's hands were freed. She slid off the horse and crossed the grass calmly. Kneeling beside Wells, she placed her hands gently on his neck and head. Almost immediately, her small body trembled. Her jaw clenched and her back arched in a convulsion.

"What the hell is this?" one of the mounted soldiers muttered, shifting in his saddle.

But then Kylee's eyes snapped open—and so did Wells'.

The young man gasped, then sat up, blinking. "What happened?"

"You fell off your damn horse, dumbass," one of the soldiers laughed, and the others joined in with nervous relief.

Schubert dropped beside Wells, his voice softer now. "You good?"

"I think so…" Wells rubbed the back of his head, stunned but alert.

Once satisfied the boy was stable, Schubert helped Kylee back onto her horse. He looked up at her. "What did you do?"

Kylee shrugged but said nothing.

Dee answered for her. "Now you know why your bosses

are so interested in this little girl."

Schubert looked at Kylee for a long moment—no smile this time. Just something cold and calculating flickering behind his eyes. Then he turned back to his horse, and the patrol moved on.

***

They had been traveling for five days since the rendezvous, eventually leaving the paved roads behind to follow a winding river Ian guessed was the Klamath. The terrain grew steeper as they climbed into the mountains. Late on the fifth day, they crested a low ridge and spotted a lake nestled in the valley below—its surface silvered by the afternoon light.

Clustered along the lake's southern edge was a compound: a handful of buildings, a stable, a few corrals, and what looked like pens for livestock. Thin columns of smoke rose from cookfires. The place was alive.

A skinny, gap-toothed militia rider drifted his horse up beside Ian and leaned in with a grin. "Hope you like farming," he said, giggling like a Deliverance reject.

Ian rolled his eyes. "Do you guys take turns saying that line?"

Some of the other riders chuckled and launched into their own jabs at the toothless kid's expense.

In the heart of the compound stood a massive building that reminded Ian of an old aircraft hangar, though even larger. No windows—just heavy doors and a wide ventilation duct running along the roofline. One of the militia had pointed it out earlier: the hydroponic farm. Smaller buildings were clustered around it—barracks, workshops, storage sheds.

The entire perimeter was ringed with a six-foot wall made of upright logs lashed together and topped with razor wire. At each corner, a narrow watchtower stood sentry over the surrounding forest.

The patrol approached a northern gate. As it creaked open, a stocky guard stepped out to greet them.

"Sergeant Schubert," he said, nodding, "Captain wants to see you as soon as you're back."

Schubert sighed. "Johnny, O'Malley—you're with me. We're taking the prisoners straight to him. Rest of you, check the schedule before you hit your bunks. Might've shifted since we left."

The guard pointed toward Ian, Dee, and Kylee. "Those three go with you. The others head to processing."

Schubert blinked. "Processing?"

"Orders from the Captain," said the guard, tone clipped. "Just follow them for once, Schubert."

"My guys have been on the road for two weeks," Schubert growled. "Send one of your POGs from the shack."

"Everything's an argument with you," the guard grumbled, then turned his head. "Cox! Get your ass out here!"

The name froze Ian in place.

Cox stepped out of the guard shack, his sunburned face sour. His eyes landed on Ian—and narrowed. "What the hell is he doing here? This the asshole who killed Taylor?"

"He's my prisoner," Schubert said calmly. "I'll take him

to the Captain."

"You're gonna drop those kids off with him?" Schubert motioned to Cox. "Really?"

"I'll take them myself," he added without waiting for approval.

"Suit yourself," the guard said. "Just don't keep the Captain waiting. Pens are next to the hydro building—follow the chicken wire and drop 'em with the lab techs."

As they walked deeper into the compound, Ian got his first good look at what "processing" meant. Behind the hydroponic warehouse, a fenced-in pen held a dozen children. They ranged from toddlers to teens, all thin, sunken-eyed, silent. A small wooden shack sat at the entrance. Through the window, Ian saw a woman in a white lab coat taking blood from a boy who couldn't have been older than ten.

Schubert stopped, staring at the pen with his jaw tight. His gaze flicked to Dee—then quickly away, as if ashamed. He knocked on the shack's door and stepped inside with Manny and Melissa. Ian and Dee remained just outside.

***

The air inside the shack was clinical—sterile, wrong. The lighting was harsh, buzzing from salvaged ceiling strips that had no business still working after a decade of collapse. Schubert noticed the distinct scent of antiseptic, copper, and something else—something too close to burnt flesh.

A row of children, no older than ten or eleven, sat on a

bench along the far wall, silent. Each had a small bandage on one arm, and a faint mark on the side of the neck—like a bruise, but more precise. Deliberate.

The woman in the lab coat—blonde, tightly pinned hair, sleeves rolled to her elbows—barely acknowledged Schubert as he entered with Manny and Melissa. She was leaning over a metal tray, organizing a set of vials marked with coded labels. Beside her, a short man in glasses and rubber gloves loaded blood samples into a mobile centrifuge humming quietly on a steel cart.

"What's this for?" Melissa asked, shrinking behind Schubert's leg.

The woman turned, her face expressionless. "Standard health screen. Just a little blood."

Melissa nodded, visibly trying to be brave. Manny said nothing, but his eyes narrowed.

Schubert stepped in. "These two are mine. They were with me the last few days. I want to know what's going on here."

The woman barely glanced at him. "Their assignment isn't up to you, Sergeant. We have orders. They are to be tested and classified. The Director requires baseline samples from all incoming minors."

"The Director?" Schubert's voice sharpened.

The woman turned fully now. "Yes. From Director Petros himself."

Schubert stood still for a moment, then took a half-step back. "And what happens after the baseline?"

The woman lifted a small handheld scanner and passed it over Melissa's arm. It beeped twice.

"Non-reactive," she said. "Likely agricultural assignment. Possibly domestic."

She turned to Manny.

Before she could scan him, Manny took a step backward.

The woman frowned. "There's no need to be frightened."

Schubert held up a hand. "Let me talk to him."

"No," the woman said sharply. "You've done your part. Leave the subjects and return to your post."

Schubert's eyes locked on hers. Something passed between them—something defiant on his part, institutional on hers. She turned her back to him.

"Take them to holding," she told the man in gloves. "The director will want to review their profiles personally before permanent classification."

Schubert didn't move. "What kind of classification?"

She paused in her work. "Biometric matching. Blood compatibility. Nanite response assays. The usual."

"You're experimenting on them," he said flatly.

The woman sighed. "They're being evaluated. If they're useful, they'll be protected. If not... they'll still serve. In time."

At that, Schubert exhaled slowly and turned to leave. But just before he exited the shack, he glanced once more at Melissa and Manny—then back at the two technicians. His fists clenched at his sides.

***

Moments later, Schubert stepped back out—alone.

"Where are they?" Dee asked.

His jaw flexed. "This isn't over."

He led them another twenty yards to a small office shack sat in the shadow of the hydro building. Schubert knocked—firmly but not rudely. A man's voice answered from within.

"Come in."

Schubert opened the door. "Captain Ferris," he said crisply. "We've returned. And we brought the ones you asked for."

"I want to see them," the voice replied—giddy, almost gleeful.

Schubert stepped aside and ushered them in. The shack smelled faintly of wax and mildew. Behind a plain wooden desk sat a gaunt man with sharp cheekbones and a long, beak-like nose. The flicker of candlelight highlighted the dark hollows under his eyes.

"Welcome," he said. "To Hoopa Farm. I'm Elijah Ferris, Captain of the Free Militia."

No one responded.

He raised a brow. "I gave you my name. It's polite to return the gesture."

Still silence.

Another voice came from the shadows. "I can name them for you."

A man emerged from the corner, dressed neatly in a North Face jacket and khaki cargo pants. Wire-rimmed glasses flashed in the candlelight. His mustache was trimmed, hair combed. Ian's stomach turned.

The man smiled. "Delilah Rosemont and Kylee Daniels."

"Riley," Dee whispered.

"Hello, Dee," said the man.

"You know him?" Ian asked.

"Yeah," she said. "That's Patrick Riley. Petros' chief of security."

Patrick stepped closer, eyes fixed on Kylee. "Are you ready to go home?"

20 – The Farm

Ferris extended a folder toward Dee. "Here, Delilah—or do you prefer Dee? This is a writ of apprehension signed by General Silas Bray himself."

Dee took the folder cautiously. Inside were two photos—one of her, the other of Kylee—alongside an official-looking document bearing a seal and a signature that might as well have been scribbled in crayon for all its legitimacy. At the bottom, in bold lettering: *Office of Silas Bray, Commander-in-Chief, Free Militia of Western Oregon.*

Ian leaned forward. "You got one of those for me? Or are we just supposed to be impressed because some self-declared warlord scribbled his name on it?"

Ferris' expression soured. He nodded to O'Malley, who stepped forward and drove the butt of his rifle into Ian's gut. Ian grunted, doubling over.

"Silas Bray is a visionary," Ferris said coldly. "Something a drifting relic like you couldn't possibly understand."

Ian coughed, but his voice remained defiant. "Yeah? What happens when your 'visionary' crosses paths with someone who's got bigger guns and actual resources? From what I've seen, Petros' people play in a different league. Your 'Free Militia' wouldn't last a week."

Riley, calm and composed, stepped forward. "And why would we do that, Mr. Hammond?"

Dee's stomach knotted. She knew that tone. Riley was dangerous when he was being polite.

"Our objectives are not territorial," he continued. "Territory is a liability. Logistics, governance, resistance... it's messy. We're interested in scientific advancement. Nothing more."

Ferris turned back to Ian, his voice cool and precise. "To answer your question: no, there's no writ for you. Not even a mention from General Bray."

"Because he's irrelevant," Riley said, almost as an afterthought. "Mr. Hammond is a disposable element. An itinerant. We have no further use for him."

Ferris glanced at Ian. "Then we're free to execute him?"

Ian met his gaze without flinching. "If you're going to do it," he said, "just make it quick."

Riley gave a thin smile. "Captain, I don't interfere in the internal policies of the Free Militia. I'm only here to recover our lost assets—which, thanks to you, we now have. Mr. Petros and I are grateful. Consider this the beginning of a promising partnership."

Ferris gave a slow nod. "Very well. Maybe we won't shoot the drifter—yet. There's always work to be done, and he looks built for it. Sergeant Schubert, call off the search and notify the Ranch. I imagine this news will brighten the General's mood."

He turned back to Riley with a nod. "We'll ride at first light. I'll escort you as far as you like."

"Thank you, Captain," Riley said. "That's very generous of you."

Schubert stepped forward as Ferris turned to leave.

"Sir, there's one more matter I'd like to discuss before you go."

Ferris gave him a sideways look. "Make it quick. Tomorrow's going to be long."

***

Schubert waited for the others to clear out before shutting the shack's door behind him. The sound of the latch clicking shut echoed louder than he expected. For a second, he stood there, gathering his thoughts, eyes locked on the back of Captain Ferris, who remained seated at his desk with that damn steamy cup of chicory brew between his fingers.

The room smelled of pine, leather, and stress. Schubert shifted his weight and straightened.

"Sir," he said. "I need a word."

Ferris didn't look up immediately. He took a slow sip of his drink, then lowered it with deliberate care. "So talk."

Schubert cleared his throat. "It's about the pens."

That got his attention. Ferris's eyes lifted, shadowed by the soft lamplight. No surprise there. He knew damn well what this was about.

"They weren't there when I left. The wire, the shack, the lab coats—none of it. Now there's kids in cages and blood being drawn like this is some pharma facility."

Ferris said nothing.

"And that woman in the coat? She doesn't wear our patch. She didn't answer a single question. Hell, she didn't even give a name."

"You're not here to vet lab personnel," Ferris said flatly.

"No," Schubert said. "I'm here to look after my men. And to make sure we're not turning into the thing we swore we'd stand against. You know, back when this was about keeping people safe."

Ferris leaned back in his chair and rubbed the bridge of his nose, like a man who'd heard this tune before. "You've been on the trail, Sergeant. Things evolve."

"Since when does evolving mean letting strangers run a prison camp for kids in our backyard?"

Ferris gave him a long look. "Those kids aren't prisoners. They're research subjects."

"Research subjects? For what? Who are we working for, sir," Schubert said quietly. "Because it sure as hell isn't just Bray anymore."

Ferris stood now, slowly, and walked to the narrow window beside his desk. Outside, the lights from the main farm building glowed like beacons in the dark. "We are building something here," he said, almost to himself. "A future. That takes compromise."

"Compromise?" Schubert repeated, disgust thick in his voice. "So we look the other way while children get poked and prodded by Petros' people?"

Ferris turned. "Riley is just the beginning. Petros can offer us stability. Medicine. Technology we barely understand. And you've seen what that girl can do."

Schubert clenched his fists at his sides. "I've also seen what happens when men start treating people like tools."

Ferris stared him down. "You brought them in. You did your duty. I suggest you keep doing it, Sergeant. Or find a different patch to wear."

The silence between them stretched.

Schubert gave a slow, stiff nod. "Yes, sir."

He turned and left the room without another word, his boots heavy on the wooden floor. He didn't slam the door—but he came close.

Outside, the mountain air bit at his face. He looked toward the pens in the distance and saw the shadows of children moving under a pale bulb.

This isn't what we signed up for, he thought. But the real question was what he was going to do about it.

***

Dee and Kylee were separated from Ian and escorted to a squat concrete building on the far edge of the compound. Inside, a narrow cell awaited—two cots pushed up against the cold, olive-drab wall that seemed to drink in what little light filtered through the high, north-facing window. With the sun dropping behind the mountains, that light wouldn't last long.

Sergeant Schubert caught up with them just after they were locked inside. Whatever conversation he'd had with Captain Ferris hadn't gone well—his jaw was tight, his words clipped.

"I'll send someone with dinner," he said. "Sorry about the accommodations. This is all we've got right now."

"What about Ian?" Kylee asked from the cot, her voice cautious but direct.

"He's fine," Schubert replied, his tone softening. He always spoke gentler around Kylee. "He's in a secure location."

"Will we get to see him before we leave?" Dee asked.

Schubert shook his head. "Probably not. I'm sorry."

Dee gave a small nod, concealing her disappointment. She was too tired to argue.

"Need anything before I go?"

"We'll be fine with some food," Dee answered, her voice low.

Schubert gave a nod and left with the other men, locking the door behind them. Through the wall, Dee could hear his muffled voice.

"How long before I get relieved?" asked a soldier—Johnny, by the sound of it.

"I'll talk to the senior watch," Schubert replied. "If no one shows up by midnight, I'll come back and relieve you myself."

"But we just got back from patrol—don't I get to eat?"

"It sucks being the boot," another soldier muttered.

"I don't work that way," Schubert said firmly. "Go eat. Straight to the chow tent and straight back."

"Thanks," said Johnny. His boots echoed as he walked off.

Dee glanced at the cots. A month ago, she wouldn't have touched something so filthy. Now, she was ready to collapse onto it without hesitation.

"Where are they taking Ian?" Kylee asked, drawing her

knees to her chest on the bunk.

"I wish I knew." Dee sat beside her. "They said he's going to work on the farm."

Kylee gave her a skeptical glance but didn't push.

Muffled voices filtered through the door again—this time a woman's giggle. Moments later, the lock turned with a sharp clunk. Johnny appeared in the doorway, stepping aside for a woman carrying a tray.

She was thin, but not frail. Mid-thirties maybe, wearing a wrinkled blouse and worn jeans. Auburn hair pulled back from her face. She wasn't familiar—but something about her eyes or mouth stirred a vague recognition in Dee.

"Thanks, cutie," she said to Johnny with a wink, stepping inside. "Evening, ladies. I brought dinner."

Her tone was bright, bordering on too cheerful for the dim cell around them. She set the tray on a splintered table between the cots and uncovered the bowls. The smell hit Dee's nose—warm, savory, hearty. Her stomach growled.

"Chicken stew," the woman announced. "Good stuff tonight."

Dee gave her a cautious nod. "Thanks."

"You're welcome," the woman said, her voice lifting slightly—loud enough, Dee noticed, for Johnny to hear outside. "You'll find the Militia boys are decent hosts, long as you do your part."

That line was for the door, not them.

Then the woman turned to Kylee. "You are just the prettiest thing, aren't you?"

"Thank you," Kylee replied, shy but polite.

"What's your name, sweetheart?"

"Kylee."

"Well, it's very nice to meet you, Kylee. I'm Marion."

Kylee's eyes widened. "You're Marion?"

The woman tilted her head. "Do I know you?"

Kylee didn't answer. She simply took Marion's hand—and didn't let go. She tugged her forward and whispered something in her ear. Marion blinked, her expression shifting from confusion to shock, then a joy so raw it cracked her composure.

She glanced at the door, saw Johnny wasn't watching, and hugged Kylee tightly.

"Thank you," Marion whispered, voice trembling. She brushed a tear from her cheek, then stepped over to Dee and squeezed her hand. "Stay strong," she whispered.

Then, louder again, with fake cheer, "Just leave the bowls on the tray when you're done. I'll come back and collect them in an hour."

She slipped through the door, and the lock clicked shut behind her.

Dee picked up one bowl and handed it to Kylee, then took the other and sat beside her again.

"What just happened?"

"I told her that her kids were safe," Kylee said casually, scooping a big piece of chicken into her mouth.

Dee blinked. "What? How?" Her thoughts immediately turned to the nanobots.

Kylee swallowed. "We saw them just over a week ago."

Dee grew even more confused.

Kylee nodded. "Heath and Anna."

Dee's eyes widened. "That was their mom?"

Kylee nodded. "She didn't know they got rescued."

Dee sat back, staring at the closed door. "You're unbelievable," she whispered.

Kylee gave a little shrug and kept eating.

***

Dee took a long time to fall asleep, but eventually, exhaustion overtook her. In her dreams, she was skiing with her parents and little sister. The slope was steep—maybe Mammoth, maybe Tahoe. Rebecca was ahead of her, laughing as she zipped downhill.

"I'm gonna pass you!" Dee shouted, crouching low to catch more speed.

Rebecca looked back over her shoulder, still grinning. "Yeah, and then you woke up. Wake up, Dee. Wake up…"

Dee's eyes opened. The dream evaporated, and she was back on the filthy cot in the concrete-walled room at the Free Militia farm.

"Wake up, Dee," Kylee whispered urgently, shaking her shoulder. "Someone's at the door."

The unmistakable sound of the lock disengaging followed. The door creaked open slowly, and a man stepped inside, silhouetted in the dim light. His voice was slurred and cruel.

"If I gotta stand here all night, I'm gonna have me some fun, dammit."

Dee's gut clenched. She recognized the voice—Cox. The same sneering bastard who tried to kill Ian near Martin's Ferry. Apparently, he had taken over as their night guard.

He came straight toward her.

"What do you want?" she asked, trying to keep her voice steady.

Cox chuckled. "A little payback for Taylor and the boys. Just sit back and enjoy it."

"Leave her alone!" Kylee shouted.

Cox shoved Kylee aside with a grunted curse and grabbed Dee. He reeked of whiskey and meat. His grubby hands found her hips, dragging her off the cot. His tongue ran across her cheek as he pinned her down.

"Stop it!" Kylee struck him with the empty dinner tray. He responded by tossing the girl against the wall and turning back to Dee.

Fueled by panic, Dee slammed her knee into his groin. Cox grunted and doubled over, but he recovered fast, yanking her back and throwing her hard onto the cot. A heavy blow cracked across her cheek, and her blouse tore as he pinned her hands above her head.

Then Kylee's voice came again—sharper, deeper, older.

"I said stop."

It wasn't a plea. It was a command.

Kylee stood on the cot, her eyes locked on Cox. She wasn't crying. She wasn't afraid. She radiated fury. And power.

Cox froze. His hands trembled. Then his eyes rolled back, and he collapsed on top of Dee like a felled tree. For a moment, she couldn't move. She could hardly breathe. Then someone yanked Cox's limp body off her.

"What the fuck are you doing in here, you piece of shit!" It was Sergeant Schubert who pummeled Cox in the face.

Cox snapped out of his trance, but it did him no good. He was on the ground as Schubert landed punch after punch, turning Cox's face into a bloody mess.

Another militia soldier grabbed both of Schubert's arms shouting, "All right Schubert! He's had enough!" Apparently, Schubert disagreed as he wrestled one arm free and got in one last punch.

Then Schubert put his hands up and said, "All right, I'm All right. It's over, I'm done."

The other Militia soldier let go of his Sergeant and bent down to check on Cox.

"I think you really hurt him boss."

"Yeah, whatever," Schubert said as he moved his head to one side to crack his neck. He looked at Dee. "You okay?"

Dee nodded. "Thank you."

Schubert shook his head. "No, don't thank me. Never should have happened. I'm going to have a talk with the Watch Officer. That turd has no business guarding prisoners." He moved to Dee and looked her in the eye but did not touch her. He must have known that after what she had been through, any contact would be unwelcome. "Really . . . you good?"

Dee managed a smile. "I'll be all right. He didn't get far before . . ." she thought about how Cox had just stopped the attack and lost consciousness at Kylee's command. She decided it would be best to keep that part a secret. "Before you got here," she finished.

"How 'bout you, girlie?" he asked Kylee.

Kylee, who was sitting back down on the cot, responded with a thumbs up.

Schubert then turned to the other militia soldier. "Help me get this piece of shit to the infirmary, then you come back and stand watch. I'll have someone relieve you in the morning." Schubert and the other soldier grabbed Cox, one man under each arm, and dragged him out the door. Dee heard the door lock, and they were once again alone in the dark.

"Kylee," Dee whispered, still sitting frozen on the edge of the cot. "You did it again, didn't you?"

"I know," Kylee said softly. She lay down, curled up, and rolled away. "Goodnight, Dee."

Dee watched her for a long moment. Kylee's breathing slowed. Her chest rose and fell in steady rhythm. As always, using her gift had drained her. But each time, she seemed to be weathering it just a little bit better. It was like Dr. Roy had said back at Martin's Ferry, as she continued to use her powers, she got stronger.

Sleep would not come so easily for Dee. Not after that.

21 – Enslaved

Whenever he moved his leg, the chain attached to the shackle on Ian's ankle jingled, keeping him awake. The room they put him in was barely large enough to lie down in. Either his feet or his head touched the wooden wall when he tried. It reminded him of a solitary confinement cell from some old prison movie. He wished he had a baseball mitt and a ball to bounce against the wall of his cell like Steve McQueen in the Great Escape.

A mouse scratched on the wood in one corner of his cell. Ian tore off a crumb from the moldy bread that came on top of the slop that was served for dinner and offered it up as a token of friendship. The little guy inched closer, sniffing cautiously with each step. When he was finally close enough, he snatched the crumb out of Ian's fingers, and then scurried off through a hole in the wooden wall. "Is that all I am to you?" Ian asked the mouse as his tail disappeared. "You little ingrate, at least you could hang out a bit!"

The door swung open. "You've got ten minutes," said the guard to someone out of view.

A figure stepped forward that Ian recognized as Riley, the man who was with Captain Ferris when they first arrived. The one that Dee had recognized from the compound she and Kylee had run away from. Riley stared at the guard for a moment. It was a clear, non-verbal message that he would take as much time as he would like. The guard stepped aside and let Riley into the cell.

Riley waited until the door closed, then said, "Hello Mr. Hammond. My name is Patrick Riley."

"I know who you are." That part was a lie. All he really knew was that this guy worked for George Petros in some kind of security role. Ian's guess was that he was the guy who applied intimidation or made examples when needed. Although he did not look dangerous, Ian knew it was the quiet guys that you needed to look out for.

"Then you know I've come to recover our organization's lost asset."

"She's not an asset, she's a little girl."

"That's where you're wrong, Mr. Hammond. May I call you Ian?"

"It's a free country. At least it used to be."

"What little girl do you know can do what Kylee can do, what you've seen her do?"

Ian stayed silent. *Where is this going?*

"She's dangerous Mr. Hammond."

"How is the ability to heal people dangerous?" Ian said. "There's a lot of good she can do out here."

"I don't mean her ability to heal."

Ian glanced at the floor. "I don't know what you're talking about."

"Oh yes you do. You've seen it. The mind reading. The ability to freeze someone with a word."

Ian kept his mouth shut. Yes, he knew but didn't want to confirm any of it.

Riley continued. "Of course, you might think that this

is an outlier. Maybe you only saw it happen once. She doesn't really control it, it's random. And I get that. But you need to ask yourself what happens when she learns to control it. When she can do these things at will. That is the power of a god my friend. In a few years she'll be going through puberty. Can you imagine a being that powerful with the emotional intelligence of a teenager? What kind of damage can she do? How many people will she hurt?"

"Have you met Kylee? I mean, have you really met her? Or have you just read the studies?"

It was Riley's turn to keep quiet.

"She doesn't have the cruelty you describe in her. Her only motivation is to help people, to save who she can. No matter what the cost to her personally. I've seen her heal so many people at one time she put herself into a coma. She will never become the monster you describe."

"I hope you're right Ian. I really do. But why leave it to chance? In our organization we have some of the most brilliant minds still left. We can guide her. We can control her more dangerous instincts and help make sure that she becomes the benevolent being you believe she will. We can give her the guidance and the tools she needs to make the best of her abilities."

"But you can't give her love," Ian said.

"What's that?" Riley was taken aback by this.

"You said it earlier," Ian said. "She's an asset. That's all you, your boss, or anyone in your organization will ever think of her. But she's so much more than what she can do. She's a beautiful, loving soul. Out here she can flourish. She can be the light to guide us out of the darkness. With you, she is nothing more than an experiment. Something to be studied and controlled."

Riley shook his head. "I can see I've wasted my time."

"What exactly is it you wanted to accomplish here, Riley? Why would you care what I think?"

"Because I was hoping to convince you to leave this alone and go back to your life as a drifter once you get out of here."

"Not sure how well you know your Free Militia buddies, but I don't think they intend to let me go. Their plan is to squeeze whatever life I have left out of me in this quaint little concentration camp."

Riley chuckled. "Please, Ian. You want me to believe that the man who led an uprising and fought his way out of a Chinese prison camp in the Philippine jungle will be kept behind these walls by a bunch of amateurs? Give me more credit than that."

"How the hell did you know about that?" *Who is this guy?*

"Ian, I respect your loyalty and your courage," Riley said, ignoring Ian's question. "But since I can't appeal to your better nature, I just want you to know that if you try to follow us or seek us out, I will have you killed. I would really prefer not to do that."

"See you soon Riley."

Patrick Riley shook his head and walked out, leaving Ian alone in his prison cell.

***

The light had long faded from the cell, and there was nothing left to do but sleep. Ian curled beneath the scratchy wool blanket tossed in with him—more of a gesture than a comfort. Exhaustion from the days on the trail pulled him under quickly.

He was deep in a dreamless haze when the thud of booted feet outside the cell snapped him awake.

The lock clanked.

The door slammed open.

Two Free Militia grunts stood in the doorway, all smirks and bravado.

"Rise and shine, sunshine," one of them said. "Time to make the donuts."

The other snorted. "Welcome to the rest of your life. Hope you like farming."

Ian blinked at them, unimpressed. That was the third time he'd heard the same line. It wasn't even worth the effort anymore to point it out.

"You guys ever think of taking this act on the road?" he muttered.

They ignored him, stepping inside to unlock his shackles with a clatter. One of them offered a warning while slipping the restraints off his ankles.

"Don't give us any trouble. Captain says if you play nice for a week, you graduate to a lumpy cot and communal farts in the barracks. No cell, no chains. Just good ol' fashioned labor with forty of your best friends."

More laughter. Ian rolled his shoulders and buttoned his overcoat, teeth chattering in the chill of early morning.

They pulled two other men from neighboring cells—

prisoners like him—and marched them across the compound toward the massive farm building. The morning sky was overcast again, but he imagined the mountains to the east, hidden behind gray clouds, would've made a hell of a sunrise.

Out near the front gate, he spotted movement—mounted patrol forming up. Horses stamped and snorted. Dee and Kylee sat behind two different riders—Dee behind Captain Ferris, and Kylee with another soldier. Patrick Riley rode at the front, calm and composed as always.

Ian's heart leapt into his throat. He broke from the group and ran toward them.

"Ian." Dee's voice carried a mix of emotions. He was relieved to see that they were safe, but terrified that they were being taken away.

There was fear in her voice. And something else. Hope.

But before he could reach them, a rifle butt cracked into the back of his skull.

The world spun.

He dropped face-first into the gravel.

Pain exploded through his scalp, and a warm wetness spread down the back of his neck. Blood. He blinked through the haze and pushed himself up, but hands grabbed him and shoved him back into line.

"Get back," growled one of the escorts.

From atop his horse, Captain Ferris turned. "They're no longer your concern, Mr. Hammond," he called. "They'll be returned safely, to where they belong."

Ian clenched his fists. Every muscle in his body screamed to move, to charge, to fight.

He took one step.

"Please, Ian," Dee called, her voice breaking. "Don't."

He froze. Five—maybe six—rifles were already trained on him. Any move would be suicide. And that wouldn't help them.

He locked eyes with Dee.

Then Kylee.

He saw fear there, yes—but also trust.

"I'll find you!" he shouted. "I'll get you out of there!"

A militia soldier stuffed a dirty bandana into his mouth and hauled him backward, his words silenced but not his intent.

He thrashed, but it was over.

All he could do was watch as they took the only people left in the world who mattered—his family—and rode away with them into the cold gray dawn.

***

Schubert stood near a man in a stained lab coat, clipboard in hand, directing workers like cattle. The crowd was being divided into two groups—half shuffled toward the massive warehouse-style building while the rest were herded by armed militia to the far end of the camp. One soldier held the warehouse door open as a line of grim-faced workers filed inside.

Ian caught Schubert's eye. The sergeant didn't react—too busy barking orders to his men to bother with a familiar prisoner.

The man in the lab coat motioned Ian inside, eyes on

his clipboard, counting heads as they passed.

Inside, the space was enormous. Rows of overhead LED lights flooded the warehouse in harsh white glare. Ian squinted as his eyes adjusted. The constant rumble of generators echoed through the room—wherever they were sourcing fuel, it had to be in large supply.

Hundreds of people milled about, maybe eighty or more by Ian's guess. They clutched bowls of steaming gray mush—breakfast. He caught a whiff: sour grain and boiled greens. Nearby, armed guards stood watch, rifles slung casually but with no illusion of disuse.

Along both walls and down the center of the building ran rows of steel racks stacked high with leafy plants. Each rack held trellises stretched with a cloth substrate, plants resting above while roots dangled into open air. Every few seconds, a fine mist sprayed from pipes laced through the framework.

Ian paused, staring.

"Aeroponics," said a voice behind him.

He turned, a little defensive. "What?"

The man stepped closer, offering a cautious smile. "That mist coats the roots with a nutrient solution. No soil, just oxygen, water, and chemicals. Efficient. This whole structure is called a growing rack."

Ian glanced back at the misting plants. "Never seen anything like it."

"You've probably eaten food grown like this and never knew it. Supermarket lettuce, tomatoes, strawberries. This tech was mainstream long before the bombs fell." He extended a hand. "Henry Wallace."

Ian shook it. "Ian Hammond."

Henry nodded, eyes scanning for watching guards. "Stick close. I'll show you the ropes."

A moment later, the man in the lab coat addressed the crowd. "Racks nine and ten—full harvest today. You know the drill. Bags are in the corner. If you're new, follow someone who isn't."

Henry led Ian to a stack of coarse burlap sacks and handed him one. Together, they climbed a narrow metal ladder that snaked through a maze of platforms built around each grow rack. Workers peeled off at various levels. Henry kept climbing.

There were four tiers total. Ian paused on the third, heart thumping as he looked down. The steel creaked faintly beneath his boots. He eyed the platform's rusted seams and the lone metal bar standing between him and a forty-foot drop.

Then someone stepped onto the ladder behind him.

He took a breath and climbed the rest of the way.

At the top, Henry showed him how to pluck soybeans from the stems, careful not to damage the plant. It was delicate work, repetitive but oddly calming—if not for the heavily armed militia pacing the catwalks, watching their every move.

As Ian worked, he kept his focus on the plant in front of him and his mind off the drop below.

Four stories up, surrounded by a humming machine of forced labor and hydroponic efficiency, Ian began to understand the deeper horror of Hoopa Farm: this wasn't chaos—it was order. Cold. Mechanical. Efficient. And they were all cogs

***

They'd picked all morning before breaking for lunch—if it could be called that. A single strip of jerky, a limp lettuce leaf, and what looked like half of an uncooked potato. Ian found an empty spot along the warehouse wall and slid down to sit, back against the cool concrete.

Henry sat beside him, unwrapping his meal without ceremony.

"What do you think of the meal plan?" Henry asked with a half-smile

"Better than what most people are eating these days."

"That's true."

"Thanks for showing me around today."

"No problem, we've all been there at one point." Henry looked around to make sure none of the militia guards were in earshot and then lowered his voice. "Where'd they get you?"

"Crescent City," Ian said. "And you?"

"Close to here. About twenty miles to the northwest. My wife and I were dumb enough to think we could track these guys without getting caught."

"Why would you want to?"

"They came through and took our kids back at this settlement we lived at along the Klamath."

This caught Ian's attention. "Along the Klamath? Did the settlement have a name?"

Henry nodded. "Martin's Ferry."

Ian smiled inwardly. "We spent some time there before moving on to Crescent City."

"We?"

"Yeah. They brought me in with a woman and a girl, that I've been traveling with."

"How is it? Is it still intact? Are the people okay?"

"As well as can be expected."

Henry's eyes shut a moment. "We lived there a while. My wife and me," he swallowed, "and our two kids. Our kids got taken in one of their roundups, claimed we didn't pay some taxes that they said we owed. It was all made up. I think they wanted our kids from the start. Anyway, we tracked them here, and before we could figure out if they still had our kids, we were captured. My wife's here too. Well, not in here, probably working the troops' mess hall."

"Are your kids in those pens with the others?" Ian thought of the chicken wire enclosure where Manny and Melissa had been taken.

Henry closed his eyes again, as if trying to hold something in. "They were. These Militia bastards sold them," his voice cracked. "They sold them to a group of traders for a couple of horses."

"Wait a minute, what were their names." Ian said as he put it together.

Henry hesitated then told him, "Heath was my oldest. He was twelve. And my little girl Anna was only eight. God knows where they are now."

Ian put his hand on Henry's shoulder. "Heath and Anna are safe my friend. They are back at Martin's Ferry, with Charles and Carol."

Henry wiped his eyes. "What? That can't be."

"We found them on the road with two vagrants who must have bought them off the traders you mentioned. We knew something wasn't right." Ian shook his head, "Or I should say Kylee knew something wasn't right."

"Is that the young girl that was brought in with you?"

"That's right."

"How did she know?"

Ian was not about to talk about Kylee's abilities with some guy he just met. For all he knew, Henry could be posing as Heath and Anna's father, just to get information. "You know kids, they can pick up on things that adults miss."

"Thank God!" Henry looked up, then back at Ian. "Thank you."

Ian shrugged.

"Are they okay? I mean, they weren't hurt or anything."

Ian let out an exhale. He didn't want to tell this guy that his kids had been abused, but he couldn't lie about something like this. "I don't think they had an easy time," was all he said.

Henry's lip quivered, and then he pounded a fist on the wall. The noise caused one of the militia guards to look their way.

Ian raised his hand and rubbed the back of his head. "I slipped," he said to the guard, who went back to eating his own lunch.

"Makes no sense though," Ian said. "Why would they take your kids just to sell them?"

"I don't know," Henry said, putting his tray down with

a look of disgust. "In the pens, they separate the kids. Some they move to another location, others they sell off."

Ian took a bite of jerky while gazing at the farm stacks.

"One thing I know," Henry said. "I'm going to get out of here and hunt those shit bag vagrants down."

"I understand the feeling, but what would that accomplish?"

"It would make sure they never hurt another kid again."

"You'll never find them. They could be anywhere."

"Fuck!" breathed Henry.

"If you get out of here, you need to head straight for Martin's Ferry, gather up your kids and head south, out of Free Militia territory."

"You bet," Henry said, his anger easing a bit. "I never want to be under the thumb of these assholes again."

***

It had been just over two weeks since Ian arrived at Hoopa Farm, and he was finally being moved out of solitary. His wrists were still sore from the cuffs, though they'd been removed hours ago, and his back ached from sleeping on wooden planks masquerading as beds. But he was walking under his own power now, unshackled, escorted by only one guard.

They passed the edge of the hydroponics building and crossed a gravel yard toward a long, windowless structure. The barracks.

The door creaked as it opened, revealing a single cavernous room filled with the stale, mingled scents of sweat, mildew, and unwashed socks. The air was warm and humid—too many bodies crammed into too small a space. Bunk beds lined either side of the concrete walls, two rows of metal frames stacked two-high. It reminded Ian of boot camp. The beds were bare except for the standard-issue wool blankets and flat pillows that looked like they hadn't been replaced since before the bombs dropped.

Fifty men, give or take, occupied the room. Most sat on bunks or lounged nearby, eating, sharpening knives, or playing cards with worn decks. All of them looked up when Ian entered.

He felt the stares. Some indifferent, others curious. A few hostile.

The guard gestured at the middle of the room. "That one's yours." He didn't wait for Ian to respond before turning and walking out.

Before Ian could move, Henry appeared from the far row of bunks, waving him over with a tired smile. "Right on time," he said. "I've been saving you a spot."

They moved through the gauntlet of eyes toward a bottom bunk near the back of the room. The mattress was thin, but clean by camp standards, and a folded blanket sat at the foot. "It's not exactly the Hilton," Henry said, "but you won't be alone."

"Feels like I just graduated from jail to summer camp," Ian muttered, setting his bag of clothes—such as they were—on the bedframe.

Henry chuckled, then lowered his voice. "You'll want to keep a low profile at first. There's a couple guys here with chips on their shoulders. One in particular—name's Del.

He was a bouncer before the war and still thinks he runs the show in here."

Ian's response was interrupted by the sound of a tray clattering to the floor. Across the room, a tall, broad-shouldered man with a buzz cut and a crooked nose stood from his bunk. "Hey, new guy," he called. "You're the one who got the special escort, right? That you?"

Ian looked over without answering.

"I heard you're tight with the girl. The one who does magic tricks." A few of Del's crew chuckled behind him.

Ian took a step forward. "Say that again."

Henry grabbed his arm. "Not now."

Del laughed and raised his hands. "Relax, I'm just making conversation. But if she ever drops by to give blessings, send her my way." He turned back to his bunk, the laughter of his lackeys fading as they resumed their game.

Ian exhaled through his nose, unclenching his jaw.

Henry nudged him with a smirk. "See what I mean?"

"Yeah," Ian said. "I've seen his type before. They pick the wrong fight eventually."

"You just make sure it's not yours," Henry replied. "At least not yet."

Ian sat down on his bunk and looked around the room again. There was no privacy, no space, and no freedom. But there were eyes here. Ears. Conversations that might lead to something.

And the work wasn't over. He'd told Kylee he'd find her.

This was step one.

***

The barracks were dim, lit only by two flickering overhead fluorescents and the dying glow of a smuggled cigarette ember. Most men were dozing. A few murmured low conversations or played cards under a hanging flashlight at the far end.

Ian sat on the edge of his bunk, lacing his boots for the early shift. He wasn't supposed to be up for another hour, but sleep had become a stranger again—just ghosts and guilt in his dreams now.

Across the aisle, Del snorted and rolled over on his upper bunk. "You always gotta make that much noise, hero?"

Ian paused. "Didn't know tying my boots qualified as a felony."

Del sat up, swinging his legs over the edge, his bulk shadowing down toward Ian. "You think because you got people talking, because Schubert pulled strings to get you in here, you're someone?"

Ian stood slowly. "I don't think anything. But I am someone who wants to survive. That's all."

Del dropped down to the floor with a heavy thud. "Yeah? Then you might want to learn a little humility. Lot of guys in here with nothing left to lose."

"Good," Ian said, stepping closer. "That means you've got nothing to gain by starting something stupid."

The tension crackled between them like a storm waiting to break. Every eye in the room shifted toward them. Cards were set down. Conversations died.

Del cracked his knuckles. "Tell you what. Let's say I just don't like the way you look. Maybe that's enough."

Ian didn't flinch. "You want to swing, then swing. But if you don't knock me out, I'm coming back harder. And I'm not stopping until someone drags us both to the infirmary."

Del's mouth twitched—maybe with amusement, maybe with menace. Then, slowly, he stepped back.

"You've got a mouth on you," he said. "Reminds me of my little brother. Kid never shut up either. Got himself shot over a can of peaches."

"I'm not your brother," Ian said. "But I'm not your enemy either."

A long pause. Del studied Ian, as if sizing up something deeper than muscle.

"You ever box?" Del asked, finally.

"Couple fights. Navy guys mostly."

"Next free night, come spar. You might learn how to keep your guard up."

"Deal," Ian said, exhaling slowly.

Del turned, climbed back to his bunk, and grunted. "Keep it quiet next time, will ya?"

As he settled, Henry appeared from behind a partition, shaking his head with a smirk.

"Well," he whispered to Ian, "that's the closest thing Del gives to an olive branch."

Ian chuckled. "I'll take it."

A few of the other men nodded to Ian across the aisle. Not a warm welcome, but a recognition. A line crossed. A barrier breached.

In this place, trust wasn't offered. It was earned—sometimes the hard way. And tonight, Ian had taken the first real step.

***

A stretch of dry, packed earth sat between the worker barracks and the farm building—just big enough to serve as a makeshift boxing ring. A few wooden crates were dragged into a rough square to act as corners. Militia guards stood in the distance, uninterested. Some of the workers had pulled up stools or crates to watch, most pretending not to care, though everyone was clearly paying attention.

Ian stood shirtless, bouncing on the balls of his feet, his breath misting faintly in the cool mountain air. Del was already stripped to the waist, cracking his neck as he stepped into the ring, fists clenched. A large scar ran across his chest like a question he never answered.

Henry tossed Ian a pair of old, taped-up leather gloves. "They're not regulation," he said with a smirk. "But neither are the rules."

"I figured," Ian said, pulling them on. "What's the goal here, Del? Knock each other out or just shake hands after a few bruises?"

Del snorted. "Let's start with bruises. Maybe move on to blood if we're having fun."

They circled each other. The onlookers leaned in.

Round One

Del jabbed first—fast for a guy his size. Ian blocked high and fired back with a hook that grazed Del's ribs. The next few exchanges were quick: jab, jab, slip, counter. Ian's military precision met Del's brawler instinct in a clash that felt oddly familiar, like two puzzle pieces punching each other into place.

Del ducked a right hook and grinned. "You hit like a Marine."

"I was one."

"Explains the posture."

Del's uppercut caught Ian just under the chin—not hard enough to drop him, but hard enough to knock him back a step.

"Also explains the jaw," Del added.

Round Two

They kept going for another five minutes, neither giving an inch, sweat flying from their brows with every dodge and counter.

Del's laughter suddenly burst through a clinch. "You ever fight someone *without* a cause, Hammond?"

Ian breathed through gritted teeth. "No such thing, is there?"

Then came the moment: Ian landed a clean jab that snapped Del's head back. Del blinked, stumbled, and then stood straight—arms wide like a showman.

"Well damn," he said, staggering toward one of the crates to sit. "Guess I just got schooled by the second-most stubborn bastard in the camp."

"Second?" Ian asked, sitting beside him, still breathing hard.

Del nodded. "Yeah. Number one's the mouse who keeps stealing my protein bar every night."

That got a laugh—not just from Ian, but from a few of the others listening nearby.

Henry stepped up and offered both of them water. "So, we calling this a draw?"

Ian nodded. "For now."

Del raised his bottle toward Ian. "To old habits, broken noses, and enemies who become slightly less punchable."

Ian clinked his water bottle to Del's. "I'll drink to that."

The moment settled. Not just between them, but among the men watching. For the first time since arriving, Ian wasn't just another outsider. He was one of them now—bloodied, bruised, and earning respect the hard way

***

The rows of aeroponic trays hissed softly, misting the roots of crops bathed under rows of humming LED lights. Most of the workers had turned in for the night. Ian stayed behind with Henry and two others, scraping nutrient sludge out of a clogged feed line beneath one of the racks.

Ian wiped a smear of compost off his face when he heard boots echo on the concrete. He froze, ducking instinctively behind a support beam. From the adjacent workroom—half an office, half a storage closet—came the unmistakable sound of Schubert's voice, low and tense.

"Captain wants eyes on the perimeter around the clock. Double watches in the towers, reinforce gate one. I want a rifle next to every pair of boots."

Another voice—older, raspy: probably one of the senior guards. "You expecting trouble, Sarge?"

"Maybe. Word came down that the *Mongrels* hit a militia convoy outside Medford last week. Burned the whole load. No survivors."

Ian felt a chill ripple through him. *Mongrels.* He'd heard the name back in the southern valleys—an elusive biker gang known for their brutal hit and run raids and mistreatment of prisoners. Militia boys talked about them like ghosts—spirits who struck fast, vanished faster.

"You think they'll hit us?" said the raspy voice.

"I don't think anything," Schubert replied. "But Lieutenant Ownsby is nervous. He doesn't want to lose another shipment."

Ian held his breath.

"What's the plan?" asked the other voice.

"We've got a runner heading out tomorrow to warn Bray Ranch. Owensby wants backup in case things go sideways. Until then—nobody in or out. And we shoot anything on the ridge that moves."

Boots scraped as the guards moved off. Ian stayed hidden until the sound faded, then emerged slowly, meeting Henry's wide-eyed stare from across the support beam.

"You hear that?" Henry whispered.

Ian nodded. "If the Collective's really coming..." He trailed off, eyes scanning the maze of crops and catwalks. "We may be able to use that distraction. We just need to survive until they get here. And be ready when they do."

***

The barracks were filled with soft snoring, wheezing, and the occasional rustle of a restless sleeper turning in his bunk. The room's pale lantern light had long since been extinguished. The air was thick with the smell of unwashed clothes and bodies, but the stillness carried an edge of alertness.

Ian lay on his bunk, eyes wide open, listening.

A faint tap. Then another.

Del.

Ian rolled out from beneath his blanket and crept toward the far end of the barracks, slipping between the rows of bunks. Del crouched near the laundry crates, and Henry was already waiting beside him, face shadowed but alert.

Two others joined them—Miguel, a wiry mechanic from Yreka, and Taye, a former schoolteacher who had somehow kept his calm even in the worst of situations.

Del kept his voice low, barely above a breath. "What's this about, Ian?"

Ian looked around at them—these were men he trusted, or at least trusted enough. "I overheard Schubert tonight in the grow house. They're doubling the watch. Preparing for something. He mentioned the Mongrels by name."

Henry stiffened. "You think they're coming?"

"I don't know," Ian said. "But if they are—if anyone attacks this place—we need to be ready. That kind of chaos might be our only shot."

Taye nodded slowly. "You want to start an escape

during a firefight?"

"No. I want to be *ready* when one starts. We don't fight. We don't stay. We vanish."

"Vanish where?" Miguel whispered. "You've seen the perimeter. Razor wire, patrols, towers."

Ian said, "There's a drainage ditch behind the barracks. The gate's welded, but it's rusted at the seams. If we have time, I can break it loose. We run through the ditch—then split."

"Split?" Del asked.

"They'll try to track us," Ian said. "But they can't follow everyone. If we all run in different directions—east into the trees, west down the gorge, even straight up toward the ridge—they'll catch some of us, but not all."

Henry scratched his chin. "And what happens to the ones who *do* get caught?"

Ian held his gaze. "Then the rest of us have to make it count."

There was silence for a moment.

"I'm in," Del said. "Always figured I'd die out here. Might as well make it trying to get free."

Henry nodded. "Me too. If my kids are still safe, I've got to get to them."

"I'll go west," Miguel said. "I know the ravine. If I can reach the river, I've got a shot."

Taye hesitated. Then quietly: "I'll head north. The old fire trails might still be clear."

Ian leaned back, lowering his voice even further. "We don't act unless it all goes to hell. But if it does—ditch, scatter, vanish. And if you make it... get as far away from

Bray territory as you can."

He looked each of them in the eye. "Now get some sleep. We might need to move fast."

***

The barracks rattled from the distant boom of gunfire and the flash of firelight outside. Men shouted and scrambled toward the windows as another blast lit the southern sky.

"They're under attack," Del muttered from his bunk, already pulling on boots.

Ian stood, eyes scanning the barracks. "This is it," he said. "We move now."

"Drainage tunnel?" Tyrell asked, already reaching under his bunk for the wire-cutter he'd stashed.

Ian nodded. "Go. Quiet. Stay low."

Henry grabbed Ian's arm. "I have to get Marion."

Ian turned on him. "We don't have time for this."

"I have to get her," Henry repeated. "You go. I'll catch up at the tunnel."

"I'm not waiting," Ian said flatly. "We're either gone or we're caught. You get there, or you don't."

"I'll get there," Henry said. His voice was firm. "Just give me the time it takes to get across the yard."

Ian hesitated, then gave a curt nod. "One shot, Henry. No hero shit."

Henry vanished into the shadows, slipping between bunk rows toward the back door as the rest of the group cracked open the drain grate and slid out into the cold night.

Ian stepped back inside the barracks and whistled to get the attention of its panicking occupants. "The guard's gone. Unless you want to stay here as a slave for the Free Militia or take your chances with whoever is trying to get through the south wall, I suggest you get the hell out of here." Most of the other farm workers bolted for the door, leaving only a handful that would rather stay. Ian was glad to see how many wanted to escape. He figured the additional distraction could only help their chances of getting out and staying out.

Minutes later, as Ian and the others reached the overgrown runoff pipe and crouched at its edge, Henry reappeared with Marion in tow. Her hair was windblown and her face streaked with ash, but her eyes were clear. Determined.

"Go!" Ian whispered. "We're not dying in a fucking pipe."

They ducked inside, single-file. Behind them, the firelight danced against the compound walls, and the distant gunfire kept time with their escape.

They got through the pipe to see that Del and the other escapees were already long gone, as planned. They quickly traversed the fifty yards to the tree line, Ian finally allowed himself to catch his breath in relief. He believed they were going to make it.

Dogs barked in the dark, followed by men shouting. It was hard to tell which direction, but Ian had to assume they were coming from the compound. The sound of motorcycles in the distance roared but quickly faded as the attackers fled. With the battle over, the Free Militia could turn their attention to finding their escaped slaves.

A gunshot rocked the nighttime forest. "I wonder if that's Del and the others?" Henry said.

"Nothing we can do about it if it was," Ian said.

A stick broke in the dark to their right. A figure was barely visible in the ambient light. "I got you now, motherfucker." The voice was vaguely familiar, and the man behind it wheezed when he breathed. "I just wish that bitch you came in with was here right now. I'd do you right in front of her, then do her." A rifle barrel was pointed straight at Ian.

It took a moment for Ian to recognize the voice. It was Cox, the Militia soldier who tried to slit his throat back near Martin's Ferry. The man looked different. His nose was out of joint, and there were cuts and bruises around both eyes.

Cox raised the sights to his bruised right eye and prepared to fire. Ian closed his eyes, thinking this was it. He just wished he could see Dee one more time; feel her, smell her. Tell her he was sorry for failing them. Tell her that he loved her.

"Cox!" The militia man lowered his rifle at the sound of his name, visibly agitated. "You got one?"

"I got three."

Sergeant Schubert drew up behind Cox. He looked from Cox to Ian to Marion and Henry. "All right, let's get them back inside."

"They'll just try again. Why don't we make an example. Scare the rest straight."

"The farm's lost enough of its labor force tonight. We'll need every one of them we recover just to keep the place running until we can grow the workforce." Ian knew that by "grow the workforce," Schubert meant kidnap more wanderers.

"What about just this one?" Cox asked, motioning to Ian with his rifle. "The General always says that examples need to be made."

"He says that." Schubert looked at Ian. "And you're right, examples need to be made."

Schubert's hand moved so quick; Ian barely knew what had happened. Before he could react, Schubert had unsheathed the knife he had taken from Ian and plunged it into Cox's neck. A stream of blood poured out, telling Ian that Schubert had located the carotid artery with perfect precision.

"What the fuck!" whispered Henry. Marion let out a surprised gasp.

Schubert wiped the knife on Cox's clothes as the now lifeless body fell. He flipped the knife and caught it by the blade, then handed it to Ian, handle first. "I'll need you to hit me hard. Take his rifle and give me a butt stroke."

Ian looked down at Cox's rifle, now lying on the ground next to him, and then back to Schubert. Was this a trick?

"Come on Marine, you remember how to give a good butt stroke!"

Ian reached down slowly and grabbed Cox's rifle. "Why are you doing this?"

"I'm starting to see what we've become. And I've seen what that girl can do. She can help people out here. Catch up to Ferris and this guy Riley before they reach his boss. Get her the hell away from those assholes."

"All right," Ian said, raising the rifle.

Schubert put his hand up. "Hold on a minute." He hyperventilated as if trying to psych himself up. He closed his eyes, hyperventilated some more, and nodded.

Ian jammed the butt of Cox's rifle into Schubert's face. The man fell to the ground, covering his face with his hands. When he pulled them away, a stream of blood came from his nose and covered his hand and shirt. He spat out a tooth.

Speaking with a lisp now, Schubert said. "Nice hit. I can sell this. Better take my rifle too, though, just to make it more believable." Henry pulled Schubert's rifle off the wounded man's shoulder. Schubert added, "Head north or west, don't go southeast. Those were Mongrels that hit us. Not sure what gave them the idea they could take down a militia outpost, but they tried tonight. You don't want to be anywhere they're going. Intel says they've gone eater in the last few years." Ian knew Schubert was right, he didn't want to be anywhere near those savages.

"I don't know how we can make this up to you," Ian said in parting.

"If I ever see you again, just send that little girl over to me. Am I right to assume she can undo what you just did?"

"She can."

Schubert let out a chuckle, along with some blood spittle. "Awesome!"

22 – The Man in the Poncho

Dee's tailbone throbbed with every jolt of the trotting horse. Sharing a saddle with Captain Ferris left her crammed against the cantle, and the rigid leather was punishing. But it beat walking.

The convoy of Free Militia soldiers moved slowly along what remained of old Route 169. Ten years of ice and neglect had broken the road into fractured slabs of crumbling pavement and overgrown gravel. At this pace, the journey would take at least two more days.

Captain Ferris rode at the head of the column with Patrick Riley by his side. Twenty mounted militia accompanied them—an escort not for Dee, but for Kylee, the "asset." Dee's stomach churned every time she thought of what awaited the girl back at the compound. Petros would not let her disappearance go unpunished. And once they returned, Kylee's "tests" would intensify.

They halted at a wide stream spanned by a rusted bridge, the sky burning red beneath a ceiling of soot-colored clouds. Ferris dismounted and gestured to a log beside the fire. "Please. Sit."

Kylee, who had been riding with another soldier, was already sitting cross-legged on the ground beside Riley, poking at a clump of moss. Her face brightened a little when she saw Dee approach.

"Corporal, untie her wrists," Ferris said. The knots bit her skin as they unwound, but the relief was immediate. Dee stayed standing.

Riley gave her a polite nod, then turned to Kylee. "Looking forward to sleeping in your own bed? I've already asked the kitchen to prepare tacos. Just the way you like."

Kylee tilted her head. "Tell them not to bother. I won't be going back. I have too much to do out here."

Riley chuckled. "I'm afraid that's not your decision."

"I'm helping people," Kylee replied with a quiet confidence. "Sick people. Hurt people. That's more important than tacos."

Riley's smile froze. He seemed unsure whether to scold her or laugh again. "What kind of work, exactly?"

"You'll see," Kylee said. "Or maybe you won't."

Riley turned to Ferris and spoke low. "I'd like a moment with the woman."

Ferris waved to a soldier. "Take the girl. Get her fed."

Dee watched as Kylee was led toward the rations tent. She glanced back once, eyes searching Dee's. Then she was gone.

"She's remarkable," Riley said once they were alone. "A true anomaly."

"She's a little girl," Dee snapped. "One you people are torturing in the name of progress."

"No permanent harm has come to her," Riley replied. "She's incredibly resilient—by design. But her ability to project the nanites externally... that changes everything."

"Why is that so dangerous? All she's done is help people."

"You're focused on what she's done. I'm focused on what she *could* do. She's projected control. Froze a trained operative with a word. What happens when she learns to do that at will? When she's a teenager? Angry? Unstable?"

"She's not a monster."

"Not now. But you're placing a child in the role of savior. That's not just foolish. It's dangerous. One Kylee might be manageable. A hundred?" Riley shook his head. "We'd be creating gods. Gods with human emotions."

Dee crossed her arms. "So now you want to *prevent* more like her?"

Riley nodded. "That part of her development was never intended. We need to understand it, contain it. Before it spreads."

"She was a child when you did this to her. She *is* a child. You created something beautiful and now you're trying to put it in a cage."

"We created a solution. But it's evolving beyond our control."

Dee leaned forward, her voice hard. "You don't want to protect humanity. You want to preserve your *control* over it. You're afraid of a world you can't dominate."

Riley's expression didn't change, but something shifted in his eyes. "You think this is about power?"

"Isn't it always?"

Riley looked away, jaw tight. "This conversation is over."

"You said you wanted to talk to me," Dee said. "What was this? Just a lecture?"

Riley stood. "I've heard all I need. You're no longer part of the plan."

"What does that mean?"

"You'll be staying here with the Free Militia. I suggest you prove your worth to them before they decide you're not worth the trouble and sell you off. Kylee and I will return to the compound tomorrow."

Dee took a step forward. "You can't do that. She needs me."

"She has other caretakers."

"None who love her."

Riley's voice sharpened. "That's the problem, Ms. Rosemont. You care too much. It clouds your judgment."

"You bastard—!"

Militia soldiers seized her arms as she thrashed against them. Riley turned to Ferris. "She's yours. Take her away."

Dee's last glimpse of Kylee was the girl turning at the sound of her struggle—just as she was dragged from the firelight

***

"So," Ferris said after he had taken Dee to where she would bed down for the night. His voice was cordial, bordering on creepy. "What am I to do with you?"

"You could let me leave with Kylee," Dee said.

"Funny," Ferris said.

"You asked."

"I was asking myself."

"You know that can be done without actually speaking." Dee knew she should try to make nice with this Ferris guy, but right now she didn't care.

A thin smile crossed Ferris' face. "You know, life in Free Militia territory is not that bad. Most folks these days are constantly fighting off cannibals and marauders. Raids are rare within our borders. The General has given us standing orders to make examples every chance we get. Word of such things tends to spread. It is human nature I suppose, even among those who have lost their humanity."

Dee stayed silent. Ferris was trying to sell her on the benefits of living among the militia while bragging about their brutality.

Ferris continued, "So, like I said, relatively speaking, life with us can be quite pleasant." Every time Ferris spoke of the Free Militia it was with reverence. He was a believer. "We're building something here. General Bray has a vision for how our nation will rise from the ashes of the old America. A free nation, a pure nation. There would certainly be a place for you here. But any civilization starts with filling man's basic need for food, shelter, and order. *We* provide that. We give people hope."

Dee knew she should keep quiet but couldn't help herself. "Is that what you're giving to those people back at the farm?"

"Building a nation is a monumental task. It requires a labor force. Besides, most of those people are vagrants and thugs. Do you think they would do it willingly?"

"Is that what you have planned for me? Work the farms for the rest of my days so that your General can get his name in the history books?"

"No," Ferris said with a shake of the head. "Of course not. That's no life for the woman of a Free Militia officer."

There it was. The little guy had a crush on her. Dee worked to keep the disgust she felt at the very thought of being with this guy from showing on her face.

Before Ferris could follow up with another question, one of his men interrupted. "Ward and Billie are missing." Dee was grateful for the abrupt ending to that uncomfortable conversation.

Ferris popped to his feet. "What? When?"

"They haven't come back from watering their horses."

Ferris was visibly agitated but said nothing.

The man continued, "I sent two three-man search parties out looking. But it will be tough to find a trail in the dark." The sun had fully set now, and twilight was fading fast.

Ferris cursed and ordered Dee and Kylee tied up again. The stress of uncertainty affected him.

Riley came into the campfire light where Ferris and some of his men were huddled. "What's going on?" he asked.

"Some of my men went missing," Ferris said.

One of the two patrols came back with no sign of the two missing militia soldiers. The other patrol did not come back at all. Ferris barked about the price of desertion.

"You don't know that they deserted," Riley said. "They might have been captured or worse."

"There's no evidence of that." Ferris sounded annoyed that Riley would question him.

"Look, Elijah, we don't know what's out there. You need to strike the camp and get us moving again."

"What are you talking about?" whined Ferris. "My men

have been riding all day, they're tired . . ."

"They'll be dead if you don't sack up and get them moving. We need to get to a more defendable position. You can start by putting that fire out. It's like an all you can eat buffet sign for cannibals." Dee did not like Riley. But right now, she wished he were in charge instead of Ferris. "Well?"

"Jennings!" Ferris' voice took on a high-pitched impudence. "Get the men back on their mounts. I want us moving again."

"All right," said Jennings with a sigh.

"Someone put out that fire," continued Ferris. "And anyone who tries to desert, I want them shot. Do you understand?"

Jennings shook his head and ignored the last remark from his captain. He began barking orders for men to get back on their mounts. Dee and Kylee were hoisted back up onto the backs of horses. Dee rode with Ferris and Kylee with Jennings.

The militia men re-mounted their horses. Four torches were lit, two at the front of the column and two at the rear.

Ferris was quiet. He was down twelve men right now and was taking it as a personal affront that they were gone. Dee did not sense any concern for their wellbeing from him, only anger at them for leaving. Riley ordering him around in front of his men could not have helped his mood much.

The horsemen at the head of the column came to a sudden stop, and Ferris's horse almost collided with the horse in front of him. "What's going on up there," Ferris barked.

Dee moved her head to get a better look around captain

Ferris' thin frame. The flickering torchlight illuminated a lone figure on the road, not even fifty yards ahead of them. At Jennings' order, two militia riders tapped their heels gently into the sides of their horses to coax them forward slowly. The figure ahead looked straight at them. He held something in both hands.

Dee could barely see him, but there was a familiarity about this guy standing in the dark on a broken asphalt road and showing no fear in the face of a Free Militia patrol. As the two mounted militia soldiers drew closer, the figure became fully illuminated by the torch they carried. He was a dark-skinned man, wearing a dark poncho. The familiarity she felt made sense now. She had seen this man before, back at Martin's Ferry. This was the guy Ian said was shadowing them. The same guy who they suspected alerted the Free Militia to their presence there. That would explain why he showed no fear if he was one of theirs.

"Get out of the road!" barked one of the mounted soldiers. "Militia patrol moving through."

The cloaked man looked up at the men on horseback but said nothing and made no move to get off the road. Dee found it strange that none of the militiamen had recognized him yet. Not even the captain.

"I said move!"

Riley trotted up next to Ferris. "What the hell are you doing?"

"There's a man on the road," Ferris said.

"One man? Run him down, this is probably an ambush."

Ferris urged his horse forward and Dee had to squeeze

tight around his chest to avoid falling. He joined his two men, conversing with the cloaked man. "Mister, this is Free Militia Territory and you're obstructing a Free Militia patrol. Unless you want to get cut down where you stand, I suggest you move. Now!"

"Nah.." the cloaked man finally responded. "I don't think I will." He had a calm, easy drawl. For a moment, Dee thought maybe he was even enjoying this standoff.

Ferris pulled a pistol from a leg holster and pointed it at the cloaked man. "My name is Captain Elijah Ferris. I'm ordering you in the name of Silas Bray, Commander of the Free Militia to step aside."

The cloaked man let out a loud howl. Dee thought he was screaming in pain, but then realized it was a loud laugh from deep in his gut. "Man, you boys seen too many war movies from back in the day." The cloaked man locked eyes with Ferris, and his face turned serious. "And you ain't no Captain. You just some punk playin' soldier and pushin' folks around."

"You've got three seconds." Ferris' voice turned hard. This man was clearly getting under his skin, but there was also a hint of fear in his voice.

"Honestly, y'all seem like a friendly bunch of fascists. Do yourselves a favor." The cloaked man's eyes moved off Ferris and locked on Dee. "Turnaround, head back to your plantation, untie these two lovely ladies and leave them here." Dee felt a chill shoot up her spine. This guy was another flesh peddler.

Ferris laughed. "And why would we do that?"

"Because if you do, and if you do it now, without making

a fuss," the cloaked man flashed a pearly smile, "I'll let you live, all of you."

Ferris barked at the soldier to his right. "I'm done with this. He's just wasting my time, get rid of him!" He backed his horse up and turned back toward the rest of his men.

The militia soldier shrugged and aimed his pistol at the guy in the poncho. "You heard the man."

The crack of a round being fired echoed through the trees. Dee turned in the saddle to watch the cloaked man, waiting for him to crumble to the ground, dead. Instead, the soldier in front of him fell from his horse, completely limp. Two more rounds cracked out of the night causing another militia soldier to slump forward in his saddle. The cloaked man scrambled to the side of the road and disappeared into the brush.

The Free Militia column became a jumble of panicked men and horses. Ferris' head jerked left to right as he searched for the source of the fire that had just killed two of his men. His horse reared in panic, and Dee felt like she was slipping off the back. She tried to wrap her arms around Ferris' bird-like chest, but he shrugged as he turned the horse, and she lost her grip. She slipped off the rear of the horse and landed hard enough to knock the breath from her lungs.

She wheezed, struggling to inhale against panic and pain. Ferris and his horse had bolted back up the road. She could not see Riley and assumed he had already taken cover.

Another crack came from behind the trees and knocked Ferris off his horse. He fell backward, but the horse never even looked back to see its rider drop like a sack of potatoes. It just kept galloping away from danger.

Finally catching her breath, Dee looked around, desperately searching for Kylee. Something bright lit up the sky. It was a flare; she guessed a few hundred feet up. It hung in the sky like a small artificial sun, barely floating downward. It had been fired by the remaining militia. Their foes were using the darkness to their advantage and the militia soldiers were doing what they could to even up the playing field.

Kylee slipped from Jennings' horse and landed on her feet. As soon as she hit the ground, she ran. Jennings spun the big animal and went straight at Kylee. He reached a hand out to snatch her up back onto the saddle. Dee tried to run toward her but fell to the ground from a sharp pain in her knee.

Jennings was on Kylee now, trying to grab her coat. A dark figure appeared out of some nearby trees; it was the man in the poncho. He swung something in his hand like a baseball bat and knocked the horseman from his saddle. Jennings tried to get up, but the cloaked man hit him with the butt of what Dee could now see was a rifle.

The cloaked man mounted the now riderless horse and offered a hand to Kylee. To Dee's surprise, she took it. "Kylee, no!" she screamed in panic. She tried again to move in toward the little girl, but barely got two steps before the pain in her knee brought her down. Dee did not know who these people were. For all she knew, they were worse than the Free Militia.

They rode past Dee and disappeared into the trees

behind her. The remaining Free Militia had scattered. Now Kylee and the cloaked man had ridden off. Alone on the broken asphalt road, unable to walk, Dee watched the flare inch its way down from the dark sky. She figured she only had a few minutes of light before she would be alone in total darkness.

A puff of dirt spouted a few yards away. Then another closer followed by a third farther off. Someone was shooting, maybe not at her, but that would not matter when she got hit. It came from uphill, from the fleeing militia. Maybe they were trying to mount a counterattack.

A quick answer came from the tree behind her as several rifles sounded off at the same time. Dee was now in a crossfire between two battling factions. She could not move. All she could do was get as low to the ground as possible and hope no one started aiming at her. More fire came from the hillside. Then there was silence.

A loud barrage of fire erupted from behind her, lighting up the hillside where the militiamen were positioned. Something burst from the trees behind her. It was the cloaked man. He ran low toward her, reached out his hand and said, "Let me help you."

Dee nodded and grabbed the cloaked man's hand. He picked her up and lifted her over his shoulder in a fireman's carry, one hand carrying his rifle, the other holding her in place by the legs to keep her from falling off. Round impacts followed them straight to the tree line. He got her down behind a knoll hidden near a stand of trees before any of the rounds found their targets.

There was a group of men all laying prone behind the

same knoll and firing at what remained of the militia patrol. They all had what looked like binoculars strapped to their heads, which projected a green tinted light onto their eyes. Most had their headgear tipped up and out of the way, unused. Dee recognized these binocular-like things from the security men back at the Petros' compound. They were night vision goggles.

The cloaked man set her down gently and looked her over. When he touched her knee, she grimaced and let out a grunt of pain. "Looks like you twisted it bad. A torn ligament for sure."

Dee looked up at the man, who had now taken the hood off his poncho. "Who are you?"

"Washington," he said. "Sergeant Louis Washington."

"Sergeant?"

He nodded.

Dee's eyes narrowed. "What are you from some rival survivalist group?"

Sergeant Washington's lips curled into an amiable smile. "No ma'am," he laughed. "United States Army."

23 – Changing Sides

The light flickered in Stephan Schubert's eyes in rhythm with the *click, click, click,* from the button on the back of the penlight. "Any nausea?" asked the Doc.

"No," Schubert said.

"What about headaches? Dizziness?"

"Nothing." Schubert couldn't control the annoyance in his voice. It had been a couple of days since he let that guy Hammond butt stroke him in the face. He played up the injury at first, but now he was tired of the whole thing and wanted to get back out on patrol. It didn't help that this *Doc*, whose only qualification was that he used to be an assistant team trainer at Southern Oregon University, kept walking down his concussion protocol checklist. It seemed to be the only thing the guy knew anything about. Schubert missed the old days when the Corpsman would give him the once over and prescribe Motrin so he could get back to playing Call of Duty.

"How are you sleeping?"

"Fine."

"Okay. Now I want you to stand up . . . that's it . . . and balance yourself on the left foot."

"What is this, a sobriety test? Jesus, Doc, I'm fine. Not even a headache, and it's been two days. Can I go now? I've got to get my guys ready to go out on patrol tomorrow."

The Doc nodded. "Well, no signs of concussion, as far

as I can tell. You lost a tooth, but that seems to be the extent of it."

"Anything else?" Schubert said.

"If you feel any of the symptoms I mentioned, headache, nausea, trouble sleeping, loss of balance . . ."

"Just give me your damn checklist so I don't have to hear you recite it again."

The Doc looked insulted. "Sergeant Schubert, this is serious. An untreated concussion could . . ."

"Okay, okay," Schubert said with a dismissive wave of his hand. "If I experience so much as a hangover, I'll be right back here. We good?"

The Doc pursed his lips like he was about to speak, but just nodded. Schubert pulled back the canvas flap on the aid tent and left.

Once outside, he saw two of his guys, Freddy and Trent, coming straight for him. Before they could open their mouths, he asked, "Everything packed, horses prepped? I want to leave at first light tomorrow."

Trent looked at Freddy and said, "I guess he hasn't heard."

"Heard what?" asked Schubert.

Freddy took a breath and said, "The patrol is delayed a couple of days."

"Bullshit," Schubert said. "Why?"

"Silas Bray's coming here. The Lieutenant wants everyone getting the place ready," said Freddy. "He should be here by nightfall."

Schubert shook his head and looked skyward in frustration. Every one of these militia officers had their priorities backward. Captain Ferris was bad enough, but with him gone, his executive officer, Lieutenant Owensby, would be extra nervous. Why in the hell would you pause the patrol schedule, effectively making the whole camp deaf and blind, just two days after a marauder attack that nearly breached the place? He took a breath to calm himself. "All right, let's get to work."

***

Silas Bray squinted up at the hydroponic growing racks, listening with lukewarm interest as a technician rattled off stats and setbacks. The man explained that recent disruptions—most notably the attack—would delay yield by a few months. But, thanks to a staggered planting strategy across rack tiers, he promised the farm could recover within two cycles.

Bray gave a distracted nod, more focused on adjusting his leather gloves than absorbing the technical jargon.

Schubert stood off to the side, arms folded. He still struggled to call this man *General*. Before the bombs, Silas Bray was a real estate speculator with a podcast, a penchant for Civil War cosplay, and a YouTube channel peddling conspiracy theories. Sure, he'd predicted the collapse—so had half the preppers in the Pacific Northwest. Bray just happened to have the land, the voice, and the audacity to claim command when everything fell apart.

Trailing behind Bray was Lieutenant Owensby, nervously gripping the strap of the General's satchel like it was a bomb about to go off. The young officer did his best to fill every silence with answers to questions Bray hadn't even asked. Schubert got some quiet satisfaction watching the blood drain from Owensby's face whenever he was stumped.

After the obligatory farm tour, Bray stepped out into the sunlight, blinking like a man who hadn't seen it in years—because, until recently, he hadn't. Schubert followed, flanked by Owensby and two junior troopers in mismatched fatigues.

Bray stopped abruptly. "Lieutenant," he said, "when do you expect Captain Ferris to return?"

Owensby froze. "Tomorrow, sir. Just before sundown."

Bray sighed. "A shame. I'll be gone by then—first light. I had hoped to speak with him. Tell Ferris I'm sorry our paths didn't cross. And remind him that he's always welcome at the Capitol. The Colonel and Mrs. Ferris would be ecstatic to host him."

Schubert fought back a grin. Bray always said *the Capitol* like it was Washington, D.C., not a half-built settlement surrounding his ranch in southern Oregon.

Owensby stiffened and said, "Yes sir. I will relay that information upon his arrival. As soon as he arrives."

Why couldn't he just say 'I'll tell him'? Schubert wondered. The kid acted like he was reciting from a teleprompter.

Bray didn't seem to notice—or care. He preferred officers who displayed nervous obedience rather than self-motivation and initiative.

"Very good," he said with a smile. "Now, let's get a look at those pens."

Schubert's jaw clenched at the word *pens*. The thought of those cages, constructed during Schubert's last patrol, where about a dozen children were being held, made him angry. Especially since he brought in two of the kids being held there. A knot formed in the pit of his stomach as he forced his anger deep down, out of sight.

"Right this way sir." Owensby motioned toward the pens."

Before they could move, the camp's First Sergeant, Tim Jefferson, jogged over, murmuring something in Owensby's ear. The young lieutenant's eyes widened like saucers.

"What is it, Lieutenant?" Bray asked, irritation sharp in his voice.

Owensby swallowed. "It's Mr. Riley, sir. He's returned… alone."

Bray's face didn't change. Not at first.

"Alone?" he echoed. "Where's the girl?"

Owensby didn't answer. But Schubert could see it in his face—Riley had failed.

Bray turned, slowly, toward the camp's gate. His lips were drawn tight, as if the wind had been knocked out of him. "Then I suppose," he said coldly, "we *will* be staying until Ferris returns."

Schubert said nothing. But inside, a single thought pulsed like a heartbeat: *Good*

***

"I don't know who they were," Riley said, his voice ragged from exhaustion. He looked like he hadn't slept in days—his clothes dusty, his face streaked with road grime. "They hit us fast, coordinated. I rode through the night to get here."

He took a breath, steadying himself before continuing. "I need men. More than that patrol you sent. We need to regroup and go back out—immediately."

Silas Bray stood in silence for a moment, his eyes fixed on Riley like he was evaluating a faulty piece of machinery. "What about the girl?" he asked at last, voice clipped and low.

"They took her," Riley said, jaw tight. "And the woman—Delilah Rosemont."

Bray muttered a curse under his breath, barely audible. His composure cracked, just for a moment. Then he turned to look out at the compound, as if the answers were hidden in the mountains beyond the fence line.

Schubert, standing nearby, felt the weight of the moment settle on his shoulders. *Hammond,* he thought. *This has his fingerprints all over it.* He didn't say it aloud. Not yet.

Bray's voice cut through the silence. "Find out who did this, Patrick. I want names. And when you have them... I want fire."

Riley just nodded, too tired to respond. His eyes burned with something colder than anger—humiliation.

And Schubert quietly began calculating how much longer this so-called "Free Militia" could keep pretending it had control

***

"Pat," crackled the voice from the PRC-117 radio, distorted by static and distance. "We can't delay Phase Two trials any longer. Have you identified and segregated viable candidates from the subjects acquired by our allies?"

Riley pressed the handset to his mouth, waited a beat to be sure the transmission was live, then responded in a measured tone. "Affirmative. Screening is complete. Viable candidates have been isolated and are ready for transport. Over."

"Good," George Petros replied, his voice cool and crisp despite the poor connection. "Have the Militia prepare them for transfer. I want them in our possession as soon as possible."

"I'll request another escort from their command," Riley said. "But we'll need to reroute—longer path, less risk. Over."

"No," Petros cut in. "I'll be sending our own retrieval team."

Riley didn't respond right away. The silence on the line stretched just long enough to suggest understanding. Petros wasn't going to say it—not over an open channel—but Riley heard what wasn't being said: *The Militia had failed.* Petros no longer trusted them with cargo this valuable. And truth be told, Riley didn't either.

"Understood," Riley said finally. "We'll have the candidates staged and ready for pickup at dawn. Over."

"Good. One more thing," Petros added, his tone shifting slightly. "I want you to remain embedded with the Militia for a few more weeks. There's additional tasking I'd like you to oversee. Details to follow."

Riley clicked the handset once in acknowledgment, then let the silence hang as the static faded.

He didn't need to ask what "additional tasking" meant. Not here. Not with Free Militia ears still too close for comfort.

***

"He's going to need double the number of test subjects for his next phase," Riley said.

Silas Bray stroked his beard, the tips yellowed from pipe smoke. "How many?"

"Ten more," Riley replied. "Viable."

Bray arched an eyebrow. "Viable?" The word came slowly, as if he were tasting it for the first time.

"I won't bore you with the science," Riley said, folding his hands behind his back. "And frankly, I'm not a geneticist. But the on-site technicians have tested each candidate for a set of traits Mr. Petros's team believes are critical—resilience, certain neural markers, immunological responses. About half pass."

"So we need twenty to get ten."

"I'd feel more comfortable gathering twenty-five. Hedge our bets."

"And those who don't pass?"

"Mr. Petros leaves that to your discretion. They're of no use to us."

Off to the side, Schubert leaned toward First Sergeant Jefferson.

"What the hell are they talking about?" he muttered.

Jefferson kept his voice low. "You've seen the pens since you got back, haven't you?"

Schubert's stomach turned. He had. The children in the wire enclosures. What he'd tried not to admit to himself was now undeniable. They were talking about *kids*.

Bray turned his head slightly toward Lieutenant Owensby. "What have we been doing with the ones who don't pass?"

Owensby stiffened. "Most have been reunited with their families, sir."

Bray's eyes narrowed. "Most?"

"Just a handful couldn't be placed," Owensby admitted, a sheen of sweat forming at his temple.

Bray waited. "And the rest?"

Owensby hesitated. "There's… a market, sir."

The room fell silent.

Schubert stared. His heart thumped in his chest as he tried to process what he was hearing. *A market. They're selling them.*

He looked to Bray, expecting fury. Instead, the old man gave a thoughtful nod.

"Sounds like a win-win," Bray said.

Schubert felt something break inside him.

Everything Dee and Ian had said was true. The Free Militia weren't protectors or rebuilders. They were kidnappers, traffickers—just another warlord's army with a different flag.

"So," Bray continued, tone almost cheerful, "where do we get twenty-five more candidates for Mr. Riley?"

Owensby stepped forward like a boy giving a book report. "A few days' ride to the southwest, sir. Just outside our border. There's a riverside settlement along the Klamath they call Martin's Ferry."

Schubert's breath caught. *Martin's Ferry.*

Bray tapped his fingers on the edge of the table. "I'll order a company to march down from the Capitol. Owensby, you'll lead the operation. Time to get your feet wet."

"Thank you, sir." Owensby practically beamed. "They'll be a welcome addition to our personnel here."

Bray shook his head. "No. Your men here are stretched thin enough trying to defend against local threats. Let's not pretend the Mongrel attack was a pack of wanderers. You'll take new men. Your current garrison will handle escort duty for the viable candidates."

"Yes, sir," Owensby said, swallowing his disappointment.

Riley nodded silently beside him. The room's business moved on, but Schubert remained still. His pulse beat in his temples like a war drum.

Martin's Ferry. They're going to hit Martin's Ferry.

He thought of Marion and Henry, of the families who had already suffered enough. He thought of the kids. And he thought of Ian, somewhere out there, ready to burn the whole damn world down if this happened again.

Something had to be done. Someone had to stop it.

And if no one else would, it would be him.

***

After the meeting, Schubert made a beeline for the camp's First Sergeant, Tim Jefferson. "They won't let us play in this Martin's Ferry operation. That's bullshit."

Jefferson grinned, "No it's not. I know you Shube, you don't want any part of marching to a village full of people you've been dealing with for years and taking their kids. So let's cut the crap. Why don't you tell me what you *really* want."

Schubert exhaled. He'd known Jefferson for over a year now—long enough to know the man could see through a lie before you even opened your mouth. It's what made him good at his job.

"Fine," Schubert said. "I want to volunteer to escort the test subjects to the pickup site. Meet Riley's people."

Jefferson's grin widened. "Already done. I recommended you to the LT this morning. It's approved."

Schubert nodded. "I've got my team picked out."

"Good, I know you have a good feel for who you can trust."

Schubert looked Jefferson in the eye. "I do."

"Take care of those kids." Tim Jefferson took a step forward and shook Schubert's hand. "And take care of yourself Schube. It has been my honor."

Stephan gripped Jefferson's hand hard as brothers do, "Mine too Tim."

***

Stephan knew his guys. He knew which ones were

true believers, the ones that defined themselves by being part of the Free Militia, and everything they stood for. He knew which ones were there just for three meals a day and a cot to sleep in. And he knew which ones were there because they wanted to serve, to help people; the ones who, like him, were bothered by the direction the Free Militia was taking.

Stephan knew his men. He could sort them into types without effort: the diehard believers who saw the Free Militia as their sacred calling, the drifters who signed up for three meals and a place to sleep, and then the ones like him—men who thought they were helping, only to watch the mission curdle into something darker. He only needed four. A patrol couldn't leave the compound with fewer than five, and Stephan needed every one of them to be solid.

Trent and Freddy were no-brainers. He'd spent long nights on patrol with them, talking about everything under the sun. He knew their skill sets, their instincts. They were in.

George Ball, the new guy, was green and clumsy but had a conscience. Stephan liked that. He'd risk it.

The only question mark was Nikolai. Quiet, brooding. Not a believer, but too closed off to read. The only way to know was to test him.

"We're going out, first light," Stephan said when George finally made it to the briefing area. It was nothing more than a circle of old beach chairs and wood stumps in the corner of the compound, away from any buildings or tents, where they would go over their plans and patrol routes with the team before leaving. It was secluded enough that they could speak freely without being overheard, but open so that Stephan could be sure no one could approach without him seeing.

The four men nodded.

"How long?" asked Freddy, meaning how many days they would be on patrol.

Stephan hesitated. Once he said it, there would be no taking it back. He took a deep breath and let it out. "Take everything you can carry… we're not coming back."

Heads tilted and eyes widened. If he did not have their attention before, he did now. "What do you mean?" asked George. "Are we moving to the Capitol?"

Stephan shook his head. "I mean we're leaving the Free Militia. If you want out let me know now." He held his breath waiting for an answer. If any of them were not on board, he could not let them leave.

Nobody said anything, they just stared at him, vacantly. Stephan was not sure if that was a good or bad sign, but he was all in now, so he kept going. "You guys have seen those pens, right? I'm sure it bugged you to see kids locked up like that, and you must have wondered what they're in there for… right?"

Trent nodded slowly, then Freddy and George followed suit. Nikolai just stared into space not speaking or giving any indication of what he was thinking.

Stephan continued, "Those people in there are testing the kids for some kind of genetic markers."

"Markers for what?" asked Trent. Stephan knew he was asking out of more than curiosity; Trent had been a medical student before the bombs.

Stephan shrugged, "I don't know exactly. But the ones that have what they want are being sent away to this secret lab run by that guy Riley's boss."

"I never liked that guy," said Freddy. Stephan wasn't surprised. Freddy didn't like anyone until he got to know them. He said the same thing about Trent when he first showed up, now the two of them were inseparable.

"So what does that have to do with us?" asked Nikolai, speaking for the first time.

"We've been ordered to escort those kids that tested positive, to a rendezvous site with Riley's people. We're to hand the kids that tested positive over to them. The ones that don't we're supposed to take down to Rio Dell and sell them."

"That doesn't sound too hard," said Nikolai. "Why all the drama about leaving?"

For a moment, Stephan wished he had waited until he was outside the compound to have this conversation. That way he could get rid of Nikolai if he refused to buy into the plan. "Because we're not doing that. We're taking the kids as we've been ordered to, but not to Riley's people or to Rio Dell."

Freddy scrunched his forehead. "How many kids?"

"There's nine total," replied Stephan. "Five have the markers Riley's people are looking for."

"What are we supposed to do with nine kids?" Freddie asked.

"I'm not asking anyone to adopt here. There's a monastery that's managed to survive southeast of

Redding. I came across it a few years back on a long reconnaissance patrol. They take in kids, Long Winter orphans. They'll take these, and they'll treat them well. I've marked it on your map." Stephan pulled a folded map out from his jacket and handed it to Trent. "I want you to take them there, then you're on your own. Stay clear of Free Militia Territory, you know the penalty for desertion.

"Wait," said Trent, "what do you mean you want *us* to take them? What are you doing?"

"As soon as we're clear, I plan to break off and head toward Martin's Ferry. Bray has ordered a company from his ranch down here to help them take more kids. If I ride hard, I can get there day after tomorrow and hopefully warn them in time to evacuate."

George shifted nervously in his seat but didn't say anything. The others stared at Stephan, probing with their eyes.

"Look," said Stephan after an uncomfortable pause. "I know this is a big ask. That's why I wanted to put it to you before we left. You can all back out, I can find others if I need to. You guys are my preferred team. I would just ask for you to stay quiet." Stephan wondered if they believed any of what he just said.

"Fuck me," said Trent, letting out a long exhale. "I'm in."

"Same," said Freddy. "If I ever see Riley again, I might put one between his eyes."

George gave a nervous laugh. "I don't like the idea of handing over kids. I'll do it. But I swear, if you guys try to make me play babysitter…"

"You'll be fine," Freddy said. "You've got the softest face. Kids'll love you."

All eyes turned to Nikolai.

He gave a crooked smile. "I've been getting bored of this place anyway. Yeah. I'm in."

Stephan let out the breath he'd been holding. "Then we ride at first light. Load light, ride fast. And God help anyone who tries to stop us."

24 – The Search

A glint of metal caught Ian's eye. He crouched and pried at something wedged into a crack in the crumbling asphalt. After a few seconds of effort, he worked it free and held it up to the light. Brass. He blew off a layer of dust and recognized the familiar shape: a spent 7.62-millimeter casing.

It confirmed what the scene already suggested.

All around him were signs of a chaotic firefight—scattered shell casings, bullet holes in trees, horse tracks that crisscrossed the road like frantic brushstrokes, and the bloated bodies of fallen militia, now claimed by carrion birds. The Free Militia had been here—and from the looks of it, they'd been on the losing end.

Ian scanned the bodies. Ferris was among the dead, crumpled near the roadside like a discarded rag doll. But there was no sign of Dee or Kylee. Relief tempered the grimness of the scene.

He'd been trailing this patrol for days, ever since he parted ways with Henry and Marion the morning after their escape from the farm. The couple had turned back toward Martin's Ferry, eager to reunite with their children. Ian had watched them disappear downriver with a mix of hope and envy. They had their family back. He was still searching for his.

What he hadn't expected was to find the Free Militia

under attack—especially not in their own territory. But someone had hit this patrol hard. Whoever they were, they were organized and well-armed enough to take out nearly an entire twenty-man mounted unit.

Two distinct trails led away from the battlefield. One was a tight cluster of horse tracks heading north—survivors, most likely. The other was a smaller set of footprints, spaced far apart, heading southwest. That group had been on foot.

Ian considered his options. The mounted group would be easier to track. And if Dee or Kylee were with them, he'd know soon enough.

He followed the horses.

The trail cut through the woods for a couple of miles before veering back onto the ruined road. Ian shook his head. Even after being ambushed, these idiots still hadn't learned to stay off the pavement.

Half a mile later, dark splotches dotted the asphalt. Blood. Ian followed it until he spotted what at first looked like a pile of rags shoved beneath a bush. As he neared, the shape resolved into a man's body, curled up beside the road. The shirt around his abdomen was soaked in dried blood—gut shot, by the looks of it. Ian guessed he'd been dead at least a day.

There wasn't much anyone could've done for him—not without training, not without supplies. Still, leaving a wounded man to die like this said everything Ian needed to know about the militia's discipline. Or lack thereof.

Then it clicked.

The man had been left behind to die. If Kylee had been

with them, this soldier would still be breathing. Free Militia or not, she wouldn't have walked away from someone in pain—not if she had a choice.

Ian stood. That was the clue he'd needed.

Kylee wasn't with the mounted survivors. Which meant she was with the other group—the ones who'd taken down the militia. The ones on foot.

And if Ian knew Dee, she'd be right there beside her.

He turned on his heel and jogged back toward the site of the ambush. He'd lost half a day chasing the wrong trail. But now he knew the direction. Southwest. He set off at a run, heart thumping with new urgency.

He was getting closer.

***

Ian had tracked the group he now believed held Dee and Kylee throughout the day, his eyes scanning the ground for signs—scuffed earth, snapped branches, a print left too clean to be natural. As the sun dipped behind the treetops, he was reluctant to stop. Every minute counted. But the light faded quickly, and without it, even a seasoned tracker would struggle. Ian knew pushing on in the dark would only get him turned around.

He found a thick pine and bedded down beneath its canopy, where the forest floor was padded with dry needles. The smell was clean and earthy, and for a brief moment, it reminded him of camping trips as a kid. He didn't let the nostalgia linger. He pulled his coat tighter, chewed a strip of jerky, and tried to ignore the ache in his legs and the worry grinding at his gut.

He woke before dawn, cold but determined. A sliver of gray light filtered through the trees, and by the time the first real rays touched the forest floor, he was moving again.

For hours, he followed the faint impressions of his quarry. But by midday, the signs vanished. The ground grew firmer, the forest thicker. Whatever subtle trail he had been following had simply evaporated. He crouched, scanned the underbrush, tried doubling back—but nothing. He wasn't good enough to pick it up again. Not here.

Frustrated, Ian stood and looked southwest.

If they had gotten away, they would head somewhere safe. Somewhere familiar.

Martin's Ferry wasn't far.

He adjusted the straps of his pack, took one last look at the direction the trail had vanished, and set off. He didn't know if he'd find them there—but it was his best shot.

***

"Ian!" the squealing voice was Anna. The little girl ran to him, arms wide open. She crashed into him with an embrace as tight as her eight-year-old arms could squeeze. He used one arm to keep the rifle on his shoulder and returned the hug with the other. Heath was close behind, still silent, but slowly waving his hand. Also with him were two other boys that he recognized as Ben and Jimmy, Charles' and Carole's sons.

Ian waved back, "Hey guys. Where are your parents?"

"They're right up there," Anna uncoupled from the tight embrace to point up the hill where Henry and Marion were waving. He knew they would not be far off. They would never let either of their kids out of their sight again.

By the time he had closed the distance with Henry and Marion, Case and Carole joined them.

"Have any of you seen Dee or Kylee come this way," Ian said, getting right to the point.

"No, I'm sorry," Case said. "And if anyone in Martin's Ferry had seen our little messiah, I'm sure we would have heard."

"How about a group of armed strangers traveling nearby?"

Marion asked, "What happened Ian? We thought they were with the militia patrol."

Ian shook his head. "No, that patrol was ambushed about thirty miles north of here. I tracked a foot mobile group as far as I could but lost the trail. They took the girls."

"Marauders?" Carole asked with a horrified shudder.

Ian pursed his lips and exhaled loudly. "Maybe. But these guys took on a twenty-man mounted Free Militia patrol. And from what I saw, got the better of them. If I had to make a guess, I would say there were about seven, eight sets of tracks. That means there were five or six fighters if you account for Dee and Kylee. I could be wrong, but I think these guys are something more than your typical marauders."

"I'm not sure if that is good or bad," Case said.

"Me neither," Ian said. "Coming back here was a shot in

the dark, but I didn't know what else to do."

"Carole," Case said. "Can you ask Clarence to prepare the cot in his back room for Ian?"

"Of course," said Carole.

"Thank you," Ian said. "But I won't be staying. I've got to keep looking."

"Where are you going to look?" asked Marion.

"Ian," Case said. "You said yourself that you lost the trail and that coming here was a shot in the dark. Are you just going to wander around hoping to find a clue?"

Ian had no response. Case was right. He was at a loss about what to do next.

"You look exhausted," Case said. "Doesn't it make sense to rest up and maybe come up with a plan rather than stumble around in a half-conscious state? You'll collapse or make a mistake that will get you killed. What good would that do for Kylee and Dee?"

Ian nodded. Maybe a good night's sleep was just what he needed to think of something, some clue or idea, that his mind was just too tired to think of right now. Besides, the cot in Clarence's back room sounded too inviting to pass up.

Case continued. "We'll put all of our heads together tonight and see what we can come up with."

"Okay," Ian said. "Just one night though."

"Very good," Case said.

***

"Wait, wait," Henry said as he passed a bottle of Maker's

Mark whisky to his wife Marion. Clarence had dug the bottle out of the back room, which he traded from a group of people passing through for a good pair of hiking boots and some socks. "We'll be spinning our wheels trying to figure out how to search the entire area. We need to figure out what these guys' motivation could be. Why did they take Dee and Kylee? If we think through that, maybe we can narrow down *where* they might take them."

"I hear you, Henry, but I have no idea who these guys are. I just know that they're excellent fighters, damn near professionals," Ian said. Clarence had arranged the chairs, everything from a recliner to a camp stool, in a circle around a large candle burning on a small table. Case, Henry, Marion, and of course, Clarence, were there batting around ideas. The whiskey served as a catalyst.

"I have to agree with Ian," Case said. "Without some knowledge of who these people are, how can we hazard a guess at their motives?"

"No, but, even the fact that they handled that Militia patrol so easily could be a clue as to who they might be," Henry said who was just drunk enough to keep pressing the point. "Ian, you're familiar with some of the warlords to the south. Who do you know that might have that capability and training?"

"No one," Ian said. "I haven't seen that kind of precision since . . ."

The door flew open, interrupting Ian, and a young man came in carrying a crossbow, one of the village lookouts. Martin's Ferry had a rotating schedule that all able-bodied residents took part in. "There's a militia soldier crossing the river."

"*A militia soldier?*" Case asked. "As in one?"

"Yes," the young man said. "Just him and his horse."

Clarence looked at Case, and asked, "What's one guy doing wandering around alone at night? I've never seen the Free Militia travel in anything less than a dozen."

"I don't know," Case said. "But we need to go find out." He turned to the young lookout. "Where is he now?"

"Coming in from the east. He should be here in about ten minutes."

25 – Allies

"Where are you taking us?"

Dee felt emboldened. They had been traveling through the night. It was late morning now, and despite all the previous night's excitement, she was growing tired and irritable.

"To a safe place," Louis said in a calm voice. "We'll talk more when we camp for the night."

Dee stopped in her tracks and glared at him, stubbornly. "I want to know where you're taking us before I take another step." These guys could force her to come along if they wanted to. But she got the feeling that was not what they were about.

"Look . . ." Louis paused, as if trying to remember something. "Dee, right?"

"That's right." Dee folded her arms impatiently.

"Look, Dee, it's not like I don't want to tell you. It's just that there's a lot of risk. It will all be clear in time. But believe me when I say it's a safe place. Safer than anywhere you've been since the bombs fell; I guarantee that. And when we get there, if you don't like it, you can leave."

"Not good enough."

"Come on, work with me here. We're not trying to keep you in the dark, it's just safer for all of us in case you fall into the wrong hands."

Dee kept quiet but didn't move.

Kylee glanced back and forth between them with a crooked smile on her face. *She knows something,* thought Dee. "They are taking us to see Dr. Schumacher," Kylee said at last.

Louis' face dropped, and he looked like he was about to say something but held back. He probably did not want to confirm what Kylee had just said.

"Really," Dee said, her irritability turned to excitement. "That's who we've been trying to find since we left the compound. How do you know her? Where is she now? How much farther?"

Louis shook his head, "We need to keep moving."

"He's right Dee," Kylee said, "It would be too dangerous for him to say where, at least not until we're safely out of Free Militia territory."

Dee cocked her head. "You know, don't you?"

"I can't help knowing," Kylee said. "But that doesn't mean we have to advertise where she and her people have moved to."

"How would telling me be advertising it?" Dee asked, getting frustrated again. "Literally everyone here knows but me."

Kylee shrugged. "Sorry Dee, it's just safer that way."

Louis laughed, then smiled at Kylee. "It's true what they say about you. Isn't it?"

"Some of what they say," Kylee said.

***

It was still night when Dee woke. The sky stretched

overhead, a seamless shroud of black—no stars, no moon. Overcast again. But at least now she knew it wouldn't last. It felt like the old days, when a cloudy night just meant rain, not doom.

Kylee was still asleep, curled tightly beneath a blanket, her face soft with exhaustion. Good. She needed rest.

Movement nearby caught Dee's eye. She tensed, heart skipping as she considered shouting to wake the camp. But then her eyes adjusted—just a lone figure pacing with slow, deliberate steps. One of the night watches.

She exhaled and stood, brushing off the blanket. Sleep wasn't coming back. Might as well stretch her legs.

As she neared the sentry, she recognized the silhouette. Sergeant Washington.

"Couldn't sleep?" he said, slicing into an apple with his field knife. He offered her a slice.

She took it without hesitation, biting in with a loud crunch. Juice flooded her mouth, sharp and sweet. "Where'd you get this?" she asked around a mouthful.

Louis grinned. "You don't think the Free Militia's the only bunch with indoor farming skills, do you?"

Dee smiled and took another slice when he offered. "Guess not."

The night was cool, the air crisp. She breathed it in slowly, savoring the clean mountain scent. "Are you really with the Army?" she asked.

"Yeah, you could say that."

"Are there others? Besides your team here?"

"Oh, yeah," Louis said. "I won't get into numbers, but we're not the last ones."

"And you're assigned to protect Dr. Schumacher?"

Louis laughed, low and easy. "Assigned is a strong word. We're survivors, just like you. We found her people. They needed help. We had the training and nowhere else to be. Plus," he added, "they had chow."

"How'd you find them? Was it luck, or did you know about them?"

The question changed his expression. His usual warmth gave way to something quieter, heavier.

"Luck," he said. "All of it."

He looked down, then out at the dark trees. The silence stretched until Dee knew not to interrupt.

"We'd just come out of the field. High-mountain training—survival stuff, horse work, rock climbing. The real deal. We were due to head back to Kentucky. I got stuck with cleanup duty, making sure our gear was packed out. I was pissed at the time... but it saved my life."

He paused, chewing the memory.

"Afterward, when we figured out what happened... we made our way down with the Marines who ran the training. We stuck with their CO until he got killed. Then we followed his XO—a Major. Eventually made our way to Crescent City. Heard rumors of a community there. That's where we found Dr. Schumacher and her people."

"And the men here tonight?" Dee asked.

"Some of them were with me," Louis said. "The rest, we trained from scratch. Civilians mostly. But smart. Tough. Good fighters. We've made it work."

Dee opened her mouth to ask more, but Kylee stirred behind them, sitting bolt upright. Her voice was urgent.

"We've got to go."

Dee turned. "What is it?"

"We need to go to Martin's Ferry," Kylee said, standing quickly, already scanning the area as if she were the one on watch. "Pack your things. They need us."

"Wait, Kylee, slow down—"

But Kylee turned to Louis. "They need you too. Get your men up."

Louis raised a brow. "Hold on, little lady. We've got a chain of command here, and I'm not—"

"You don't understand," Kylee said, stepping toward him. "There's no time. They need you now. You have to come with me."

Her voice had changed—not frantic, not demanding, but filled with something else entirely. Certainty.

Louis glanced at Dee. "She always like this?"

Dee nodded. "When she says go, you go."

Louis exhaled and muttered under his breath. "All right. Let's move." He turned toward the sleepers and started shouting orders. "Up and armed, boys! We've got a mission!"

Within minutes, the camp was coming to life.

Kylee just stood in the center, watching the treeline—already looking far ahead of everyone else

26 – Warning

Ian recognized Stephan Schubert the moment he rode into view. Even in the fading light, there was no mistaking the man who'd let him escape the Free Militia's labor camp. But this wasn't the sharp-eyed squad leader he remembered. This Schubert was gaunt, sunburned, and hollow-eyed—drained in every sense of the word.

"What the hell are you doing here?" snapped Robbie, one of the younger men who had taken up night watch in Martin's Ferry. "Pretty ballsy showing up alone."

"There's a Free Militia company headed this way," Schubert said, voice hoarse from the road.

"Bullshit," Marion spat before anyone else could speak. Her voice was hard, cutting. She stepped forward, eyes narrowed with fury. "You're one of them. What's your game?"

There was no mistaking the loathing in her tone. Marion and Henry had every reason to hate the Free Militia—after what they'd done to their children, and to so many others. The crowd gathered fast, angry murmurs growing louder.

"I had a head start," Schubert said. He swayed slightly in the saddle. "But they're coming. A couple days out, maybe less. You don't have long."

"Long for what?" asked Case, his voice steady and low, a grounding presence amid the rising tension.

"To get out," Schubert said simply. "To pack up and

evacuate. They're coming for your kids."

That brought a collective intake of breath. Eyes widened. Muscles tensed. But then someone spoke.

"You expect us to believe that?" said a big man in stained coveralls. Ian didn't know his name, but the intent behind his words was clear. "Give me ten minutes with him in Clarence's basement. I'll get the truth out of him."

More voices agreed. The crowd surged forward.

Ian stepped between Schubert and the nearest men before anyone could lay hands on him.

"Stop!" Ian shouted. "Just—hold on."

He raised both hands, turning slowly to face the others.

"Look, I get it. You don't trust him. Hell, I wouldn't either if I were in your shoes. But hear me out. This man didn't just let me walk away from that farm. He helped me. Helped *us*—me, Henry, Marion. He risked everything to make sure we got out."

Henry had joined the group and nodded reluctantly. "That part's true," he muttered. "Doesn't mean I like it. Doesn't mean I trust him."

"I'm not asking you to trust him," Ian said. "I'm just asking you to listen. That's all."

A hush fell over the crowd. Case stepped forward again, calm and reasonable as always. "That sounds fair," he said. "Let's hear what the man has to say. Then we'll decide what to do."

Schubert opened his mouth—but didn't speak. His eyes unfocused, and he staggered. Then he collapsed, knees buckling.

Ian caught him before he hit the ground.

"Doc?" he called over his shoulder.

Case was already moving. He knelt beside the unconscious man, fingers at the pulse in Schubert's neck. "He's dehydrated. Severely. And looks like he hasn't eaten or slept properly in days."

Clarence stepped forward. "Want to use the back room again?"

"Please."

Ian nodded and hooked his arms under Schubert's shoulders. Another man stepped in to grab the legs.

"On three," Ian said. "One, two, three—"

They lifted Schubert and carried him toward Clarence's shop as the villagers parted, watching silently. Some still looked skeptical. Others, worried. A few already glanced at the treeline beyond town, as if expecting riders to crest the ridge at any moment.

Ian didn't blame them. Because this time, the warning felt real.

***

When Schubert woke, he looked confused. His eyes wandered, then settled on the intravenous fluid bag hastily hung from a hook on the ceiling with a line running down into his left arm.

"Doc," Ian said, calling over his back shoulder into the main room while keeping one eye on Schubert. "He's awake."

Case entered the room, followed by Marion Wallace and Clarence. "How are you feeling, young man?" asked Case.

"Like dogshit run over by a wagon wheel," Schubert said. "But better than when I came in. How long have I been out?"

"Approximately twenty-six hours."

Schubert shot up in bed. "Oh shit. We've got to get you folks moving, they're not far behind. Have you started packing?"

"We're not about to leave our home because you tell us to," Marion said. "You need to explain to us the real reason you're here. What is it the Free Militia wants with Martin's Ferry? Why do you need our people to leave?"

"Anyone with kids needs to pack up and leave right now," Schubert said.

"What the hell do our kids have to do with it?" Marion said. The Free Militia had taken her kids once. Ian guessed she would fight to the death before letting that happen again.

"Look," Schubert said. "I don't have the full plan. I just know that Silas Bray is working with some scientists, the same people who are looking for that little girl that came through here a few weeks ago. They want pre-teen children to give them a blood test. If they pass the test, they want to take those kids with them back to their headquarters, wherever that is."

"I can tell you," Ian said, "he's right about these guys that the Free Militia has partnered up with. I met a dude named Riley who works for George Petros." Ian saw the look of recognition in Case and Marion's eyes at the mention of the billionaire entrepreneur celebrity. "These are the same guys Dee and Kylee were running from."

"You say the militia is coming here to take children," Case said. "For what purpose?"

"I'm not clear on that," Schubert said. "I just know they want ten kids, and they're coming here to get them. If they can find ten to pass their test."

Case nodded. "You must understand, Sergeant, this is a little farfetched. What would they need to administer a blood test for? What are they trying to find?"

"You're asking the wrong guy, Mr.—" Schubert started.

"Doctor!" Marion grumbled.

"Okay," Schubert said. "You're asking the wrong guy, Doc. You might understand what they're looking for, but I sure don't. It's all above my paygrade, anyway. I just know they are coming, and they want to take ten kids with them."

"Case," Marion said. "They had an enclosure where they kept about a dozen children at their farm in recent weeks. That could be linked to what the Sergeant is saying."

"It is," said Schubert. "They say they need more."

"Those poor kids," said Marion, "I wish we could have gotten them out. Have they already been sent to this guy Riley's people?"

"As far as the Free Militia knows. In reality, they're on their way to a monastery with some friends of mine."

Marion squeezed Schubert's arm. "Well done, you were always one of the good guys back there."

"Does that mean you believe him?" asked Clarence.

"All I know is, this guy was one of the ones that did what he could to help the farmers and other laborers. If I was to believe any militia man, it would be him."

Case looked at Marion and rubbed the stubble on his

chin. "This is a lot to ask people to do based on the statement of one man. A man whose loyalties are questionable."

"I agree with the Doc," said Clarence. "He could be trying to flush people out. Maybe they figure it'll be easier to grab the kids on neutral ground instead of riding into Martin's Ferry where we might have an advantage."

Schubert let out an exasperated breath. "If Silas Bray wants your kids, there's nothing you can do to stop it. If you try, he'll burn you out and take the kids anyway. You've got to run."

"We'll have to put it to a vote," Case said. "Give people the information and let each family decide for themselves."

"We don't have that kind of time," pleaded Schubert.

"This is not the Free Militia, Sergeant," Case said. "We do not dictate to people what to do. That's not something I would do even if I thought I could. Clarence, can you get the word out? Tell people to gather in front of the trading post as soon as they can."

"You got it Doc," said Clarence before leaving the room to get the word out.

"What will you do?" whispered Marion to Case.

"I don't know," Case said. "I have no family left. But, I can't see sending all these people out there without a Doctor. I guess I'll have to see how many opt to leave. What about you?"

"The Militia took my kids once. Never again. I'm going to take my family and run."

***

Case stood atop the wooden platform outside the Martin's Ferry trading post, addressing the gathered crowd of sixty men, women, and children. Lanterns hung from hooks, casting flickering halos across weathered faces as Case calmly relayed everything they'd learned from Sergeant Schubert. He took care not to editorialize. His role was to inform, not persuade. If people were going to leave their homes, they needed to do so with clear minds—and without coercion.

Schubert stood beside him, answering questions when asked, his voice hoarse but steady. Case occasionally stepped in if the tension escalated—particularly when the crowd turned accusatory. Emotions ran hot: confusion, skepticism, and quiet panic rippled through the assembly. The idea that the Free Militia might return to take their children sounded absurd—until someone inevitably mentioned Heath and Anna. Their story was still fresh, still raw. That alone gave Schubert's warning weight.

Within the hour, most of the town had made up their minds. The few who insisted on staying did so out of fear, stubborn pride, or the belief that the Free Militia would pass them by. But most, especially parents, began quietly preparing to leave.

"You ought to go with them," Schubert said to Ian, pulling him aside as the crowd began to disperse. "They still want that girl, and chances are they'll try to get some info out of you."

"I have no idea who took them," Ian said. "I found the ambush site and tried to track them but lost the trail."

"Doesn't matter," Schubert said. "They'll work you over anyway just to make sure you're not lying. You not having anything to give them will just make it harder on you."

Ian knew Schubert was right. "I don't think they'll go any easier on a deserter who leaked their plans."

"They won't, I know I wouldn't. I'll go with these folks for a while, then break off."

"Where will you go after that?" Ian asked.

Schubert shook his head. "I don't know. I can't go back home. Free Militia are all over southern Oregon. Can't go south, it's too hot. I'll go east. There's wilderness and open sky that way. Maybe find a quiet corner and disappear."

"Stay clear of the roads. Marauders like to hang out anywhere that has pavement. I know you militia boys are used to going where you want in an armed patrol, but you're alone now. It'll be a tough slog over the mountains."

"I've been surviving in the woods since I could walk," Schubert said with a dry smile. "I'll be fine. Just need to stay frosty."

A shout broke the air, sharp and frantic. Ian turned toward the far end of the camp, where a cluster of canvas tents had become a makeshift village. People were gathering, murmuring anxiously. The mood shifted like a rising wind.

Ian moved quickly toward the noise. Schubert followed.

By the time they reached the crowd, Case was already there, speaking in a measured voice to someone obscured by the growing wall of townsfolk. Ian pushed his way forward—and froze.

Three armed men stood facing Case.

They wore the green and brown field uniforms of the Free Militia.

"Damn," Schubert muttered beside him. "We're too late. They're here."

27 — Ultimatum

"How do we know it's not just the three of you?" a voice called out from the crowd.

The Free Militia sergeant smirked, brought two fingers to his mouth, and let out a sharp whistle. Across the river, shadows moved. Then came the clatter of hooves. One by one, mounted soldiers emerged from the treeline. Ian counted at least two hundred—maybe more still hidden beneath the canopy.

He turned to look for Schubert, but the militia deserter was gone. Ian didn't blame him. Schubert had delivered his warning. Now, survival was his own priority.

"That's half our company," the militia sergeant announced, jabbing a thumb at the opposite bank. "The rest are positioned on the ridgeline south of your little town. Nowhere to run. Nowhere to hide. All we want is a simple blood test."

"You want to take our kids!" someone shouted.

"Just ten of them," the sergeant replied with a shrug. "You've got plenty."

"We'll fight you!" another voice yelled.

"No," Case said. His tone cut through the clamor—calm, loud, authoritative. "They'd wipe us out and take what they want anyway."

"Smart man," the sergeant said approvingly.

"There has to be another way," Case said. "Look, I'm a

doctor. What exactly are you looking for?"

The sergeant shrugged. "Beats me. Orders are orders."

Henry Wallace appeared from behind a tent, raising a hunting rifle. "You took my kids once. You won't do it again."

The sergeant lifted his left hand, then dropped it in a quick chop. Henry jerked and fell backward. A blossom of blood spread across his chest.

"Henry!" Marion shrieked, dropping to her knees beside him.

Ian tore open Henry's shirt to reveal a bullet wound dead-center. "Put pressure on the wound!" Case commanded. Marion, trembling, pressed both hands to Henry's chest.

Ian stood and faced the militia sergeant. "Snipers?"

The sergeant spat tobacco juice into the dirt and grinned.

"What's wrong with Daddy?" a small voice cried. Anna and Heath stood near their tent. Anna sobbed. Heath, pale and wide-eyed, said nothing.

"Come on," Ian said to the sergeant. "Is this really who you are? Shooting unarmed civilians? Taking people's kids? We're all Americans."

The sergeant raised his voice for the whole village to hear. "Orders come straight from Silas Bray. Nothing can stop this. You have two hours to bring us all children between the ages of four and twelve. Three adult escorts only. If we think you're holding out, we come in—all of us."

He and his men turned their horses and rode off.

Two villagers carried Henry into his family's tent, Case

following close behind. The crowd stood frozen in stunned silence.

Ian's instincts screamed for him to disappear. A few weeks ago, he would have. But Martin's Ferry had sheltered Kylee. These people had stood with her, protected her. He couldn't walk away now. Not when everything was on the line.

A young man spoke up. "We need to gather the kids."

"The hell we do," said Charles, voice sharp with emotion. "We need to sack up and fight."

"You saw what's across the river!" the young man snapped. "There's no way we can win."

"You don't have kids," said Tina, Travis's mother. "I'd rather die than hand over my son or daughter."

"They're only taking ten," said Gwyneth, an older woman wrapped in a wool blanket. "Is it worth sacrificing the rest of us for ten? They're not going to hurt them."

"They took Heath and Anna and sold them to a pair of perverts," Charles said, voice tight with fury. "Heath hasn't spoken since."

"Ten kids," Gwyneth insisted. "Think of the greater good."

"Jesus, Gwyneth," Carole said. "This isn't some ethics seminar. These are our children!"

"Maybe it'll be someone else's kid," Gwyneth muttered.

"What if they choose yours?" Carole snapped back.

Case emerged from the tent, wiping blood from his hands. All eyes turned to him.

"How is he?" Clarence asked.

Case exhaled. "He's alive—for now. But he won't last if

I can't get that bullet out. I don't have all the surgical instruments I need to go in and get it. Not to mention anesthesia. As for the rest of us... what have we decided?"

"We won't give up our kids," Charles said.

"Most of us won't," someone added.

Case nodded. "You understand what that means?"

"We're ready to fight," said Charles.

Ian stepped forward. "Oh no, you're not. Not against that." He pointed across the river. "That's not a fight—it's a slaughter."

"Ian," said Clarence. "You used to be a Marine, right?"

Ian nodded. "That was a lifetime ago."

"Then help us," Clarence said. "You know tactics, how to prepare."

"I know when we're outgunned. Maybe a dozen functioning weapons in the village? Crossbows? Knives? The militia has modern rifles, better range, better firepower. We wouldn't last five minutes."

"Then what do we do?" someone asked.

A voice cut in from the edge of the crowd.

"You don't worry about the snipers."

All heads turned. Stephan Schubert stepped into view, his overcoat stained with blood and dirt. He looked rough, but he grinned.

"They're gone," he said. "Took care of them."

"What?" Ian said. "How?"

"I know that lieutenant. Predictable prick. I knew exactly where he'd put them."

Clarence grinned. "Then maybe we've got a chance."

Case turned to him. "Clarence, maybe it's time to open

up your basement."

Clarence's smile widened.

28 — The Battle of Martin's Ferry

Clarence led Ian and Schubert down into the basement of the old ranger cabin that now served as Martin's Ferry's trading post. Charles followed close behind, along with two others—a man and woman in their thirties—both wearing the wary, determined expressions of people who'd survived a long time in a brutal world.

At the bottom of the narrow stairs, Clarence struck a wooden match from a pocket-sized box and lit a mostly burned-down Yankee candle. Its flickering light cast long shadows over rows of metal shelving.

The basement smelled of old wood and engine grease. On the shelves were survival treasures: canned food, vacuum-sealed fruit, boxes of matches, rust-resistant tools, and battered flashlights. Odds and ends that would've filled a garage sale ten years ago, now worth their weight in silver. Clarence had collected it all through years of careful trading.

In the far corner, tucked behind the stairs, stood a dusty bookcase crammed with old paperbacks. Clarence reached over and slid it along the wall, revealing a narrow opening carved into the concrete. Crouching, he reached inside with both arms and carefully dragged out a black hardened-plastic case the size of a guitar amp.

He laid it on the floor and popped the two metal clasps. The lid opened with a hiss.

Schubert gave a low whistle. Nestled inside the foam padding were five rifles, sleek and matte black, like something from the future.

"I hate to admit it," Ian said, eyeing the weapons, "but I don't recognize these."

"I do," Schubert said, kneeling and lifting one from the case like it was a holy relic. "These are the XM-92s. I was on the user trial for them. They were supposed to replace the M-86—never got widely issued before the sky fell in. Where the hell did you get these?"

"My day job used to be warehouse manager down at the logistics base in Barstow," Clarence said. "When the bombs hit, I loaded up my F-150 with five cases and headed north."

"Where's the truck?" Ian asked.

"Traded away the parts before folks realized gas was about to go stale."

Schubert chuckled, pulling back the charging handle and checking the action. "You've kept 'em oiled."

"Every week like clockwork."

Schubert nodded in approval. "Nice trick with the bookcase, too. I must've searched this basement half a dozen times. Never saw that crawlspace."

"That was the point," Clarence said, smiling faintly.

Ian stared down at the rifles. "Okay, this helps. But it's five rifles."

"I got three more cases," said clarence, motioning to the remaining contents of the crawlspace.

"Okay, twenty. That's still a drop in the bucket against a company of two hundred, all armed with M-86s and AR-

75s."

"That's because you haven't fired one of these," Schubert said, standing up. "These are game changers—accurate out to six, maybe seven hundred meters, and I only saw two jams in three days of field testing."

Ian's eyes narrowed. "You're saying we have range on them now."

"Exactly."

"But how do we train people to use these in—what—an hour?"

The woman behind them finally spoke. Her voice was cool and edged with steel. "Really?" she said. "You two think you're the only ones in this town who've ever fired a rifle?"

Schubert blinked. Ian looked her over again and caught something in her stance: the squared shoulders, the weight balanced evenly on the balls of her feet.

Maybe she'd carried a rifle long before Martin's Ferry.

Clarence grinned. "Gentlemen, meet Lily Cruz. National Guard, back before the Fall. And her friend Dale over there used to teach marksmanship in Alaska."

Schubert nodded slowly. "Guess we're not starting from zero after all."

Ian allowed himself a grin. "Looks like the militia's in for a hell of a surprise.

***

There were four sealed cases hidden in Clarence's basement crawlspace—twenty rifles in total. Clarence explained that the rifles were designated J-92s: "J" for Joint Service, and "92" for reasons even he didn't know. Behind the rifles sat several ammo cans—nearly 5,000 rounds by Clarence's guess—and two full gallons of Cleaner, Lubricant, Protectant.

It took twenty minutes to distribute the weapons. Volunteers outnumbered rifles two-to-one. Schubert gave a crash course in loading, chambering, and clearing jams, while Ian, Clarence, and a dozen others got to work stuffing magazines.

By the end of the militia's two-hour ultimatum, Martin's Ferry defenders had taken up positions in cover along the perimeter. Ian posted small teams on the rear flank in case the blocking squad moved in from the west. The children and those too injured or elderly to fight were hidden in Clarence's basement. Ian knew they were as ready as they could be.

"I wish I still had my binoculars," Ian muttered. His old pair, along with most of his gear, was confiscated back at the farm.

Clarence ducked away and returned with a compact monocular. "Best I could do."

Through the scope, Ian saw the Free Militia company mounted and milling about, restless. Among them stood Patrick Riley, deep in conversation with a man in officer's dress. Ian passed the monocular to Schubert.

"That's Riley, talking to someone who looks like he's in charge," Ian said.

Schubert narrowed his eye. "Owensby. Lieutenant. First-class prick. Guy's a Bray loyalist through and through. Was still in high school when the world ended, but I bet he was already dreaming about commanding troops from his basement."

Ian frowned. "What the hell are they waiting for?"

"Probably disagreeing over who gets to play war hero."

Just then, Case arrived behind them.

"Doc, you shouldn't be up here," Ian said.

"They're still out of range. Besides, someone's got to keep you idiots hydrated."

Ian nodded. "Fair enough. But fall back to the trading post once it starts."

The Klamath cut a jagged line through the east, forcing any mounted advance through a narrow bend of shallow water. Trees hemmed the north and west, making those flanks dangerous—whoever held the forest, held the fight.

As if on cue, the Free Militia began crossing the Klamath, funneling into a narrow, shallow stretch. "That's a beautiful chokepoint," Ian muttered. "Think we can range them from here?"

"Barely," Schubert said. "Better chances once they're on this side. Owensby will stop to line them up like a parade. He doesn't think we've got anything that can touch him at distance."

Ian smirked. "Let's not tip our hand."

Schubert adjusted his scope. "They're at 750 meters."

"Hold fire," Ian said. "Let them bunch up."

Behind them, a runner raised a green shirt tied to a stick—the signal to prepare to fire.

Ian lined up Owensby in his sights, paused, then asked, "You want me to take him out?"

Schubert blinked. "Now's when you ask that?"

"Better now than after he's dead."

"Leave him. He'll make dumber decisions than whoever's behind him."

Ian nodded, shifted aim, and squeezed. A soldier slumped in his saddle.

Then the line exploded in sound as the defenders opened fire. Most missed their first shot—new rifles, new nerves—but a few found their marks.

The militia formation broke. Horses bucked, soldiers dismounted or scrambled for the trees. Chaos spread across their line.

Owensby, still mounted, flailed his arms before someone yanked him into cover.

"We're not done," Ian shouted. "That was round one. They'll regroup, and they'll come again."

"What now, boss?" Schubert asked.

"Stop calling me that."

"You're calling the shots, Ian."

Ian scanned the terrain. "They'll try to close the distance from the tree line. We lose our range advantage then."

"So?"

"I want to take a group into the trees—hit, fall back, hit again. Bleed them and buy time."

"That's risky," Schubert said. "These people aren't trained."

"They've got guts," Clarence said, stepping up. "And they've got no choice."

Before Ian could respond, an explosion tore through their line. He ducked, shielding his head from raining debris. Two defenders were down—one with her legs blown off, another clutching his face where shrapnel had struck his eye.

Ian froze, his mouth dry, his heartbeat pounding in his ears.

Case appeared, checked the wounded, then looked at Ian. "What happened?"

"I—I don't know. Something exploded."

A drone buzzed overhead, square-bodied and loud. A speaker crackled.

"Ian Hammond," the voice called.

Ian stiffened. He recognized that tone, even through distortion.

Riley. It made sense now. The Militia didn't have drones, these were under the control of Petros' lapdog Riley.

"You're leading this effort," the voice said. "I have four armed drones above you, each carrying Hellfire missiles. You've seen what they can do."

"What do you want?" Ian asked.

"To avoid more bloodshed. Lay down your arms. Surrender the children. Only ten. They'll be safe. Fed. Cared for."

"Like you cared for Kylee?" Ian shouted back.

"Kylee's abductor skewed your understanding," Riley replied. "We're on the verge of a breakthrough. She could help change everything."

"You're lying," Marion Wallace shouted. "You won't take our kids again!"

"You have one more chance," Riley said. "Otherwise, the Free Militia will take what we've come for."

The drone veered east. From above, a missile flashed down—but it missed. Another drone followed, then a third. Ian braced for impact.

Instead, smoke trails streaked up from behind Martin's Ferry.

"What the hell?" Schubert asked, his eyes wide.

The drones exploded mid-air—one, two, three—brought down by missiles from the ground.

"Who's firing those?" Ian asked.

"Not us," Clarence said, amazed.

The villagers cheered. For a moment, there was hope.

But then Riley's voice returned, colder now. "You've delayed the inevitable. The militia are angry. They're coming."

The crowd quieted. The threat loomed larger now.

Ian looked to Schubert. They both knew—once the Free Militia got close, even their new weapons might not be enough.

Then a small voice rang out.

"No!"

Kylee stepped forward, her coat too big, her chin held high.

"You will not take any of these children, Patrick."

"Kylee," Riley said. "Time to come home."

"My home is out here."

"You're needed. With us. For the future."

"I am needed here."

"You could lead a new generation."

Kylee's smile was calm, radiant. "That's a beautiful thought, Patrick. But it's a lie. You don't want more like me. You want to make sure there never are."

A beat of silence hung in the air after Kylee's declaration. The hovering drone bobbed gently, as if even it were stunned.

Then Riley's voice returned, but it had lost its performative calm. The tone was flatter, clipped—each word measured, but tightly wound.

"You've made your choice," he said. "I hope—for all our sakes—that it doesn't become the world's burden."

A faint hiss of static followed. Then he added, quieter, but with unmistakable sharpness, "You're not as untouchable as you think."

The drone began to rise, angling southeast, its rotors humming louder as it climbed.

Ian looked at Kylee. "Was that a threat?"

Kylee shook her head, but her jaw was set. "That was a promise. And a man who just lost the only thing he ever wanted to control."

The drone peeled away.

Movement stirred in the trees.

"They're coming," Ian said.

And everyone knew—the final test was moments away.

29 – Evolution

Militia rifles cracked in the distance—slow at first, then faster, like popcorn over flame. The rounds struck all around them, snapping branches and kicking up dirt. Outgoing fire answered back, but it was disorganized and thin.

Ian scooped Kylee into his arms and ran toward the safety of Clarence's cabin.

"It's good to see you again, Ian," Kylee said, as if they were meeting for coffee instead of during a gunfight.

"What are you doing here?" he asked, breathless.

"I came because I knew you needed help."

He almost asked how she knew—but stopped himself. There wasn't time.

"Where's Dee?"

"She's with our new friends."

That was enough. Dee was safe, and Kylee—somehow—was back. He shifted her weight to one arm and opened the door to the cabin.

"I'm taking you to the basement. The other kids are there. It's the safest place."

Kylee shook her head. "I think I'll go see the wounded instead."

"No, they're in the back room. But it's above ground—"

"Ian." Her voice was soft but immovable.

His arms went slack. She slipped down gently to the

ground, as if he had simply decided to let her go. It wasn't forced, but it wasn't entirely voluntary either. The sensation left him wondering if this was how those men in Rio Dell had felt when she stopped them with just a word.

Something had changed in Kylee. Something powerful.

She looked up at him with calm eyes. "Go. The defenses need you. I'll be fine."

Ian stared for half a second, then nodded. Without another word, he burst out of the cabin, rifle in hand.

The Free Militia had pushed forward. Their fire was steady and advancing, forcing the defenders to fall back behind whatever cover they could find. Ian ducked behind a stack of firewood near the cabin where Schubert was waving his arms, directing fighters.

"Welcome back," Schubert called out.

"What's the plan?"

"We're slowing them down," Schubert said, "but not stopping them. They're coming no matter what we throw at them."

Militia gunners found better angles now, bracketing the barricades with withering fire. Schubert ducked a round that bit into the wood near his head. 'These guys are learning,' he muttered.

Ian peeked over the barricade. The militia moved with methodical discipline, using cover and suppressing fire. A direct frontal assault, even well-defended, wouldn't hold for long. He cursed the lack of mortars, grenades—anything to apply pressure from above.

"We've got to surrender," Ian said. "We can't hold."

Schubert turned to him, expression grim. "It's too late.

You don't know Silas Bray. If anyone resists, he makes an example of them. If resistance goes unpunished, it spreads. That's his gospel."

Ian shut his eyes for a moment, seeing Dee's face behind his lids. Then—an explosion.

It shook the ground. Dust kicked up around them. Ian's head jerked toward the blast. "They've got mortars?"

Schubert blinked. "No. And that wasn't aimed at us."

Another explosion rocked the Free Militia lines. Then another.

"What the hell?" Ian said, peeking over cover.

"Hot damn!" Schubert grinned. "It's hitting them!"

The militia fell into chaos. Rifle fire erupted from their right flank, pinning them between two fronts. The disciplined advance crumbled into confusion and retreat. Some ran for the trees, others fired blindly.

Ian stood, clenched fist raised to signal a ceasefire. "Hold fire! Don't shoot unless they regroup!"

He wanted to pursue—capitalize on the moment—but he didn't know who their allies were. Without coordination, a charge could be deadly.

Figures emerged from the tree line—dozens of them in digital camo. One wore a pink down jacket.

Ian lifted Clarence's telescope and laughed. "It's Dee."

Relief flooded through him, but his grin vanished at the sound of fresh gunfire from behind Dee's group. A new force was attacking from the rear. Whoever these allies were, they were pinned down now.

Ian scanned quickly. They had no clear shots, no angle. He stood to lead a charge—but froze as Kylee walked calmly from Clarence's cabin.

Even the birds fell silent. A static charge crept across the clearing like the calm before lightning. She raised her hands, palms forward, and spoke one word that thundered across the clearing:

"Stop."

Everything stopped.

The militia froze mid-motion. Several dropped to the ground as if strings had been cut. The fighting ceased.

Schubert's mouth fell open. "What the hell is happening?"

"Kylee," Ian said. "She's doing it."

"I thought she was a healer."

"She is," Ian replied. "And apparently... more."

Ian looked around at the villagers catching their breath, at the unconscious soldiers, and finally at Kylee. She wasn't a child anymore—not just a healer. She was a force. And he wasn't just a survivor anymore. He was hers to protect. And to follow

For a moment, silence reigned. Then Dee and her escorts began collecting weapons from the paralyzed soldiers. Martin's Ferry fighters followed suit.

Dee walked toward them flanked by two soldiers, rifles slung barrel-down. Her stride was steady, sure. Ian dropped his own rifle, slinging it the same way.

He walked toward her, heart pounding. As soon as they were close, Dee sprinted forward. Ian met her halfway, lifting her off the ground in a tight embrace. He spun her once, then set her down gently.

She pulled him in by the back of his neck, and their lips

met—unspoken love, fierce and long-awaited, sealed between them.

For the first time in days, Ian breathed. Really breathed. They had survived the storm.

But as he held her close, he knew: the war wasn't over. Not yet

**

This time, Kylee didn't lose consciousness. But after the Free Militia collapsed and fled, she was spent. Dr. Roy believed she was growing stronger—or perhaps just learning how to better manage the strain of her gift.

"What you did was incredible," Ian said quietly. He stood just behind Dee, who sat beside the bed holding Kylee's hand. The girl lay beneath a light blanket in the back room of Clarence's cabin, her breathing slow but steady.

Ian gave her a faint smile, then turned to Dee. "I'll go check on things outside." Dee nodded without looking up, brushing a strand of hair from Kylee's forehead.

Outside, the mood had shifted. The surviving Free Militia troops had come to, but not before every one of them had been disarmed. Lieutenant Owensby and four senior noncoms were now in custody, under the watch of the uniformed soldiers who'd accompanied Kylee and Dee to Martin's Ferry.

The rest had been allowed to go free. There were too many to imprison, and the townsfolk lacked the supplies—and stomach—to execute vengeance. They left in a scramble, spurred by fear. Some mounted whatever horses remained. Others, less fortunate, waded into the Klamath, dragging themselves across or letting the current sweep them downstream. Their retreat was clumsy and panicked. The memory of being frozen in place—powerless—had broken their will.

Schubert stood near the barricade, arms folded, watching the last of them vanish over the ridge. He shook his head slowly.

"That might be the first time the Free Militia has ever been beaten in open combat," he said. "Ambushes, sure. But not like this. Not a whole company routed." He gave Ian a sideways glance. "I'm just glad she's on our side."

Ian followed his gaze toward the cabin. "Yeah," he said. "Me too.

30 – Moving Day

"Wash, we've got five prisoners," called one of the soldiers as he and three others marched the captured Free Militia into Martin's Ferry. One man had his arm in a sling, another wore a bloodied bandage across his shoulder.

"Bring them here, Chip," Sergeant Louis Washington said.

"Who the hell are you?" snapped Lieutenant Owensby. Dee recognized him immediately from the farm compound.

"My name is Sergeant Louis Washington," Louis replied evenly. "United States Army. And you?"

Ian's head jerked up at the words *United States Army*. Not some survivalist fantasy, but the real thing.

"Bullshit," Owensby barked.

Louis stared at him with bored contempt.

"I'm Lieutenant Jeremy Owensby of the Free Militia," Owensby continued. "In the name of Silas Bray, I demand to know what the hell you think you're doing on Free Militia soil."

That earned a chuckle from Louis. "This is *American* soil, junior." He stepped forward and casually tore the gold bar from Owensby's collar. "Impersonating a military officer's a federal offense, Mr. Owensby."

"What? No, I— You're kidding, right?"

Louis ignored him. "Zip-tie them and keep them under guard," he ordered his men. "We'll take them back with us when our ride comes. The Major's going to want a word."

"You got it, Wash," Chip replied.

Dee slipped her arm through Ian's and guided him closer. "Louis," she said, "this is Ian Hammond. He was with us before we were captured."

Louis extended a hand. Ian shook it. "I heard you helped organize the defense. You prior service?"

"Yeah, a few years in the Corps. Before the bombs."

"Well, folks around here sure think highly of you. Hell of a job."

"Honestly, we got lucky. But what brought you here anyway?"

Louis nodded toward the main road. "Your little friend. Said she wouldn't go anywhere unless we stopped here first and gave you a hand."

"Kylee?" Ian smiled. "I'm not surprised."

Dee laughed. "Told you—she just knows things."

Schubert was led forward in zip-ties, and Dee stiffened. "That's the one who took us in Crescent City. Claimed he was a Marine on leave when the bombs hit."

"Wait," Ian said, stepping forward. "That guy's a defector. He warned us. Without him, we'd never have been ready. He fought with us."

Louis gave the man a long, hard look. "We'll take that into account."

"You mean let him go," Ian said.

"Easy now," Louis snapped. "You're not in charge here."

"And you are? What gives *you* the right?"

"Ever heard of the UCMJ?"

"What does that have to do with—"

"If your boy was active duty when the bombs hit, he's *still* active duty. If he joined the Free Militia and fought against U.S. forces, that's not desertion. It's treason."

"He was just trying to survive like the rest of us. You're not taking him."

"Back off, Hammond, unless you want to wear zip-ties too."

Ian took a threatening step forward. Louis didn't flinch.

"Would you two stop measuring your dicks?" Dee snapped.

Louis exhaled, calming slightly. "Look. We're just taking him back to the Major. You can speak for him. I *promise* that'll count for something."

Ian paused. "Where are you taking him?"

"Same place we're taking all of you—our base of operations."

Ian opened his mouth, but Dee cut in. "Ian—these are Dr. Schumacher's people. They're who we've been trying to find. And they've been looking for Kylee."

At that, Case emerged from Clarence's cabin, one arm around Kylee, helping her walk. Her face was pale and drawn, but her eyes were alert. Dee rushed to her and hugged her tightly.

"She needs rest and fluids," Case said. "She saved two more lives. Just can't help herself I suppose. At least this time, she won't slip into a coma."

"Thanks, Doc," Ian said.

Case shook his head. "No, *thank you*. For everything."

***

The aircraft vanished briefly behind the trees before rising back into view, its oversized propellers rotating upward like great mechanical wings. Through the handheld telescope Ian had passed her, Dee watched in awe as the massive machine transitioned from forward flight to hover. The propellers, now functioning as rotors, spun with thunderous authority as the tilt-rotor descended toward the clearing just east of Martin's Ferry. A second aircraft circled above, waiting its turn.

To her left, Louis was hunched over a handheld radio, calmly issuing instructions. Dee couldn't make out the words, but Ian had explained earlier—it was called a "talk-on," guiding the pilots in verbally. Why military people always needed their own terms for everything, Dee didn't know, but it seemed to work; everyone else understood it without question.

Earlier that morning, just a few hours before the aircraft's arrival, Louis had gathered the people of Martin's Ferry to address them directly. He'd told them they were welcome to join him and his team at their operating base. They had to make up their minds quickly—two hours, no more.

The aircraft they were sending was called a CV-44 *Emperor*, a tilt-rotor heavy-lift bird capable of vertical landings and takeoffs, just like a helicopter. Ian said each one could carry around thirty-five passengers plus a crew of four. With two aircraft and plans for two round trips, everyone in Martin's Ferry could come if they chose.

And most did.

Of the roughly 120 residents, the majority accepted the offer. The promise of security, food, and medicine was too compelling after so many years surviving the Long Winter. A few chose to stay behind—Clarence among them—but every family with children chose to go.

The first *Emperor* flared and slowed, hovering briefly before setting down in the field. The downdraft from its rotors whipped across the grass and pressed hard against Dee's chest. She stumbled a step before bracing herself and planting her boots firmly.

Louis ran beneath the roaring blades, meeting a flight-suited crewman at the ramp. The tail section yawned open to reveal a wide non-skid ramp and dimly lit cabin beyond.

The villagers had been organized into four boarding groups. Dee, Ian, Kylee, and Schubert—still technically a prisoner—were in the first. It had taken some persuading from Ian, but Louis had agreed to let Schubert ride without restraints.

"He'll be held temporarily until Major Rodriguez finishes his review," said Louis to keep Ian from going off again.

Two other Free Militia prisoners were not so lucky: their hands were zip-tied, and black hoods covered their heads.

Dee caught the scent of oil, sweat, and turbine fuel as she stepped up the ramp. It reminded her of the old regional airports from her childhood, filtered through a decade of ash and hardship. She paused at the top of the ramp and turned one last time toward the settlement. The Klamath River wound quietly through the valley. Clarence stood on the porch of the ranger cabin that had become Martin's Ferry's trading post, one hand raised in farewell.

She had begged him to come—him and Doc Roy and a few others. But Clarence had declined. Said someone needed to keep the lights on for the next lost soul that wandered in from the woods. He'd stay, along with the others who couldn't bring themselves to let go.

Dee settled into a seat along the cabin wall, strapping in next to Kylee, who had barely spoken since the battle. Ian climbed in a moment later, settling into the seat on Dee's other side.

As the aircraft lifted off vertically, the village receded beneath them. The tilt-rotor banked and began accelerating westward, and that was when Kylee's small hand slipped into Dee's.

A moment later, Ian's arm wrapped around her shoulders.

And for the first time since she'd seen her parents alive almost a decade ago, Dee felt something she hadn't in a long time.

Safe.

Loved.

Home.

EPILOGUE

The rear of the large aircraft opened like the jaws of a great whale. A ramp settled onto a concrete pad, providing an avenue for debarkation. The passengers unstrapped and exited when instructed by the crew, starting from the seats closest to the ramp. Once clear of the aircraft, they were shuffled into a nearby warehouse where they were met by a medical team of nurses, doctors, and various assistants wearing scrubs and masks.

Ian cast a glance behind and saw Schubert being quietly led away from the rest of the group. He made a mental note to find out where they were taking him

In-processing began with a barrage of medical tests and invasive questioning. Ian paused midway through answering a question about pre-war vaccinations when the rumble of the two *Emperors* rising for their return trip to Martin's Ferry drowned out all sound. He waited for the noise to subside before continuing, then endured questions about everything from his name, last known address, any known surviving relatives, any known deceased relatives, occupation, previous occupations, allergies, medical conditions, whether he had chicken pox, been vaccinated for polio, hepatitis, the mumps, the measles, meningococcal disease, and rubella.

The best he could tell them about the vaccinations was, *probably*. They wanted to know if he had ever traveled outside the United States. When he answered yes, this led to a whole other series of questions about everything from herbicide exposure to had he ever burned the shit from a field latrine.

At the next station, a nurse administered a half-dozen injections, including flu and COVID vaccines. Across the room, Ian caught Dee's eye. She winced as a needle jabbed into her arm and gave him a weary smile.

"Any of those for the bloody flu?" Ian asked the nurse.

The man, mid-thirties and clearly running on too little sleep, shook his head with a tired smile. "Not yet. Rumor is someone in your group has a resistance marker. Maybe we'll learn something."

"Just a rumor, huh?"

"Exactly," said the nurse, pressing a bandage to Ian's shoulder. "Go through that door and wait for your name to be called."

"You mean there's more?"

"Afraid so. Welcome aboard."

"Thanks," Ian said as he headed to the next waiting area.

After several more hours of poking, prodding, and being asked to recall long-forgotten details about his life before the bombs, Ian and the rest of the newcomers were escorted to temporary housing—refurbished Conex containers converted into clean, functional living quarters. A central bathhouse served the cluster, and when Ian saw the flushing toilets, he nearly cried. The working showers almost did him in.

Ian, Dee, and Kylee were quartered together—thanks,

apparently, to Kylee's insistence. When they walked in, Dee flipped on a light switch by the door, flooding the room with brightness. Ian flinched—he hadn't seen electricity used on this scale since before the bombs. For a moment, he wondered where the power was coming from.

Their unit held two cots and a small loveseat. Ian offered to take the loveseat, but both Dee and Kylee vetoed him. The kid fit perfectly; Ian would've had his legs dangling over the armrest all night.

They each took showers before heading to the communal dining area. Dinner was scheduled for 4:30, with the residents of Martin's Ferry eating first, then the rest of the base an hour later. Despite vaccinations and bloodwork, the administrators still wanted to minimize contact between the newly arrived and the long-term residents. No one who had seen the effects of the Bloody Flu questioned the caution.

At 3:30, Ian returned from the shower and sat on the loveseat, towel still around his shoulders. Time—real, mechanical, wall-clock time—was something he hadn't kept in years. Out there, it was just light and dark. But he could get used to the structure again if it meant hot meals and a roof overhead.

Dee and Kylee came in a few minutes later. Without a word, they all squeezed onto the loveseat. Ian's head rested against the wall, eyes slipping shut. No one spoke. No one needed to.

A knock came at the door.

Dee stirred. "What's that?"

Ian blinked, still half-asleep. "No idea." He got up and

opened the door.

Louis Washington stood on the other side, flanked by two men—one in a slightly faded Marine Corps uniform, the other in civilian clothes. The man in uniform wore the insignia of a Major. He had a hard face, leathery skin, and a lean build that said he had endured the last ten years with resolve and discipline.

"You Ian Hammond?" the major asked.

"I am."

"That the girl in there with you?"

Ian's hand went instinctively to the doorframe. "Who's asking?"

The major held up a calming hand. "Name's Major Javier Rodriguez. I'm senior officer here on the Joint Military Contingent."

"And where's here?" Ian asked, squinting.

"Eastern Oregon," Rodriguez replied. "That's as specific as I'm going to be right now."

Fair enough, Ian thought. He didn't expect more.

Rodriguez motioned toward the civilian beside him. "This is Dr. Farrow. We're here to escort the girl and the woman—Delilah, right?—to see Dr. Schumacher."

"Oh, hell no," Ian said. "I'm coming too."

Louis chuckled. "Told you he'd say that," he said to Rodriguez.

Rodriguez shot Louis a look—a brief, subtle exchange between two men who'd clearly been through a lot together. Then he turned back to Ian. "You're welcome to come. I only meant it wasn't required. If you're tired, you're free to rest."

Kylee's voice rang out from behind him. "He's coming."

Her tone left no room for debate.

Rodriguez nodded once. "All right then. Let's go."

***

The double doors opened to reveal a sleek, spotless office. One side was dominated by a standing desk with twin monitors; the other, a modest sitting area with couches arranged around a low coffee table. But it was the west-facing wall that stole the eye—not a wall at all, but a massive window overlooking a mountain range bathed in orange and maroon light from the setting sun.

A woman stood at the desk—tall, poised, and radiating quiet authority. The blonde of her youth had surrendered to gray, and fine lines traced outward from her mouth like the echoes of command. Her wire-rimmed glasses sat low on her nose as she looked up over them, eyes a piercing shade of blue.

"Dr. Schumacher," said Rodriguez, gesturing toward the group. "May I present Delilah Rosemont, Ian Hammond, and—"

"And Kylee Daniels," the doctor finished for him, her voice gentler than Ian expected—yet practiced, precise. A woman who could read any room and match its tone. She extended a hand to Kylee.

"You're very welcome here," she said.

Kylee shook her hand formally. "Thank you, Doctor."

Schumacher turned her gaze to Ian and Dee. "All of you are welcome."

"Thank you," Dee said softly, uncharacteristically

unsure.

Ian nodded his thanks, keeping silent. Whatever else could be said, these people had saved their lives and offered them shelter. Still, he knew none of this would be happening if it weren't for Kylee.

Schumacher's smile returned as she looked back at the girl. "I hope they've been treating you well. There's an ice cream machine in the cafeteria, you know—between meals. Soft serve. I'm partial to vanilla. Have you ever had any?"

"I had some," Kylee said with a small smile. Then, after a pause: "Dr. Schumacher, thank you for sending Louis and his team. You saved us."

"Thank Louis," Schumacher replied. "Major Rodriguez and I were just back here eating ice cream. But really—it was the least we could do. You risked everything to get out of Petros' compound. The least we could do was meet you halfway." Her expression darkened. "I still have friends inside Owens Valley. I know what he put you through. I'll never forgive him."

Kylee looked down briefly, then met Schumacher's gaze with quiet strength. "It doesn't matter now. We're safe. That's what matters."

Schumacher studied her for a long moment. "You're nine," she said, almost to herself. "I have to keep reminding myself. The way you speak, the way you carry yourself... It's astonishing."

Kylee's smile returned. "You're thinking about the nanobots and their effects on early cognitive development, right?"

Schumacher laughed—surprised and delighted. "You're

reading me, aren't you?"

"Sorry," Kylee said, sheepish.

"We've met before, you know," Schumacher said. "You wouldn't remember. You were only six months old."

"I remember," Kylee said.

The room went still.

Schumacher's mouth opened slightly. "Of course you do," she said softly. "Incredible."

Kylee's tone shifted. "I like your idea to study how the nanobots in my body affect the Bloody Flu. Bringing in infected people for treatment and observation—that's smart."

Rodriguez stiffened. "You never said anything about bringing in infected patients."

"I haven't finalized the plan," Schumacher replied, still calm. "But if we want to develop a vaccine, we need real data."

"That's a massive security risk," Rodriguez said, voice tight. "I can't support that."

"You misunderstand," Schumacher replied, now on firmer ground. "Kylee's already demonstrated she can eliminate the EVD-34 virus. If we can learn how, we might save what's left of humanity. It would be immoral not to try."

"I think your idea is bold and noble," Kylee said. "But I have a better one."

Schumacher's expression cooled. "What kind of idea?"

"Instead of bringing sick people here, I'll go to where they already are. I'll help treat them in the field, and your researchers can come with me. You'll get all the data you need, faster and more efficiently."

Schumacher shook her head. "That's too dangerous. We can't risk losing you."

"I didn't leave Petros to hide," Kylee said evenly. "I left to save lives. And that's what I'm going to do."

"You can do that by letting my team work, here."

"Even your best projections say a year or more for a vaccine. My way increases your sample size exponentially and accelerates your research. Fewer people die. Isn't that the point?"

She let the silence settle, then added, "You have a choice, Dr. Schumacher. Work with me—on my terms—or continue your research without me after I leave."

"You'd just walk away?" Schumacher asked, though there was no anger in her voice—only fatigue. "I wouldn't stop you. Even if I could."

"Then I'm asking you to work with me."

Schumacher let out a long breath. "It's a big ask. I'll need some time."

"You have until tomorrow morning," Kylee said. "If you say no, we'll leave after breakfast."

"That's fair," Schumacher said at last. Then, turning to Louis: "Please see them back to their quarters."

"That won't be necessary," Kylee said, taking Ian's hand. "We can find our own way."

***

"What do you think?" Jane Schumacher asked, turning to the once-brash young Marine who had, over the years, become her most trusted advisor.

"You don't want to know what I think," said Major Rodriguez.

Jane sighed. "Rod, I really wish you'd stop saying that. There's no one whose opinion I value more." It wasn't flattery—she meant it. Javier Rodriguez was one of the rare few who never held back when asked for his thoughts but always delivered them with measured reason. It often took a bit of coaxing, but when he spoke, it was clear, grounded, and sincere.

"She's dangerous," he said.

"Because she wants to help people?" Jane countered. "Right now, we need a healer. Our population's been dwindling for a decade—we're weak and getting weaker. Ending the dying is step one. Then we prepare."

Rodriguez leaned forward, his voice rising slightly. "You know that's not what I mean. What else can she do, Jane? I know you're not telling me everything."

She didn't answer right away.

Rod pressed on. "Maybe we should give her back to Petros and his people. At least they've figured out how to control her—how to harness her. They can replicate her, weaponize her. That's what we need."

"Kylee doesn't need Petros' cruelty to become who she's meant to be," Jane said, calm but firm. "She'll get there on her own."

Rod glanced sideways at her and gave a half-smile. "You already made your decision before you asked me, didn't you?"

"Yup," Jane replied without hesitation.

"Then why bother asking?"

Jane shrugged. "Because I knew you'd disagree. And sometimes, you need to work through the counterargument to be sure you're right."

Rod was quiet for a moment. Then he asked, "When are we going to tell her everything—about what really happened, and what's still coming?"

Jane stared out the window for a beat before answering. "There's no need," she said quietly. "She already knows."

***

Prometheus Command – Sublevel 6, once a cutting-edge research complex, now thrummed like a heartbeat withing the Sierra Nevada Mountains providing the western wall to the Owens Valley. The air was filtered, the lights dimmed to conserve power—though vanity kept the glass conference wall perfectly reflective.

Riley stood rigid, the silence around him more punishing than a reprimand. George Petros leaned forward slowly, the motion precise, deliberate.

"She's gone," Riley said. "Schumacher has her."

No reaction.

"She's outside Initiative control. The militia failed. The villagers fought back." He hesitated. "Kylee Daniels is... beyond our reach."

Petros remained still for a long time, then swiveled his gaze to the wall console.

"You were supposed to secure her," he said finally. "Not give her a cause."

"We tried."

"You underestimated her."

"We all did."

Petros rose, smoothed the collar of his charcoal-gray shirt, and activated the communications panel. The black glass shimmered, then resolved into the grainy silhouette of a man seated before an old American flag. His hair was neat, his voice sharp, familiar. Too familiar.

"Well, well," the man said, eyes flashing with performative concern. "You've lost her, haven't you?"

Riley tensed. Petros didn't blink.

"She's out of reach," Petros said. "For now."

"You let them build something," the man replied. "A story. A spark."

"They'll need more than stories when Arclight comes out of the dark."

That made the man pause—just briefly. His voice lowered.

"You're watching them, I trust?"

"Always."

"Then here's the plan: take their hope, and show them fear. Remind the world why you're necessary. Let Kylee heal a village or two. Then burn one."

Riley turned toward Petros, startled. But Petros said nothing.

"You know what they say," the man continued, with a smirk that didn't reach his eyes. "Forward, always forward."

The screen blinked off.

Petros stood for a long moment, staring at the empty

wall. Then, quietly, he spoke to Riley.

"Prepare a new list. We start with anyone tied to Schumacher. And keep eyes on Arclight."

"They're just ghosts now."

Petros finally turned to him.

"No, Riley. *We're* the ghosts now."

***

"Wait," Kylee said, pausing mid-step. "Let's go this way."

She led them outside and down a narrow path that opened onto a westward-facing overlook. The sun was a molten disk sinking behind the mountains, casting the sky in rich bands of amber and crimson.

"That's quite the game of chicken you're playing with Dr. Schumacher," Ian said, folding his arms.

"Not really," Kylee replied calmly. "She'll agree to our plan."

"And if she doesn't?" Dee asked with a note of concern in her voice. "Do you really want to go back out there—just the three of us?"

"If that's what it takes to save lives," Kylee said, her voice steady. "Then yes. But it won't come to that."

"I hope you're right," Dee murmured.

"She is," said a deep voice from behind.

They turned to see Louis Washington making his way down the path toward them, a grin already tugging at the corners of his mouth. "Doc Schumacher took all of five minutes to agree to do it your way."

"That's wonderful!" Kylee beamed, throwing her arms

around the big soldier.

Louis chuckled as he hugged her back. "Hey now, I'm just the messenger. But she does have one condition—you three are to stay and rest here for at least a week before heading back out."

"We can do that," Kylee said without hesitation. Then she turned back to the sunset, her face serene in the fading light.

Ian glanced at Louis. "Is she usually this easy to convince?"

"Never," Louis said with a smirk.

Ian laughed and slid an arm around Dee's shoulders. She leaned into him, slipping her arm around his waist. Together, they stood in the glow of the setting sun— watching the day fade, knowing the world outside still waited. But for the first time in ten years, Ian allowed himself to relax.

For now, they were safe.

And that was enough.

Printed in Dunstable, United Kingdom